*A Silent
Ocean Away*

By DeVa Gantt

A Silent Ocean Away

A Silent Ocean Away

COLETTE'S DOMINION

DeVa Gantt

AVON

An Imprint of HarperCollins*Publishers*

A SILENT OCEAN AWAY. Copyright © 2008 by DeVa Gantt. All rights reserved. Printed in the United States of America. No part of this book may be used or reproduced in any manner whatsoever without written permission except in the case of brief quotations embodied in critical articles and reviews. For information address HarperCollins Publishers, 10 East 53rd Street, New York, NY 10022.

HarperCollins books may be purchased for educational, business, or sales promotional use. For information please write: Special Markets Department, Harper-Collins Publishers, 10 East 53rd Street, New York, NY 10022.

FIRST EDITION

Designed by Rhea Braunstein

Library of Congress Cataloging-in-Publication Data
Gantt, DeVa.
   A silent ocean away: Colette's dominion / DeVa Gantt.—1st ed.
     p. cm.
   ISBN 978-0-06-157823-6 1. Family—Fiction. 2. United States—History—19th century—Fiction. I. Title.
   PS3607.A59S58 2008
   813'.6—dc22

                              2008018316

08 09 10 11 12 WBC/RRD 10 9 8 7 6 5 4 3 2 1

A Silent Ocean Away is dedicated to our readers—those who enjoyed our self-published version of the Colette Trilogy and enthusiastically spread the word. If not for them, and the many booksellers who invited us into their stores, this edition would not be in your hands.

DIRECTORY OF CHARACTERS

In Richmond, Virginia:

Charmaine Ryan—heroine of the story (born 1818)

Marie Ryan—Charmaine's mother, abandoned as a young child at the St. Jude Refuge

John Ryan—Charmaine's father and dockworker

Father Michael Andrews—Pastor of St. Jude's Church and Refuge

Sister Elizabeth—Nun and teacher at the St. Jude Refuge

Joshua Harrington—Charmaine's first employer

Loretta Harrington—Joshua's wife

Jonah Wilkinson—Captain of the *Raven*, the Duvoisin merchantman

Edward Richecourt—Duvoisin lawyer

On Charmantes:

The Duvoisin Family:

Frederic Duvoisin—Patriarch and master of Les Charmantes; son of Jean Duvoisin II, founder of Les Charmantes (deceased); brother of Jean III (deceased)

Elizabeth Duvoisin—Frederic's first wife (deceased 1808)

John Duvoisin—only son of Frederic and Elizabeth; heir to the Duvoisin fortune (born 1808)

Paul Duvoisin—Frederic's illegitimate son (born 1808)

Colette Duvoisin—Frederic's second wife (born 1810)

Yvette and Jeannette Duvoisin—twin daughters of Frederic and Colette (born 1828)

Pierre Duvoisin—youngest son of Frederic and Colette (born 1834)

People living in the Duvoisin Mansion:

Agatha Blackford Ward—older sister of Frederic's late wife, Elizabeth; John's aunt

Rose Richards—elderly nursemaid to Yvette, Jeannette and Pierre; formerly nanny to John and Paul; originally hired by Jean II to care for Frederic as a young boy

Professor Richards—Rose's deceased husband; formerly tutor to John and Paul; initially hired by Jean II as a tutor for Frederic

George Richards—Rose and Professor Richard's grandson; close friend of John and Paul; production manager and overall supervisor of island operations (born 1809)

Duvoisin Servants:

Jane Faraday—head housekeeper

Travis Thornfield—butler and Frederic's personal valet

Gladys Thornfield—Travis's wife; Colette's personal maid

Millie and Joseph Thornfield—Travis and Gladys's children

Felicia Flemmings—housemaid

Anna Smith—housemaid

Fatima Henderson—cook

Gerald—head groom

Islanders:

Dr. Robert Blackford—Island physician; Agatha's twin brother; older brother to Frederic's first wife, Elizabeth; John's uncle

Harold Browning—Charmantes' overseer

Caroline Browning—Harold's wife; sister of Loretta Harrington

Gwendolyn Browning—Harold and Caroline's only daughter

Stephen Westphal—Charmantes' financier; manager of the town bank

Anne Westphal London—Stephen's widowed daughter; resides in Richmond

Father Benito St. Giovanni—island priest

Jake Watson—harbor foreman

Buck Mathers—dockworker

Jessie Rowlan—dockworker

Madeline Thompson (Maddy)—mercantile proprietress

Wade Remmen—lumbermill operator

Rebecca Remmen—Wade's younger sister; friend of Gwendolyn Browning

Martin—town farrier

Prologue

Fall 1833
A Prayer

$\mathcal{A}$N evening mist settled over the moss-scarred walls of the stone church, shrouding it in hopelessness. A solitary man slumped forward in one pew, muttering disparaging phrases to the looming shadows. He needed another drink. Expensive whisky hadn't yielded peaceful oblivion, hadn't even dulled his senses. And yet, if he wasn't drunk, what the hell was he doing in a house of God? What, indeed! He chortled insanely, the inebriated laugh ending in a dizzying hiccup. He'd come to pray—pray for death. Not his own death. He wasn't quite so noble. Not yet, anyway. Instead, he petitioned the Almighty to bring about the demise of another. Retribution—justice. His lips twisted with the delicious thought of it. *Death . . . So simple a solution.*

"Put him out of his misery. Put me out of *my* misery," he slurred, confronting the wooden crucifix that hung above the barren altar. *"Do you hear?"*

His sudden movement sent the walls careening, the statues a nauseating blur of spinning specters. He grasped for the bench, attempting to right his toppling world, but his hand missed its mark.

Not so his forehead. It met the back of the wooden pew with a re-sounding crack. With a groan, he crumbled to the stone floor, his agony blanketed in a palette of smoky-blue, a vision that dissolved into the consuming void of blessed unconsciousness.

Marie Ryan hurried along the dimly lit courtyard, her heel catching sharply on the stone pathway and echoing across the vacant enclosure. In all her years at the St. Jude Refuge, deep in the heart of Richmond, Virginia, she had never acquired the soft footfalls of the diminutive nuns who routinely tread the very same cobblestone in their contemplative procession toward vespers. This evening was no different.

She was very late, and the interview awaiting her tardy arrival had been arranged for her. Now it would have to be canceled. She would not leave the refuge again. This was her home, where she belonged, and neither the threat of her husband, nor her ill-fated past, would send her scurrying from its protective walls. Tonight she had received a sign.

From the day she had been abandoned as a young child on the steps of St. Jude's thirty years ago, the Almighty had intended she serve Him. For the past sixteen years, she had ignored His call; tonight she would not. Life beyond the church walls no longer lured her with empty promises. The real world comprised two separate, yet contingent, factions of humanity: those who suffered life's travesties and those who ministered to them. On this eve, she would circumvent the former and embrace the latter. Her penance had been paid in full.

She entered the rectory and nodded demurely to its three occupants: Sister Elizabeth, Father Michael Andrews, and Joshua Harrington. The latter was an elderly gentleman and prosperous businessman, who was seeking a suitable companion for his wife.

With five sons married and moved away, Loretta Harrington was suffering the effects of an empty nest.

"Please don't think me ungrateful, Mr. Harrington," Marie apologized when the introductions were over, "but I'm afraid I've changed my mind."

Father Andrews stood stunned. The gentlewoman had shown great interest in the Harrington position and had asked him to set up this appointment. He knew its handsome salary would prove a blessing. "Marie, is something wrong?"

She hesitated. "I've finally realized this is where I belong, here at the refuge. Yes, I know I have a home, but I want to work at St. Jude's with those who really need me."

The priest's astonishment doubled. Though Marie's daughter attended the rudimentary school that Sister Elizabeth conducted, Marie rarely crossed the church's threshold herself. "But your husband—" he began.

"Will be made to understand," she replied.

"I'm not certain *I* understand. I thought you needed this employment."

Marie sighed. "There was a man in the church tonight. He was ill."

"Another beggar," Father Michael scoffed, his voice unusually harsh.

"No, not a beggar," Marie refuted, surprised by his reaction. "He was dressed in fine clothing. And yet, he was in a sad state: unconscious. I believe he struck his head on the pew. I had Matthew carry him to the common room, and I remained with him until he awoke. I fear he has suffered greatly, and not just physically. I want you to look at him, Father."

"I fail to comprehend how this man has influenced you."

"It was something he said," Marie remarked distantly. "I believe the Good Lord sent him not only to St. Jude, but to me, to make me see this is where I'm needed, where I belong. Again, I apologize, Mr. Harrington. I shouldn't have drawn you away from your wife. But I must remain at the refuge. I hope you understand."

With a mixture of relief and dread, exultation and pain, Father Michael Andrews smiled down at Marie. He'd been denied this woman's presence for sixteen years. Tonight she had returned.

Rising from the rickety chair he had perched before the window, John Ryan strutted across the small kitchen like a proud peacock. He massaged his inflated chest, then raked long yellow fingernails through his graying hair. It fell back over his indelible scowl.

Turning away in disgust, Charmaine Ryan threw herself into preparing dinner. Her father's pompous promenade repulsed her to the core, and when he paraded so, she thanked the Lord for making her a girl.

She sighed. Her mother was unusually late. The appointment with Joshua Harrington had begun over two hours ago, and though her father deemed the lengthening delay a favorable sign, she did not.

"What time did your mother say she was supposed to meet with 'em?"

Charmaine jumped. "I think she said five."

"*Think?* Jesus Christ, girl, don't you know?"

"No, I don't know for certain," she responded peevishly, her eyes hardened until he, with a grumbling shake of the head, meandered into the bedroom.

Charmaine struggled to gain control of her ire. These days, anything her father said brought her to anger. Unlike her mother, who cowered under John Ryan's verbal assaults, they incensed Charmaine. Perhaps she was brave because he had never raised a hand to her. Marie was less fortunate. Educated in the folly of questioning her husband's supremacy, she kept silent in order to preserve a fragile peace.

With mind revolting, as it always did when she pondered the union of John Ryan and Marie St. Jude, Charmaine stared absently across the humble kitchen, beyond the dilapidated walls of the three-room cottage, and past the barriers of time, hoping to perceive some understanding of nature, the twist of circumstance that had sanctified the marriage of her parents. If she knew little about her mother's past, save the fact she had been abandoned on the steps of St. Jude Thaddeus Church, she knew even less about her father, a man who appeared and disappeared as the mood struck him, often leaving his wife and daughter for days at a time, which suited Charmaine just fine. The less she saw of him the better. Did he have a family aside from his wife and daughter? It was only one of many unanswered questions. All she really knew of John Ryan was that he was an ill-bred, uneducated drunk. He rarely worked, and then, only when he needed money for spirits, sauntering about the Richmond docks seeking odd jobs.

How had such a scapegrace won the heart of her mother? Another unfathomable question. Marie should have entered the novitiate, taken sacred vows that would have wed her to God and His Holy Church. Instead she had left St. Jude's at the age of eighteen to marry a man whom she claimed had been kind to her. A single child had been born of their union. Charmaine had been christened Haley Charmaine Ryan after her paternal grandmother, a woman she had never met. However, only her father used the name Haley, and now it was all but forgotten, for her mother fancied the name Charmaine, a name that still haunted the older woman's memory from a time and place she couldn't quite recall.

"Maybe we oughta eat without her."

Charmaine flinched. The man had perfected his penchant for

sneaking up on people. "Yes, perhaps we should," she agreed, setting the meal on the humble table. She'd purchased a small slab of pork with the money she'd saved from running errands for the elderly spinster next door. Tonight they'd celebrate her mother's good fortune.

"I hope that Harrin'ton fella knows a good thin' when he sees it," he said, straddling the stool at the head of the table. Charmaine held silent as he pulled the wooden platter and knife nearer and proceeded to manicure the fat from the steaming roast. Then, he set aside the choice slices for himself and placed the remaining cuts on his daughter's dish. "Your mother is a hard worker," he continued. "There ain't none that can match her skill when she puts her mind to it, and I wouldn't want this fella thinkin' otherwise."

"No, sir," Charmaine whispered sullenly, appalled by his demand that a stranger respect the virtues of a woman whom he continually debased. His convoluted reasoning would never cease to amaze her, and if the situation weren't so decidedly sad, she would have laughed outright at his pathetic proclamation.

"I just hope he intends to pay her well," he proceeded, his words muffled as he shoved a forkful of meat into his stubbled mouth. "I ain't allowin' no kin of mine to work cheap. No, sir. For his sake, I hope he ain't some high-and-mighty a-ris-to-crat who thinks he can get away with payin' some miserly amount, 'cause I won't have it."

Again Charmaine bit her tongue. It was pointless to accuse him of sending his wife to labor for wages he would assert his right to claim. Besides, it would benefit Marie to hold such a position, one that would grant her a life apart from her derelict husband. Charmaine attended the St. Jude School with the other orphaned children. It was an escape from her father's cruelty. But what did her mother have? Up until today, nothing but the bungalow in which they lived and dared not hope for anything better to come along. But something *had* come. The Harrington household offered Marie a refuge of her own.

"Jesus Christ, woman, how could you *be* so goddamn dumb?"

"I'm sorry, John," Marie placated, "but there was nothing to be done."

"Nothin' to be done?" he sneered. "You expect me to believe that? I know what you've been up to. You didn't want that job! Workin's too good for you."

"That's not true, John. I told you, Mr. Harrington was seeking someone younger and more impressionable, someone his wife could take under her wing."

The remark elicited another oath. "Then send Haley," he said.

"What?"

"You heard me," he responded with a growing grin, the infant idea taking root. "She's young enough for all them things you been sayin' them Harrin'tons want. She oughta suit his fancy wife jus' fine."

"No, John. Charmaine is too young, and she has her schooling to finish."

"Schoolin'!" he spat. "She's had enough of that damned church. What good has it done her, 'cept to teach her how to sass me? It's time she earned her keep!"

"That won't be necessary," Marie unwisely rejoined. "I'll continue to look for a job, and until I find something suitable, we'll get by on the money you earn at the warehouse. I know it isn't much, but we've managed before and—"

"I ain't workin' there no more," he cut in.

"Why not?"

"John Duvoisin is a drunk, and I ain't workin' for no drunk. So we're just gonna have to let Haley work for them Harrin'tons and live on what she brings home. Then when you find somethin', we'll be sittin' pretty."

"But, John, she's young," Marie reiterated softly, praying she could calm him. "Surely they won't pay her well. No, there are other options. If need be, we'll use the money I've—" *Too late!*

"And what money might that be, Mother?" he accused, his calculating eyes assessing her as if she had somehow managed to scheme behind his back.

"The money I've earned taking in laundry."

"The money you've earned taking in laundry?" he mimicked cruelly. "And how did you manage to keep all this money a secret up until now?"

"It wasn't a secret, John. It was my money, and I was saving it in case—"

"*Your* money? *Your* money?" he bellowed, his face suffused with rage. "That money belongs to me. All of it! I'm your husband! I'm the one who clothes and feeds you and your daughter and puts a roof over your heads, ain't I?"

"Yes, John, but—"

"Shut your yap! And don't be givin' me them saintly looks, either!"

"Stop it!" Charmaine shouted. And then, fearing how the ensuing row would ultimately end, she reined in her anger. "Please, just stop it!"

Her unexpected outburst only succeeded in diverting her father's fury. "Now let me tell you somethin', young lady. I'm sick and tired of them looks you been givin' me—looks you think I can't see—believin' you're better than your pappy. It's about time you showed me some respect instead of sassin' me with that spiteful tongue of yours. As long as you're livin' under my roof, you'll be doin' as I say without any lip. You hear?"

Her pulse quickened. "I hear, Father, and I'll do just as you say."

He showed great surprise, and his rage ebbed.

Charmaine raised her chin. "I would love to work for the Harringtons. That is, if they'll have me."

"Oh, they'll have you, all right," he reasoned, "unless your mother here has been lyin' 'bout what them folks are lookin' for."

Marie ignored her husband's remark. "Charmaine, you can't do this."

"Why not?" she queried.

"Yeah, why not, Mother?"

"Because of your life at St. Jude's, your education."

"What life?" Charmaine countered. "I don't have a life there, and I certainly don't have one here." Ire and pain sparked in her brown eyes, daggers of hatred she shot at her father. "I want to leave, because once I'm employed by decent people, I'll no longer be living under *your* roof!"

But the declaration did not rile him, for he had gotten exactly what he wanted.

Chapter 1

Friday, September 9, 1836
Richmond, Virginia

JOHN Duvoisin watched the *Raven* labor from the landing
stage. As her towboats released their lines, the cargo ship lost
all momentum, and she sat indecisive for a moment. Then her
canvas sails bellied out, harnessing the wind. She groaned as she
cut across the current of the James River; her destination: three islands nestled in the northeastern waters of the West Indies. The
islands, called Les Charmantes, were often considered the foundation of the Duvoisin fortune. To John, Les Charmantes meant
much more. He tracked the vessel as she sailed off, and his mind
meandered with the James. She was now but a toy on the wide
river, and still, he stared after her as if, by mere eye contact, he
could transport himself to her decks. A raging frustration had
kept him from boarding the vessel this morning, his reward: bitter reflection, which chastised him for doing nothing. His inter-
nal war reached its pinnacle as the *Raven* traversed the river's bend
and vanished from view. He drove rigid fingers through his tou-
sled hair as if to liberate his turbulent thoughts, then strode from
the bustling wharf, oblivious of Richmond's busy waterfront. He

mounted his horse and turned it into the crowds, leaving thoughts of the *Raven* and Les Charmantes behind.

"We're moving! We're finally moving!" Charmaine exclaimed as she peered through the porthole of her small cabin. Turning, she smiled triumphantly at Loretta Harrington, who sat complacently on the only anchored chair. "Won't you come and see?"

"No, thank you, my dear," Loretta replied, returning the radiant smile. "I'll allow the ship to take care of itself and pray that my stomach does the same." It was the one reservation the middle-aged woman had about this entire trip: seasickness. But Charmaine Ryan was well worth any discomfort she might endure in the next four or five days, so she bent her mind to the task at hand. "Why don't we practice a bit more for the interview, Charmaine? It will take my mind off the rocking of the ship."

"I'm quite prepared," Charmaine replied, but she did as Loretta suggested and came and sat beside the woman who had become a second mother to her . . .

Charmaine had been welcomed into the Harrington house nearly three years ago. Marie Ryan had contacted the couple when she realized her daughter would not be talked out of her decision to leave home, and Joshua Harrington had taken an immediate liking to the sensitive yet talkative fifteen-year-old. In her large brown eyes, he saw a determination rarely found in one so young, and in her words, noted a firm conviction for what was right and good. After that first meeting, he was certain Charmaine Ryan would make an excellent companion for his wife, who sorely missed her five grown sons. He hoped the girl would become the daughter Loretta never had.

Within a fortnight, all the arrangements had been made, and Charmaine left one life behind to begin another. She moved into a pretty, whitewashed house in a residential section of Richmond, taking her meager belongings with her. She would live with the Harringtons during the week and spend the weekends with her parents.

Charmaine's only regret was leaving her mother to fend for herself. But Marie began spending more and more time at the St. Jude Refuge, drawing solace from the work there, content to shoulder the woes of others rather than dwell on her own, happy in fact. Thus, Charmaine found it strange when she grew unusually distant one weekend, surmising some misfortunate troubled her. Though Marie avoided the details, she said, "I used to think only the poor suffer, but I was wrong. Perhaps the greater the wealth, the deeper the pain."

Within the month, John Ryan decided to put a stop to his wife's "charity" work. Charmaine was determined to thwart him, thanking heaven her wages had exceeded what he'd expected her to earn and that she had had the good sense to secretly retain half. Now she insisted her mother use it. "Tell father the church is paying you," she conspired. "Then he will be happy you are working there." Sure enough, his grumbling ceased when the cold cash was placed in his hand.

Life with the Harringtons was a breath of fresh air. Under their roof, Charmaine felt secure. In this home, the husband treated his wife with respect and adoration. Joshua Harrington was everything a spouse should be. Likewise, Loretta was devoted to him. A dear and kind woman, she never had a harsh word for anyone. Charmaine benefited the most from the matron's fine character, blossoming in her affection.

"You are more than a companion to me," Loretta had said within the first year. "I consider you a part of my family, Charmaine."

Charmaine came to believe this, and it was only when the Harrington sons ventured home that she felt unhappy, envying the relationships between husbands and wives, children and parents, fathers and daughters. Although she was always included in their gatherings, Charmaine was careful to remain aloof, for this loving family didn't belong to her, not as long as her own parents lived. Her mother and father were a constant reminder of who she really was.

For two years, she guarded her background, frightened the Harringtons would send her packing if they learned the truth. Though her mother was a good woman, she was but an orphan whose only stroke of fortune had been her adoption and education at the St. Jude Refuge. Marie's parentage was probably no better than John Ryan's, and he was nothing more than white trash in the eyes of civilized Richmond gentry.

Loretta and Joshua pondered her pensive moods, which usually occurred after her visits home. They sensed she suffered, yet reasoned she needed time to overcome her reticence. Time, however, was not on Charmaine's side.

Her father confronted her one weekend. "You been workin' for them Harrin'tons gone two years now. When are they plannin' on payin' you more?"

Charmaine *had* received an increase, but since she continued to share half her wages with her mother, she'd set the additional money aside for herself.

"I'll ask them, Father," she blurted out, the vow apparently appeasing him.

Not so; her hasty response fed his suspicions, and for a week, he mulled it over. Then, late one Friday night, he decided to set things right. It took him a bottle of whisky to muster the courage to lumber up to the Harrington house on wobbly legs and pummel the front door. When the maid opened it, he pushed his way in, demanding to see Joshua Harrington.

"I wanna know how much you been payin' my daughter," he

slurred when Joshua appeared, "and I also wanna collect her wages personally from now on. I ain't gonna be cheated outta what's my right to claim!"

"Man, you're drunk!"

"You're damn right I'm drunk! But I'll tell ya one goddamn thing, drunk can make a man see clear. I know Haley's been tryin' to rook her ol' pappy, and I'll be havin' none of it! Do you hear?" He slammed his fist into his hand.

"Go home and sleep it off," Joshua cajoled, taking Ryan by the elbow and leading him to the door. "We can discuss this when you're sober."

"Oh no, you don't!" John Ryan objected, twisting free. "I know what you're up to. You're in on this little conspiracy. I want them extra wages I ain't been gettin', and I want 'em now!" He tried to grab Joshua's lapels, but lost his balance and staggered into the wall.

Joshua flung the door open and spoke in a low, clipped tone. "I've not withheld any wages from your daughter. Clearly, this is a matter to discuss with her, but now is neither the time nor the place. Charmaine has retired for the evening. Now, I ask you politely to leave. Go home and sleep off your sorry state." Joshua pointed toward the walkway.

John Ryan shuffled from the house, mumbling under his breath. "If you ain't part'a this rotten scheme, then my wife must be behind it. I should'a known she was lyin' to me."

Charmaine remained unaware of the confrontation; Joshua thought to spare her the humiliation. But he regretted this decision when the following Monday arrived, and she did not return from her visit home. Loretta grew worried. They didn't know where the Ryans lived and had no way of contacting her. After a second day passed without word, Joshua went to see Father Michael. The priest had, after all, arranged the initial meeting between the Harringtons and Marie. But Michael had no idea where they lived, either. Apprehension set in when Joshua related the story of John Ryan's drunken tirade. Marie had been absent from the refuge for four days. Michael had suspected her home life was unhappy, and though he had asked her about bruises that appeared overnight, she would brush his concerns aside with excuses. "Just a fall I took . . . I'm very clumsy." Michael feared the truth, but what could he do? Today, his anger eclipsed the priestly vows he had taken twenty-five years ago. If John Ryan had hurt Marie and Charmaine . . .

Late Wednesday night, Charmaine gathered the courage to return to the Harringtons. Her mother was dead. Slowly, painfully, she described the squalid life she had endured under her father's roof, culminating with the past weekend when she had found her mother lying unconscious. Even though her father was nowhere to be found, Charmaine knew what had happened. She'd run from the house, crying for help. The neighbors had taken pity on her, summoning a doctor. For three days, her mother lay clinging to life, words occasionally spilling from her lips, begging her husband to stop. Charmaine wept when she learned a dispute over her wages had instigated the fatal beating.

The following morning, Joshua visited the local sheriff, demanding the immediate arrest of John Ryan. Because Joshua was an upstanding citizen, the sheriff quickly issued the necessary warrant. If John Ryan were in the area, he would be apprehended.

Marie was buried the next day, a quiet funeral attended by the Harringtons and friends from the refuge. Many mourners cried, including Father Michael. As the last prayers were spoken and the small crowd departed, the priest took Charmaine aside. "I'm sorry, Charmaine," he murmured. "Your mother will be deeply missed. If you're ever in need, please don't hesitate to come to me."

"I will be fine, Father," she said. "The Harringtons have offered me a permanent home, but thank you all the same."

One week passed, followed by the next, and it became clear John Ryan was either far from Richmond or cleverly hiding. The chances of making him pay for his heinous crime grew slimmer by the day. Many nights Charmaine lay awake, fearful he might be waiting for the opportunity to corner her alone. Although the Harringtons assured her he would never show his face again, she was ever wary of the shadows, especially when she walked down the city streets. Was he lurking between the buildings, in the doorways, watching and waiting? To calm her fears, she prayed for her mother, resolute in her belief that Marie had found peace in the afterlife and watched over her from paradise.

A year went by and Charmaine began to relax. In that time she had become a daughter to Loretta in nearly every way. The truth about her background *had* changed the Harringtons' opinion of her. They loved her all the more.

Loretta took her further under her wing, determined to mold her into a graceful lady, certain she would recognize her value if her station in life were elevated. To this end, an elaborate tutelage commenced. Loretta prided herself on etiquette, and Charmaine found that by following this gentlewoman's perfect example, grace and dignity became second nature. Loretta built upon Charmaine's rudimentary orphanage education, introducing her to literature, fine art, and music. She taught Charmaine how to dance, how to sew, and they spent many happy hours in front of a blazing hearth with needlepoint in hand.

Of all the subjects she studied with Loretta, Charmaine cherished her music lessons most. She excelled at the pianoforte, her talent perfected by the melodies themselves and the happiness and sense of well-being she experienced each time she mastered a particular piece. The salubrious effect did not go unnoticed, and one day, Joshua surprised them with a most unexpected and extravagant gift—the "improved" pianoforte, or piano, as it was now being called, touting it as the innovation of the century. Unlike its predecessor, this piano had additional octaves and a deeper, full-bodied resonance. Loretta took to the new instrument like a duck to water. Inspired, Charmaine strove to fine tune her skill, and with time, had to congratulate herself, for whenever the Harrington sons came to call, their children would gather around the keyboard, requesting *she* play.

She looked forward to these convivial visits, though they led to new yearnings. Loretta saw it and knew Charmaine wondered where her life was leading. "She needs a husband," Loretta told Joshua one evening. "Don't you see how longingly she looks at our boys and their children?" When Joshua snorted, she fretted the more. "If only one of our sons weren't married . . ."

Loretta began inviting eligible young men to the house; but none of them caught Charmaine's fancy. In fact, Loretta was certain the girl remained ignorant of her plan until one day Charmaine put a stop to it. "Mrs. Harrington, I'm not interested in the gentlemen you've invited here to meet me." When Loretta feigned confusion, she continued with, "I don't think I'll ever marry. I never want to live the life my mother lived."

Loretta anguished over the declaration. "Charmaine, not all men are like your father. Take Joshua, for instance. He is kind and loving. You can have such a husband someday, too. But it won't happen if you see your father in every man."

"Better I remember the likes of my father than turn a blind eye to reality. I felt my mother's pain—lived with it. I cannot forget that so easily."

"Charmaine, you're too young to give up on all mankind. There is someone out there for you, but you must open your heart." One look at Charmaine's stormy countenance, and Loretta knew it would take more than words to convince her.

From that day forward, Loretta was determined to change

Charmaine's way of thinking, to nudge her from the safe but isolated haven of the Harrington house into the world of the living. Easier said than done. Just as exasperation was setting in, a novel opportunity presented itself. Loretta knew if she failed to capitalize on it, Charmaine's life was destined to stagnate and turn bitter.

A letter from her sister mentioned that Frederic and Colette Duvoisin were seeking a governess for their three young children. Loretta knew the name well. The Duvoisin family owned large stretches of land in Virginia. In fact, her brother-in-law was an overseer to the Duvoisin holdings on the Caribbean island where the family lived. Les Charmantes was a fabled paradise. Although Loretta had never made the journey there herself, her sister's occasional letters always praised its beauty. Loretta began to believe Les Charmantes was just what Charmaine needed: a new home far away, with children, new acquaintances, and God willing, a future!

Her mind made up, Loretta began her artful maneuvers to win Charmaine over to the idea. "I've had a lovely letter from Caroline," she casually mentioned one evening as they sat in the front parlor. Charmaine's eyes lifted from her needlepoint, and Loretta continued. "She's written of the Duvoisin family."

"Duvoisin family?" Charmaine queried, and because she pronounced the surname incorrectly, Loretta repeated the French name: Doo-*vwah*-zan.

"Apparently, Frederic and Colette Duvoisin need a governess for their twin girls and young son. According to Caroline's letter, they are considering only young applicants. It would be a wonderful opportunity in such a fine house and serene setting. Something like this only comes along once in a lifetime, if that." Loretta looked up from her sewing to find Charmaine studying her intently.

"You think *I* should apply?" Charmaine asked, certain Loretta had broached the subject for a very definite reason.

"Yes, I do."

Joshua cleared his throat. "I don't think that advisable, my dear."

"And why not?" *If he says one word to waylay me, he will regret it!*

"The Duvoisin men are a wild lot," he said, despite the look his wife was giving him.

"Charmaine would be caring for three young children."

"It is not the children who warrant concern," Joshua rejoined.

Loretta shook her head, dismissing his protestations with, "Now, Joshua, we don't live in the Middle Ages. Besides, I intend to accompany Charmaine to the island. If we find the position unsuitable, she need not accept it."

"Island?" Charmaine queried. "But I thought—"

"Les Charmantes," Loretta explained. "Or just Charmantes as the islanders refer to the main island. I've mentioned it before, Charmaine. It is where Caroline, Harold, and Gwendolyn have lived these past ten years. It is also the Duvoisin homestead."

"Yes, I know where your sister lives, but I thought the position would be here, in Virginia. The island"—she breathed deeply—"it must be very far away."

"Only as far away as a letter, and Duvoisin vessels are constantly en route between Richmond and the islands. The family is as much involved in shipping as it is in tobacco and sugar." Loretta paused before continuing. "Of course, it is your decision, my dear, and it needn't be hastily made. Think on it for a while. Isn't that right, Joshua?"

"Absolutely," he mumbled facetiously, cognizant of his wife's tactics.

Days passed with no mention of the island or the position available there. But Charmaine thought long and hard about traveling to Les Charmantes. Governess of three small children. It was better than maid or housekeeper. She wouldn't always have Lo-retta. Where would she be twenty years hence? This opportunity was before her now, and another might never come her way again. More important, if she moved away, she'd no longer be fearful of her father's whereabouts.

Loretta seemed to sense when she was ready to capitulate and broached the subject from another angle. "You are an incredible young woman, Charmaine."

"Incredible, indeed," Charmaine scoffed.

"I'll hear none of that," Loretta scolded. "Your worth is in your heart. The Duvoisin children would benefit from the love brimming there. If you speak as if you are unworthy, you make it so."

That fervent declaration left an impression. Perhaps Loretta was right. This was an unusual opportunity, and something might be waiting for her there. It couldn't hurt to visit Les Charmantes and see. Maybe her mother *was* watching over her. She'd leave it in God's hands.

Within the week, Loretta sent a letter to Caroline informing her sister of their impending visit. By month's end, Joshua had booked passage for the three of them aboard the *Raven*, one of the Duvoisin cargo vessels, which would be delivering supplies to the island.

On the eve of the journey, Charmaine had worried over her decision. But today, with the sky so blue, the river so calm, and her anticipation riding high, she was caught up in the exuberance of the moment and happy she had favored action over complacency, chosen the new over the old. If Loretta felt she could claim the coveted position of governess to the Duvoisin children, claim it she would. So, she sat beside her mentor in the small cabin and prac-ticed the answers she would give to the questions that might be asked during her upcoming interview.

"That's fine," Loretta smiled. "And remember, Charmaine, you don't have to tell them everything."

"But what if they ask about my family?"

Loretta patted her hand and said, "My mother, God rest her soul, died a year ago. Unfortunately, my father left us long ago."

"But is that acceptable? Will they be satisfied?"

"As I told you before, I will see to it they are."

"All is well!" the robust Joshua Harrington boomed as he fell into the chair his wife had vacated.

Charmaine and Loretta looked up from the small bunk, the skirt they had been mending momentarily forgotten as they considered the man turned boy. It was clear he had enjoyed the last five hours above deck as the vessel forged into the Atlantic.

"Jonah Wilkinson tells me he foresees no difficulties with our crossing, and, my dear wife, you will be glad to hear the good captain believes we will sight the islands in under four days, provided the winds remain with us."

"That *is* good news," she replied cheerfully.

"You know, my dear, we can't really call your affliction seasickness," he pointed out. "After all, you've never actually been—"

"Please, Joshua," she implored, "let us not speak about it."

"How thoughtless of me. Would you prefer to hear about our departure?"

"That would be lovely," she replied enthusiastically, winking at Charmaine.

"I knew it was going to be an exceptional voyage the moment we hoisted sail and started to move," he began. "And not due to the gusting wind. Luck was with us from the start. Captain Wilkinson had expected to be delayed by Mr. Duvoisin, but a message was delivered stating he would not be boarding the *Raven* to inspect the cargo as planned. Needless to say, that saved precious time. But the true good fortune lies in the fact that we were not subjected to Mr. Duvoisin's deplorable comportment and snide comments."

"Joshua!"

"Now, Loretta, I've spoken of the man's questionable character before. Everyone in Virginia knows: where John Duvoisin travels, ridicule follows. I tell you now, if he were residing on Les Charmantes, I would have grave misgivings in allowing our Charmaine to live there."

John . . . Charmaine thought . . . *How I despise that name!*

Saturday, September 10, 1836

Jonah Wilkinson charted his ship's passage, pleased with the favorable weather. The *Raven* would make excellent time if she did not encounter the tropical storms that often brewed in these waters in late August and September. But if yesterday's winds were any indicator, the voyage to Les Charmantes would be uneventful and completed in less than four days' time. From there, he would steer his ship to New York, then to England, and eventually back to Virginia, completing a four-month-long journey. Although he did not own the decks upon which he trod, Frederic Duvoisin had made him feel as if he alone were master of the *Raven*. For that reason, he'd work for no other.

He was scrutinizing his charts when Charmaine walked over to him. Although he knew every inch of this part of the Atlantic, he found it comforting and oftentimes commanding to pore over the well-worn maps. The rustle of clothing distracted him, and he turned to look at her. They'd been introduced amid the confusion and flurry of their departure, and he hadn't given her a second thought, until now.

She did not have a stunning face like the rare beauties he'd seen during his travels. It did, however, possess a captivating quality if one cared to look. Well-shaped eyebrows highlighted her most alluring feature—her large brown eyes, framed to perfection by sooty lashes. Her nose was long and slim and turned up on the end. Her lips were neither thick nor thin, coming to life when she spoke. As Jonah stared down at her, he realized her loveliness would never truly be appreciated as long as her dark locks were subdued in a severe bun. But that was for the best, as was her plain apparel, which detracted from her trim figure. Any overt displays of femininity would unleash the uncouth manners of his wild crew.

"Good afternoon, Captain." She smiled up at him, making him feel much taller than his five feet seven inches. "I didn't mean to disturb you, but Mr. Harrington encouraged me to come above deck while he sees to his wife."

"How is the dear woman?" Jonah inquired, remembering that one of his passengers was not faring so well, even during this calmest of voyages.

"She's much improved, thank you. The first day was the worst. When she occupies her mind with a distraction, her constitution is the better for it."

"That's the way of it with many people, until they get their sea legs. But with you, Miss . . . ?"

"Ryan," Charmaine supplied.

"Miss Ryan," he smiled, "you don't seem the least unsettled by this maiden voyage. I'm correct in assuming this is your first time at sea?"

"Yes, but it's too beautiful to upset me." A radiant smile lit the whole of her face. She drew a deep breath, grasped the railing, and looked out at the endless expanse.

"It is breathtaking, is it not?" he asked, turning to the horizon as well, applauding the young woman's fledgling admiration.

"It makes me realize how small I am in comparison."

"Just as the waves crashed to shore before our birth," he

observed in kind, "they will pound the sand after our death. Our passing will make no difference."

The words displeased her. "You think not?"

"There are those who would disagree. Are you one of them?"

"I'd like to believe everyone makes a difference, if only a small one."

Jonah marveled over the philosophical statement. She couldn't be more than eighteen. "Once you've reached my age, you may begin to wonder. But that's neither here nor there. Let me show you my pride and joy."

He motioned toward the stern, and Charmaine realized he meant the ship. Inclining her head, she indulged him, spending an hour walking the upper decks, learning each by name: forecastle, waist, and quarter. He told her the one-hundred-twenty-five-foot vessel had been commissioned in Britain and had, since her maiden voyage over thirty years ago, traversed the high seas with him as her captain. He pointed out everything, from helm to capstan, describing the manpower required to raise the *Raven*'s great length of chain and heavy anchor. Her masts were square-rigged, raked at a slight angle aft for optimum propulsion. Charmaine shielded her eyes and looked up at the three sky-piercing spars, politely humoring him as he went on with a litany of sails, from flying jib, soaring on the bowsprit and spearheading their journey, to the spanker, which acted with the rudder and forged their course. Unfortunately, he mistook her smile for interest and rambled on with his detailed dissertation.

Joshua joined them, and Charmaine sighed in relief, ready to escape to her own cabin. But the conversation unexpectedly turned to the Duvoisins, piquing her interest, so she hugged the rail instead.

". . . very wealthy," the captain was saying, "ten ships, three islands, thousands of acres, and God knows what other investments. But that fortune comes at a high price. Frederic and his sons have been dealt their share of turmoil, a weighty load I'd not care to carry . . ."

The greater the wealth, the deeper the pain . . . Charmaine thought.

". . . There are many who resent their power and covet their money, but those very same men would likely abuse such power and wealth. At least the Duvoisin men come by it honestly, with hard work and acumen."

Joshua grew circumspect. Over the past two days, Jonah Wilkinson had proven to be a man of integrity, and Joshua had come to respect his opinion. "You speak highly of them," he commented dubiously.

"I'm not placing Frederic on a pedestal, but he is a fair man, as fair as any I've known. It's a trait he's passed on to his sons."

"Even John?" Joshua snorted. "A few words came to mind when we were introduced last year, but 'fair' was not one of them."

Jonah chuckled. "I'm not surprised. John can be decidedly caustic, his tongue as quick as his mind, but more often than not, he *is* fair. His sarcasm is just a shield."

"A shield?"

"Against the anger, against the guilt," Jonah replied. "It is rumored he brought on a severe seizure that left his sire crippled. The stroke, or whatever it was, victimized both father and son. Frederic was once a strong and forceful man. Now he never leaves the confines of his estate. John suffers, too. He fled the island three years ago and hasn't returned. As far as I know, he's had no contact with his father. He continues to manage all the Virginia and shipping assets out of Richmond, while Frederic relies on his other son, Paul, to run Charmantes. Unfortunately, that has created more problems."

"How so?" Joshua queried, enthralled.

"The brothers view matters differently. At times, their conflicting ideas pull those in between in opposite directions. There can only be one captain of a ship, lest it founder."

"So, the two sons struggle for the upper hand."

"It goes back to childhood rivalry. Paul enjoys a bond with his father that John, the legitimate son, never had."

"Legitimate?"

Jonah cleared his throat. He'd said too much, yet felt compelled to explain. "Frederic adopted Paul as an infant and raised him as his own, but his was an illegitimate birth. He's Frederic's son," Jonah finished, anticipating the next query. "Of that I'm certain."

"But why would a man favor a bastard child over—"

The inappropriate epithet was out before Joshua could catch himself. He reddened and looked at Charmaine, but her composure remained intact; apparently, she hadn't understood.

Jonah, however, did not seem pleased with the crude appellation. "Frederic respects both of his sons, but Paul works harder than John, so I suppose that has forged a stronger relationship."

"And John's mother?" Joshua asked, further surprised. "What is her reaction to all this?"

"Elizabeth died in childbirth over twenty-five years ago. Some say Frederic blamed John for her death, but that's nonsense. Canards of that kind stemmed from the fact that Frederic grieved for many years after her death."

Charmaine was suddenly confused. "But I thought"—she faltered—"then Colette Duvoisin is Mr. Duvoisin's *second* wife?"

"He remarried ten years ago," Jonah answered succinctly.

Frederic grieved for many years after her death . . .

Charmaine canted her head, sensing evasiveness, unable to pinpoint the heart of her perplexity. Frederic Duvoisin, clearly an older man, had two grown sons, one by his first wife, another by a lover, and he had three other children, the youngest a baby, really, these brought forth by a *second* wife.

"Is she an islander?" Charmaine asked.

"Who? Miss Colette? Oh, my, no." The captain chuckled. "She is French, pure aristocrat. Arrangements were made by her mother, I believe," he added, uncomfortable with Charmaine's intense frown, attempting to thwart the idle talk he knew she was bound to hear.

"Her mother?"

"Colette was quite young at the time."

"How young?"

Jonah, who had waxed loquacious for the past hour, grew laconic. To Charmaine's further trepidation, Joshua Harrington allied himself to the man. "Arrangements of this sort are made all the time by the upper classes, aren't they, Captain Wilkinson?"

"Just so," Jonah hastily agreed.

Charmaine shivered in the blazing sun. She had thought the wealthy enjoyed unlimited choices, yet here was a young woman, much like herself, imprisoned more surely than she would ever be.

"An arrangement?" she mused. "A more apt word would be bondage."

"Bondage?" Jonah objected with a false laugh, then added, "Miss Colette may have borne her husband three children, but I assure you, she enjoys a most comfortable life," as if that fact made their coupling palatable.

Charmaine bit her bottom lip, terribly troubled, and her mind ran far afield, to an island she had yet to tread. *A loveless marriage.* Her mother had suffered such a union. Suddenly, Charmaine's life no longer seemed suffocating. She had never appreciated how free she truly was.

The evening meal was served in the captain's cabin with Charmaine and the Harringtons as his guests. The food, though mediocre, was tempered with good conversation. Even Loretta ate without discomfort, quickly approving of their warm host. Charmaine had shared all the things she had learned that afternoon, so Loretta didn't hesitate to ask her own questions, artfully starting with the Duvoisin's more distant past, one that seemed shrouded in a web of mystery. Jonah, who'd spent many evenings in the company of three generations of Duvoisin men, was happy to oblige . . .

In the early 1700s Jean Duvoisin left his native France and traveled to the American colonies. The younger son of a wealthy and politically connected family, he set out to find his own fortune, taking with him a sizable sum of money, a fast ship, and his father's blessings. He settled in Newportes Newes, a thriving community and burgeoning shipping center at the mouth of the James River. When he heard of William Byrd II's plans to establish a new town some ninety miles northwest, he moved his young family to the site in 1737. Richmond was so dubbed in honor of Richmond on the Thames, England, and it was Jean Duvoisin who helped bolster her success. The Byrd trading post and warehouse, or Shocco as the Indians called it, was in need of a full-time shipper. Jean saw financial potential in assuming such a role and had a second ship commissioned in Newportes Newes. Byrd sanctioned the lucrative endeavor, then guaranteed its success by awarding him substantial acreage west of Richmond. In less than ten years, the entire parcel had been cleared and planted. In addition, Jean now owned three merchantmen that not only brought him wealth through the supplies he shuttled from Europe, but enabled him to transport his own tobacco inexpensively and expediently. When he died some twenty years later, both ventures had exceeded his wildest expectations. The plantation had tripled in size, he owned vast stretches of land throughout the Virginia territory, and the shipping operation belonged exclusively to his eldest son.

Jean Duvoisin II followed in his father's footsteps of expanding the Duvoisin empire, but he took to the seas to do so. The shipping industry became his obsession, the prosperity of the future. Upon his sire's demise, the family plantation was left to the care of other men. Jean II had already conquered the deserted islands he named Les Charmantes (pronounced "lay shar-mont," meaning "the charming ones"). Searching for a base location amidst the expanding routes of his ever-growing fleet, he tamed the wilderness of the largest island and built himself a villa that would allow him privacy. Rumors spread that the house, the very isle, was nothing more than a prison where he locked away his beautiful wife, earning him the title of gentleman pirate. Island lore held that he had kidnapped her from under the nose of a Richmond rival and feared losing her while he was at sea, so he brought her to his isolated paradise so she'd never escape him.

She was the first to give birth on Charmantes, as the main island was being called, bringing into the world six children. The three middle sons perished in a fire that claimed her life as well, leaving behind an eldest son, Jean III, a daughter, Eleanor, and a youngest son, Frederic, twelve years his brother's junior. Years later, Jean and Frederic both traveled to Virginia, taking charge once again of the investments there.

When Jean II fell ill in 1796, his elder son returned to Charmantes and became involved in the American and French West Indies dispute. It cost him his life. Within the year, Jean II died as well, and the Duvoisin fortune fell into Frederic's lap. He was only twenty-three. Finding it impossible to guard Charmantes while residing in Virginia, and fearing its possible loss, he journeyed back as well, expanding his father's farming enterprise into a full-fledged sugarcane plantation run on the work of slaves and indentured servants whom he personally hand picked.

He was already in his thirties when he married Elizabeth Blackford, a young Englishwoman fifteen years his junior. She left her family—a mother, father, brother, and sister—and traveled from Liverpool to the islands where she began her life with her new husband. But she died in childbirth less than a year later, leaving behind an embittered husband.

"The island has grown over the years," Jonah went on to say. "The sugarcane operation led to the building of a harbor where ships could unload supplies and take on raw sugar for transport. From there a town emerged, built by the freed bondsmen. Having served their time, Frederic encouraged the better men to continue on in his employ for set wages. These were the first men to truly settle Charmantes, some sending for families. Frederic's close associates maintained he was mad, his idea sheer folly; in Europe, these men were criminals. But many had been punished for petty crimes. Poverty can make a man do foolhardy things. On Charmantes, they had an opportunity to start over, and most were happy to take it. They are rough around the edges, but there is little crime on the island. In a manner of speaking, they keep the peace. As the population multiplied, Frederic sponsored other businesses. First Thompson's mercantile was built, supplying the islanders with the staples. After that, a cooper opened up shop, crafting all the watertight casks necessary for sugar transport. Of course, Dulcie's was next."

"Dulcie's?" Loretta asked.

"The saloon," Jonah explained, stopping to take a sip of his black coffee. "Then a livery went up, and next a meetinghouse which serves as a church on Sundays. That was constructed about ten years ago. Miss Colette is a devout Catholic and insisted on it for the townspeople."

"Do they truly have a reverend to conduct services?" Loretta queried, astonished. "I thought my sister exaggerated when she mentioned Sunday Mass in one letter."

"No exaggeration there. The man is a Roman Catholic priest and has resided on Charmantes for years now."

"Isn't that a bit strange?" Joshua asked. "It seems to me the Church wouldn't be sending priests to small, distant islands."

"You underestimate the size and scope of Charmantes," Jonah replied. "They even have a bank. It's run by one of Frederic's friends from Virginia. Many influential men have invested in Duvoisin enterprises, primarily the shipping end of his business, while a good many islanders are purchasing land on the outskirts of town, an option open to them as long as they build a house or business on it. The Duvoisin wealth intrigues them, whets their appetite. They feel they can grasp Frederic's good fortune just by owning a parcel of his land."

"And have they?" Joshua asked.

"In a day or two you'll set foot on Charmantes and see her people. Then you can decide if they live the good life or not."

Loretta leaned forward. "I know my sister and her husband are pleased with their move to the Caribbean. And I must admit, after your description, Captain, I'm looking forward to arriving. It sounds wonderful, doesn't it, Charmaine?"

But the girl was pensive, deaf to their conversation.

"Charmaine?"

"I'm sorry—what did you say?"

"Les Charmantes sounds like a lovely place to call home," Loretta prompted. "But you seemed awfully far away."

Charmaine rubbed her brow. "No," she murmured, "I'm listening."

Loretta knew better. The girl had lamented Colette and Frederic Duvoisin's courtship throughout the afternoon, imagining the most wretched scenarios, refusing to consider other possibilities. Loretta was determined to ascertain the truth before Caroline had a chance to bend their ears.

"Captain Wilkinson," she began, "if I'm not being too presumptuous, could you tell us a bit more about Colette Duvoisin?"

Jonah responded with a frown, and Loretta diplomatically digressed. "My sister loves to prattle, but hates to write. Her short letters are few and far between. Charmaine may soon be working for Mr. and Mrs. Duvoisin. Surely you can appreciate her eagerness to become acquainted with them."

"What would you like to know?" he relented, realizing there was no point in trying to avoid what they'd eventually find out.

"Charmaine seems to think Miss Colette is young enough to be Mr. Duvoisin's daughter."

"She is. Younger than his two sons, in fact."

Charmaine gave Loretta an "I told you so" look.

Jonah read it, too. Folding his arms across his chest, he said, "Miss Colette's family was suffering from financial difficulties. Frederic saw them through all of that. There was also a brother, who was quite ill. Frederic's wealth defrayed the expenses from his prolonged malady. Now, some might call such an arrangement 'bondage,' but I'm sure it's not the word Miss Colette would use."

Charmaine ignored Jonah's final assertion, horrified. Her mother's life had been deplorable, but at least that had been Marie's choice. Colette Duvoisin, on the other hand, had been married off for monetary reasons, like chattel. Charmaine felt terribly sad for the woman.

Jonah leaned back in his chair. "Miss Colette is not as unhappy as you imagine her to be, Miss Ryan."

"That is something I will have to decide for myself, Captain," she replied.

Loretta patted Charmaine's hand, certain the captain was

right. "At least the mistress of the manor will be someone closer to your own age," she placated. "You may become friends."

Charmaine hadn't thought of this and hoped that might come true.

Monday, September 12, 1836

She awoke early the morning of her fourth day at sea. Captain Wilkinson expected to sight the islands with the break of dawn, and she wanted to be above deck as they came into view. She dressed quickly, choosing her best Sunday dress of pale green, and was brushing out the last tangles in her thick, unruly hair when the awaited shout resounded from above. "Land ho!"

Indecisive for only a moment, she threw the dark brown locks over her shoulder, where a cascade of curls fell to her waist. No bun today, lest she forfeit the coveted sight. Let the wind take the tresses where it would; they'd not spoil this glorious day, which promised the start of a new life. Stealing a final peek in her hand mirror, she smiled in satisfaction, then hastened from the cabin.

Captain Wilkinson took no notice of her when she reached the upper deck, his eyes raised to the rigging and the crew that prepared the *Raven* for docking, some climbing the ratlines to adjust the sails. Surmising Joshua was still abed, Charmaine moved out of harm's way to a vacant spot at the port railing.

The tarrying men began to ogle her, and she bowed her head to their crude comments. Although she'd turned their heads a number of times during the voyage, their perusal had never come close to a leer. She glanced down at her dress wondering if her attire was somehow indiscreet, but finding nothing there, she focused on the great expanse of ocean, hoping to catch sight of land. They were forging into a stiff headwind, and the gales swirled round her, capturing her unbound hair one moment and molding her skirts against her legs the next.

When one man whistled, Jonah's attention was snared. He chuckled. By all outward signs, the girl was trying to ignore his surly crew. Wiping the sweat from his brow, he walked over to her. "Good morning, Miss Ryan."

Relieved, Charmaine faced him.

Jonah took in her ebullient smile, the sparkling eyes alight with anticipation, and the wild tresses that framed her delicate face, evincing a comeliness thus far obscured. No wonder his men were behaving this way.

"I heard the heralding of land, but I can't see it," she complained. "Are the islands still so far away I need a spyglass?"

"No, my dear, but you are searching the wrong part of the sea."

Embarrassed, she dropped her gaze, but he took her elbow and led her to the opposite railing, pointing to the southeast. There, on the horizon, was land.

He returned to his work, but she remained starboard side, watching the dark smudge grow larger until the whitest of beaches came into view, a great expanse that seemed tremendous for a mere island. Beyond the shore, she detected shrubs and long grasses that meandered into shaded areas cast by huge, bowing palm trees, willows, and silk cottons. She marveled at its untouched beauty, suddenly realizing she had yet to see any human habitation. There were no docks, no houses, and no people. She looked over her shoulder to question the captain about this, but he was nowhere to be found, so her curiosity would have to wait. They were now riding parallel to the seemingly deserted island. She felt much like Jean Duvoisin II, discovering his paradise for the first time— untamed, yet free. There couldn't be a more serene place on earth, she thought, concluding that this couldn't be the main island, but rather one of the smaller two that had not been settled.

By and by, the beaches turned rocky, and cliffs dominated the coastline, jutting ever higher as they trekked east. Huge waves sent sea spray spiraling upward as they bombarded the palisades, showering a mist that reached as far as the decks. They closed in on a lighthouse that marked the northernmost point. Once they passed it, her eyes fell back to the bluffs, which curved to the right far into the distance.

The hour lengthened, and Captain Wilkinson returned, Joshua Harrington at his side. "We're circling Charmantes," he said, "and should reach the cove shortly."

"The cove?" she asked.

"That is where the dock is built, on the eastern coast. Most Caribbean islands have a leeward or western port. During hurricane season, they are safe from those storms. But Charmantes boasts an almost landlocked harbor, a bay that is protected by a peninsula. Because he was able to construct his harbor in the east, Jean II chose the safer western side of the island to erect his mansion, where the beaches are sandy and beautiful. When we enter the inlet, this untouched beauty will be replaced by the bustling town I spoke of the other evening."

He pointed to the eastern horizon. "If you look carefully, you'll see the other two islands that comprise Les Charmantes." Shielding their eyes, Charmaine and Joshua were able to discern two tiny landmasses.

Shortly thereafter, the main island curved sharply away, and the *Raven* tacked south, hugging the peninsula now. Charmaine was once again left alone as Joshua accompanied the captain. Seabirds appeared from nowhere, darting between the towering masts, swooping low and hovering over the water, squawking loudly as if welcoming their approach.

They reached the cape's tip, and Charmaine's eyes returned to the spider-web rigging. Ropes groaned as the triangular sails were trimmed. Instantly, they billowed taut, harnessing the wind. The stern veered out, and the vessel pivoted right, completing a wide one-hundred-eighty-degree loop starboard side. "Wearing ship," the captain called it, and Charmaine marveled at how the huge merchantman was navigated north and into Charmantes' estuary. She gasped when the deserted land gave way to a busy wharf and thriving community.

As the captain skillfully maneuvered the *Raven* closer to port, angling the packet against the largest of three docks, Charmaine ran hungry eyes over every visible portion of the island, buildings everywhere. When she had her fill, her gaze turned toward the people, ordinary people she quickly assessed. Why had she thought they'd be different?

The crowd was increasing; the merchantman's arrival of paramount interest, the pier a sea of faces now—white, black, and every shade in between—all modestly garbed, though far from impoverished. There were women among them, some clutching infants to their breasts as they waved to their sailor husbands. These crewmen were not the wanderers Charmaine had supposed them to be, but had families waiting for them here.

The *Raven* was secured in a frenzy, as scores of men labored with the massive vessel. At last, the gangplank was lowered, and those on the quay scurried to her decks. Friends slapped callused hands across the backs of those they had not seen for many months. Plans were already being made for a night at the town's saloon. Husbands rushed to the wharf to hug their wives and children. For the moment, all thoughts of labor were suspended as handshakes, embraces, and stories were exchanged.

A hush came over the throng as a tall, dark man boarded the vessel and came to stand in their midst. He radiated a magnetism that commanded everyone's attention, and Charmaine's eyes were riveted, admiring him in a way she had never admired a man before. His face was swarthy, testifying to many hours spent under the tropical sun, his jaw, sharp. Intense eyes hinted of a keen mind.

Chestnut-brown locks fell on a sweaty brow, and his straight nose plunged down to a dark moustache and full lips. His stance was easy, yet his bearing was self-assured, proud—aristocratic. "Let's go men!" he bellowed, white teeth flashing against his bronzed skin. "The sooner we get this ship unloaded, the sooner the drinks are on me at Dulcie's!"

Loud cheers went up, and all was in chaos as the men fell into their work. The tall stranger stood his ground, feet planted apart, issuing a spate of orders to all quarters of the deck. The main hatch was thrown open, equipment was rolled forward, and a pulley and boom were quickly assembled. He smiled broadly as he surveyed the enthusiastic laborers before him.

Charmaine could not tear her eyes away, pleased she'd gone unnoticed.

With a sweep of his forearm, he mopped the sweat from his brow. Then, in imitation of the seamen and longshoremen, he ripped off his own white shirt, revealing a broad, furry chest and wide shoulders. He flung the garment over the railing and threw himself into unloading the vessel.

Charmaine's heart took up an unsteady beat. In Richmond, gentlemen never doffed their shirts, and astounded, she gaped at the play of muscles across his tanned back and arms. Obviously, he was not afraid to work; rather, he enjoyed it. She felt the blood rise to her cheeks as her eyes traveled down his back, which glistened with sweat, to his muscular legs, sculpted against his form-fitting trousers. She turned away, overwhelmed. She couldn't breathe. He was, by far, the most handsome man she had ever beheld.

"Charmaine!" Joshua called, pushing his way through the commotion to reach her. "I've located Harold and Caroline Browning."

"They're here?"

"Waiting on the wharf," he answered, taking hold of her arm

and leading her to the stern of the ship. "Apparently, they expected us to be on the *Raven* once they realized it was coming from Richmond."

Charmaine nodded, though her regard rested on the captivating stranger. He and three other men were rolling the first casks across the deck, one to the other.

"Who is that man?" she asked.

"Paul Duvoisin," Joshua replied gruffly, noting the blush on Charmaine's cheeks. "We've already been introduced."

"When?"

"Just a few moments ago on the wharf. But come, Charmaine, we must hurry. The ocean breezes are all but gone, and I do not care to spend the remainder of the day in this heat. It's only going to get worse as the sun rises higher."

They neared the gangplank, and Joshua gestured over the side of the ship to a pleasant-looking couple waving up at them. "I have to fetch Loretta. Why don't you make your way down to her sister?"

"But I have to get my belongings," she replied. "They're still in my cabin."

"Not to worry. I'll fetch them for you."

"Don't be silly! You go ahead and help Mrs. Harrington, and I'll meet you on the pier with the Brownings in ten minutes."

Joshua departed, taking the stairs of the companionway quickly down. But Charmaine's steps were halted as her gaze fell once again upon Paul Duvoisin. Her heart raced, awed by the realization that a fortune rested in the hands of someone so young and handsome. Best not to dwell on it. With that thought, she descended to the deck below and collected her baggage.

When she once again stepped into the midday sun, Joshua was nowhere in sight. Certain she had finished her packing before him, she began her search for Captain Wilkinson. It would be impolite to leave without thanking him.

She learned from one of the seamen that he was in his cabin. Crossing to the quarterdeck, she knocked on his door and was invited in. He was seated at his desk, with Paul Duvoisin leaning over his right shoulder. Neither man looked up from the sheets spread before them, but the captain motioned toward her with a brusque command, "Don't dally boy! Bring them here!"

Charmaine was stunned and didn't answer.

He looked up. "Oh, Miss Ryan, I apologize," he said. "I thought you were Wagner. He was fetching some documents for me."

With the mention of the unfamiliar name, Paul straightened, his attention instantly snared. *This is unusual—a comely lass: wavy hair, pretty face, and curvaceous figure. Why is she on the* Raven? He inhaled. He had never seen her before. "Is this a beautiful niece you've kept hidden from us, Jonah?"

"You know I have no kin, Paul."

"So you've said," Paul mused, dissatisfied with the response.

His eyes remained fixed on the young woman, but before he could pose another question that might reveal her identity, the cabin boy rushed in. Paul snatched the documents from him, sat down, and began reading them.

Dismissed, Charmaine's heart sank, but she thanked Jonah Wilkinson for his hospitality. He, in turn, kissed her hand and wished her well. Glancing toward the desk, she quietly left his cabin.

Above deck, the heat had intensified. She retrieved her trunk and lumbered toward the gangway, certain the Harringtons were waiting for her.

Joshua spotted her and boarded the vessel, taking her luggage in one hand and her elbow with the other. In no time, she was standing on the solid dock, though her unsteady feet reacted as if she were still on the rocking ship.

"So, you are Charmaine," Caroline said as introductions were made, her husband smiling pleasantly. "You're as lovely as my sister wrote."

"I'm afraid Mrs. Harrington is too kind."

"Nonsense," the plump woman replied. "You are nearly as pretty as my Gwendolyn."

Her husband cleared his throat, but she silenced him with a cold glare.

Charmaine was glad to climb into the Brownings' carriage. "Is it always so hot here?" she complained, dabbing at her brow.

"There's normally a breeze," Harold replied, "but you get used to it."

"Not if she wears her hair that way," Caroline countered.

Charmaine lifted the tresses off her neck. "I was trying to wrap it in a bun—"

"Charmaine," Loretta interrupted, squeezing her hand, "it's lovely."

Caroline raised her nose, but quickly turned her attention to the road. "Look—over there!" she exclaimed, pointing across the thoroughfare, motioning for her sister to shift to her side of the coach. "That's Dulcie's. Oh, the goings-on at that establishment! But men will be men. Isn't that right, Harold?"

"I wouldn't know," he mumbled, talking to his lap.

"What did you say?"

This time he answered clearly. "I said, only you would know."

She eyed him suspiciously, then ignored him altogether as the town continued to roll by. "And over there is the mercantile. It carries a wide variety of goods, nearly as fine a selection as any general store you'll find in the States. But you don't want to shop there on the weekends. That's when the bondsmen make their purchases. What a filthy lot they are!"

"Caroline," the man reprimanded, offended, "many of them are good men."

"How can you say that?" she demanded, every bit as offended as he. "Murderers—that's what they are!"

"They're not murderers. They wouldn't be working here if they were. You know that. Most are poor men paying the price of a minor offense."

"Oh, don't be so addle-brained!" she accused, insulted by his contradictions. "They're common criminals. Why must you always make excuses for them?"

"I know them, or have you forgotten I oversee most of their work?"

"Ssh!" she hissed, her indignation and revulsion surpassed by her shame. "Do you want everyone to know you associate with those people?"

"I'm not going to hide what I do for a living on this island," he replied in exasperation, "or worse still, lie about it, as you do."

"Harry, please," she protested, her nervous eyes flitting over those in the coach, "not in front of my family!"

When her bottom lip stopped quivering, she peered out the window and complained anew. "Now look what you've done! We're on the outskirts of town and have missed all the sights!"

She remained petulant for all of a minute, then warmed to a new topic. "It's a shame you missed meeting Paul Duvoisin, Loretta. Quite a fine specimen of a man he is, but a rogue, if you know what I mean, with an eye for the ladies. They say the apple doesn't fall far from the tree. Following in his father's footst—"

"Caroline!" Harold objected again, appalled by her audacity.

"Well, it's true!" she returned in kind, annoyed that her husband dared to quash the bit of gossip that begged telling. "Imagine, remaining a widower for all those years—sampling his fill—only to up and marry a girl young enough to be his daughter! And to think that Colette—"

"Caroline!" Harold exploded. "Hold your tongue!"

"But Harold!" the virago mewled, shaken by his uncharacteristic outrage.

His ire cooled as swiftly as it had spiked, and he pulled at his shirt collar in evident distress. "I'm sorry," he apologized lamely. "But my wife shouldn't be spreading rumors."

Caroline clicked her tongue, muttering, "They're not rumors, they're facts."

The remainder of the trip was passed in silence, leaving Charmaine to wonder over the woman's temperament, so unlike that of her sister. Beyond that, Charmaine's thoughts traveled to Colette Duvoisin, the same questions resurfacing, no less troubling. Was the young woman content bound to a man old enough to be her father? What revelations would the next few days bare?

When they arrived at the Browning cottage, a girl of perhaps fifteen emerged from within. Like her mother, she was plump, but she had a charming smile and rushed forward to greet them. "Aunt Loretta? Uncle Joshua?"

"Gwendolyn?" Loretta queried. "My, how you've grown!"

As embraces were exchanged, Harold drew his wife aside and whispered to her in heated tones. "If I hear so much as another syllable concerning Frederic and Colette, I swear I will send you packing." When Caroline's mouth dropped open, he rushed on. "Do you want me to lose my position here? Would it please you to see me banished like Clayton Jones? Remember what happened to him?"

Caroline's eyes grew wide as saucers. "Yes—but no—of course not."

"Or perhaps you'd like to be the next Alma Banks? That would really give the townspeople something to talk about."

Caroline's expression bordered on the horrific.

"Yes." Harold nodded with a satisfied grin. "You'd best think about that the next time you feel like wagging your tongue. Frederic might be ill, but I have it on good authority he's not as incapacitated as everyone seems to believe. Beyond that, I respect Colette, as much as I do her husband. If not for them, who knows where we would be today? Therefore, you will cease your prattling!"

She nodded meekly, took a moment to compose herself, and finally beckoned everyone inside.

Chapter 2

Sunlight poured into the bedroom Charmaine shared with Gwendolyn Browning. Her eyes opened and she stretched, enjoying the gentle breezes that whispered through the windows. In just a few hours, the coolness of the early morning would yield to the intense rays of the Caribbean sun. This was summer on Charmantes, but according to the Brownings, the other seasons were not much different, just a bit milder.

Crawling from the small double bed, Charmaine looked down at her slumbering friend. Yes, she could call Gwendolyn her friend. The girl was talkative and bubbly, her gaiety infectious.

Yesterday, they had toured the town with Caroline. Today, Gwendolyn wanted to show Charmaine the other, more beautiful spots Charmantes had to offer. Charmaine was looking forward to it. She didn't relish Mrs. Browning's company and was happy to leave the woman with her sister for the day.

As she sat at the dressing table and unbraided her hair, Gwendolyn stirred. "Good morning," she greeted with a yawn. "Why are you up so early?"

"I couldn't sleep. So, what do you have in store for me today?"

"The beaches. They're lovely compared to the ugly town."

Charmaine brushed out the riotous locks. "I didn't think it was ugly." In truth, she had been quite impressed by it. Even with Captain Wilkinson's description aboard the *Raven*, she had not been prepared for the self-sufficiency she'd witnessed yesterday. Besides the mercantile, saloon, meetinghouse, and bank, the town had a skilled cooper at the cooperage, a farrier and blacksmith at the livery, a tanner, potter, and cobbler sharing space in one of the three large warehouses, and a lumberyard of sorts, which supplied various building materials for all the cottages being erected. According to Mrs. Browning, most of the wood came from the northern pine forests and was milled right there. Additional hardwoods were transported from Virginia. Jonah Wilkinson had been correct; many families intended to make Charmantes their permanent home. Construction was visible everywhere, and only the sea stood as a reminder that this bustling "city" was on an island and not part of a greater country.

Gwendolyn watched Charmaine coif her thick tresses into a respectable bun. "Your hair is so unusual, Charmaine. How ever did it get so curly?"

"I don't know. My parents had straight hair, and I curse my misfortune."

"But it's beautiful! If I had your hair, I'd set my sights for Paul Duvoisin!"

"Oh, Gwendolyn, you do have high aspirations!"

"Maybe I'd have to lose a bit of flesh around my middle," the girl sulked, looking down at her plump figure. "But after that—well—there'd be no stopping me!" When Charmaine shook her head, she pressed on. "If you saw him, you'd understand what I mean!"

"I have seen him, and I know what you mean."

"You have?" Gwendolyn asked, jumping from the bed. "When? Where?"

"The day we arrived, on the ship."

"Oh . . . isn't he the most handsome man you've ever seen?" she declared dreamily. "I could just swoon every time he looks my way. Only, when he does look my way, he's never looking at me." She pouted until struck by a new thought. "If I had your curves and hair, I'd have a chance, a real chance!"

"A chance at what?"

"A marriage proposal, of course! And I'd accept immediately, before he could change his mind!"

Charmaine smiled at the juvenile declaration. Her friend babbled on.

"I know I'm only romancing. But look at you. You have all those things a man looks at, especially your lovely figure and beautiful hair."

"I'm sorry to say you are wrong, Gwendolyn. I was wearing my hair like this when Mr. Duvoisin and I first met, and he wasn't interested in introductions."

"He was probably busy," the girl reasoned. "He's always like that when a ship comes into port. All work, all business. But wait until you're living under his roof, seeing him every day, perhaps taking meals with him. Things are bound to change, aren't they? And then you will be the envy of every girl on this island, because you'll have that once in a lifetime chance we've all been pining for. You mark my words if Paul doesn't notice you then!"

Paul Duvoisin's house . . . living under his roof . . . taking meals with him . . . seeing him every day! The full import of working for the Duvoisins took hold. Why hadn't she thought of him living there? It was his home! Charmaine felt giddy, seized by a host of paradoxical emotions: apprehension and expectation, dread and elation.

They left the bedroom some time later, dressed and ready for a day's excursion. Loretta sat at the kitchen table, finishing a letter of introduction she would send off to the Duvoisin manor. In it, she had requested an audience with Madame Colette Duvoisin, stating that her companion, Charmaine Ryan, had traveled to Les Charmantes from Richmond in order to apply for the position of governess.

"That should do it," she said, patting the folded missive. She set her hand to another, informing her housekeeper they had arrived and would spend no more than a month abroad. By the time the girls had eaten, she was finished and asked Gwendolyn to post the letter. "Here is some money," she added. "Caroline tells me there will be a fee to have it shipped to the Richmond post office."

Gwendolyn nodded. "What about the other one to Mrs. Duvoisin?"

"Your father said he will deliver it today," Loretta replied.

The waterfront town wilted in the morning sun, but it did not seem to impede any of the islanders. Charmaine and Gwendolyn ambled toward the general store, and still Charmaine felt faint, reaching the shade of the mercantile porch none too soon. The heat had not affected her companion.

"Come, Charmaine," she encouraged, "I see Rebecca Remmen. Her brother doesn't generally allow her to walk about town on her own."

"You go," Charmaine said. "I have to rest a minute. Why don't you give me your aunt's letter and I'll post it while you talk with your friend?"

"Very well. I'll meet you inside in a few minutes."

Charmaine entered the general store and was surprised to find it empty, save its proprietress, Madeline Thompson, the comely widow introduced to her yesterday. "May I help you?" the woman asked, her sultry voice laced with a mild, Southern accent.

"Yes, please," Charmaine replied. "I have a letter I'd like to post."

Madeline scrutinized the item she handed over. "Richmond . . . Hmm . . . It's a shame you didn't get this to me sooner. The post was carted off yesterday. But I suppose I could deliver it to the *Raven* myself, after I close up my shop."

Charmaine nodded gratefully and began fishing in her reticule for the coins Gwendolyn had passed to her. She was oblivious to the mercantile bell. "Now if you'll just tell me how much—"

"Excuse me one moment," Madeline said, moving around the corner of the counter. "May I be of some service?" she inquired of her newest patron.

"No thanks, Maddy—"

Charmaine's stomach lurched as she recognized the voice of Paul Duvoisin.

"—I can find the things I need. But if you'd like," and he removed a piece of paper from his shirt pocket, "you could gather the items on this list. Miss Colette requested them this morning."

Madeline smiled and slipped the paper from his fingers, her hand lingering a bit longer than necessary near his. "And may I ask a favor of you?" she queried coquettishly. "That is, if you're headed to the *Raven* today?"

"I am. What would you have me do?"

The woman looked down at the correspondence she held in her other hand. "I've just received a letter intended for Virginia, but Gunther took the post already. Could you possibly give this to the captain? I'd be eternally grateful."

"Eternally, Maddy? You're not using your feminine wiles on me, are you?"

"If only they would work!"

"All right, Maddy," he chuckled, pocketing the letter. "I'll deliver this if you'll have Miss Colette's items ready by the end of the day."

"Perfect," she purred. "I'll have the pleasure of your company not once, but twice today."

Paul winked at her, then stepped away. Charmaine looked on. He seemed to have enjoyed the woman's coy overtures. He glanced in Charmaine's direction, and her heart missed a beat. At that moment, she fervently wished she were as adept at conversation as Madeline Thompson, flirtatious as it might be. She shook her head, knowing such thoughts could only lead to trouble. Suddenly, he was standing next to her, depositing a handful of items on the counter. Charmaine realized how foolish she looked just lingering there. "I believe I owe you money for the postage on my letter, Mrs. Thompson." He was staring down at her, but she didn't look up, her bonnet concealing her face.

"That will be two cents," Madeline said as she moved behind the counter.

Charmaine quickly produced the coins, but before the proprietress could take the money, Paul was asking if she could add his items to those he would retrieve later that afternoon. With her nod, he bade them a good day. To Charmaine's relief and disappointment, he walked out the door and into the blazing sun.

She stepped out of the mercantile a few minutes later, but there was no sign of him. Gwendolyn waddled over to her, exuberant. "Charmaine, you've just missed Paul Duvoisin! And he even spoke to me! 'Course, he rushed right off, but Rebecca was ecstatic. If you think I'm bad, you should hear her talk. She's so in love with him . . ." And so it went. Gwendolyn's happiness was contagious, and despite the heat, Charmaine had to smile and enjoy herself.

"This last week has been unusually warm," Gwendolyn confided. "Our weather is normally beautiful all year long. Wait, you'll see, and I know you'll come to love it here!"

They headed southwest and within an hour were walking along white beaches where it was quiet, the town a distant memory. They collected seashells while Gwendolyn chatted away. Charmaine found it amazing so many people inhabited Les Charmantes, yet no one bothered to enjoy its most wondrous spots, for they were alone on the long expanse of sand, save the gulls that scattered with their approach, caterwauling in objection, soaring high on extended wings, then landing moments later in the wake of their steps.

When the searing sun of midday became too intense, they found refuge among the many overhanging boughs of the palm trees. They rested in their shade, their low voices the only indication they were there. Charmaine smiled as a pair of flamingos walked along the water's edge, but seeing the young women, turned direction and disappeared into the shaded wood.

"Now," Gwendolyn breathed, "where would you like to go next?"

"I don't know," Charmaine answered, looking up at the girl who had stood to brush away the moss and sand that clung to her skirts.

"It's your choice," Gwendolyn continued. "We're close enough to walk to the Duvoisin mansion. It's probably only a half-hour away from here. Of course, we won't be allowed on the grounds. It's fenced off. But you could get a good look at where you'll be working."

"Where I'll be working?" Charmaine queried with raised brow. "I haven't even gone on an interview yet, Gwendolyn. You sound so sure I'll get the governess's position."

"You will. Your name alone guarantees it."

Charmaine frowned bemusedly. "What do you mean?"

"Charmaine . . . Charmantes . . . It's destiny, don't you think? How many other girls have a name so similar? It's as if the island were calling you home."

Charmaine shook her head with a laugh. "I hope you are right, because I think I will enjoy living here, especially with you as a friend."

She declined the visit to the Duvoisin mansion, fearing someone important might see her. They were getting hungry, and Gwendolyn suggested they go back to town and eat at Dulcie's. "I brought some money."

"The saloon?" Charmaine asked, aghast.

"It's not that bad, not during the day, anyway, and the food is very good."

Charmaine disagreed. "It's a gaming establishment and worse."

"Only at night, Charmaine, and mostly on weekends. During the day, we'll be fine. None of the indentured servants or freed slaves are allowed in there."

"Freed slaves?" Charmaine queried, finding the statement strange. She had noticed quite a few Negroes walking the streets without restriction, but just now wondered about it, for such sights were uncommon in Richmond.

"All the islands in this area of the West Indies are under British rule," Gwendolyn explained as they meandered back the way they had come, "and a few years ago, slavery was abolished both in England and on the islands."

"But I thought Frederic Duvoisin owned and governed Charmantes."

"He does," Gwendolyn affirmed. "But according to Father, he also wishes to appease the British. He transports a great deal of sugar to them. He also receives British protection against pirate attacks on the high seas and here on Charmantes. His cargo would not be well received if the English felt it was bought and paid for with slave labor."

"So, he's keeping the peace."

"And not just with the British monarchy. His wife holds slavery as an abomination as well."

"Really?" Charmaine was surprised. She'd grown up with slavery all around her and accepted it as commonplace.

Gwendolyn delved into a sketchy tale about a Negro named Nicholas and a severe beating. Apparently, Colette Duvoisin had come to the man's defense, which fed some nasty gossip. Frederic Duvoisin put a stop to it, making an example of two islanders at the heart of the problem by expelling them from Charmantes. There were also rumors of a murder, and Gwendolyn insisted a great taboo still clung to the story, frightening people into silence. Eventually, all the Negroes were liberated.

"If we're not going to Dulcie's," Gwendolyn said, "what about the harbor?"

Charmaine regarded her quizzically. Within the hour, she was being pulled along the boardwalk. As they drew nearer the dock, Charmaine wrenched free, comprehending her friend's scheme. Gwendolyn intended to spy on Paul Duvoisin. But the capricious girl hurried ahead, closer to the *Raven*, which was still moored there, her quick step unhampered by her girth.

"Gwendolyn—no!" Charmaine called. "We shouldn't be here!"

The girl only giggled, stopping to catch her breath. "Don't be silly! He'll never see us, I promise. Leastwise he never has before!"

"Before? You've done this before?"

Gwendolyn nodded persuasively. Though Charmaine shook her head, she realized the busy wharf offered them a measure of anonymity: the passersby ignored them. They were soon concealed in a small alcove formed by one of the huge warehouses and an empty toolshed, a reasonable distance from the ship and the long-shoremen who tarried at loading the packet. Barrels and crates obstructed the men's view of them more than their view of the men, for they peered through the slats, hungrily searching the ship for some sign of Paul Duvoisin.

"This was foolish," Charmaine whispered. "What if he *does* see me?"

"He won't," Gwendolyn promised. "Besides, if you watch for a while, you'll get used to seeing him and won't be nervous when you start living at the mansion. After all, it will probably be deliciously difficult those first few days in the house."

A series of loud oaths put the discussion to rest. "Jesus Christ Almighty! Not that way! The other way!"

Standing not fifteen feet away at the foot of a beveled gang-plank was a disheveled man, his eyes hardened, his yellow teeth grinding down hard on a wad of tobacco. "Goddamn it! I told you to roll it the other way!" He threw down the rope he'd been at-tempting to loop around a huge oak cask and motioned to a boy of perhaps twelve. "Stand over here, goddamn it! I'll push while you slide the parbuckle underneath. Then we can hoist it up."

The lad, whose shoulder was braced against the horizontal barrel, did not budge, his neck taut and face reddened. "This one's gotta weigh five-hundred pounds. The wharf ain't level, I tell ya. I think it's gonna run away if I let go!"

"I got it!" the dockworker sneered. "Now grab the goddamn rope!"

Reluctantly, the youth obeyed. The barrel instantly broke loose and rolled down the pier. The boy grimaced as it hit three other casks standing on end, his face breaking into a smile when it stopped, undamaged.

"Jesus Christ, boy!" the man cursed lividly. "How could you *be* so goddamn dumb? Why didn't you wait until I got me a proper grip?" Cold hatred gleamed in his eyes, but the lad did not take heed and snickered in relief. "You wouldn't be laughin' if I kicked your damn ass!"

Charmaine had seen enough. "Let's go, Gwendolyn. That man reminds me of someone I'd rather forget—"

"What goes on here?"

The older man drew himself up as Paul Duvoisin approached. "This young snip don't know how to be puttin' in a day's work," he grumbled.

"Is that so?" Paul queried. "What do you have to say for yourself, boy?"

"I'm just learning, sir. Today's my first day. I need some trainin' is all."

"What you be needin'," the older man hissed, "is a good swift kick in the pants. Maybe that'd wipe that brazen smile off your goddamn face!"

"All right, that's enough!" Paul commanded. "Since the boy is new, I expect you to be patient with him. If you don't think you can manage that, I'll place him with someone else who can instruct him properly."

"That's fine by me. No way in hell I need help like that!"

"Good," Paul said coolly. "What's your name, lad?"

"Jason, sir. Jason Banner."

"Well now, Jason, we'll see if Buck Mathers can use you today."

"*Buck?*" the older man expostulated. "Why the hell are you givin' him to that big nigger? He don't need no help!"

Paul raised a dubious brow. "If Jason is more of a hindrance than a help, that shouldn't matter to you, should it, Mr. Rowlan?" Receiving no answer, Paul turned back to Jason. "You'll find Buck at the bow of the ship. He's the biggest black man on deck, so you shouldn't have any trouble spotting him."

"Yes, sir. I know who he is."

"Good," Paul replied, clapping a hand on the boy's shoulder. "Do whatever he tells you to do. Tell him I sent you along, and I'll speak to him later."

"Yes, sir! Thank you, sir!" In a moment, he was gone.

Paul faced Jessie Rowlan. "Back to work."

"You're gonna find someone else to help me, ain't ya?"

"You had help, but you turned it aside. Now, finish this job without further incident or collect your wages from the Duvoisin purser. Either way, I don't want to hear your foul mouth again!"

Rowlan received the ultimatum, but could not contain his outrage. "The Duvoisin purser," he grumbled under his breath as he shuffled over to the awaiting barrels. "Don't that sound fancy? We all know it's 'Do-voy-sin.' Leave it to the rich to take an ugly name—"

"It's 'Doo-*vwah*-zan,' Mr. Rowlan, fancy or not," Paul responded smoothly. "Pronounce it correctly or don't bother looking for work here."

Rowlan's eyes narrowed, his hatred poorly concealed.

"Was there something else you wanted to say—to my face this time?"

The man didn't answer, though his manner spoke volumes as once again he readied the cask for hoisting.

Paul rubbed the back of his neck and walked away.

Charmaine watched Paul return to the *Raven*'s deck, and she imagined a similar confrontation. Her lips curled in delight as she envisioned John Ryan cowering before Paul, and the fear that had stalked her in Richmond was gone.

"Wasn't he wonderful?" Gwendolyn whispered in adulation.

"Yes," Charmaine sighed. Paul Duvoisin was suddenly more than just handsome.

Rowlan coaxed another worker into helping him. A length of rope was doubled around the heavy barrel, the ends of which were pulled through a loop to form a sling. Eventually, it was hoisted up the concave plank with a pulley. Once on deck, it was released and rolled across the waist of the ship to the hatch.

The hour lengthened. Men tarried at the same operation fore and aft, but with ease and camaraderie. Quite abruptly, work shifted from loading the vessel to unloading two crates of tea. Charmaine wondered why, but Gwendolyn only shrugged. A buckboard drew alongside the vessel, ready to receive them, but splintering wood rent the air and the pulley let go, one large container plummeting to the pier below. The men on the quay shouted and scattered, stumbling with the shuddering impact. The crate hit the wharf just shy of the wagon and split open, spilling tea leaves everywhere. The horses reared, and the driver clutched the reins tightly to keep them from bolting.

Paul appeared at the starboard rail. His scowl was black, his jaw clenched by the time he reached the wharf. "Whose work is this?"

Jake Watson, his harbor foreman, shook his head in disgust. "I don't know."

Paul glared into the circle of men who gathered around the damaged goods. "Who's at fault?" he demanded again, his voice cutting the air like a whip.

A towering Negro stepped forward, Jason Banner at his side. "It was ol' Jessie Rowlan's fault, sir. I saw him liftin' that crate with the wrong pulley."

Paul gritted his teeth. "Where the hell is he?"

The black man pointed toward the deck, and all eyes followed. Jessie Rowlan was leaning on the railing. Paul strode purposefully up the gangway, his irate regard unwavering.

Jessie Rowlan turned to meet the attack, wearing a vengeful grin. "What can I do for you, Mr. Doo-*vwah*-zan?" he queried snidely.

"Are you responsible for that mess down there?"

"What do you mean 'responsible'? The way I sees it, ain't no one 'responsible.' Just a little accident, is all."

"The way I see it," Paul growled, "the wrong equipment was used. We have block and tackle for crates and we have block and tackle for casks, something you might have remembered if you weren't so drunk! But since you were the one working the pulley, I'm holding you directly responsible for the 'accident' as you call it. I cannot abide such stupidity, and I certainly can't afford it. To-morrow you may collect your wages from Jake Watson, out of which I shall deduct the money not only lost on the damaged goods, but on the equipment as well. After that, I never want to see your sorry face again."

Renewed loathing welled up in Jessie Rowlan's eyes. "Well, if it ain't the high-and-mighty Paul Duvoisin, who thinks he owns the whole goddamn place. Well, sir, I got me some friends, and you'll be regrettin' you ever said that. You think you're better than everybody else. Well, you ain't. You ain't even as good as most of the men here. At least we ain't *bastards*—rich or otherwise!"

Paul seized him by the throat, lifting him clear off the deck. "Utter that word again and I swear you're a dead man! Hear me? A dead man!"

"Yes!" Jessie Rowlan choked out.

In an instant, Paul sent him sailing, and he lay sprawled on the deck. He jumped to his feet and dashed off the ship, the dock-workers stepping back as he retreated, all unusually quiet.

"What was that all about?" Charmaine whispered.

"I'll explain later," Gwendolyn hushed, straining to hear.

"All right, Jake," Paul called down to the pier, "let's see what the men can salvage with a few shovels and a couple of barrels. I should have sent the lot back to John when I realized it was still in the hold."

"I don't think it was your brother's fault, sir," Jake shouted up. "I should have checked the labeling more carefully. I thought it said—"

"No matter, Jake! It looks like a storm is rolling in, and we'll have a bigger mess on our hands if it pours before that tea is cleared away. There's a bonus if the job is finished before the first drops hit!"

Hearing this, the men scrambled to do his bidding. Satisfied, Paul turned back to his work.

"Why did Jessie Rowlan call Paul that nasty name?" Charmaine pressed as she and Gwendolyn rushed home.

"What name?"

"You know the name, Gwendolyn. Mr. Harrington used it during our voyage here and grew uncomfortable when he remembered I was present. I know it's not a nice word. Why won't you tell me?"

"There's nothing to tell," Gwendolyn said, embarrassed by a subject she was not supposed to know about. "The man was cussing, and Paul became angry."

"No, it was more than that. Paul didn't lose his temper until Jessie Rowlan said *that* word." Still, Gwendolyn refused to shed light on the subject. "Is it because Paul is adopted—illegitimate?" she pressed.

"How did you know that?"

"Captain Wilkinson mentioned it."

"Did he also mention what the townspeople whisper?"

"He didn't gossip, if that's what you mean."

Gwendolyn lifted her nose. "And that's exactly why I won't repeat it."

The gleam in Gwendolyn's eyes told Charmaine the girl was dying to tell all. "It won't go any further than me, if that's what you're afraid of."

"Well," Gwendolyn hesitated, looking around. "People say

Paul is Frederic Duvoisin's *bastard* son," and she whispered "bastard" as if the wind had ears.

"What does that mean? Isn't that the same as illegitimate?"

"Yes, but worse! It means his father had an affair with a prostitute, and Paul was born of it. Otherwise, Frederic Duvoisin would have done the gentlemanly thing and married the woman. They say the infant came from abroad, and Frederic adopted the baby because he was certain *he* was the father."

Charmaine's heart swelled in sadness for Paul. He was wealthy, handsome, and from all outward signs, an honorable man, and yet, he had to endure the scandalmongering and rebuke of those around him.

Pelting rain washed her mind clean.

"Come quickly, Charmaine! We're going to get soaked to the bone!"

They raced through the streets, coming to the residential section of town as swiftly as their legs would carry them. But they weren't fast enough, for their clothes were drenched before they reached the Brownings' front porch.

"Goodness me!" Caroline protested as she took in her daughter's appearance. "Just look at yourself, young lady! Your dress is ruined!"

"I'm sorry, Mother, but Charmaine and I ran as fast as we could."

"*You what?*"

"We ran from town."

"You ran from town? And what will my friends think?"

"Mrs. Browning," Charmaine placated, "everyone was running for shelter."

"Well, let me tell you something. Dignified young ladies do not run in public, rainstorm or not! What would Colette Duvoisin say if she saw you?"

Loretta stepped from the sitting room. "She would say, 'There go two intelligent young women. Unlike the dignified ladies on this island who traipse slowly about town during a rainstorm in wet, clinging clothes, these two run for cover so as not to be struck by lightning.'"

Miffed, Caroline flounced past her sister, but Loretta smiled at the bedraggled girls. "To your room and out of those dresses before you catch cold."

Caroline remained in a huff until dinner, when her true anxieties were revealed. Though she loved the island, she feared her daughter would never learn the social graces necessary to obtain a respectable husband some day. By the end of the meal, Loretta empathized with her sister and, much to the dismay of Gwendolyn and Charmaine, agreed to take Gwendolyn back to Virginia when she and Joshua departed. Noting her niece's downcast eyes, she said, "You will come to love Richmond, Gwendolyn. Think of it as an extended holiday, and if you are not happy after a week or two, you can always return home."

Gwendolyn brightened; however, Charmaine felt empty. She had hoped to have a friend on the island whom she could visit and in whom she could confide. It seemed she was destined to be alone.

Chapter 3

THE open carriage rocked gently from side to side as it turned off the main thoroughfare and proceeded at a leisurely pace through the tree-lined passage that led directly to the Duvoisin mansion. The four occupants soon sampled the tranquility of Charmantes. Very few people traveled the isolated road, and the quiescent forest enveloped them. Heading west, their destination was the opposite side of the nine-mile-wide island, the paradise of Jean Duvoisin II preserved. Although the eastern coast was heavily populated, the western shore remained the sole dominion of one family: the Duvoisins. Not even the far-off sugarcane fields and orchards to the south, nor the lumber mill and pine forests to the north trespassed on the serenity to the west, where the island remained untamed save for the mansion they were swiftly approaching.

"What is the matter, my dear?" Loretta whispered.

Charmaine inhaled. "I'm very nervous. What if they don't like me?"

"We shall leave."

"Oh, Mrs. Harrington, you make everything sound so simple."

"That's because it is," she stated with a fortifying smile.

Yesterday, they had received Colette Duvoisin's reply, written in her own hand, suggesting the interview be held on the sixteenth of September at four in the afternoon. Charmaine had found it exceedingly difficult to sleep last night, smiling weakly when Harold Browning suggested accompanying them. "Less formal," he had said. She knew he hoped to ease her mind, and she had thanked him, but his presence did not lessen her anxiety.

When it seemed the ride would go on forever, the pine trees began to thin. Charmaine was the first to see it—the magnificent mansion nestled on a lush blanket of rich green, a white pearl set on an emerald carpet. As the carriage closed the distance to the metal fencing that guarded the grounds, it loomed larger than any edifice she had ever seen, grander than any of Virginia's great estates. Palatial and breathtaking, it required no words of compliment or description; in truth, only the greatest poet would do it justice.

Ten Doric columns rose heavenward from a wide portico, supporting not only a second-floor veranda, but a third story as well. The massive colonnade ended beneath a broad, red-tiled roof with dormer windows. Both porch and balcony ran the length of the main structure and wrapped around either side, disappearing along the wings set at right angles. They boasted evenly spaced French doors, all thrown wide to catch the afternoon breezes. The manor's main entrance luxuriated in the shade of two towering oak trees that grew on either side of the central drive. The entire edifice was framed by papaya and palm trees, which extended along the side wings of the house from front to back. But the eye was drawn back to the enormous oaks, unusual, yet majestic. Harold told them Frederic's father had transplanted saplings from Virginia in memory of his deceased wife. Now, some fifty years later, they flourished on Charmantes, a reminder the Duvoisin fortune had its origins in America. The pair accentuated the symmetry of the stately mansion, and not even the small stone structure attached to the south wing could mar the perfect balance and beauty.

No one spoke as the carriage passed through the main gates and rolled along the cobblestone driveway. It stopped in the shade of the oaks, where the company of four alighted, each acutely aware of their station in life. With stomach churning, Charmaine allowed Harold Browning to escort her up the short, three-step ascent, across the porch, and to the only set of oak doors.

The butler was awaiting their arrival, for the door swung inward before they could knock. "If you will kindly step this way," he said, "I shall tell Miss Colette you are here."

The spacious foyer had a lofty ceiling, crown moldings, an ostentatious chandelier, marble floors, and an enormous grandfather clock. Directly opposite the main entryway was an elaborate staircase. Its ornate railing followed curved steps up to a wide landing, above which hung a stunning, life-sized portrait of a young woman. There, the stairway split in two, each rising to opposite wings of the house. Overlooking these were huge mullioned windows, capturing the afternoon sun and bathing the awed assembly in its golden light.

They were led through the north wing and into the library where they were invited to make themselves comfortable. Volumes of books lined three of the four walls. A huge desk, sofa, and armchairs graced the center of the room. It was dark within, but not unpleasantly so, for the dimness embraced the cool ocean breezes that whispered through the open French doors.

Loretta settled in a wing chair. "It's quite humbling, is it not?"

"Yes," Charmaine murmured, doing the same.

"And did you notice the painting in the foyer?" Loretta asked. "I wonder who the beautiful young lady might be?"

"That is Miss Colette," Harold offered.

Loretta smiled. "Well, Charmaine, now we know why Mr. Duvoisin married her. I don't think you'll have a problem convincing Mrs. Duvoisin to hire you."

Charmaine was astounded. "Why do you say that?"

"Didn't you study her face?"

"I didn't have time!"

Loretta's smile deepened. "It's something you should have seen immediately. If the painter captured his subject, as I'm certain he did, Mrs. Duvoisin is a warm and loving individual who will recognize the same qualities in you. She should be very pleased when we leave today. I doubt she's had many applicants who are as young, caring, and vibrant as you."

Charmaine began to respond, but the door opened, and the woman of the portrait preceded Paul Duvoisin into the room: quintessential femininity and rugged masculinity, Colette and Paul Duvoisin, stepmother and stepson. Their relationship struck everyone instantaneously. They were close in age and looked more like husband and wife. In truth, they would have made the most handsome couple gracing Richmond society. Yet theirs was a stranger connection. All eyes traveled to the doorway in expectation of Frederic Duvoisin, but he did not cross the threshold.

Colette broke the suspect silence with a gracious "good afternoon," the French lilt in her voice enthralling. She suggested they move to the adjacent drawing room, where it was brighter. This room looked out onto the front and side lawns with two sets of French doors thrown open. It contained a brace of sofas, a number of armchairs and end tables set along the perimeter of an intricately woven Oriental rug, and a massive fireplace, seemingly out of place in a house situated on a Caribbean island. Above the mantel hung a portrait of a man holding a small boy upon one knee, with another boy off to one side. But Charmaine's gaze did not linger there. It was drawn to the grand piano of polished ebony, unlike any she had ever seen, nestled in a corner of the room, between the two doors that opened onto the foyer and library.

As Harold Browning made all the introductions, Colette encouraged everyone to sit as she herself had done. She was clad in an unadorned, yet becoming gown of pale blue. Her flaxen hair was pulled to her nape, framing her face. Her slate blue eyes were spellbinding, her nose slim and delicate, her lips full and inviting. But it was her smile that brought all the exquisite features to life and, as Loretta Harrington had averred, put everyone at ease, everyone that is, except Charmaine.

Colette sat with hands in lap, lending complete attention to her guests, while Paul elected to stand close behind her, feet planted apart, much like that day on the *Raven*. It was as if he were protecting her from some unknown misery. His darkly handsome features contrasted with her graceful fairness, and once again, Charmaine thought of them as husband and wife.

"Miss Ryan," Colette began, "how do you like our island?"

"It is very beautiful," Charmaine answered.

Colette saw herself in Charmaine. Without warning, she was reliving her own arrival at the Duvoisin mansion nine years earlier, those overwhelming feelings that assaulted her as she entered this very room. Of course, her meeting was not an interview for the post of governess. On the contrary, she was to meet Frederic Duvoisin and make a first impression. Even now, she could feel the quickening of her pulse and the racing of her heart when he turned to greet her. He had been exceedingly handsome and extremely intimidating. The intensity of his regard had pierced her soul. He had taken her breath away. Yes, she knew what it was to feel ill at ease in the presence of the Duvoisins. She extended a smile to Charmaine. "You've been here for . . . three days now?"

"Four," Charmaine corrected. "We arrived Monday morning on the *Raven*."

That's where I've seen her! Paul mused, her elusive face suddenly recalled and attached to the unidentified woman in the captain's cabin. But her hair had been unbound—long, and curling about her face, and down her back. That's why he hadn't been able to place her immediately. Now it was clear how she had come to be on Jonah Wilkinson's ship. She'd traveled from Richmond. He wondered if John knew her, perhaps met her on the vessel before its departure. But, no, he reasoned, she wouldn't be acting the trapped rabbit if she had met his brother first. Then again, John may have put her ill at ease for the entire family. *It's a shame she wears her hair pinned up . . . She was so lovely with it down and unruly.*

". . . isn't that correct, Paul?" Colette was asking.

"I'm sorry. What were you saying?"

"Miss Ryan has seen the most beautiful parts of Charmantes if she has seen the beaches," she answered, turning in her chair to better look at him.

"Yes," he murmured, but said no more.

Charmaine shuddered under his scrutiny, wondering if she had offended him in some way, for his scowl had darkened. She was grateful when the door opened and another woman joined their company, turning Paul's attention aside.

"Agatha," Colette greeted, "please, come and meet our guests."

The woman was older, yet every bit as striking and statuesque as Colette. Her dark auburn hair was coiled in a thick coiffure. Her face possessed high cheekbones, perfectly shaped eyebrows that arched over piercing green eyes, and a long aristocratic nose, which ended above expressive lips. She swept into the room with an air of authority and smiled pleasantly at the assembly.

"I didn't know you were entertaining visitors today," she said in a thick English accent. "Do you think this wise after Robert's instructions of yesterday?"

"Agatha, I'll adhere to your brother's advice when it is reasonable."

The woman responded by insisting on refreshments. She rang for a servant, who was instructed to prepare a pitcher of lemonade.

Introductions were once again made. Charmaine learned Agatha Blackford Ward was the sister of Frederic Duvoisin's first wife, Elizabeth. Recently widowed, she'd taken up permanent residence on Charmantes in order to be near her twin brother, Robert Blackford, the island's sole physician, and her closest living relative.

"Miss Ryan is inquiring about the governess position," Colette finished.

Agatha Ward's manner, which had been decorous and welcoming, grew rigid. "Really? She seems very young."

Paul cleared his throat. "I believe Colette is conducting this interview, Agatha. Why don't you allow her to ask the questions?"

The older woman was startled by the polite reprimand, but maintained her aplomb as she went to the door and received the arriving tray of lemonade. She poured a glass for everyone, and took a chair near Colette.

Colette regarded Charmaine once again, her gaze assuasive. "May I ask about your background, Miss Ryan?"

"Please, call me Charmaine."

"Very well, Charmaine. Where have you been employed?"

"I've been working for the Harringtons these past three years, since I was fifteen."

"And your duties there?"

"For the most part, I acted as companion to Mrs. Harrington."

"And before you began working there?"

"I attended school in Richmond. In addition to reading, writing, and mathematics, I am quite proficient in a great many scholastic disciplines."

"Which school?"

"St. Jude's."

Colette's eyes lit up. "St. Jude Thaddeus . . . patron saint of the hopeless."

"Yes," Charmaine concurred in surprise. "Many people don't know that."

"The hopeless do," Colette breathed. "Are you Roman Catholic, then?"

"Yes. My mother was devout, and I try to follow her example."

Colette nodded in approval. "And have you had any further education? Attended a lady's academy, perhaps?"

Charmaine hesitated, but Loretta quickly interceded. "Charmaine's education continued throughout her years living with me. She enjoys fine literature and music, is proficient at needlepoint, and is able to sew her own clothing. She knows a great many dance steps and demonstrates a fine hand at the piano. In addition, you'll find she embraces all the finer points of decorum you will expect her to impart to your daughters."

"I see," Colette replied. "And do you speak French?"

"Do I have to?" Charmaine said in alarm.

"No." Colette chuckled. "It is not a requirement. I was just hoping we could converse in my native tongue."

Charmaine sighed, but her relief was momentary, for Agatha spoke once again. "You may not be interested in my advice, but I feel it would behoove you to search for someone more mature when considering your children's education. Miss Ryan may very well know all the things Mrs. Harrington insists she does; however, that does not ensure her capability of conveying that knowledge to the children. I'll warrant her education has not included pedagogic training. With Frederic's money, you could procure the most learned professor to instruct the girls and Pierre. Why rush into such a decision? Why not advertise in Europe?"

Charmaine's face fell. She could not fault the woman's observation. In fact, what she said made perfect sense. Why would Frederic Duvoisin hire someone like her when his money could purchase so much more? To her utter dismay, Paul spoke next, and his remarks were no less devastating.

"Perhaps Agatha is right, Colette. Father can well afford the most expensive tutors money can buy, as he did with John, George, and me. When Pierre gets older, it will greatly benefit him to have learned what a true scholar can edify. Why not hire someone like Professor Richards? Thanks to Rose's husband, our education was expansive, and we were well prepared for university. Miss Ryan, on the other hand, has acted as a lady's companion for three years. For all her education, where is her experience with children? It appears to be deficient."

"On the contrary," Loretta argued. The conversation had taken a wrong turn, and it was time to intervene. "There have been many occasions when Charmaine has been left in charge of my grandchildren for days at a time. She is excellent with them, and they beg to come and visit just to spend time with her."

Charmaine was momentarily stupefied, and Paul noted her unguarded surprise. *So, Loretta Harrington is playing games here. No matter, I can play, too.* "Still," he pondered aloud, his eyes sparkling victoriously, "Miss Ryan seems better equipped to fill another role in this house—something less demanding than running after three young and energetic children who are active from morning 'til night. Perhaps a maid?"

"I am quite strong, thank you," Charmaine snapped, "and capable of running after three children. Before I began working for the Harringtons, I used to lend a hand with the orphans at the St. Jude Refuge. I was good at it. I enjoyed playing with them. It wasn't that long ago I was young myself."

"Exactly," Colette interrupted irenically. "I am seeking more than a governess for my children. As Agatha inferred earlier, my health is not what it should be. And when I am not feeling well, I want to know I have placed my children in capable hands, hands that will do more than educate them. The governess I hire *must be* energetic, loving, and compassionate, and eager to engage in all those impetuous things that young children do. I want my children to run free, I want them to learn to ride a horse and swim in the ocean. I want them to dance—to live! I don't want them closeted in their nursery day in and day out, never enjoying Charmantes' gentle breezes. We live in a paradise. I want my children to embrace that paradise—to grow healthy in body as well as in mind, to be happy. Do you appreciate what I'm saying?"

Her rhetorical question was not directed at anyone in particular, but rather everyone in the room. The query held for a moment.

"That being understood," she proceeded. "I have just a few more questions for Miss Ryan. Your family"—she paused as if she knew she were headed for stormy seas—"you have not mentioned them. May I ask why the Harringtons have accompanied you all the way from Virginia?"

Charmaine bowed her head. For all her hours of practice, the memories were incredibly painful. "My mother passed away last year. My father left us long ago. I don't know where he is." She raised glistening eyes to Colette. "If it weren't for the Harringtons, I don't know where I would be today. They have been very kind. They are my family now."

Very good, Loretta thought, *honest and to the point*. One look at Colette and she knew Charmaine had touched the woman's heart.

"I'm so sorry," Colette murmured, embracing a moment of silence. Then she was speaking again. "I would like my children to meet you. I shall base a portion of my decision upon them. Would you indulge me, Miss Ryan?"

"Please, call me Charmaine. And, yes, I was hoping to meet them."

Agatha stood. "Shall I have Rose bring them down?" she asked.

Colette nodded and the older woman departed.

"Rose Richards, or Nana Rose as the children call her, is our nursemaid of sorts," Colette explained. "She's been in the Duvoisin employ for nearly sixty years, raising not only Paul and John, but their father as well. Rose's husband, Professor Harold Richards, educated two generations of Duvoisin males. She is a dear woman," Colette concluded, "but getting on in years. Certainly not the person to run after three youngsters.

"Now, let me tell you a bit about my children. The girls are the oldest and turn eight the end of this month. Although they are identical twins, they are completely contrary to one another, as different as night and day, so you shouldn't have any trouble telling them apart. Yvette is precocious, unlike her sister, Jeannette, who appears quiet and shy. My son is two and a half, usually a troublesome age to be sure. Not so with Pierre; he's very dear and brings only happiness."

The door opened, and a pretty girl with pale blue eyes entered the room. Her flaxen hair was only half plaited, but she seemed oblivious to it as she surveyed each stranger and singled out Charmaine. "Who are you?" she demanded.

"Yvette," her mother reproved. "Our guests will think you've no manners. That is not the proper way to introduce yourself."

"But I don't want to introduce myself, Mama. I would like her"—and the girl pointed a finger toward Charmaine—"to tell me who she is."

"Yvette," Paul corrected curtly, "pointing at someone is not polite, either."

Yvette scowled briefly, then plopped into a chair, sulking.

Colette ignored her and invited Jeannette and Pierre to join them. The young boy immediately ran into his mother's out-stretched arms. When Jeannette, Rose, and Agatha were settled, Colette proceeded to introduce her children to the visitors. "This is Mr. and Mrs. Harrington of Richmond, Virginia—"

Yvette perked up. "That's where Johnny lives."

"—and this is Miss Ryan, a friend of the Harringtons."

"Do you live in Richmond, too?" Yvette asked.

"I grew up there," Charmaine replied.

"Do you know my older brother?"

"No, I'm sorry to say I don't."

Yvette was not deterred. "Do you think you could track him down?"

"Yvette," her mother chided, "that's enough."

The girl smiled sweetly. "But, Mama, you said the Duvoisin name is well known. Maybe Miss Ryan could find out where Johnny lives."

Charmaine laughed. "I suppose I could, if I tried."

This seemed to please the girl. "Good, because when you go back to Richmond, I wonder if you might take a letter to him. I've wanted to write to him before, but Mama says she doesn't know where to send his post, and Father . . . well, he and Johnny had a terrible—"

"Yvette!" Paul barked. "Our guests have no interest in such matters!"

The girl rolled her eyes and turned aside in her chair, pouting the harder when Rose Richards cornered her. "Next time," the el-derly matron whispered as she began brushing Yvette's golden hair, "you're not to run out of the room until you look presentable."

Charmaine's eyes traveled to Jeannette, who had remained ever so quiet. The girl smiled timidly and said, "You're very pretty."

Charmaine chuckled. "Thank you, Jeannette. And may I say, so are you?"

"How did you know my name?"

Yvette grunted. "Mama told her before we came into the room, silly!"

"Your sister is correct," Charmaine concurred. "But your mother didn't have the chance to tell me much more than that. And I'd like to know more about both of you, unless of course, you'd like to know something about me."

"I'd like to know your name," Yvette replied.

Colette clicked her tongue. "Yvette, you've been told Miss Ryan's name."

"I mean her first name. What is your first name?"

"Charmaine."

Jeannette canted her head. "That's funny! It sounds like Charmantes."

"It does, doesn't it?" Charmaine agreed. "My friend said the same thing the other day, but I hadn't thought of it before."

"Can we call you Charmaine?" Yvette asked.

"No," Colette interjected, "but you *may* call her Mademoiselle Charmaine."

Yvette attempted to pull away from Rose, but succeeded in yanking her hair. "Ouch!" she squealed, gaining another scolding from her nana.

"If you'd stop your fidgeting, I'd have plaited your hair already."

"Why do I have to have it brushed and braided, anyway? I've told you, I'd rather be a boy and cut it off!"

Charmaine chuckled again. "I sympathize with you, Yvette. I hate brushing my hair and think about trimming it short nearly every morning."

Yvette studied her with something akin to admiration. "Why haven't you?"

"I've been told it is my most beautiful possession."

Yvette seemed displeased with the answer.

"Besides, what would I do if I looked horrid when I was finished? I'd be in a fine fix. It would take years to grow back."

"True," Yvette ceded, crossing to Charmaine now that her second braid was finished. "When do you begin taking care of us?"

Colette was astonished. "Why ever did you ask that, Yvette?"

The girl faced her mother. "Nana's been saying she can't keep up with us the way she did with Johnny, Paul, and George. And I heard Mrs. Ward suggest a governess."

Colette frowned pensively. "And how did you overhear that, young lady?"

"I don't know," Yvette shrugged. "I just did."

"And would you like Miss Ryan to be your governess?"

"*I* would," Jeannette answered eagerly. She turned to her baby brother, who sat contentedly in his mother's lap, and asked, "What about you, Pierre? Would you like Mademoiselle Ryan to come and take care of us?"

The little boy smiled, rubbed his eyes, and yawned.

"He's tired," Jeannette supplied, "but I think he likes her."

"And what about you, Yvette?" Colette asked. "Would you like Mademoiselle Charmaine to come and live with us?"

"I guess so," she replied flippantly.

Paul spoke sharply. "Yvette, your mother is asking for your opinion. It would be polite to give it."

"It's difficult to say," Yvette returned, finger upon chin, "but I think I'll like her better than I do Felicia."

One look at Paul, and the entire company realized Yvette had said something best left unmentioned. It was equally evident Colette knew exactly what her daughter meant. Before Paul could reply, Colette said, "Yvette, I am very disappointed in you."

The girl burst into tears, her impertinence swept away with

her mother's disapproval. "I'm sorry, Mama," she cried. "I'm sorry, Paul!" Humiliated, she ran from the room.

Colette exhaled. "I think it best to end the interview now. I know you are anxious, Miss Ryan, but I must consider the matter at greater length. I shall send word to you by Monday, if that is agreeable?"

Charmaine smiled weakly. "Yes, of course. That will be fine."

Sensing Charmaine's chagrin, Jeannette walked over to her. "I like you very much. I promise to help convince Mama and Papa to offer you the job."

Papa—Frederic Duvoisin—Charmaine had forgotten about him. Of course Colette would want to discuss this with her husband. Suddenly, all did not seem so bleak, and she smiled at the child. "Thank you, Jeannette, and I hope to see you again very soon."

Caroline Browning was eagerly awaiting their arrival. "Come quickly," she beckoned as they alighted from the carriage. "What happened? Did it go well? Did you get the position?"

Charmaine breathed deeply. "I don't know. I mean, I won't know until Monday. Mrs. Duvoisin wants to speak to her husband first."

"Frederic wasn't there?" Caroline asked as if scandalized. "Then it *is* true."

"What is true?" Loretta asked.

"That Frederic doesn't leave his chambers."

"We don't know that, do we?" Loretta replied. "He could have been attending to business elsewhere."

Such speculation seemed implausible to Charmaine. Paul had found time to be there, and according to Gwendolyn, he was always busy.

Caroline echoed her thoughts. "Everyone knows he never ventures from the mansion. Isn't that so, Harold?"

Her husband did not disagree.

"No, his condition must be grave." Her mind continued to work. "And what of Miss Colette? Is she also as ill as everyone whispers?"

Loretta frowned. "You knew her health was failing and didn't tell us?"

"I can't think of everything," Caroline said, drawing herself up and running a hand down her bodice. "Was it important?"

"It would have explained why Mrs. Duvoisin is seeking someone young and energetic to assist in the care of her children," Loretta stated, her annoyance apparent. "We went to that interview believing education was the primary qualification for the position, when in fact, the children's supervision is Mrs. Duvoisin's greatest concern. Had we known that, Charmaine could have been better prepared."

"So you think it went badly?" Gwendolyn timidly asked.

"On the contrary," Loretta replied. "It went very well."

Sunday, September 18, 1836

The day was cool, refreshing in its promise of milder weather, but it was drizzling, and Colette sighed as she realized the rainy season was upon them. They'd have overcast weather on and off now until December. She sat at her desk in her private chambers, reveling in the gentle breezes that swirled past the palm and pawpaw branches beyond the balcony and wafted through the French doors. Moments such as these were rare, and she had come to guard this precious time, insisting she have an hour to herself after Mass every Sunday. So far, everyone had respected her wishes. With Pierre sound asleep in the center of her bed, she was almost content.

Returning to the business at hand, her eyes fell to her partially penned letter:

Dear Miss Ryan,

> *Having reflected on our interview of Friday afternoon, I feel it would be beneficial to meet once again in order to discuss more fully the requirements designated to the care of my children. I would, therefore, like to extend a second invitation. If possible, could you meet with me privately this afternoon at four o'clock? I'm certain if this visit includes just the two of us in my chambers, it will give us the chance to become better acquainted.*

What else to write? She didn't want to alarm the young woman by asking her to come alone, but there had been too many people present on Friday afternoon, hardly the proper way to conduct an interview. She liked Charmaine Ryan and, in all probability, would offer her the governess position before the day was over.

A knock fell on the outer door. *Is it noon already?*

"Come in," she beckoned, grimacing when Agatha Ward opened the door.

She despised the woman. But Agatha had made herself at home from the moment she crossed the mansion's threshold six months ago. Unlike past visits, this one had never come to an end. According to Rose Richards, the dowager had been making her sporadic treks to the island since Paul and John were young boys. With her parents dead and herself barren, she made a point of staying in touch with her only living relatives: specifically her brother, Robert, and nephew, John. From the day of her first visit some twenty years ago, Frederic had welcomed her, and she would often stay for weeks at a time, usually when her mariner husband, an officer in the British Royal Navy, put to sea. That husband died in January, leaving Agatha alone in the world. By March, she had swept into Colette's world, taking up quarters in the north wing of the Duvoisin manor—permanently. When Colette unwisely suggested a separate residence, Agatha informed her that long ago Frederic had extended a standing invitation to live in the manse, should the need ever arise. The need had arisen, and Agatha Ward was there to stay. To make matters worse, she had masterfully ingratiated herself to the staff, insisting she was Colette's personal companion of sorts. Colette had neither the will to fight the woman, nor the courage to discuss her misgivings with her husband. Today, she chastised herself for her faintheartedness.

"I thought you were resting," the woman chided lightly.

Fighting an instant headache, Colette attempted to be civil. "I am."

"But you are writing a letter."

"Yes," Colette breathed. "Hardly a strenuous activity." She folded the missive as Agatha approached. "Is there a reason why you are here, Agatha? I thought I'd expressly stated an hour—that I'd like one hour to myself."

"The girls were asking for you."

"How can that be? George took them into town today."

Agatha's brow gathered in confusion, yet she shrugged nonchalantly. "I'm sorry. I thought Fatima had complained about them running around the kitchen. Perhaps she was referring to yesterday. But after last week's incident in Paul's chambers, I thought it best to inform you of any inappropriate behavior as soon as it arises. Yvette is the one who takes advantage of your private time."

"Agatha, we've discussed this before. She is only a child."

"And as such, should know her place. After all, what type of young lady will she grow to be if she is allowed—"

"You are speaking of my daughter."

"And of course you would defend her," Agatha continued with hardened voice. "Colette, I don't mean to upset you, but Yvette does so on a daily basis. According to Robert, it is the worst thing for you. Listen to me!" and she held up a hand when Colette attempted to argue. "Yvette's unruliness grows worse by the day. I realize your failing health, your inability to supervise her at all times, has exacerbated the problem, but that is no reason to ignore it. As your friend, your companion, I feel I must warn you of the consequences. She's in need of a firm hand to eradicate—"

"Mrs. Ward!" Colette blazed. "You are my husband's guest in this house."

"On the contrary, I am your companion."

"That is your title, not mine. You are a guest in this house, nothing more. Therefore, take heed: I love my children. Tread carefully where they are concerned, lest I revoke the gracious invitation my husband has extended to you. Do you understand?"

"My dear," Agatha rejoined condescendingly. "It is you who do not understand. Your husband is distressed over your failing health and has expressed his concerns not only to Robert, but also to myself. It is owing to Frederic that I have agreed to remain on Charmantes. He has requested I not only tend to your every need, but make certain you follow my brother's every instruction. You are, for all intents and purposes, my charge." She smiled triumphantly. "Don't look so chagrined, Colette. Frederic is only worried for you—and his children."

Defeated, Colette bowed her head, unable to comprehend her husband and the further suffering he would now inflict. But then again, she knew all too well the hold Agatha had over him, and she hated the woman for it. When the dowager departed, Colette walked out of the stifling room and onto the balcony, welcoming the rain that kissed her face, washing away the tears that were suddenly there. *Frederic—why? Why would you choose her over me?*

Colette could still remember that night. The twins had just turned one, and Frederic hadn't once, in all that time since their birth, made love to her. It was her own fault, she knew. He thought she hated him. *She* thought she hated him. But she also loved him, loved him fiercely, loved him until it hurt, a love that frightened her in its paralyzing intensity. In addition, there was the doctor's insistence she never attempt to have more children. Agatha had arrived a few days earlier. She'd come with a number of business associates of her deceased father. Frederic was interested in commissioning a new ship, the *Destiny*, for his ever-growing fleet. These were the men who would take back the specifications and see the vessel built. There was one gentleman in particular, a younger, handsome man, quite taken with Colette's youth and beauty. It had been easy to flirt with him. She enjoyed watching Frederic across the table: jaw set in tight lines, brow furrowed, his volatile temper perilously close to the surface. Perhaps it was just what he needed to push him over the edge and bring him back to her arms. She gave him a coquettish smile, daring him to speak. Later, in her sitting room, she paced a frightened trek across her carpet, fearful she'd overstepped her bounds. He'd come to her tonight, of that she was certain, but would she be equipped to deal with his wrath? Her pulse raced with the thought of his lovemaking, heart thudding in her ears. But the hours accumulated, and Frederic did not come. Frustrated, she abruptly decided to go to him. She would swallow her pride and admit she wanted him, loved him. Heavy breathing came from his bedchamber. There was no need to go farther. Agatha's clothes were strewn on the dressing room floor. Frederic had found release in the arms of his sister-in-law. Colette tiptoed back to her own suite, finding release in the many tears she shed on her pillow, her heart dead.

Frederic never knew what she had seen. But every time Agatha came to visit, Colette surmised he welcomed her to his bed. She wondered if, even now, in his crippled state, he embraced the woman who had come to stay.

Colette returned to her letter. It would be pleasant to meet with Charmaine Ryan, even more pleasant to have someone closer to her own age residing in the manor. She decided to hire the young woman.

"Charmaine, whatever are you doing?" Loretta questioned from the bedroom doorway. "It's nearly half-past three. You'll be late for your appointment."

"I must look my best, but I can't seem to get this clasp."

"Here," Loretta scolded lightly, "allow me."

The brooch was secured, and Charmaine stepped back for inspection. "How do I look? Will I pass the final test?"

"You look lovely," Loretta answered, taking hold of Charmaine's hands in reassurance. "My goodness, you are shaking like a leaf in a windstorm. No wonder you couldn't fasten that clasp."

"I'll be fine," Charmaine said tremulously, her smile faint, her eyes beseeching. "And if I fail to get the position . . . ?"

"It will be their loss," Loretta replied. "But, you must think positively. And remember, a white lie here or there is not beneath you."

"Oh, I couldn't!"

"Nonsense. You saw how effective my fibbing was. And no one in the Duvoisin household was the wiser for it."

"But what if they were to discover the truth?"

"How could they, Charmaine? You must learn to deal with people as you find them, use their tactics, so to speak. Take Paul Duvoisin, for example. He exploited your inexperience, and I answered in kind. You *are* capable of caring for my grandchildren, even if you haven't had the opportunity to do so."

"You don't like him, do you?" Charmaine queried.

"Who? Mr. Duvoisin? On the contrary, he's most likely a fine gentleman. However, until you know him better, be on guard." Loretta smiled encouragingly. "Now, come, Charmaine, the carriage is waiting to take you to a new life, and in my heart I know you won't be disappointed."

Charmaine settled into the landau Colette Duvoisin had provided. Sitting alone, she was left to contemplate her fears. Loretta was so sure of her future, but Charmaine could not muster the same confidence. She'd always found comfort in silent prayer, yet those she'd offered at the noon Mass did not help. The island priest, Father Benito St. Giovanni, had delivered a long-winded, inauspicious sermon, and although Colette Duvoisin's letter seemed favorable, Charmaine experienced a sense of impending doom. Perhaps the magnitude of the Duvoisin dynasty blotted out the importance of her humble existence. What did she matter? But more important, if Paul disapproved of her, what real happiness could she hope to find within the mansion's walls?

The master's and mistress's chambers were located to the rear of the south wing, far from the noise and activity of the thriving house. One story above the dormant ballroom, these lavish chambers provided the quiet solitude both master and mistress sought, and those who were intent upon living did not trespass there.

This was Frederic Duvoisin's self-imposed prison, a place to brood over the life he had lived. Seated in the massive chair that occupied his outer chamber, he would often contemplate the oak door closed before him. There were three doors leading from the room: one that opened onto his bedchamber and another leading to the hall. But they were of no interest to him. The heavy door sitting directly across from him, not more than ten paces away, the door that opened onto his wife's sitting room—*that* was the one he cared about.

He was acutely aware of her movements on the other side of that barrier, as he was every night when he lay abed, listening to the ritual of her nightly toilette. And when the chamber was plunged into a despairing silence, he would turn to stare at that door as well, the one connecting bedroom to bedroom, but not husband to wife . . .

He found himself grinding his teeth, unable to control the fulminating anger that seized him. In all his sixty years, he had never been a man to sit idly by and allow time or circumstance to control him. He had always forged forward: relentless, demanding, and above all else, stubborn. These traits had led to this hell of non-existence: half man mentally as well as physically, a decision fashioned eight years ago, a decision cemented five years later on the day he learned the devastating truth, the day of his seizure. Colette . . . how he loved her.

But dwelling on his love scorned would do him no good. It was the very emotion he fought to control. He had no rights where his wife was concerned. He had renounced them long ago, a punishment he hoped would gain her forgiveness. But had she? Even the memory of his first wife, Elizabeth, no longer brought him solace, for he had failed her as well.

"What must you think of me?" he mumbled, his heart aching for her gentle understanding. Why wouldn't she come to him in his greatest need? He knew the answer. Even now, Elizabeth remained with Colette.

"Enough!" he grumbled, his guilt tangible today. Mustering his minimal strength, he repressed the revolutionary thoughts, lest they destroy his sanity as well. If after three years he hadn't died, he must force himself to live. "I've sat too long and relinquished too much."

With enormous effort, he stood, his height mocking his crooked frame. The stroke had not completely purloined his strength. In days gone by, he had been a formidable opponent to any man, the envy of his peers, and many would be amazed at his determination now, yet those who knew the man of old would be repulsed.

His left side remained partially paralyzed, the leg giving him more trouble than the arm, and he scowled deeply as he leaned on the black cane he required for support. Trapped inside a useless body, he half limped, half dragged himself to the oak door. As always, his eyes traveled to the full-length mirror that had been placed, upon his order, in the corner of the room. And as always, he was revolted. Even so, it served its purpose, a constant reminder of what he'd become, why he must remain closeted away. He'd not endure the stares, the whispers, the comments, and most destructive, the pity.

Colette displayed none of these. In fact, she was the only person who did not avert her gaze, choosing instead to meet his regard directly and without repugnance. Yet, in her eyes, he read the most pain of all, was certain she blamed herself. He knew she longed for his forgiveness, but he could not bring himself to utter the words that would sever the only tie that bound them. Funny how he thought about it every time he prepared himself to see her . . .

Colette surveyed the sitting room, satisfied that everything was in order. She turned to her personal maid, a smile lighting her blue eyes. "That's fine, Gladys, just fine. I'm certain Miss Ryan will find the room inviting. Perhaps you could ask Cookie—I mean, Fatima—ask Fatima to prepare some refreshments."

"Yes, ma'am," Gladys replied, retreating from the chamber.

Colette stood in the balcony doorway, the breeze buffeting her face. *When am I going to forget?* The sound of the door reopening drew her back to the present. "Did you forget—"

The query died on her lips as Frederic hobbled in. It had been three years since he had entered her boudoir, and this unexpected visit disturbed her. Of late, their only common ground was the neutral territory of the children's nursery.

"I didn't mean to disturb you," he apologized, his speech slightly slurred.

"You didn't," she replied, forcing herself calm, her eyes fixed on him.

He limped closer. "I see you are preparing for a guest. Someone I know?"

"A woman I'd like to hire as governess to the children."

"And the woman's name?"

"Charmaine Ryan."

"Paul says she's very young. Most probably inexperienced."

Astonished and instantly agitated, Colette spoke without thought. "He discussed this with you? How dare he go behind my back?"

"I may ask the same of you, Madame," Frederic snarled derisively. "I am your husband and master of this house. Paul shouldn't be informing me of matters concerning the children—you should. Or is that too much to ask?"

"No," she whispered, lowering her gaze to the floor, fighting the tears that rushed to her eyes, "it is not too much to ask."

Frederic heard the tremor in her voice and gritted his teeth, his outrage engulfed by self-loathing. "Tell me about Miss Ryan," he urged.

Colette composed herself. "She is from Richmond and heard of the governess position through Harold Browning. Harold's wife is related to her previous employers, the Harringtons. She worked for them for three years and has had quite a bit of experience with their grandchildren. She is well educated and—"

"—you highly recommend her for the position," he finished for her.

"Yes," Colette murmured. She was losing this battle of wills.

In an attempt to regain her poise, she retreated to a chair a few feet away from him.

But he moved to where she sat, towering above her. "This is all fine and good, Colette, but it doesn't make one whit of sense to me. You, who have never left your children unattended for even a moment, are looking for someone else to tend them? And don't tell me this has anything to do with their education. You could teach them all they'd ever need to know. Why, then, are you situating a stranger in this house, forfeiting the care of our children to someone else?"

"I'm not forfeiting their care, but I'm not as strong as I was a year ago. Robert insists the children are a burden. Though I do not agree, I don't want my limitations to restrict their activities."

"You should never have had the boy," Frederic stated sharply. "You were told no more children after the twins."

"It wasn't Pierre. I was fine after his birth. It was the fever last spring."

Frederic's scowl deepened, forcing her mute. The minutes ticked uneasily by until he cleared his throat. "And Robert recommended a governess?"

"His sister did."

"She doesn't approve of this one."

"And how would you know that?" Colette asked suspiciously.

"She asked Paul to speak with me. According to Agatha, Charmaine Ryan is too young and vivacious." He limped back to the adjoining door, paused, then faced Colette again, his eyes briefly sparkling. "I'd say Miss Ryan is exactly the type of governess our children need."

Colette smiled, and for the first time in months, Frederic's heart expanded. Tears sprang to his eyes, and he swiftly turned away. "I promised Paul I would speak to you on Agatha's behalf, and I have." When she didn't respond, he opened the door and returned to his own chambers. Colette had won his approval.

Despite her tardy departure from the Browning house, Charmaine arrived at the Duvoisin doorstep on time. Shaking her skirts free of any wrinkles, she faced the formidable manor and, with the deepest of breaths, began the short ascent up the portico steps. The front door opened, and a man rushed out, head down, oblivious of her. His pace increased, and Charmaine stepped aside to avoid the collision. Too late! He ran headlong into her, nearly knocking her to the ground. Impulsively, he grabbed her arms and steadied them both.

"Excuse me," he chuckled self-consciously, but as he set her from him, his perusal turned fastidious, and his smile deepened. "My, my!"

Charmaine couldn't help but smile in return, completely at ease with this lanky stranger.

"I shouldn't have come galloping out of the house like that, but bumping into you made it all worthwhile." Without further ado, he grasped her elbow and assisted her with the remaining steps. "And might you have a name?"

Her eyes never left his lean face. "Charmaine Ryan."

"Oh, the new governess."

"Am I?" Charmaine queried.

His face sobered, and he groaned inwardly. "Not exactly, but you are being considered. I'm sorry for getting your hopes up, though I'm certain—"

"George, weren't you supposed to help Wade sharpen the saw at the mill?"

Paul Duvoisin stood in the main doorway, arms folded across his chest, a scowl marring his face. Charmaine hadn't noticed him there, and suddenly her cheeks burned crimson. "Well?" he queried.

"It's Sunday," George replied defensively. "The saw can wait until tomorrow. Besides, I've spent the better part of the afternoon with *your* sisters, having just now returned them to my grandmother. The rest of the day is mine."

Paul didn't respond, yet Charmaine read the silent exchange that passed between the two men. "I guess I could look in on Alabaster," George added.

Paul's brow lifted. "Why?"

"Phantom bit him a little while ago."

"How in the hell did that happen?" Paul demanded.

George cleared his throat, adding emphasis to the slight nod he effected in Charmaine's direction. But Paul ignored the gesture, unmoved by her presence. Finally, George answered. "Yvette was—"

Paul held up a hand, highly perturbed. "I don't want to hear it! But I promise you this—and you can tell Rose for me—one of these days Yvette is going to go too far, and when she does, I'm going to put her over my knee and take the greatest pleasure in giving her a damn good spanking!"

George coughed again, louder this time, and glanced at Charmaine, whose face was scarlet. Paul was looking at her, too, a smile replacing his scowl, and she became the recipient of his remarks. "But, perhaps, where everyone else has failed, Miss Ryan will have some positive effect on my sweet little sister. If she does, it will attest to her experience with children."

"I'll check on Alabaster," George broke in. "Good day, Miss Ryan. I hope to enjoy your company in the near future. Good luck!"

"Thank you," she said, grateful that someone was interested in putting her at ease. "It was nice to meet you, even though we were never introduced."

"I'm George," he replied. "George Richards."

"Mr. Richards," she nodded. "And thank you, again."

"The pleasure was all mine," he said. On impulse, he grabbed her hand and kissed it. Then he was striding happily down the steps and across the lawns, unable to suppress the urge to give Paul a backward glance. His friend's jealous scowl did not disappoint him. Yes, Paul *had* been warning him off.

"Miss Ryan," Paul said as he dragged his eyes from George, "I see you have arrived promptly."

"It was very kind of your family to send the carriage for me," she answered, her voice steadier than she believed possible.

"Yes . . . Shall we go into the house? I know Colette is anxious to see you." He didn't wait for a reply, stepping forward to fill the spot George Richards had vacated. With the slightest pressure to her elbow, he prodded her forward.

Her breathing grew shallow with the trip-hammer of her heart. No words were spoken as he directed her through the doors, across the foyer, and up the south staircase, presumably to the Lady Colette's private chambers. Charmaine welcomed the silence, for it gave her time to compose herself.

"It's not much farther," he said. "Colette thought you'd be more comfortable in her suite. Unfortunately, it's at the far end of the house."

"I knew the manor was large, but . . ."

"You didn't realize how large," he concluded, a hint of a smile tugging at the corner of his mouth.

"This is the south wing," he explained, stopping at the crest of the massive staircase. "The rooms on this side of the house are relegated to the family. The north wing"—he motioned across the empty cavity below, where the staircase dropped and rose again on the other side—"is vacant for the most part, and used only when my father entertains guests."

"I see," Charmaine said with great interest, noticing that a hallway ran the length of the front of the house, connecting north wing to south wing. Ten other rooms opened onto this gallery.

Paul's eyes followed her avid gaze. "The rooms at the front of the house face east and receive the sun in the morning. My brother's former room"—he pointed out, not far from where they stood—"and the children's nursery, complete with bedchamber and playroom," which sat opposite the south wing corridor, "and if you follow this closed hallway, you enter the south wing of the manor."

He led her down that passageway now. She was becoming accustomed to his voice. Without thinking, she asked, "What of your room?"

If he thought her brazen, he gave no such indication. "We just passed them. They are directly opposite the staircase."

"You have more than one?"

"Yes, a dressing room and a bedroom. Most of the rooms on the second floor were designed that way. It allows the occupants freedom and space."

"Freedom from what?" Charmaine asked, astonished by the grandeur.

"The world, if they choose. But if they decide differently, the sitting room can be changed into a dressing room, as I have done."

"It is good to know you're not escaping from the world," she answered a bit too enthusiastically.

They had reached the end of the hallway, and Paul turned toward her, smiling roguishly. He was so close she could see the flecks of green in his olive eyes.

"No, I'm not doing that," he reassured softly, sending shivers of delight up her spine. "Shall we?" he asked, inclining his head toward the last door on the left. When she nodded, he knocked, and at Colette's insistence, they entered the mistress's private quarters.

Colette Duvoisin's sitting room was elegantly appointed, yet far from grandiose. There were only a few items of great and expensive beauty, catching the eye quickly and holding it. In the center of the chamber was an Oriental rug, a miniature of the huge carpet that adorned the oak floor of the drawing room. To one side there was a high-backed ottoman, and in front of it, a serving table with marble top. Two mahogany chairs were set to either side, facing the divan. Across the room was an armoire and a chest of drawers adorned with fresh cut flowers arranged in a tall vase. Next to this was a dressing table with jewelry chest. On the far wall, nestled between two sets of French doors, was a desk. Colette had moved its chair slightly and sat in front of the open glass doors.

She rose slowly, allowing Charmaine a moment to admire the room, then suggested they sit on the sofa. Paul bade them good afternoon and left, allowing them the private meeting Colette had promised in her letter.

They spent an hour together, alone: no children and no introduction to the master of Charmantes. Charmaine surmised this interview had been arranged to ease her anxiety and to reach an understanding that Colette would remain an active participant in her children's lives as long as her health permitted.

"Mrs. Duvoisin," Charmaine dared to say, "excuse my impertinence, but from what illness do you suffer?"

Colette leaned forward. "Please, you must call me Colette. I insist."

"Very well," Charmaine ceded, "Colette."

Satisfied, Colette said, "It is not an illness, really. I had a difficult delivery with the girls, and the doctor recommended no more children. When I realized I was expecting again, everyone grew concerned. Thankfully, my son's birth proved easy. But when I fell ill earlier this year, Dr. Blackford claimed the strain of carrying

Pierre made it difficult to fight the unknown malady. I fear he is right, for I have yet to recover. Robert is optimistic and foresees an improvement if I don't exert myself. Hence, daily Mass has been suspended, excursions into town forbidden, and the need for a governess a priority. And with that accomplished now, I leave the rest in God's hands."

Charmaine sat stunned, uncertain of Colette's meaning until she stood and extended her arms with the words, "Welcome to the Duvoisin family." Charmaine laughed outright, then cupped a hand over her mouth, rose, and fell into Colette's embrace. She had the job!

While sharing tea, they discussed her salary, a figure tantamount to a king's ransom in Charmaine's eyes. Her wages would be nearly thrice what she had earned while working for the Harringtons. Once a month, the money would be deposited in the town's bank where she could draw upon it whenever she liked. Her services would be required seven days a week, although only the weekdays would be dedicated to lessons. The weekends could be spent in any manner she wished, so long as the children were included. Neither her room and board, nor her meals would be deducted. After a few years in the Duvoisin employ, Charmaine would be an independent woman.

As she rode back to the Browning house, she was both happy and relieved and about to embark on a new life.

Chapter 4

Monday, September 19, 1836

CHARMAINE arrived at the mansion early the next morning. Colette had insisted she take a full day to settle into her room on the third floor. Thus, she wouldn't step into her role as governess until Tuesday. Loretta and Gwendolyn had accompanied her, and together, they entered the huge foyer, where Charmaine stifled the first of many giggles. Gwendolyn's "oohs" and "aahs" were plentiful.

"It is beautiful, isn't it, Gwendolyn?" she whispered, awaiting Colette's introductions of the house staff.

Charmaine met Mrs. Jane Faraday, an austere widow and head housekeeper of the manor. Falling directly under her authority were Felicia Flemmings and Anna Smith, two maids, a bit older than Charmaine, whose duties included housecleaning, laundry service, and table waiting at each meal. Next, there were the Thornfields, Gladys and Travis, and their two children, Millie and Joseph. Millie was Gwendolyn's age, and Joseph twelve. They accomplished odd jobs around the mansion and its grounds while their parents attended to the personal needs of the master and mistress.

When Travis was not serving as Frederic Duvoisin's valet, he assumed the role of butler. Unlike Mrs. Faraday and her two charges, the Thornfields seemed very pleasant. But of all the servants Charmaine met, Mrs. Fatima Henderson, the rotund black cook, became her favorite. Warm and loud with a devilish twinkle in her eye, Charmaine liked her from the start.

With Travis and Joseph's help, Charmaine's belongings were carried up to the third floor via the servant's staircase at the back of the north wing. She spent the morning unpacking and arranging the bedroom more to her liking, the finest she had ever slept in, Loretta and Gwendolyn offering their advice.

Just before noon, Millie invited them downstairs for lunch, not in the servant's kitchen, but rather, the family's dining room.

Forty feet long and nearly as wide, it was situated between the library and kitchen of the north wing's ground floor. Two of its four walls were comprised of continuous French doors, all open, leading out to the wraparound veranda on one side and an inner courtyard on the other. Like a crystal palace, the chamber dazzled the eye in the midday sun. In the center was a lustrous red mahogany table, with matching chairs to seat fourteen. The table could accommodate twice as many, yet was dwarfed in the magnificent room. Suspended above it were three chandeliers, sparkling in imitation of the French doors. On the wall abutting the library was a liquor cabinet, opposite that, a baroque cupboard displaying an array of fine chinaware.

A splendid meal awaited them. The children were there, and in a matter of minutes, the discourse turned spontaneous, the girls delighting in the company they were entertaining. When Charmaine marveled over the manor, they insisted on showing her the entire house, but Colette told them that would have to wait for the next day, as Charmaine's duties didn't begin until then.

When the last dish was cleared away, Charmaine walked

Gwendolyn and Loretta to the front portico, taking a deep breath when Loretta turned to hug her goodbye. Charmaine read joy in her eyes.

"You are going to be fine here, Charmaine."

"I know I am," Charmaine concurred, battling a pang of melancholy. "You'll be leaving for Richmond soon, won't you?"

"Not until I'm certain you're happy. I can withstand my sister's company for another week or two." When Gwendolyn laughed, so did Loretta and Charmaine. "Besides," Loretta added, "we don't know when the next ship will put into port."

Charmaine watched as they boarded the carriage and drove away. Turning back into the mansion, she realized the rest of the afternoon belonged to her. With nothing to do, she wished she had taken the girls up on their offer to investigate the house. Nevertheless, Colette had told her the manor was her home now and she was free to roam wherever she liked.

She ambled into the front parlor and was drawn to the piano. Ever so carefully, she lifted the lid and stroked the beautiful ivory keys. But before she could sit down to play, a voice came from the doorway. "There you are!"

It was Yvette, and she was alone. Paul's words of yesterday surfaced: *One of these days Yvette is going to go too far . . . But perhaps Miss Ryan will have some positive effect on my sweet little sister. If she does, it will attest to her experience with children . . .* Obviously, Paul's opinion of her remained unfavorable. What Charmaine wouldn't give to prove him wrong and, in the process, demonstrate that children could be handled without need of a spanking.

"Yvette?" she queried. "You are Yvette, aren't you?"

"Yes, it's me," the girl replied. "Have you finished unpacking?"

With Charmaine's affirmation, she continued. "Perhaps you can spend the rest of the day thinking of some fun things to do with us tomorrow."

"Fun things?" Charmaine asked. "Why do you say that?"

"Everything has been so boring lately. Nana Rose is old, *very* old! And with Mama feeling ill all the time, we never do anything that's fun or exciting anymore. We're always cooped up in that silly nursery!"

"I see. I will think about it. How does that sound?"

Unconvinced, Yvette's shoulders sagged. She flung herself into a chair and mumbled, "It sounds wonderful."

Charmaine took stock; the child's discontent might work in her favor. "I've an idea. You look like the kind of a girl who enjoys a good bargain."

She had Yvette's complete attention. "Yes?"

"I've heard you can be very difficult."

"Who told you that?"

"It's not important. But if we could come to an agreement, I'm certain we'd both be happy with the outcome."

"What sort of an agreement?" Yvette asked suspiciously.

"Last Friday you mentioned your brother, John, in Richmond."

"What about him?"

"I could possibly get a letter to him."

Yvette's eyes widened. "Really?" Then, as if she knew she was being duped, she said, "How? You're staying here now."

"But my friends, the Harringtons, are returning to Richmond in a few weeks. And Mr. Harrington has met your brother. He could locate him."

"*Truly?*"

"I believe so," Charmaine replied, tickled by the girl's renewed exuberance.

Yvette grew cautious again. "What do I have to do?"

"Be well behaved," Charmaine answered simply.

"Well behaved? That's it?"

"From what I've heard, that will be a great deal for you. You are to obey and respect me the way you do your mother. No mischief making."

A myriad of expressions ran rampant across the girl's face as she weighed the pros and cons of the pact.

"Of course," Charmaine pursued, "it might be too difficult for—"

"I'll do it!" the girl cut in. "Do you want to shake hands?"

Charmaine nodded, reaching for Yvette's extended hand, puzzled when it was abruptly withdrawn. "One other thing," Yvette said, arm tucked behind her back. "You had better not tell Mama or Papa, or I won't be allowed to send it."

Charmaine was perplexed. Certainly the child's parents wouldn't forbid her to write a simple letter to her older brother. "Why would they mind?"

"They are angry with Johnny. That's the real reason I haven't been able to send him a letter. I'm not supposed to tell you this, but he caused Papa's seizure. It's the big family secret! But you were bound to find out. Everybody in the house knows what happened. Johnny didn't mean it, I know he didn't. At least Papa didn't die." The girl sighed. "Now I'm not even allowed to mention his name. I know they won't let me write to him."

"I'll speak to your mother about it," Charmaine reasoned gently.

"No!" the girl persisted. "No secret, no deal! Because if you tell her about the letter, it will never leave this island."

Charmaine frowned. She didn't like being manipulated, and she certainly didn't want to go behind Colette's back. "I shall have to think about it."

"Never mind," Yvette groaned, clearly upset. "I knew you'd be too scared to do something daring."

"Yvette," Charmaine cajoled, certain she was courting an enemy now rather than a friend, "if it means that much to you, I promise we'll get a letter to your brother one way or another."

A long silence ensued. Charmaine stood her ground, allowing Yvette her assessment. She smiled hesitantly. "Are you certain? You're not just saying that?"

"I'm certain, and I do promise. Now come, I'll take you back to the nursery before Nana Rose or your mother comes looking for you."

Yvette artfully turned to the piano. "Do you play?"

"Yes, I do."

"Would you teach me?"

"I suppose I could. You'll be my first student, though."

"I don't care. I'd like to learn. Johnny plays very well," she imparted, striking one key. "He'd be very surprised if he came home and could hear me play. I'd really like to surprise him."

Charmaine smiled down on the girl, who so obviously cherished her elder brother. "Very well, Miss Duvoisin. If you are willing to practice an hour a day, by Christmastide you should be able to play a number of simple melodies. Would you like to begin now?"

Receiving an alacritous nod, they sat at the piano. "Now, this is middle C."

It was thus Colette found them. She smiled contentedly.

When Yvette tired of the piano, Charmaine accompanied her back to the nursery and insisted the girls give her the grand tour. She was in awe of all the things they pointed out, most especially the water closet situated near the crest of the south wing staircase and its companion washroom on the first floor directly below. Complete with washstand and chamber seat, its interior plumbing was fed by a water system devised by the girls' grandfather at the time of the mansion's construction. Rainwater was collected off the roof and funneled into a holding tank one story above. Charmaine jumped back when Yvette cranked a huge lever and a surge of water "flushed" the toilet. The girl laughed merrily. "Haven't you ever seen a privy before?" This type, she hadn't. Not even the Harringtons had so modern a lavatory facility.

In the south wing, she was shown the grand ballroom and banquet hall, huge and empty, comprising the entire ground floor of that wing, echoing their hollow footfalls as they crossed to a side doorway that led to the family chapel. The stone edifice was built eight years ago, and was the only structure oddly out of balance with the entire house.

Next, the girls took her to the gardens nestled in the courtyard between the north and south wings. Frederic's father had hired a gardener to plant out the nearly enclosed area with various shrubs and exotic flowers. Travis and Gladys tended it now. It was remarkably cool amongst the many overhanging boughs of scarlet cordia and frangipani trees, their abundant blooms of deep orange, white, pink, and yellow vibrant and sweet smelling. Marble benches were placed along the cobblestone walkway, beckoning any wanderer to sit and enjoy the placid beauty and fragrant flowers. A grand fountain graced the very center, water spurting upward, dropping back to marble basins of graduating diameter, three melodious waterfalls spilling to a shallow pool below.

"You have a little paradise right here," Charmaine said to the girls.

"Still," Yvette commented, "once you've gotten used to it, it's boring."

"Yes," Jeannette agreed, "it's much more fun to go on picnics or riding the way we used to before Mama became ill."

So, Charmaine thought, there is the crux of the matter. They were tired of the same old thing, and she couldn't really blame them. Children were meant to run free. Tonight, she would start planning how she could make their lives more adventurous. Though she knew their studies were important—Colette had already made certain her daughters could read and write—Charmaine remembered the manner in which they spent the weekends would be up to her choosing. Perhaps a few picnics would be nice, so long as the rainy weather they were due to experience cooperated.

At seven o'clock, everyone headed for the dining room. Charmaine was to have her first supper with her new family. As at lunch, Rose and Yvette walked to the far side of the table and took two center seats. Colette helped Pierre into the chair adjacent to her own, there at the foot of the table, nearest the kitchen. Charmaine assumed that when Frederic joined them, he would sit opposite his wife at the head of the table. Colette beckoned Charmaine to once again take the chair to Pierre's right, and Jeannette quickly sat next to Charmaine.

"Is this all right, Mama?" she asked politely.

"As long as Nana doesn't mind being cast aside."

Rose shook her head. "Let Jeannette sit near Charmaine. That's fine."

Voices resounded from the hallway, and George Richards and Paul appeared. To Charmaine's utter surprise, Paul sat at the head of the table, while George took the chair to his right. Evidently, Frederic Duvoisin would not be joining them. Unbidden came the thought of Paul and Colette as husband and wife.

Agatha Ward was the last to enter the room. Charmaine had only seen the dowager once the entire day, when she had insisted Colette take a nap. She graciously greeted everyone, then sat across from Pierre.

The family fell into easy banter, and dinner was served. Charmaine enjoyed the food immensely, not realizing how hungry she was, although the noontime fare had been delectable. She helped with Pierre's plate, while talking with the girls, Rose, and Colette. Halfway through the meal, George spoke to her. "Well, Charmaine Ryan, how was your first day as governess?"

"It was wonderful."

Colette chuckled. "Charmaine wasn't supposed to begin her duties until tomorrow. However"—she sent a mock frown down the table toward her daughter—"Yvette took it upon herself to obtain a piano lesson from Miss Ryan."

All eyes went to the girl, save Paul's, whose gaze rested on Charmaine.

"That's right," Yvette piped up, "Mademoiselle is teaching me how to play."

"She's going to teach me as well!" Jeannette chimed in.

Paul leaned back in his chair. "Miss Ryan is full of surprises, isn't she?"

Charmaine looked directly at him. "There is nothing surprising about playing the piano, Mr. Duvoisin. Mrs. Harrington spoke of my ability to do so during Friday's interview."

"So she did," Paul agreed with the hint of a smile. "Tell us, Mademoiselle, what else do you intend to teach my sisters and Pierre?"

"Whatever they would like to learn."

As his smile broadened, butterflies took wing in her stomach. Flustered, she looked away.

"We've shown Mademoiselle Charmaine the entire house," Jeannette supplied. "And she thinks it's beautiful."

"Yes," Paul mused, "I'm certain she does."

Charmaine was grateful when the conversation turned to other things. Having dinner night after night with Paul in attendance was going to be disconcerting. But at least he had noticed her, and of course, his presence at the table was preferable to his absence.

She wondered why George was there. Then his last name registered. *George Richards, Rose Richards . . . I've just now returned your sisters to my grandmother.* George was Rose's grandson. She remembered Yvette's remarks during her interview. *She can't keep up with us the way she did with Johnny, Paul, and George.* Apparently, Rose had been a surrogate mother to all three boys. Now she understood why George was at the table and why there appeared to be a great camaraderie between him and Paul. Like his grandmother, he was more than an employee; he was considered a part of the family.

When the meal was over, Anna and Felicia cleared the dishes away. Charmaine watched as the latter fawned over Paul a second time. Earlier, Charmaine had been uncertain of the serving girl's intentions, but there was no mistaking the signals Felicia was sending now: the batting eyes and swinging hips. With olive skin, dark hair, and shapely curves, Felicia Flemmings was fetching. More than once, Paul leered at her.

Colette noticed it, too. "Felicia," she sharply remarked, "I'd like to speak with you tomorrow morning, in my chambers."

The maid's face dropped. She curtseyed and scurried away, not to be seen again for the remainder of the evening.

After dessert, Colette rose, and the family retired to the drawing room. Paul and George declined to join them. "We have a number of things to accomplish in the study," Paul told Colette. "Unfortunately, a few of these matters I need to discuss with Father. Nothing taxing, just—"

"That's fine, Paul," Colette interrupted. "It would be good for him to get involved in Duvoisin business, the more taxing the better. He's sat too long."

With a nod, he and George entered the library. Charmaine suddenly realized the library and the study were one and the same room.

By nine o'clock, the children were asleep, and Charmaine returned to her room on the third floor. So much had happened during her first day in the grand house, and both her mind and heart were full. It had been a good day, and she looked forward to tomorrow. With a sigh, she climbed into bed and fell swiftly to sleep.

But her dreams were disturbing. At first, she was on the wharf, watching Paul scowl at Jessie Rowlan. Then, Jessie Rowlan was her father, and Paul was lifting him clear off the dock, his fist knotting the shirt at the base of her father's neck. Next, John Ryan lay sprawled on the floor of the meetinghouse, and Paul was snarling to the island priest, "Tell Mr. Ryan who his daughter is married to."

She awoke in a cold sweat. Though her heart fluttered with Paul's insinuation that *she* was his wife, images of John Ryan remained vivid. *You're safe now . . . Paul will protect you. That's what your dream was telling you. He will protect you.* Even with that thought, it was a long time before she fell back to sleep.

Sunday, September 25, 1836

Charmaine's first week as governess passed without incident. True to her word, Yvette was the perfect child, and Charmaine began to wonder if Paul's anger of the Sunday past had been exaggerated. Nevertheless, Rose and Colette commended the girl on her good behavior. When her praises were sung, Yvette's eyes would travel to her governess, a silent reminder of Charmaine's end of the bargain. A wink sufficed to confirm their pact.

Yvette continued with her piano lessons, her sister in attendance. Their interest had not diminished; both girls practiced over an hour each day, and by Friday, they were able to play a few simple tunes with ease.

When Saturday proved sunny, Charmaine decided to take them on a picnic. Dr. Blackford had arrived early in the day, and Colette was closeted away with him. When Rose insisted on caring for Pierre—"You'll have a better time with the girls if he stays behind"—Charmaine and the girls set out for the nearby southern beaches, a hearty picnic lunch in hand. They collected seashells, waded knee-deep in the warm water, ran and laughed and told stories. The girls wanted to hear all about Charmaine's past, which she recounted, omitting the sordid details of her family life. They were interested in "being poor" as they put it and decided it would be a far more exciting life than the one they led "being rich." Charmaine snorted. She wished she'd had so terrible a childhood as they.

On Sunday, everyone attended Mass in the small stone chapel, everyone except Frederic. Charmaine began to wonder if she were ever going to meet the Duvoisin patriarch.

Like the week before, Father Benito's verbose sermon was uninspiring and fraught with condemnation. Charmaine's mind wandered to Father Michael Andrews. His homilies had been eloquent, his redeeming message of love and forgiveness, fulfilling. She thought of her mother, recalling her words of praise whenever she spoke of the spiritual priest. Father Benito could derive some inspiration from Father Michael.

Charmaine was glad when the Mass came to a close. The girls had fidgeted, Pierre was cranky, and Paul's eyes were constantly upon her, leaving her ill at ease. Did he think it was her fault the children could not sit still? Colette withdrew to her chambers, saying she was not feeling well, and it fell to Charmaine and Rose to care for the children for the remainder of the day. After the noonday meal, Charmaine took Pierre upstairs for his nap. The girls wanted to practice their piano lesson, so Rose decided to remain downstairs with them.

The boy fell asleep almost immediately, and Charmaine tiptoed from the room to retrieve a book from her bedroom. Fear gripped her when she returned to the children's chambers: Pierre's bed was empty. *Where is he?* She ran from the nursery in a panic, reaching the stairs in a heartbeat. Then she heard it: giggling coming from the apartments directly behind her. Relief flooded in. The door was standing slightly ajar, and Charmaine pushed it open. There stood Pierre, thigh-deep in Paul's riding boots.

"Pierre!" she scolded, her eyes darting about the dressing room. "Come here this instant!" He only giggled again, attempting to walk with the boots on. "Pierre, you're not supposed to be in here. Come here, please!"

He tripped and laughed harder, wriggling out of the boots and scurrying into his older brother's bedroom. The chase was on; she had no choice but to dash across the suite, stopping just shy of the bedroom doorway. Thankfully, it was empty as well, save a huge, four-poster bed, under which Pierre was crawling.

"Don't make me come after you, young man!" Charmaine futilely admonished. Groaning, she rushed forward, realizing the faster she got the boy out of Paul's private quarters, the better. Lying flat on the floor, she caught hold of his legs and was just pulling him out from under the bed, when a cough startled her. Afraid to look, but knowing she must, she let go of Pierre and, standing, turned to face Paul, her cheeks flaming red.

"Have you lost something, Miss Ryan?" he asked devilishly, his shoulder propped against the doorframe, arms and legs casually crossed. "Or perhaps you've come to my chambers for another reason?"

"No, sir—I mean—yes, sir," she stammered, her mortification nearly unbearable. "I've lost something, sir."

"Have you?"

Mercifully, Pierre wriggled out from under the bed and ran directly into his older brother's arms. Paul scooped him up, his brow cocked in Charmaine's direction. "So, it's Pierre you've lost? Amazing . . . Rose is minding the girls in the drawing room, and you were supposed to be caring for Pierre. Tell me, Miss Ryan, is it too difficult to keep track of one small boy?"

"I thought he was sleeping, sir," she answered, highly offended. "I left him for only a moment to—"

"No need to explain, Miss Ryan. As I mentioned during your interview, running after a child can be quite demanding, perhaps too much for you."

"Sir, you are wrong," she bit out, "and someday, you will eat your words."

He burst into hearty laughter, inciting another round of giggles from Pierre.

Charmaine's temper peaked, and she had to quell the urge to step forward and slap the mirth from his face.

He recorded her anger, and though his eyes remained merry, his demeanor changed. "I think you've proven your worth to my family, Miss Ryan. You've done a fine job with the children, especially where Yvette is concerned."

His unexpected words were sincere. She didn't know what to say.

"Do you accept my compliment, then?" he asked with a lopsided grin.

"Yes, sir," she replied, her throat dry and raspy.

"Why don't you call me Paul? That is, if you'll allow me to call you Charmaine? We're not so formal on Charmantes, leastwise not as formal as Richmond society can be. I promise, it is quite easy to pronounce."

The mild barb prompted her to reply. "Paul," she said softly.

"Charmaine," he returned with a slight nod. "Now, *Charmaine,* let's get Pierre back to his playroom. We wouldn't want Mrs. Faraday to find us alone in my bedchamber. I fear she'd be scandalized."

Charmaine's cheeks burned anew, and again Paul chuckled.

In a matter of minutes, Pierre was back in his bed and Paul had left them. But Charmaine trembled for a good hour afterward, her insides pleasantly warm. Paul approved of her, he finally approved of her!

Later that afternoon, Gwendolyn and Loretta paid her a visit. They spent an hour on the portico while the girls and Pierre played hide-and-seek nearby. Gwendolyn nearly suffered the vapors when Paul emerged from the manor and greeted them. He headed toward the stable and carriage house, which comprised the southern front lawns of the compound. When he was out of earshot, she said, "You are so lucky, Charmaine!"

Loretta frowned disapprovingly. "Charmaine had best keep a level head."

"Don't worry, Mrs. Harrington. I know I'm only the governess. But it is nice to dream."

"So long as it remains a dream."

Soon it was evening, and Charmaine's first week in the Duvoisin employ came to a close. But as she tucked the girls into bed, Yvette whispered to her, "You haven't forgotten about my letter, have you?"

"No, I haven't forgotten," Charmaine whispered back.

"Good, because I finished it yesterday. I even drew a picture! When are your friends leaving for Richmond?"

"Not for another week or so. They have to wait for a ship to make port. But I haven't forgotten, Yvette, and I promise I'm sticking to our pact. May I read your letter tomorrow?"

Yvette's eyes widened. "Of course not! It's private."

Charmaine chuckled and gave her a kiss. "You've been a fine girl this week, Yvette. I hope that after your letter leaves the island you'll continue to behave."

"Don't worry, Mademoiselle," she yawned. "I like you, so I'll be good." With a contented smile, she snuggled under her blankets.

Jeannette was already asleep, but Pierre grew obstinate, crying for his mother, whom he hadn't seen for most of the day.

Thankfully, Colette appeared, her face pallid, her legs unsteady. It didn't look as though Dr. Blackford's Saturday visit had done her much good. She stayed only long enough to rock her son to sleep. Charmaine decided that as soon as Colette seemed up to it, she would broach the subject of Yvette's letter.

Monday, September 26, 1836

The second week began much like the first with the exception of her newly won respect from Paul. She was glad he no longer treated her with indifference. During that first week he'd been courteous to a fault: *Good morning, Miss Ryan. Good evening, Miss Ryan.* By Saturday, Charmaine had been certain the man didn't know how to be friendly, only polite. All that had changed on Sunday, and she smiled with the memory of it. By the end of Monday, she had become comfortable calling him Paul, and he in turn called her Charmaine, inquiring pleasantly as to how her day had been with the children.

Her new "friendship" with Paul did not go unnoticed by the two maids of the manor, and late that night when she reached her room on the third floor, Felicia and Anna cornered her there. "So it's Paul, is it?" Felicia sneered. "You wouldn't be falling into his bed now, would you?"

Charmaine was appalled by the maid's vulgarity. "Are you jealous, Felicia? I don't suppose Paul respects a woman who throws herself at him. I know Miss Colette doesn't approve."

The housemaid's eyes flashed. "I don't care about *Miss* Colette. And what would you know of Paul's likes or dislikes, anyway? Just stay away from him, you hear me? Stay far away!"

"Please step aside," Charmaine replied condescendingly.

Stunned, the voluptuous woman threw a vexed look to her

cohort, the considerably plainer Anna Smith. Charmaine seized the moment and pushed into her room, shutting the door in the servant's face. Leaning back against the door, she closed her eyes and breathed deeply, wishing her room wasn't on the same floor as Felicia Flemmings's. She didn't think the taunting would end with this one confrontation. Annoyed, she grabbed her book and decided to read until her eyes were tired and she'd be able to sleep.

Tuesday, September 27, 1836

Where Monday had been rainy, Tuesday dawned sunny. On Colette's request, Charmaine spent the morning in town. Tomorrow was the twins' birthday, and Colette needed someone, preferably a woman, to travel to the mercantile. She provided the carriage, and Charmaine had the driver stop at the Browning house to see if Gwendolyn would like to join her. They had great fun fetching the gifts Colette had ordered for her daughters months ago, the most remarkable, two miniature glass horses to add to their animal collection. "The girls love the stable," Colette had said. "Now they'll have horses of their own."

As noon approached, Charmaine said goodbye to Gwendolyn and had the driver take her back to the manor. Once there, she rushed up to her bedroom and deposited the packages on her bed. She reached the table just in time for lunch.

"Where have you been?" Yvette demanded.

"You'll find out tomorrow," was all Charmaine would say.

Later that evening, when everyone was abed, Charmaine wrapped the gifts, spending a great deal of time on the ribbons. Colette had recommended she hide them in the back of the girls' armoire, behind all their dresses. It was best if she crept down there now, when they were sound asleep. Sure enough, no one stirred. When she was finished, she headed down to the library, crossing paths with Jane Faraday on the stairs.

"Is there something you require, Miss Ryan?" the head housekeeper queried brusquely.

Charmaine decided not to take offense. The older woman's comportment was generally curt. "I was going down to the library."

"At this time of night?"

"I'm not tired, but I find reading by lamplight makes me so."

The woman eyed her suspiciously. "Then I suggest you choose a book quickly and take it back to your room on the third floor." Without further explanation, she continued her ascent.

Puzzled, Charmaine proceeded on her quest, selecting a novel entitled *Pride and Prejudice.* The study was inviting, the lighting good, and because she had spent a great deal of time in her bedroom already, she ignored the matron's directive and settled into one of the high-backed chairs. For an hour, she was lost to the story, unlike any she had ever read, and the characters of Mr. Darcy and Elizabeth Bennet, imagining Paul and herself as the hero and heroine. Oh, to live such a romance!

Muffled giggles interrupted her revelry. Mrs. Faraday thought everyone was abed. Not so. Charmaine recognized the voices: Felicia and Anna were scurrying about. Paul hadn't dined with them this evening, and Charmaine wondered if he had just come in. Whenever he was in the house, Felicia and Anna were never far away. *What are they doing?*

Charmaine lit a candle and doused the lamp, then crossed the room and cautiously opened the door. The hallway was surprisingly empty and dark, though light cascaded through the French doors in the dining room. She walked toward them, head cocked. No one was there either.

She stepped into the courtyard, breathing in the soft fragrance of the garden flowers. The breeze was a bit chilly, yet refreshing. The cool air carried the scent of ocean spray, sweet against her face as it washed away the remnants of the hot day. On impulse, she wandered along the garden path, her candle unnecessary, for lamps were lit here and there and a full moon bathed the sanctuary in heavenly light. She blew it out and set it atop her book on a nearby bench.

She sat down and closed her eyes, thinking about her new life and all that happened over the past month. So many changes, all for the better, she realized. Was she happy? Yes, she answered; she had made the right decision in coming to Charmantes. Like Yvette and Jeannette, she had yearned for adventure and had miraculously found it. Her life was no longer dull, but exciting.

The hour grew late. It was time to retire. Sighing, she finally rose.

"Going so soon?"

Startled, she spun halfway around to confront the deep voice that spoke from the shadows. "I'm sorry," Paul said as he stepped away from the tree he had been leaning against, "I didn't mean to frighten you."

"How long have you been standing there?"

He walked closer. "Long enough to watch you meander through the gardens and sit down on that bench. Actually, I've been intrigued. So many emotions crossing your brow, some of them quite vexing, I'd say."

Charmaine stepped back, her legs connecting with the bench she had just vacated. "Vexing?" she queried. "They weren't vexing, I assure you."

"What could someone so young be worrying about?" he pondered aloud, ignoring her remark to the contrary, stilling the hand that wanted to caress her cheek. Her blushes were intoxicating, and he had found himself thinking of her often during the past week, more often since Sunday.

"I told you, sir, I wasn't worrying about anything."

"Sir?" he queried. "I thought we'd dispensed with that formality."

"Paul," she acquiesced, heart hammering in her chest.

"Are you content here?"

"I think so," she whispered. "Actually—I *am* content. That is what I was thinking about before you spoke."

"You've been here less than a fortnight. How can you be certain?"

"I can't, but for now, my heart tells me I'm content."

He chuckled softly as if he approved of her conclusion, then stepped in so close their bodies were nearly touching. Charmaine closed her eyes, certain of his next move. She was desperately frightened, yet scintillatingly excited. But he didn't take her in his arms, and her eyes flew open, both relieved and annoyed to find he was now sitting on the bench.

"Stay awhile longer," he demanded, grabbing hold of her wrist and pulling her down beside him. "There's no reason why we should feel uncomfortable in one another's presence. I know you think of me as your employer, but I'd much prefer our relationship to grow into that of . . . *friends*. Would you like that?"

"Yes," she replied. "I'd like that very much."

"Good . . . And perhaps, in time, our *friendship* will blossom into something more. Would that be agreeable to you?"

He edged closer, his warm thigh coming in contact with hers, branding her through her dress, making it difficult to concentrate on his words. "I think so," she whispered tremulously.

He threw his arm around the back of the bench and leaned forward. "Life can be full for you here, Charmaine. I can see to that. You're a very beautiful young woman, and I can offer you fulfillment." With a rakish smile, he leaned back, allowing her to take his lead. She seemed to puzzle over his words, leaving him to contemplate the depth of her innocence.

"You've been too kind already, Paul. Just this past Sunday, you could have been angry when I allowed Pierre to run into your rooms, but you weren't. You've insisted I use your given name. I couldn't ask for more than that. Between you and Colette, I've been made to feel very welcome."

So, she believed him to be a gentleman, he mused, in the strictest sense of the word. He had played the game well thus far. But she had been living under his roof for nearly ten days now, and governess or not, she had caught his fancy. He knew she found him disconcerting. How many times had she blushed in his presence? More times than he could count. But those blushes were born of an attraction as well. Just now she was longing to have him kiss her. But he wanted more than a casual kiss. He would have preferred bedding a housemaid than the children's governess. When his efforts to hire her on as a servant had been thwarted, he'd changed his tactics. He had played the gentleman, until tonight. Suddenly, his need to have her was great, the time for the plucking, ripe.

"I'm not speaking of kindness, Charmaine. I'm speaking of comfort."

"I'm quite comfortable, Paul," she replied, completely misreading his cue. "My room is immaculate and finer than any other I've ever had. As for the rest of the manor, it's beautiful, and I feel fortunate to be allowed to roam about, using the library and the piano whenever I wish. From the very first day, everyone has made me feel at home."

Paul ran his hand through his hair in mild derision. *Must I spell my meaning out for her? Has she no knowledge of men?* He found that hard to believe; her comeliness must have captured many a young man's eye. It wasn't as if she were a Southern belle, smothered every minute of the day by a hovering chaperone. No, Charmaine Ryan must have had experience in the realm of domination and submission. She was only playing her own game here, perhaps to further her own reward, but that would soon end.

"Miss Ryan," he began again, "I'm certain you are not as naïve as you would lead me to believe. I'm pleased you find my house satisfactory. At present, however, that is the furthest thing from my mind. Let us say I'm more interested in our sleeping arrangements—yours and mine."

Slowly, the light began to dawn, and Charmaine's cheeks flamed scarlet. She tore herself away from the bench and the hand that had come to rest on her thigh. "How dare you suggest such a thing?" she spat out, her ire conquering her shame. "I'm a good girl, and I'd never, *never* do what you are suggesting. I was hired to see to the children's care—not yours!" Her eyes flooded with unwanted tears, and she suppressed the urge to run from the courtyard; she'd not grant him the satisfaction of laughing at her as well.

Groaning inwardly, Paul cursed himself for the fool he was. He had known she was different, but in his eagerness to have her, he'd ignored the signs of her possible virtue. Was he so conceited to believe every girl on the island would eagerly jump into his bed? He should have waited. But no; he had overstepped the bounds of propriety. She would leave the gardens tonight with her chastity intact, and he, with the brand "cad" stamped across his chest. From this evening on, she'd be wary of him. Somehow, he must mitigate the damage done, perhaps purge her mind of its dark conclusions.

"Charmaine, whatever is the matter?" he asked with great concern. "Is it something I said? What has brought you to tears?" He stood, produced a handkerchief, and moved toward her.

"Don't come near me!"

Her tone, rather than her command, stilled his advance. With five paces between them, he spoke. "Please, tell me what I've said to upset you."

"You know what you've said. I'll not explain it to you!"

"I fear you misjudge me," he cajoled, a simple plan germinating. "Surely you don't think I was suggesting you . . ." He allowed his shocked query to trail off as if embarrassed. "Charmaine," he breathed, braving a step closer, "you've misconstrued my remarks. Please believe me when I tell you I was only considering the "sleeping" arrangements. There, I've said it again!"

She eyed him skeptically, uncertain of herself. He seemed bent upon exonerating himself. If his intention had been to proposition her, why would he bother? She relaxed somewhat, accepting the handkerchief he held out to her.

"Charmaine," he whispered again, taking another step forward. "I'm sorry, truly I am. I didn't mean to offend you. We're blunt on Charmantes. But if you'd indulge me a moment longer, I think I can explain. I've been considering your room on the third floor. You're far too removed from the children there, and with Colette's poor health, it seems more practical for you to take up quarters next to the nursery. In that way, you'll be able to comfort them, especially little Pierre, should they awaken in the middle of the night."

He was winning her over. He could see it in her eyes, in her very being, her body no longer rigid. Inspired, he pressed on. "In fact, if you took the room adjacent to the children's bedchamber, I could have a door installed between the two, opening your room onto theirs." He stepped closer still, watching her dab at her eyes. "If that would be agreeable?"

"I don't know, sir," she faltered, relying on a formal address for fortification.

"Charmaine, you're not going to revert to calling me that again, are you?"

"I think 'sir' is more appropriate. Perhaps you think I'm naïve, and I suppose I am. However, being naïve does not make me a fool. I know right from wrong, decency from indecency. If I accept your offer, the move will be for the children's comfort, not yours. I hope *my* meaning is understood."

He *had* misjudged her. By the end of her reproof, he was simmering. *Who does she think she is, berating me as if I were a schoolboy? Why did I attempt to placate her? I should have kissed her passionately and been done with it—to hell with her objections.* But the moment was lost, and now he said, "Our meanings are the same, Mademoiselle. What is your answer?"

She hesitated. "Yes, but—"

"But what?" he queried snidely.

"The playroom abuts the children's bedroom on one side, and according to Yvette, your brother's chambers, the other side. Certainly either room is out of the question."

"John's room sits unoccupied. I'll have George break through the wall and mill a door for the frame."

"But what if your brother should return? Surely he won't be happy to find the governess in his room."

"He won't."

"He won't what?"

"Return. John won't return." The declaration was delivered with such conviction that the matter was closed as quickly as it had been opened. "Now," he proceeded, his temper poorly concealed, "if we're in agreement, I'll say good night. The hour grows late, and I have to be at the dock at sunrise. I'm expecting a ship from Europe."

"Yes," she replied. "Good night and thank you . . ."

Her words were directed at his back. He'd already dismissed her, quickly retreating through the gardens and leaving her perturbed.

Paul was glad to reach his room, fulminating over the wretched scene he had generated. He was grateful for only one thing: his brother John hadn't witnessed the complete ass he'd made of himself; otherwise, he'd never live it down. *Well, Miss Ryan,* he thought as he stretched out on his bed, *tomorrow you can have your fancy room and your fancy airs all to yourself! I want no part of them. There are too many women on the island just clamoring for my attention. I have no need of one lovely governess. But when you grow lonely, when you're ready to become a woman, then you can come crawling back to me, and perchance, I'll take you to my bed.* Satisfied with that thought, he slept.

Chapter 5

Wednesday, September 28, 1836

ONSTRUCTION on the new door began the next morning. The sound of splintering wood echoed throughout the house, confounding those at the breakfast table. The twins dropped their spoons and ran from the room, ignoring their mother's admonition to wait. Charmaine and Colette found them in the nursery, wide-eyed over the hole in the wall and the debris littering the floor.

"What is this?" Colette demanded as Rose and Pierre drew up alongside her.

George peeked through the opening from the bedroom beyond. "The new doorway," he offered.

"Doorway?" Colette queried, clearly irate. "What doorway?"

"The one Paul told me to begin working on today."

"Why would Paul ask you to break a hole through that wall, George?"

George's eyes flew to Charmaine, and she cringed. "For the children's benefit," he replied. "Paul thinks Miss Ryan should be nearer the nursery, so he's given her this room—and a door in order to provide easy access should they awaken during the night."

"That's John's room!" Colette fumed. "You've no right to desecrate it."

"*Desecrate it?* I'd hardly say I was desecrating it. And it's not my idea, anyway. I'm just following orders."

"And what if John were to come home?"

"He's not coming home, Colette. You know that."

"Someday he will," she murmured, her anger spent, "and he'll be hurt to find his chambers have been given to someone else."

Jeannette grabbed hold of her mother's hand. "Don't be upset, Mama. There are so many rooms in our house, I'm sure Johnny won't mind using another one. Besides, it will be nice to have Mademoiselle Charmaine nearby. Maybe that was Paul's birthday gift to us."

Colette smiled down at her daughter. "Perhaps you are right. I just wonder what your father is going to say when he sees this mess."

George said, "According to Paul, he approved the project."

Colette rubbed her forehead. "Yes, I suppose he would." She motioned to the children. "Come, let us step out of George's way."

"Oh, please, can't we watch?" they begged.

Colette relented, advising them to remain seated on the far bed.

For a full hour, they chatted happily away. George, Travis, and Joseph indulged them whilst sawing, banging, and removing the wood and plaster that seemed to be everywhere.

When Pierre tired of the spectacle, Colette and Charmaine withdrew into the adjoining playroom. Realizing she was not needed, Rose excused herself.

Charmaine inhaled. "Colette," she said, "I'm sorry Paul didn't speak to you about the room. I didn't know he was going to start on it immediately. I should have insisted he get your permission first."

Colette's brow dipped in consternation. "You knew about this?"

"Paul mentioned it to me last night. He suggested—"

"Last night? Paul arrived home late last night."

Charmaine was too embarrassed to reply, and Colette deduced the obvious.

"Charmaine," she began, folding her hands as if in prayer and bringing them to her lips. "I think I should warn you about Paul. Perhaps I should have done so sooner. He's a ladies' man." When Charmaine hung her head, Colette attempted to ease her distress. "I don't want to see you hurt."

"Don't worry, Colette, I won't bring shame to your home."

"I'm not speaking about shame, Charmaine. I'd hate to see you give your heart to someone who has no intention of returning your love."

Charmaine was stung by the words, though she knew they rang true. Her initial assumption had been correct: Paul *had* propositioned her. When he'd realized she was not about to be compromised, he'd enacted a grand charade of misunderstanding. Her mother had warned her of such men, and Colette was doing the same. There was only one thing Paul desired from her, and it wasn't "friendship," not even love.

"I'll take heed," she whispered and added as a dismal afterthought, "If you don't want me in that room—"

"Nonsense," Colette countered. "Moving you into John's room is actually a fine idea, and the damage to the wall is done."

Charmaine reflected on the Duvoisin son she had yet to meet, the strange reaction his name had evoked that morning. Her thoughts circled to Yvette and the letter she'd written. Best to ask now and get it over with. "Yvette would like to send a letter to her brother in Richmond. I promised if she were good, and you gave your permission, I'd ask Joshua Harrington to deliver it."

"Let Yvette write her letter," Colette answered without hesitation. "I'm certain John could use some happy news from home."

Relief washed over Charmaine. "She already has."

Colette didn't seem surprised.

After a time, she called to the girls, insisting they do a bit of reading. Together, they finished a narrative on Eleanor of Aquitaine, the French noblewoman of the twelfth century, who, at the age of fifteen, married the king of France, and later, the king of England. The girls pestered their mother for details, knowing Colette's family, the Delacroix, hailed from Poitiers, the same village where Eleanor grew up. When Colette spoke of the death of Eleanor's twenty-seven-year-old mother, Jeannette lamented. "That is so sad, Mama. You will be twenty-seven soon."

Colette squeezed her, promising to live a long life, then sent them over to Charmaine, who had been preparing a series of spelling lists. The girls were already good readers, but she was showing them the letter patterns in words.

Not five minutes later, Yvette was complaining. "This doesn't make sense!"

Charmaine looked over her shoulder. "What doesn't?"

"This stupid list," she grumbled. "Oil, boil, soil, foil . . ."

"Yes, what about it?"

"Well, if 'o-i' makes the 'oy' sound in those words, Du-*vwah*-zan should be pronounced Du-*voy*-zan . . . and Mademoiselle . . . Madum-*oy*-zel."

Charmaine chuckled. "Very good, Yvette," she praised. When the girl eyed her skeptically, she added, "It shows you're paying attention and really learning. As for your surname and Mademoiselle, I think the 'o-i' is pronounced differently because both words are French."

Colette looked up from where she was now reading to Pierre. "Mademoiselle Charmaine is correct, Yvette," she interjected. "In the

French language, 'o-i' is pronounced 'wah.' But you know that. There are quite a few French words that have made their way into the English language: 'armoire,' 'reservoir,' and 'repertoire,' for instance. Your papa's other island 'Espoir' is also pronounced with the 'wah' sound."

"It's very confusing," Yvette grumbled.

"That is English," Charmaine concluded. "Some say it is the most difficult language to learn because it has so many variations."

"Is that true, Mama?" Jeannette asked.

"Is what true?"

"That English is difficult to learn?"

"Yes, I suppose it is. I learned the rudiments when I was young, but I didn't become proficient until . . . until I moved here."

"Did Papa teach you?"

Colette grew reticent. "A bit," she whispered. When Jeannette probed further, she said, "It is nearly lunch time. Let us finish up."

After the meal, the girls rushed to the piano for their daily lesson. An hour later, everyone retreated to Colette's chambers where it was considerably quieter. The promise of birthday gifts was more enticing than the construction site. Charmaine volunteered to get the presents from their hiding place. She had just reached the end of the corridor when Agatha Ward appeared.

"Miss Ryan," the matron criticized, "are you being employed to decorate the hallway or were you hired to care for the children?"

The obtrusive statement left Charmaine dumbfounded, for she had had little contact with the woman, passing a friendly "good day" now and then, but nothing more. Agatha avoided the children, and Charmaine only saw her at mealtimes or when she insisted Colette rest. Most days, Colette politely ignored her.

"Well, Miss Ryan?" she pressed.

"I've been sent on an errand"—Charmaine stammered—"for Miss Colette."

"An errand?" Agatha scoffed. "And where are the children?"

"With Miss Colette, in her chambers."

"Young lady," she scolded, "Miss Colette is not well. *You* are the one who should be looking after the children, not she! They continue to contribute to her failing health."

Charmaine's ire had been primed. "Miss Colette seems most indisposed after she passes an afternoon with your brother, Mrs. Ward. On the other hand, her health always improves when she spends time with her children."

Agatha Ward's eyes widened briefly, then narrowed into slits of animosity. Charmaine realized too late she had just made an enemy. "What are you inferring, Miss Ryan—that my brother is incompetent? Let us hope you are never in need of a physician's care while on this island. I don't think Robert would appreciate ministering to someone who eagerly maligns his good name."

"I didn't mean—"

"Didn't you?" the widow hissed. "You had better scurry back to your—"

"What goes on here?"

Startled, Agatha's hostility faded, her attention focused over Charmaine's left shoulder. "Why Frederic," she recovered, "isn't this a surprise?"

Charmaine pivoted around, stunned to find the splendid Frederic Duvoisin standing before her. He leaned heavily on a polished black cane, his posture crooked. Even so, he radiated a power that negated the rumors she had heard. He was taller than Paul, his attire casual, yet finely tailored, and he was handsome, positively handsome. Liberal touches of gray highlighted a full head of hair, not quite as dark as his son's. He was clean-shaven, with squared jaw, long, curved nose, and thin lips. His steely eyes were keen and bore through her, scrutinizing her more surely than she did him.

"Are you pleased with your assessment, Miss Ryan?" he asked, irony lacing his deep voice, his speech slightly slurred. He knew who she was! "I asked you a question, Mademoiselle. Does the invalid meet your expectations?"

"You're not an invalid, sir," she answered truthfully.

The remark surprised him, but he snorted derisively, then confronted Agatha. "Has Miss Ryan done something to annoy you?"

"She has left the children unattended."

"Where?"

The dowager lifted her nose a notch. "In Colette's chambers."

"And where is my wife?"

"With them."

"I'd hardly call that unattended, Agatha. Colette is, after all, their mother."

"Yes, Frederic, but she is not well. That is the only reason Miss Ryan was hired. What is the point of a governess, if she does not tend to her pupils?"

"Miss Ryan?" Frederic queried, giving her the chance to defend herself.

"Your wife asked me to get the twins' birthday gifts, sir."

"I see," he said, focusing on the widow again.

"Had I known," Agatha lamely objected. "Miss Ryan said nothing of gifts."

"You didn't give me a chance," Charmaine rejoined.

Agatha gritted her teeth. She was losing this debate. Best to swallow her pride, apologize, and quickly excuse herself.

Charmaine watched her hasten down the stairs, then faced Frederic again. Suddenly, she understood why Colette might be attracted to a man old enough to be her father. Unlike Paul, who at times possessed a youthful mien, this man was hardened, lordly, and completely disarming. In his younger days, she could only wonder over the women who fell at his feet. Did he know how intriguing he was? Yes, he definitely knew. Even now, in his crippled state, he knew.

Presently, he was awaiting her next move. "Miss Ryan," he said, breaking the prolonged silence. "I believe you were sent to retrieve something for my wife?"

"Yes," she said and headed toward the nursery, intimidated when he followed her, acutely aware of his handicap now that he attempted to walk. She knew he would not appreciate her pity, so she kept her gaze averted, rummaging instead inside the armoire for the girls' presents. When she turned around, he was standing before the broken wall, studying it. According to Paul, he'd agreed to the door's installation. She wondered what he was thinking now. Work had come to a halt; the men must have gone off for lunch.

As if reading her thoughts, he said, "I heard all the banging and wanted to see for myself the progress. I also wanted to spend time with my daughters."

He faced her. "My wife is very pleased with you, Miss Ryan."

"I'm happy to be here, sir. I like your children very much, and Miss Colette is a lovely woman."

"Yes, she is," Frederic agreed, his eyes intense. "And with your new room, she shall sleep soundly knowing you are not far from the children."

"Yes, sir," she replied, thinking, he *had* given his permission. Although Frederic Duvoisin might not often leave his chambers, he was fully aware of everything that happened in his home. Most of the gossip was untrue.

"I see you have all your packages. Shall we?" He inclined his head toward the hallway, intending to accompany her.

"Yes. The girls will wonder what has kept me."

Again, Frederic followed, and she slowed her pace in an effort to diminish his incapacity. The gesture annoyed him. "Hurry up, Miss Ryan, we don't have all day!" Flustered, she quickly complied.

When they reached Colette's suite, he asked if she might fetch another three parcels. "There are additional gifts in my dressing room."

The master's apartments were congruent to Colette's boudoir: the same dimensions, doors equally positioned. Yet the similarity ended there. These lavishly appointed quarters were masculine: bold and ornate, dark and somber, with heavy, elaborately carved furniture.

Charmaine didn't dally. She skirted across the spacious room, re-stacked the parcels, and returned to the passageway moments later. The packages were cumbersome, and she shifted them uneasily, relieved when Frederic rapped on his wife's door.

Yvette opened it, clearly surprised to find him there. "Papa?"

He raised a dubious brow. "Yvette, am I to stand forever in the hallway? Or will you invite us in? Miss Ryan is overburdened with birthday presents."

"Come in, Papa," she invited, stepping aside. "We didn't expect you to visit us today. Mama promised to take us to your room after dinner tonight."

"The schedule has been changed," he said, limping into the chamber. "I heard the racket coming from the nursery and went to have a look at the door being installed for your benefit. But you weren't there. Instead, I have had the pleasure of meeting your new governess."

Yvette wasn't listening, her attention diverted. "Oh, my!" she exclaimed, scanning the packages Charmaine carried. "How many are there?"

"Allow Miss Ryan to put them down, Yvette."

Frederic reached the settee and fell into it with an exhaustive "oomph," his face drawn as if in pain. When the moment passed, he looked about the room. "Where is your mother?"

"In the bedroom, with Pierre. He needed to have his nappy changed. There is an odd number of packages here," she observed, lifting the largest.

"One is for Pierre," her father explained.

"Pierre? Why does he get a present? His birthday isn't until March."

"Now, Yvette, would you deny him the pleasure of opening a gift? I realize it's not his birthday, but he'll be upset if there's nothing for him to tear into."

Charmaine was taken by the man's thoughtfulness, his tender voice.

"May I open one of them now, Papa?"

"First, tell your brother and sister I have come for a visit."

She jumped to do his bidding, calling from the doorway, "Papa is here."

Jeannette scampered into the room and embraced him. "Papa!"

"You are looking well, Jeannette."

"So are you, Papa. I'm glad you came to visit us today! Does this mean you are getting better?"

"If I am, it is because of you." He stroked her hair, his eyes glowing.

The endearing moment was broken when Colette stepped into the room, Pierre in her arms. Frederic looked up, missing her smile of greeting, and spoke sharply. "Do you think that wise, Colette?"

Her face dropped. "Wise?"

"Carrying the boy so," he replied. "You've been told not to exert yourself."

She bit her bottom lip and immediately set Pierre on his feet. He was off and running, crying, "Mainie's back!"

"Mainie?" Jeannette and Yvette asked in tandem.

Colette understood and laughed, shaking off Frederic's stern disapproval and reveling in Pierre's candid joy. "I think you have a new name, Charmaine."

Charmaine scooped the child up and gave him a hug. "And I like it."

"Mainie," Pierre said again, before giving her a big, wet kiss.

Charmaine returned the affectionate gesture, which elicited a repeat performance from the lad. After a moment, she walked over to the sofa. "Your father has come to see you, Pierre," she said, placing the boy on the man's lap.

Pierre immediately began to squirm, and Frederic struggled to hold him in place. Before he could wriggle free, Colette crossed the room and sat next to them. Frederic shifted closer to her, their thighs touching, eyes meeting. He relaxed his grip, and Pierre crawled into her lap, happy again.

The minutes gathered in silence, an uneasy quiet. Charmaine grew uncomfortable. No words had passed between the couple, and yet much had been said, the tension mounting. Even the girls could feel it, for they remained mute, waiting for someone else to speak. Only Pierre appeared oblivious, happily playing with the buttons on his mother's dress.

"Perhaps you'd like some time alone," Charmaine suggested awkwardly and, not waiting for a reply, turned to leave.

"A moment longer, Miss Ryan," Frederic commanded. "Would you please distribute my gifts to the children? Each one is marked."

Charmaine attended to his request. Yvette ripped the wrapping from the present. Jeannette held her parcel a moment longer, studying her parents instead.

Frederic looked up at her. "Aren't you going to open your gift, Jeannette?"

"Yes, Jeannette," Yvette urged, "open it quickly. I want to see if you got something better than a silly old doll so we can trade." She held up a lovely china doll with eyes that opened and closed.

Charmaine winced, wary of Frederic's reaction. Would he admonish the girl? He only chuckled, as if the declaration were ingenuous, rather than pert. "What is this, Yvette? I thought all little girls played with dolls."

"No, sir. I'd much prefer to have a horse!"

"A horse?" he pursued in jest. "And how would I manage to get him in a box of that size?"

"He wouldn't have to be in a box, Papa," she replied in earnest. "You could have him hidden in the stables, with a big blue ribbon around his neck!"

"Really? And what would you do with him once you'd found him?"

"Ride him, of course!"

"But horseback riding isn't ladylike."

Yvette mistook his facetious remark and wrinkled her nose disdainfully. "I don't want to be a lady, Papa. I'd much rather be a boy."

"Would you now? And why is that?"

"It's no fun being a lady, that's why! You always have to worry about keeping your dress clean. You always have to wear a dress! Boys can wear trousers. They can be rude and spit. They can learn to swim and climb trees! But if you're a girl, you're not allowed to do any of those things. A girl has to have proper manners, and I hate it! I want to do the things my brother does."

"Pierre?" Frederic asked, baffled. "Surely you're allowed more than he?"

"Not Pierre, Papa. Johnny. He always does fun things. When he was living here, we had such a wonderful time! Every day we did something new, and he never once told me I couldn't because I was—"

"Yvette," her mother remonstrated, "that's enough."

"No, it's not enough! I'm tired of being told not to mention his name. I love Johnny!" With arms akimbo, she turned accusatory eyes on her father. "And when is he coming home, anyway? When are you going to stop being angry with him? *When?*"

"Not for a very long time," Frederic snarled irascibly, jaw clenched.

"*Why?*" she demanded, stomping her foot.

"He is a menace to certain members of this household. Now, you'll not speak of him again! Is that understood, young lady?"

Undaunted, Yvette's eyes flashed fire for fire, refusing to answer.

"*Is that understood?*"

"No—it's not!" she shouted, throwing down the doll. Its head shattered into a thousand pieces, shards of glass flying everywhere. She tore from the room, ignoring her father's repeated bellows of: "Yvette, come back here!"

Colette appeared to weather the storm, speaking softly yet firmly when he leveled his wrathful gaze on her. "There was no need to speak to her that way."

"You think not?"

"She loves her brother and doesn't understand—"

"Damn it, woman!" he roared, as if astounded by her audacity. "Why do you defend him? It is time you taught the children to respect me! I refuse to tolerate such insolence from an eight-year-old child. My daughter will not decide *if* she obeys. She *will* obey!"

Colette bowed her head to his public chastisement.

Belatedly, Frederic seemed to remember the governess was there. "Where is Pierre's present?" he asked gruffly.

Charmaine relinquished the package she held for support, and Frederic extended it to his son. "Look, Pierre, I have a gift for you. Come, sit here and open it with me."

The boy would not budge from Colette's protective lap.

"Come," Frederic persisted, "sit on my knee so you can open this. Your mother is right here. She would like to see what's inside."

The more he cajoled, the more the child withdrew, balled fists holding tightly to his mother's dress, face buried in her bosom, his muffled whimpers echoing in the turbulent room. He had no interest in the package with its pretty ribbons.

Colette began her own appeal. "Here, Pierre, I will help you. *Voici, mon caillou,* your father would"—the statement caught in midsentence, a minute flinch as her gaze clashed with Frederic's —"come, Pierre, we can open it together."

Clearly, Frederic had had enough. "Give me my son!" he demanded, grabbing hold of the boy's arm. "Give him here—now!"

Defeated, Colette allowed Frederic to pry Pierre loose. At last, she was free and stood quickly. She averted her face, squared her shoulders, and walked with dignity from the room.

The door closed, and Colette ran—ran to escape the demon that chased her, ran down the passageway, the stairs, ran until her side hurt, coming up abruptly as the main door in the foyer swung open and Paul strode in. She turned from him and ran again, to the back of the house and into the gardens.

"Colette?"

Jeannette was silently weeping when her father spoke to her. "Come, Princess, help your brother open his package."

The girl looked from Frederic to Charmaine as if she hadn't heard. "What was the matter with Mama?" she asked.

"I don't know, Jeannette," Charmaine whispered.

Hoping to still her quaking limbs, she scooped up the discarded doll and began picking up the pieces of glass that littered the floor. Perhaps it could be mended. Jeannette crouched down to help.

"Leave that!" Frederic barked.

Charmaine dropped the fragments. "I'd best see to Yvette," she said, determined to escape the wretched room. But unlike Colette, who had maintained her composure, she fled like a petrified rabbit, the broken doll still in her arms.

Jeannette was right on her heels, until Frederic stopped her. "Jeannette, come help your brother." With a sigh, she complied.

Paul walked briskly into the dining room; it was empty. Noise from the kitchen sent him in that direction. He was surprised to find Travis, Joseph, and George sitting at the rough-hewn wooden table. Fatima was serving the three men a late lunch, the very meal that had brought him home. "Have you seen Colette?" he asked.

"No," George replied. "Why?"

"She wasn't upset about the new door, was she?"

"In the beginning. But not anymore. Why?"

"She was crying. Just now—in the foyer."

George shook his head. "She wasn't that upset."

Paul ran a hand through his hair. She *was* upset. He had to find her. *The gardens—she must have gone into the gardens.*

Charmaine found Yvette on her bed, toying with an envelope she tapped on her knee. She looked up, her eyes red. "I may as well burn this," she said, and Charmaine realized it contained the letter she had written to John.

"No, Yvette. It's being sent directly to your brother just as I promised. Your mother gave her permission this morning."

Yvette frowned in momentary disbelief, then smiled, wiping away the last of her tears. "Thank you." She turned serious again. "I don't know why Papa is so angry with Johnny. His seizure happened three years ago! Johnny is his son. Why won't he forgive him?"

"It's not just a matter of forgiveness, Yvette. I think your father is embarrassed about the way he looks right now. His arm, his leg, the way he walks, the cane he has to use for support. He sees himself as a cripple, and that's not an easy thing for any man to live with. If an argument with your brother caused that condition, I can understand his bitterness. The pain and humiliation that's deep inside of him has turned into anger."

"He's more than angry, Mademoiselle Charmaine. He hates Johnny."

Charmaine shook her head. "No, Yvette, I don't believe your father hates him. No man hates his own son." Even as she spoke the words, she wondered if she were wrong. After all, she hated her father. And if that were possible, why couldn't Frederic hate John? She shuddered with the thought of it, for in this relationship, so many others were involved.

"Yvette," she began cautiously, "I'd like you to do something I know will be difficult. I'd like you to go back to your mother's apartments and apologize to your father."

Yvette's face turned crimson. "*Apologize?* You want me to apologize after what he said? He should apologize to me and to Johnny! I'll never apologize to him! He'll be lucky if I ever speak to him again! I thought you understood!"

Charmaine allowed the barrage of protests to ebb before she attempted to explain. "Do you want your brother to come home again, Yvette?"

"Of course I do!"

"The only way you're going to get your father to change his mind about John is by setting the example you want him to follow."

Yvette weighed the wisdom of her governess's supposition and grimaced in revulsion. "*But apologize?* I don't see how that can possibly help."

"Your father is resentful, Yvette. How much greater will that resentment become if he thinks he's lost your love to John as well?"

"He'll only hate him more," she muttered, realizing she'd only make matters worse if she stayed angry with her parent. "I suppose I have no other choice," she groaned. "And I've ruined that silly doll. I can't fix that!"

"I don't think your father cares about the doll. But he does love you."

"I know he does," she ceded. "Will you come with me?"

"I'll be along in a minute," Charmaine promised as the girl walked to the door. "But Yvette, don't mention the letter to your father."

The girl rolled her eyes. "Don't worry. I'm not that stupid!"

When Yvette had gone, Charmaine went in search of Colette.

Was there nowhere to turn? No quiet haven where the past wouldn't haunt her? How much longer would she bear this heavy burden of guilt? How much more could she endure? Colette was in the courtyard before the kaleidoscopic questions converged into one ostensible answer, too terrible to face. *Peace, there will be no peace until I die.* She sat hard on a bench deep in the garden, buried her face in her hands, and wept.

Where is she? Paul scoured the pathways, hearing, rather than seeing her first. He knew who had reduced her to tears. This had nothing to do with the new door. Or did it? He regarded her for countless minutes, uncertain how to confront her misery. It had been years since she'd cried on his shoulder. His chest ached at the sight of her anguish.

"Colette?" he called, his throat constricted.

The golden head lifted, and her face glistened with moisture, her eyes red and swollen. Embarrassed, she stood and quickly attempted to wipe her cheeks dry. But the tears spilled forth faster than she could brush them away.

"Colette," he breathed again, this time stepping closer, gathering her into his strong arms, a bulwark to shoulder her pain. When she tried to push him away, he pulled her tighter into his embrace, murmuring tender words to soothe her. "Ssh . . . there now . . . Cry . . . cry if you need to cry."

It had been too long since she'd been held—too long. Relinquishing the battle, she collapsed against him, crying until it hurt, until the well was dry and a strange calm settled over her.

"*Cela est fini,*" he murmured against the top of her head.

Charmaine reached the gardens through the ballroom. She didn't want to meet Mrs. Faraday, or worse still, Agatha Ward along the way, so she took a route that avoided the main house. Surely Colette would be there, for the courtyard offered a secluded sanctuary.

Soft words spoken in melodic French caught her ear. Colette used it every day when instructing her children, and Charmaine had learned quite a few phrases, but this was the first time she had been privy to an entire conversation. She peered through the branches and watched Paul lead Colette to the very bench they had shared the night before. And like the night before, he produced a handkerchief, pressed it into her hand, and said, "*Tu vas mieux maintenant?*"

"*Me pardonnera-t-il jamais?*" came her desperate response.

He shook his head, studying the delicate hand he held. "*J'éspère que je pourrais te donner la réponse que tu désires entendre.*"

She lowered her eyes. "*Comment est-ce-que je peux demander pardon quand je sais ce que j'ai fait? Je ne devrais pas te demander d'être compréhensif. Tu devrais me reprocher aussi . . .*"

His voice grew hard, and he released her hand. "*Tu sais que cela n'est pas vrai! Je ne t'ai jamais reprochée.*"

She began wringing the handkerchief. "*Je ne m'attends pas à ce qu'il me pardonne,*" she whispered, her eyes raising to his. "*Peut-être pourrais-je supporter sa douleur ainsi que la mienne.*"

"*Sa douleur?*" he snorted.

"*Oui. Je lui ai fait plus de peine qu'à moi-meme.*" She inhaled and shuddered. "*Il m'a aimée. Le savais-tu? Il m'a aimée, mais j'étais trop aveugle pour le voir. Je croyais que ma vie était terminée, alors j'ai choisi de mener une nouvelle vie, plus désastreuse que la première . . . Mon Dieu . . . Je me suis mentie à moi-même pendant si longtemps, je ne sais pas où se trouve le vrai bonheur.*"

"*Avec les enfants,*" Paul answered. "You have the children."

"Yes," she sighed, "I have the children."

The words were spoken reverently, as if she were drawing sustenance from them. But as the conversation continued in English, Charmaine tiptoed away, not wanting to eavesdrop. She knew Colette was in good hands.

She returned to the mistress's chambers, surprised to hear happy voices. Yvette was nestled next to her father, his arm around her shoulders. Someone had cleaned up the mess; there was no sign of the madness that had trespassed there only a short time ago.

Realizing Charmaine was there, Frederic struggled to his feet. He stared down at his children, then at her. "Thank you," he eventually murmured, and she knew he was speaking of Yvette. She nodded slightly.

Saturday, October 1, 1836

Charmaine woke to the sun in her eyes. She blinked once and, realizing she'd overslept, jumped from her bed. Muttering under her breath, she flew about the room, splashing water in her face, dressing quickly, and brushing her hair haphazardly. She had no time to pin it up; instead, she tied it back with a ribbon, unmindful of the curly wisps that refused to be tamed.

The Harringtons were leaving at seven, and Paul had promised to take her into town to see them off. She was supposed to be ready at the crack of dawn, but she hadn't slept well. Felicia had cornered her in the hallway again, making ribald comments about her new sleeping quarters. "Couldn't be much closer to Paul's." Now Charmaine was terribly late. She ran from her room on the third floor and down the servants' stairwell that led to the kitchen.

Fatima Henderson bustled between table and woodstove, the smell of bacon and eggs filling the air. She was humming to herself, but one look at Charmaine and she clicked her tongue. "Miss Charmaine, why are you running like that?"

"I'm late!" she heaved, completely out of breath. "Have you seen Master Paul? He hasn't left without me, has he?"

"Slow down. He's in the dining room waiting for his breakfast. Now, sit yourself down and I'll fix you something, too."

"I couldn't eat a thing. Are you certain Master Paul hasn't left?"

"See for yourself."

Paul was indeed at the table. As she entered the room, he stood, his eyes raking her from head to toe, causing her heart to race.

She hadn't spoken two words to him since the night in the gardens, save a courteous good morning or good evening. That had changed last night when he informed her the *Destiny* would be leaving with the tide first thing in the morning. Her beloved Harringtons would be aboard, and it would please him to accompany her to the harbor to bid them farewell. When she had fretted over the imposition, withholding her reservations about riding into town with him alone, he brushed her objection aside, saying he needed to inspect the cargo. It was all arranged; he would escort her.

He was still staring at her, a lopsided grin that amplified the leering quality of his perusal. Charmaine glanced down at her dress, wondering if something in her appearance was amiss. "Is something wrong?" she asked.

"On the contrary," he answered, coming around the table and insisting she join him. "You look lovely."

She blushed. Suddenly, she felt lovely.

He led her to the chair on his left and pulled it out for her. When she hesitated, he said, "Charmaine, we don't have all day. I promise, I won't bite."

She cringed and sat quickly, cursing her Irish blood, which advertised her every emotion. Obviously, her blushing amused him. She must learn to control her feelings. *But how?*

"I'm sorry I've kept you waiting," she said when he was seated again.

"You haven't. I've just come in to eat," and he took a sip of his coffee.

Fatima was there, filling his plate. When she made her way round the table, Charmaine declined the aromatic food. "I'm not hungry, really I'm not."

Paul's brow raised. "You'll be famished by lunchtime."

"I'll have coffee instead. I don't want to miss the ship's departure."

"The captain won't set sail until I give the order."

When they left the house, she was surprised to find a chaise waiting for them. "I was busy while you were sleeping," he needled as he helped her in. This time she willed her face passive. He circled round the back of the vehicle and climbed in, taking up reins and flicking the horse into motion.

The trip was pleasant, and Charmaine was amazed at how easily Paul drew her into casual conversation. By the time they reached the town, she felt comfortable with him, more comfortable than ever before.

The *Destiny* was waiting just as he had promised. With heavy heart, she boarded the ship, knowing this farewell was going to be difficult.

Loretta and Gwendolyn were just emerging from their cabins, and Charmaine's eyes immediately filled with tears. She fell into Loretta's embrace and hugged her tightly. Finally, she drew away, wiping her face.

"I'm going to miss you," she whispered hoarsely.

"And I you, Charmaine. But you have a new life here. I will write." Loretta faced Paul, who had stepped to one side, permitting them their maudlin farewell. "Charmaine is like a daughter to me, Mr. Duvoisin," she imparted pointedly. "Today I leave her in your care. I pray I am not remiss in doing so."

Paul responded urbanely. "Your misgivings are unwarranted, Madame. Miss Ryan will be well protected while residing in my home."

"Good," Loretta replied.

Charmaine went in search of Mr. Harrington who was with the ship's captain. She was glad she had stuffed Yvette's letter in her apron pocket the night before. After bidding the man farewell, she pressed the correspondence into his hand, asking if he would see it delivered. He nodded and gave her another hug. She looked up to find Paul closely watching her, a strange expression on his face.

Then it was time to leave. She forced a smile from the boardwalk as the *Destiny* cast off. Paul remained at her side, watching as she continued to wave to her friends. As the vessel slipped farther south toward the mouth of the cove, she turned away. Loretta and Gwendolyn were no longer visible; there was no point in staying.

She was frowning when she faced Paul. "I thought you had to check on the ship's cargo before she left."

Paul rubbed his chin. "Everything was in order, just as I had hoped."

"So you weren't needed to see the *Destiny* off."

"Now, Charmaine, if you had known that, you would have insisted upon journeying to the harbor on your own this morning, and I would have been denied the pleasure of your company."

"Are you saying you lied to me?"

"Something like that." He was smiling, his deviltry irrepressible.

"Come, Charmaine. There is another reason I accompanied you into town today." He read her confusion and took hold of her elbow, leading her away from the wharf. "Colette asked me to take you into the bank and introduce you to Stephen Westphal. He is the town financier and will calculate the deposits made to your register each month. Unconventional by Richmond standards, but expedient on Charmantes. I'd like to check and make certain the account is in force and you are able to withdraw your salary whenever you like."

They spent the next hour conversing with Mr. Westphal, a strange man by Charmaine's estimation. He was of medium height, balding, probably a bit younger than Frederic Duvoisin, but not at all handsome. His eyes were too small, his eyebrows too feminine, and his lips too thin. He looked every bit the European aristocrat, which Paul confided he was; his family boasted a duke as a distant relative, though he himself was born in Virginia. His fingers were long and perfectly manicured. His clothing was expensive and accentuated his paunch, attesting to his own wealth and good fortune. He knew who Charmaine was. News of the Duvoisin governess had spread rapidly on Charmantes.

"Why don't you join us for dinner this evening, Stephen?" Paul asked. "In fact, come a bit earlier, perhaps six? My father and I have a few matters we'd like to discuss with you."

The man eagerly accepted the invitation, then nodded to Charmaine.

As they left the bank, Paul inquired whether she'd like to get a bite to eat. They strolled across the street, and Charmaine felt many eyes on them. She was thrilled knowing she was the envy of every young maid today. However, the pleasant feel of Paul's arm beneath her own evaporated when they reached the saloon. "I can't go in there!" she gasped.

"It's not a brothel, Charmaine," he chuckled. "I assure you, Dulcie's food is quite good."

"I—I didn't suggest it was!" she stammered. "I must get back to the house. The girls are waiting to help me move my belongings into the new bedroom."

"Ah yes, the new bedroom." He chuckled again, but said no more.

The ride home was disconcerting. Unlike their earlier conversation, Paul set her heart to palpitating, touching on indelicate subjects best left alone. Did he enjoy making her uncomfortable now that the Harringtons were gone? Was he reminding her she had nowhere to turn with them far from Charmantes?

"I hope you find your new bed pleasing," he began. "It might be overly large for just you."

Charmaine's cheeks burned. "If Pierre awakens in the night, there will be plenty of room for him to join me," she courageously returned.

"Hmm . . . best not to nurture that type of habit. He'll become spoiled."

"I doubt Pierre will ever be spoiled. He's a dear little boy."

To Charmaine's dismay, Paul revisited the subject of her new bedroom. "Now that you are on the second floor with the rest of the family, you will enjoy having the French doors at your disposal." When she didn't respond, he expounded. "During the summer, they are left open to catch the ocean breezes. The rooms on the second floor are always pleasantly cool. And of course, there is the *other* convenience they afford."

Charmaine knew he wanted her to ask him about that *other* convenience. She resolved not to, then did. "What convenience?"

"Every room opens onto the balcony: my bedroom, the children's rooms, even your room now. It's an inconspicuous way to travel from one chamber to the next . . ." His gaze, which had remained fixed on the road in front of him, now rested on her. "Just another convenience."

The lecherous overture evoked Colette's warning: *He's a ladies' man, Charmaine . . . I wouldn't want you to get hurt . . .* Was Paul propositioning her here, in the chaise, in broad daylight? "What are you suggesting, sir?" she bit out.

"Sir?" he queried. "Charmaine, when are you going to drop the formal title? What is it going to take to have you call me Paul permanently? You're not still upset by what you *think* happened in the gardens the other night, are you?"

He was trying to confuse her again. "I shall never call you Paul."

"Perhaps an agreement," he continued, completely ignoring her declaration, his brow raised in thought. "What if I promised to never again say anything to embarrass you?"

"I would say—that is impossible for you."

He threw back his head and laughed. When his glee subsided, he pressed on in the same vein. "What if I vowed to never do anything you yourself didn't want me to do? Would you drop the title 'sir' then?"

Is he serious? What should I say? She decided it was safer to say nothing.

"Well, Charmaine?" he probed. "We're almost home. Perhaps you'd like to think on it. But when you do, remember what I said to your Mrs. Harrington this morning. I meant every word."

They were home, and Charmaine inhaled before facing him. The buggy stopped, and their eyes locked as each tried to read the other's thoughts. The approach of another carriage intruded upon the moment. Dr. Robert Blackford had arrived for his weekly visit. Paul swore under his breath, jumped from the chaise, and rushed around to help her down. The faintest "thank you" fell from her lips as she hastened up the steps and into the house.

Paul stared after her, a wide grin mirroring his mood. She was something to behold, and all the more enchanting in her innocence and ire. Yes, she was innocent. He was certain of that now, and for that reason alone, he couldn't remain angry with her. She was too lovely for that. Today, he had enjoyed teasing her, but he also wanted her to feel at ease in his presence. Perhaps this "agreement" he'd contrived was the best way to do that. He also had to consider what Colette asked of him in the courtyard the other day. *I don't want you toying with Charmaine's affections. I don't want her to become another conquest. The children will need her should anything happen to me. Please promise me you won't hurt her.* Because he respected Colette, he had reassured her he would be on his best behavior. As for Charmaine, he'd make good his "agreement." He was certain if he did, she would come to enjoy his company. It would only be a matter of time before she recognized her own desires, and he'd be there when she was ready to enjoy them. *Yes, Charmaine Ryan, I can wait.*

Robert Blackford interrupted his musings, and they exchanged a few words before going into the house. The doctor was early; it was just after twelve.

"Quickly, Jeannette!" Yvette implored on a strained whisper. She was crouched near the top of the staircase, peering through the rungs of the balustrade into the nursery. "If you don't hurry, we shall miss it!"

"Miss what?" Charmaine asked from the landing.

Yvette swiftly straightened up. "Mademoiselle," she said sweetly.

Perhaps it was the manner in which the girl smiled, or the fact she didn't give Charmaine a direct answer, but Charmaine knew trouble was brewing.

"Miss what?" she asked again.

Yvette knew how to handle this: be as truthful as possible without telling the truth. She gave a big, healthy, exasperated huff. "There's a horse in the corral I want Jeannette to see."

The explanation sounded veracious enough, yet Charmaine wasn't convinced. "Why were you sneaking?"

"I wasn't sneaking. I was just telling Jeannette to hurry."

Jeannette appeared, smiling just as sweetly, but her demeanor was natural and honest.

"Where are your mother and Nana Rose?" Charmaine asked suspiciously.

"In the dining room, finishing lunch," Jeannette answered.

"And they've given their permission? This horse isn't dangerous, is it?"

"Oh, no," Jeannette answered sincerely. "Chastity is quite tame."

"Chastity?"

"Mama's horse," Yvette supplied with foot tapping.

"And why is this horse of such interest to you?"

"George has something he wants to show us," Yvette replied, inspired.

"What do I want to show to whom?"

Yvette grimaced. *Rotten luck!*

George joined the threesome, a biscuit in hand, another in his mouth. "Was someone talking about me?" he asked, swallowing.

Charmaine turned a critical eye on him. "You know nothing about this?"

"About what?"

"The horse in the corral. The one you want to show the girls."

"No."

Yvette was more than exasperated now. "Yes, you do, George," she argued, arms akimbo. "Remember, last time, when Paul said we were too young? You promised next time we could watch. Well, now it's next time."

George shrugged. "I don't know what you're talking about."

"Let's have it out, Yvette," Charmaine demanded. "What mischief are you making?"

Jeannette sighed. "Tell her, Yvette."

"Oh, all right," she capitulated with a huff, "but George did promise! Joseph said Gerald and the other stable-hands are helping Phantom and Chastity mate, and I want to watch."

Charmaine's hands flew to her face, her fingers fanning her cheeks.

But George's convulsive coughing surpassed her mortification, the biscuit he'd been eating lodged firmly in his throat. "I think—I'd better—go now"—he sputtered, fist thumping his chest—"if you'll—excuse me."

Once he was gone, Charmaine turned her humiliation on the girls. "What a disgusting remark! Why, in heaven's name, would you want to see such a thing?"

"I was just interested." Yvette shrugged lackadaisically.

"I suggest you become uninterested. Whether you like it or not, Yvette, you are a young lady. Even gentlemen don't speak of such things—"

"What things?"

Charmaine winced.

"Charmaine?" Paul queried, drawing up behind her, his eyes shifting to Yvette when she refused to look at him. "A gentleman doesn't speak of what things?" he probed further, the context of the conversation dawning.

"Horses mating," Yvette supplied without shame.

Charmaine held her breath against his certain anger, surprised when he said, "Mademoiselle Charmaine is correct. Gentlemen don't speak of such things, not freely, anyway. I'm surprised you are causing her grief today. This is hardly the way to show your appreciation. If I'm not mistaken, she delivered a letter to the *Destiny* for you, didn't she?"

Yvette's stormy eyes turned contrite. The moment held, the silence growing awkward. "I'm hungry," Charmaine said.

Colette was wiping Pierre's mouth clean when they entered the dining room. Agatha's face brightened at the sight of her brother. "Why, Robert, you've arrived early today." He seemed equally pleased to see her, an unusual smile breaking across his face.

Colette straightened. "Dr. Blackford," she breathed. "I do not require your services today."

The man bristled, throwing back his shoulders. "Madame, that is not a decision for you to make. Your husband has requested I restore you to good health. I cannot do so unless I minister to you on a regular basis. I thought you understood that when we agreed on weekly treatments."

"I'll tell you what I do understand, Robert," she returned heatedly. "I felt fine before you arrived last Saturday. But after you left,

I was dreadfully ill for the remainder of that day and well into Sunday."

The man took offense again, his brow severe. "It must be the new compound. It's quite potent. But it needs to be, especially since you refuse to take it when I'm not here."

Colette's eyes shot to Agatha, and Robert nodded. "Yes, I've heard how difficult you can be. If you'd be reasonable and consume the elixir as prescribed, a lower dosage might be more appropriate. I'll have to consult my medical journals to see what can be done."

"Consult all you like, Doctor, but you will *not* be treating me today."

Agatha clicked her tongue. "It's the governess," she accused, indicating Charmaine. "She has been filling your head with her medical opinions."

Colette frowned. "I don't know what you are talking about, Agatha. But I do know how poorly I've been feeling."

"Exactly," the older woman agreed, "and that is why Robert is here. Think of your children and how it will affect them if your condition worsens."

Colette faltered, and Agatha capitalized on her reaction, nodding toward Charmaine again. "If Miss Ryan thinks my brother is incompetent, I would like to hear why she feels that way."

All eyes rested on Charmaine who was forced to defend herself. "I never said Dr. Blackford was incompetent, Mrs. Ward. I merely suggested the best therapy for Miss Colette was the company of her children."

Paul cleared his throat. "Why don't we leave your visit until next Saturday, Robert?" he suggested in an attempt to placate all parties. "In that time you can consult your journals and determine the proper dosage for Colette. Meanwhile, she can see how she fares without her weekly treatment."

Robert gave a cursory nod, clutched his sister's arm before she could protest, and led her out of the house.

When Colette heard the front door close, she sighed. "Thank you, Paul."

He responded with a suave smile, then spoke of a different matter. "I've invited Stephen Westphal to dine with us this evening. My father has agreed to meet with him. I think you are right. It *will* do him good to get involved in island business again."

Colette's eyes lit up. "Did Frederic mention dining with us?"

"Not that involved," Paul replied flatly, "not yet, anyway."

Charmaine and the girls spent the better part of an hour transferring her belongings to her new room. Certain she'd never use the dressing room, she had asked George and Travis to move the armoire into the bedchamber where her dresses would be within easy reach. When the girls had finished tucking the last handkerchief away, she stood back to survey the final result, pleased.

Yesterday, the suite had been aired out. The masculine tones were all but gone: feathery curtains replaced the heavy draperies at the French doors, and the dark quilt that had covered the huge, four-poster bed was exchanged for a downy white comforter. Colette had removed all of John Duvoisin's possessions. Charmaine prayed Paul and George were correct when they declared the man would never come home. She fretted over Colette's assertion that he'd be upset to find his quarters given to someone else, let alone the governess.

The dinner hour arrived. Colette reminded her daughters they were to have a guest at their table, and they promised to be on their best behavior. When they reached the dining room, Paul and Stephen Westphal were already there. They had spent an hour in Frederic's apartments, but as Paul had predicted, his father did not join them. Colette was annoyed to find Agatha positioned directly to Paul's left and opposite Stephen, but said nothing. George arrived and said quite tactlessly, "Mr. Westphal, you are in my seat."

"Mr. Richards, really!" Agatha castigated. "Stephen is Paul's guest this evening and has important business to discuss with him. There are plenty of other chairs from which to choose."

George's face reddened, but he didn't respond. Instead, he took a place near Charmaine and avoided glances toward the head of the table. A sumptuous feast was set before them, and though he fell into the meal, he simmered at Agatha's insult.

Agatha Ward—how he despised the woman! For as long as he could remember, he and John fell in her disfavor. They stayed far out of her way whenever she came to visit. But Paul, ever polite and the apple of his father's eye, gained her approval from the start. Agatha was always trying to please Frederic, and if Paul were his father's favorite, Agatha would champion him as well. But today, something else was brewing. *Today? Bah! For months!* Perhaps it was Frederic's malady, perhaps it was Paul's good looks, so much like those of the older man. Evidently, Agatha's eyes had been diverted from father to son. George snorted in revulsion. Maybe he should warn his friend before the hag dug her claws in too deeply. He snorted again. *Paul didn't come to my defense tonight, didn't put the shrew in her place the way John would have, so no, I won't speak to Paul about Agatha Ward.*

The meal progressed and the banter was pleasant. Duvoisin business did not dominate the discussions, though Agatha attempted to direct the conversation to that issue. Paul avoided the topic of sugarcane crops and the shipping industry. After a time, it became obvious he either didn't want Agatha to know anything about island operations or had covered all the important elements earlier in his father's chambers.

Charmaine considered Colette. Though she played the perfect hostess, she seemed agitated. At first, Charmaine thought Pierre was the source of her irritation, for he played with his food and couldn't be coaxed to eat. But one glance at George, and Charmaine read the same expression there. She felt bad for him, knowing he didn't deserve Agatha Ward's sharp rebuke.

Hoping to mellow his mood, she struck up a conversation, pleased when he responded impishly. In no time, they were chuckling over his whispered comments. "I think Agatha and Stephen make a handsome couple. He looks like a proud rooster. Perhaps he fancies being pecked to death by a clucking hen."

The gaiety at the foot of the table chafed Paul. He threw George a nasty scowl, but the man's head was inclined toward Charmaine, and he missed it. Charmaine noticed, however, and quickly straightened up. Reading her expression, George looked round, finally making eye contact with Paul.

Satisfied the tacit message had been received, Paul turned back to the banker. "So, Stephen, have you any news from Anne?"

The man swallowed, then patted his mouth with his serviette. "Why, yes. She is in fine spirits and no longer wearing widow's weeds."

"Anne London is Stephen's daughter," Paul elaborated for those listening. "She lives in Richmond, but was recently widowed—last year I believe?"

The banker smiled down the table, growing garrulous now that he'd been offered the floor. "A year ago, May. She was quite distraught over the loss of Charles, God rest his soul, but he left her a small fortune, and for that, she is grateful. She has begun socializing again. Of course, I've cautioned her a level head when receiving suitors. She must be wary of blackguards who will be after her money and not her heart."

"I'll bet," George mumbled, eliciting a giggle from Charmaine.

Again Paul scowled, his jaw clenched.

Charmaine blushed at her own impropriety, especially when Yvette demanded, "What's so funny?" She was glad when Agatha piped in.

"Has your daughter been receiving anyone, Stephen?"

"I'm not supposed to say," he chuckled, looking from one face to the other, his gaze coming to rest on Paul, "but, in her last letter, Anne wrote that your brother has been paying her court."

Paul was surprised. "John? She's been receiving John?"

"That's what she writes."

"Johnny?" Yvette inquired. "Does your daughter know Johnny?"

He began to respond, but was cut off by Agatha. "Children should be seen and not heard. This is an adult conversation, young lady."

Colette's restraint wore thin. "Agatha—I am Yvette's mother and will do the reprimanding when necessary." She ripped her turbulent eyes from the widow and spoke to Stephen. "Mr. Westphal, please answer my daughter's question."

"Yes," he said, clearing his throat, uncomfortable with the clash of wills across the table, "my daughter knows your elder brother. She writes fondly of him. Perhaps she will be your sister-in-law someday."

Colette's smile did not reach her eyes. "Tell me, Mr. Westphal, does your daughter have any children by her deceased husband?"

"No, Madame," he answered, confused by the question. "She never really liked children, so I suppose it was for the best. Why do you ask?"

"I was just wondering." She sipped her wine, her gaze traveling to Paul. He considered her momentarily, then returned to his dinner.

The meal ended without further incident, and much later, when Charmaine retired to her second-floor chamber, her thoughts were far from Stephen Westphal, Anne London, or Agatha Ward. She was thinking of the Harringtons and George and Paul. The dreams she would dream tonight would be wondrous in her new bed, for the mattress was luxurious, the pillows soft, and the comforter warm in the cool night air. Bravely, she left the French doors open and fell into a blissful slumber.

Paul and Agatha sent Stephen on his way and climbed opposite staircases to their chambers. Only Colette and George remained behind in the parlor. "George," she said when he rose to retire, "I must speak with you."

"Yes?" he said on a yawn.

"Have you noticed the way Agatha is mooning over Paul?"

He laughed with the comment. "You've noticed it as well? I thought it was just me! I was going to warn him about it, Colette, really I was." He shook his head, disgusted. "I could have wrung her neck tonight! Who does she think she is, talking to me like that?"

"I know, George. I was angry, too. Aside from that, I'm uncomfortable with the way she's been looking at Paul. For weeks now, I've tried to convince myself I've been misreading it. But tonight, when I saw her seated near the head of the table, leaning close to Paul, interested in his every word, I know I'm not."

"Don't worry, Colette, Paul is not going to fall for Agatha Ward. And if he does, what does it matter?"

"*What does it matter?* Do you think I want her living in this house permanently? She's at least ten years older than he."

"More like twenty. Elizabeth was her younger sister, and if I'm not mistaken, *she* was eighteen when she had John. That would make Agatha fifty."

"One would never know. She's a handsome woman."

George only snorted. "Looks are only skin deep, Colette. Paul will be considering more than her beauty if he looks her way."

Colette rubbed her brow. "He never has before."

"Colette, don't fret over it," George soothed, just now realizing how upset she was. "I don't see how you can think any man would be interested in Agatha. She's downright cruel. Besides, Paul is far more taken with Charmaine Ryan. Did you see how angry he was with me tonight? He's been giving me that 'she's mine—I saw her first' look for two weeks now. If you want to place some distance between Paul and Agatha, make certain Charmaine sits next to him at the table. He won't be looking at anyone else in the room. I guarantee it."

Colette forced a smile, and George knew he had not put her at ease.

"I'll talk to him about it. Is that what you want?"

"I don't know, George . . . But I would like Agatha Ward out of my life."

George nodded in understanding.

Much later, when she was abed, Colette mulled over her predicament. If only she could talk to her husband the way she had during their first year of marriage. They'd been quite happy then, certainly able to communicate once they'd worked their way through those first stormy months. What had happened? She knew: The twins . . . the birth of the twins had happened, and she had been forbidden to have any more children. Frederic was a passionate man, and the strain this placed on their relationship had been destructive. How often had she caught him ogling her in the months following the birth of their daughters, those months when he had never once made love to her? But it was more than that. Much more. Frederic had longed to hear her speak three simple words, words he had often murmured when he climaxed inside of her. Why then had she withheld the love she knew he craved, the love she readily possessed? Why hadn't she told him she loved him in return? *Because I was frightened,* her mind screamed, *frightened of yielding him a greater power over me!* And so, she had remained silent, allowing him to believe the worst, that she was still very angry with him, hated him. And then something else happened. Agatha Ward had come to visit, and Agatha Ward had found his bed. Frederic's intense perusals stopped, and Colette was left desolate.

Tonight, she worried anew. She'd been mistaken in believing Agatha still sought Frederic's embrace. Evidently, the disabling effect of his stroke had left the woman wanting. Was Paul her next target? Colette shuddered with the thought. Not that she cared about Paul's sexual proclivities. She did, however, fear the possibility of an enduring relationship. The woman was devious and capable of manipulating a younger man. Colette was strong enough to combat Agatha today, but what of tomorrow? What would happen to her children if she were not well or, worse still, not there to protect them? If Agatha gained a greater foothold in the Duvoisin home, her children would suffer. Colette prayed to God she was wrong, but she wouldn't wait for God to answer. Though she didn't want to send Charmaine to the wolves, she did have Paul's promise to respect the young governess. Perhaps with time, he would look beyond Charmaine's lovely face and see the beauty beneath. Yes, Colette sighed, finally able to close her eyes in pursuit of sleep . . . *Beginning tomorrow, before Agatha becomes accustomed to sitting next to Paul, there will be a new and permanent seating assignment at my table. Let Agatha fume.*

Chapter 6

Friday, December 16, 1836

I T was Charmaine's nineteenth birthday, though no one in the house knew.

As soon as she was dressed, she went into the nursery. The children were still asleep, but Pierre sensed her standing over his bed, for he sat up, rubbed his eyes, and stretched out his arms. Charmaine cuddled him, as she did every morning. She had come to cherish him as if he were her son, and he reciprocated that love, an ever-growing bond that made his mother's frequent absences bearable.

Colette's health was deteriorating. Robert Blackford had indeed consulted his journals, changing the compounds he'd been prescribing to a more potent tonic. Throughout October, Colette had improved dramatically. Unlike September, she'd be up and about after his Saturday visits, maintaining she felt fine. Over the last month, however, the fatigue she'd experienced in late summer began setting in again. Charmaine noted that by week's end, Colette's cheeks were pale and her meager energy depleted. She often complained of headaches and dizziness. By Saturday, she desperately needed another dose of the doctor's elixir. She no longer spent Fridays with the children; she was too ill.

Therefore, Charmaine was surprised when she swept into the nursery this morning, proclaiming she felt fit as a fiddle. "I think it did me good to see the doctor yesterday. As much as I hate to admit it, perhaps I should allow him to visit twice a week."

I just wish his ministrations had a lasting effect, Charmaine thought as she smiled at Colette, her friend. Over the past two months, they had grown so close Charmaine couldn't imagine life without her. Their similar age had a lot to do with it, but there was something deeper that drew them together: an unspoken, almost reverent, sympathy for one another.

"Good morning, my little Pierre."

Pierre held out his arms to his mother. When she sat on his bed, Charmaine deposited him in her lap. "Mama, I missed you!"

Colette chuckled. "How could you have missed me, *mon caillou*? You were sleeping."

"I dreamed you was far away, and I was wookin' for you," he said in earnest. "It was scary!"

"Oh, my!" Colette replied, feigning fearful eyes. "What happened?"

"There was so many peoples I couldn't find you. And someone was callin' me, but I was scared so I kept runnin'." His brow, which had furrowed over stormy eyes, suddenly lifted, and his face brightened. "But I found you."

"Where was I?"

"In heaven," he answered simply, happily. "It was very boo-ti-ful there."

A baleful chill rushed up Charmaine's arms, but Colette's countenance remained unscathed. She hugged her son and laughed. "Oh, Pierre! Someday, we'll all be in heaven together, with everyone we love. It's a wonderful place."

Once the girls were up and dressed, they went down for breakfast. Paul was at the table, an unusual sight. He was normally gone long before they had risen and wouldn't return until evening.

Complying with Colette's strange request, Charmaine sat down next to him. Two months ago, she had approached the new seating arrangement with demure reluctance. But she had survived that first day and the day after that. Today, she could honestly say she enjoyed sitting near him. Ever since their private carriage ride home, he had been the perfect gentleman, and though Charmaine often noticed that assessing look in his eyes, he hadn't once embarrassed her. True to his word, she was safe in his home. Any indecent proposition remained a memory of the past, and she could now spend an entire evening in his presence without blushing. Colette seemed pleased with their blossoming "friendship," and Charmaine wondered if she were now playing matchmaker.

"What keeps you at home this morning, Paul?" Colette asked while helping Pierre into his chair.

"I've been into town and back already," he answered. "Now I have an important matter to discuss with my father."

His voice was hard, and they realized he was irate. His fingers drummed a short stack of letters on the left side of his plate. Charmaine wondered if they were the cause of his anger.

"Is something wrong?" Colette asked in genuine concern.

"Just my brother."

Yvette perked up. "Johnny? Did he write to you?"

"He wrote to me all right," Paul replied. He leafed through the correspondence and pulled two letters from the rest. "Here, Yvette, Jeannette, at least someone will be happy today."

"From Johnny?" Jeannette queried, her face radiant as she accepted the post.

"Why did you get one?" Yvette sulked. "I'm the one who wrote to him."

"Yvette," her mother remonstrated lightly, "don't be envious. It's not becoming. Besides, you received a letter, too. Why don't you read it to us?"

The girl wrinkled her nose. "It's private, Mama. That is the only reason I learned to read and write in the first place, remember? So that Johnny could send me my own *private* mail."

"Very well," her mother said. "Maybe Jeannette will read *her* letter to us."

The girl was quietly devouring the missive. When she looked up, her eyes twinkled. "Oh no, Mama," she breathed, "mine is a secret, too!"

Getting nowhere with the twins, Colette turned back to Paul. "What has John done this time?" she asked.

He'd begun to eat and didn't answer. If Charmaine didn't know better, she would have thought the topic dismissed, but she had learned to read his moods. He remained agitated, his scowl similar to the one he'd worn the day he'd confronted Jessie Rowlan.

Colette buttered and handed Pierre a piece of toast. He ate it greedily. "Slow down, *mon caillou,* you have too much in your mouth, and you will choke!" Pierre tried to respond, but with his mouth so full, no one could understand what he said. Colette just shook her head, smiling.

She regarded Paul again, seemingly unable to let the matter rest. "Well?"

"John has changed the shipping routes," he replied curtly, shuffling through the letters again and producing one addressed to Charmaine. "You wanted to know why the mails were delayed," he said, tapping the envelope on the table before passing it to her. "The ships that usually come directly to us from Virginia have now been redirected. Since November they've traveled to Europe first, and *gradually* make their way to us en route back to Virginia. In short, we have to wait on our post and our supplies."

"Why?" Charmaine asked.

"John loves to interfere."

"That is not true," Colette objected.

"Isn't it?" Paul demanded, full-voiced, his temper unleashed.

Charmaine sat stunned. He had never spoken a harsh word to Colette.

Colette responded calmly. "If John changed the routes, he had good reason."

"Why are you always defending him?" he growled, his query strikingly reminiscent of Frederic's remark on the twins' birthday.

"I'm not defending him," she argued diplomatically. "I'm merely stating a fact. John will inherit his father's fortune someday. Why would he jeopardize it by setting up shipping routes that would undermine Duvoisin enterprises?"

Paul was chafed by her logic. "Clearly you are blind to his maneuverings. Therefore, there is no point in discussing it."

"Paul—you and John were close once," she rejoined, unaffected by the fury in his eyes. "Why are you allowing money to come between you now? When I think of the three of you, George included, I can't believe what I see and hear."

"I said I don't want to discuss it!"

Colette sighed, but did not press her point.

Yvette finished eating quickly and ran from the room, saying she was going straight to the nursery to write another letter.

"You have lessons!" her mother called.

They had developed a routine. After breakfast, the children returned to the playroom. For two hours, they read, did arithmetic problems, and studied geography or world history. If Paul or Frederic were available, they would question them about the travels of the newest ship that had put into port. After lunch, Pierre took his nap while the girls had their piano lessons. Most days, Colette would listen to them, happy with their progress. Other days, she would retire to her own room to rest. The late afternoon was left for the outdoors. The rainy season of autumn was behind them, the weather beautiful, a bit cooler than the summer, and quite unlike the Decembers in Virginia. Now that the children had a governess, Nana Rose had more time to herself. Nevertheless, she was available when the weekends arrived and Charmaine chose to take the girls into town or on a picnic. Sometimes it was best if Pierre stayed home, and if Colette was indisposed, Rose stepped in.

Presently, Charmaine stood from the table. She looked to Paul, who hadn't said another word to anyone; he was reading a periodical that accompanied the perplexing letters. "Thank you," she whispered.

It was a moment before his head lifted and another before he realized she had spoken to him. "Excuse me?" His eyes were grave, but not angry.

"I said, 'thank you'—for the letter from my friends in Virginia."

"You're welcome, Charmaine. I hope they are well."

"I'll soon find out," she said. "How much do I owe you for the postage?"

"Nothing," he replied with a debonair smile. "Any charges are taken out of the island account."

"Are you sure?"

"I'm sure."

She nodded a second "thank you" and, with heart thumping, called to Jeannette. "Come, sweetheart, it is time we got on with today's lessons."

Jeannette complied, grasping her own letter. But as she passed behind her mother, she stopped as if remembering something and hugged her, capping the capricious gesture with a kiss.

Stunned, Colette laughed. "What was that for?"

"It's a secret, too," she whispered, turning to Pierre next.

He struggled against the embrace until Colette said, "Your sister is trying to give you a kiss."

Charmaine heard tears in Colette's voice and realized she was trying not to cry. But the moment passed, and she was lifting Pierre to the ground, speaking to Paul at the same time. "Please don't upset your father with talk of John."

He frowned. "This is all about John, Colette. I can't pretend he doesn't exist—leastwise not while he controls the purse strings from Virginia."

It was futile to argue, so Colette took Pierre by the hand and followed Charmaine and Jeannette from the room.

Later, while the girls were busy working, and Pierre was playing with his blocks, Charmaine turned pensive. *John Duvoisin.* Any time his name was mentioned, emotions ran high. The men of the family spoke of him as if he were an adversary, the women, his proponent. Charmaine began to wonder if she were ever going to meet the man and form her own opinion of him.

"Mademoiselle Charmaine?" Jeannette queried, cutting across her thoughts. "You haven't read your letter. Look, it's under my paper!"

Charmaine was embarrassed. For the better part of a month she'd complained over the delayed mails. Yet here she was, a letter in hand, daydreaming about someone she'd never met. Chuckling, she broke the seal and began to read, happy to find all was well with the Harrington clan. The letter had been a wonderful birthday present. She'd write to them tonight.

Paul entered his father's chambers, nodding to Travis as the man left them alone. Frederic sat in his abominable chair, staring out the French doors, past the gardens and toward the pine forest that ensconced the family's private lake. Beyond that was the ocean and, farther still, the States—Virginia in particular. His eyes did not waver as he said, "You needed to speak with me?"

"Yes, sir," Paul answered, purposefully placing himself between his father and the glass panels. When the man eventually looked up, Paul handed over the documents he carried. "John has changed most of the shipping routes."

"Why?"

Strange question . . . Paul had expected a furious reaction. "According to his letter, it's an issue of the trade winds. But that has never been a factor before, not when we were in need of supplies."

"How have the routes changed?" Frederic asked, disregarding the papers.

"He's established two circuits: a Richmond, Europe, Charmantes course, and a Richmond, New York, Europe course. More often than not, we won't see half the fleet, and those that do eventually reach us will be hauling staples all the way to Europe first. It's ludicrous. Furthermore, sugar bound for New York may have to change ships in Richmond."

"Is this such an ill-advised decision?"

"It's an annoying one, Father!" Paul railed. "John is looking for an excuse to upset the apple cart. It is his way of exacting retribution."

Frederic rubbed his brow. "Those are harsh words."

"Don't tell me *you* are defending him!" Frederic's eyes narrowed, and Paul cringed. "I'm not trying to stir up trouble, Father. But I am tired of John controlling *everything*—at his whim, I might add."

Silence prevailed, and Paul could see the man's mind working, a mind unaffected by the stroke that had damaged him in every other way. Paul, in turn, experienced a wave of righteousness, Colette's assertion surfacing. "To be fair, John may have rerouted the ships for another reason."

Frederic showed surprise. "Really? What is it?"

"For the past two years, the sugar crop has been deplorable.

I've had difficulty filling the ships' holds to capacity, sending quite a few back to John with room to spare. In our need to meet the increased demand, we've overworked the soil, using fields that should have lain fallow. This season alone, the yield was two-thirds what it was three years ago, and that with more acres harvested. The land is effete and requires a more relaxed rotation if the necessary elements are to be restored. We should either suspend planting for a year or two, or turn the next few tracts over to tobacco."

Frederic grunted. "Tobacco is just as taxing on the land, and then we'd have to consider the other adjustments we'd be forced to make: training the bondsmen, equipment, buildings. And even if it were to flourish, we'd be placing all our coins on one bet. I'll not have the Duvoisin fortune left to the whim of one crop. The Virginia plantation is relegated to tobacco. Charmantes produces sugar."

Paul threw up his hands in exasperation. "Tobacco is just a suggestion, a crop the family has experience with, but if some dramatic changes aren't made, Charmantes will be in deep trouble. She's bringing in minimal revenue now."

"I can see you have something else in mind. What is it?"

Paul inhaled. "Go back to the other island and finish what you started there four years ago."

Frederic's countenance blackened. "The land is cursed."

"That's ridiculous, Father. What happened on Charmantes had nothing to do with Espoir."

"If I had been here—"

Paul's own anger flared. "We're not going to go over this again! What's done is done! The other island is there. It's fertile. It's partially cleared. You've built a bondsmen keep—constructed a dock. It's begging to be developed!"

"You do it," Frederic interrupted.

"What?"

"You heard me. I give it to you. It's yours, Paul. Do with it as you will."

Paul frowned in disbelief. "You're serious? You'll allow me free rein?"

"I'll do better than that. I'll give you enough money to contract the building of three ships—your ships—expressly designed to transport your sugar. You will also need a fourth vessel for the treks between Espoir and Charmantes. Purchase a considerably smaller packet, something ancient. In addition, I'll supply the funds to acquire an indentured crew. How many men will you need: twenty, thirty?"

"Twenty will be more than sufficient," Paul breathed, his jaw slackened in amazement.

"Very well, then," Frederic continued, his mind working rigorously now. "Set up a meeting with Stephen Westphal. We'll need to liquidate some funds, but for the balance, our bank seal and the Duvoisin name should hold some weight in the States and Europe. I suggest you commission the ships in Newportes Newes or Baltimore. Best to check with shipbuilders in New York as well. If the southern costs come in too high, quote the New York estimates to them."

"American-built vessels? But the British tariffs—"

"Construction costs should come in at least twenty percent lower than any bark you could commission in Britain. From what I've been reading, European shipbuilders can't compete with the States' plentiful lumber. If you contract the building of three vessels, the savings should be considerable. That alone will outweigh any British import tax. The newest clippers have proven advantageous to many shipping magnates, and America seems to be leading the fray in perfecting them. Speed, not imposed tariffs, should be the deciding factor."

"What of steam propulsion as opposed to fully rigged sail?"

Paul asked in waxing excitement. "They are cutting crossing times in half. I'd like your permission to look into that as well."

Frederic nodded, feeding off his son's exuberance. "By all means. You'll have to travel to Britain for the bondsmen. While there, contact the Harrison shipping firm. They can vouch for progress with the paddlewheel. Perhaps they could be persuaded to share information concerning the success of their own steam fleet. Now, if you are as excited about this as you appear to be, it is prudent not to delay. I suggest you leave as soon as monies are made available through Stephen."

Paul's mind was reeling. This couldn't be happening! All these years, he had dreamed of owning a piece of the Duvoisin fortune. To John, the prospect meant nothing. John was the legitimate heir, therefore, the Duvoisin fortune had always been there for the taking. Paul, on the other hand, had labored long and hard for his father, and still, after ten years, remained his loyal son, nothing more. Today, the long journey had come to an end. Somewhere along the way, he had proven himself worthy; he was finally being offered his deepest desire—his rightful share of the Duvoisin holdings. Suddenly, he was smiling broadly, and Frederic was happy to know he had pleased at least one son this day.

"It will be mine?" he whispered. "Not to be shared with John?"

"It will be yours, Paul," his sire avowed, "all yours. No interference from John, no conferring with John, no dependence upon John. I should have done this a long time ago. You've been a good son. You deserve more."

"Thank you, sir," Paul said with the utmost respect. "I'll contact Stephen."

Paul's mood was far different when everyone gathered at the dinner table that evening. The children were equally lighthearted, and Charmaine regarded George, Rose, and Colette, who seemed part of the same merry conspiracy. As the meal progressed, she grew more befuddled and petitioned Jeannette for an answer. "Why is everyone so happy?"

"You'll see," was all the girl would say, and Charmaine caught Colette's wink. But Pierre was unable to keep silent and blurted out, "Mainie's birfday!"

"Pierre!" Yvette scolded. "You've gone and spoiled the surprise!"

"The surprise?" Charmaine asked, her eyes arcing around the table until they rested on Paul, who raised a brow in pretended confusion.

"Da-tay . . . da-tay . . . *ta*-day is Mainie's birfday!" Pierre happily repeated.

The kitchen door swung open, and Fatima barreled into the room carrying a cake. In unison, the children shouted, "Happy Birthday!"

Charmaine's hands flew to her mouth. "How did you know?" she asked, missing Agatha's disdainful scowl.

Colette smiled. "You mentioned it to Jeannette months ago during your first picnic, and she told me right away. I just hoped she wasn't mistaken about the date, but I had no way of asking without making you suspicious."

"I don't know what to say," Charmaine murmured, realizing just how much this family had come to mean to her.

"You don't have to say anything," Jeannette piped in.

"Yes, she does," Yvette insisted. "She has to say how old she is!"

"I'm nineteen. And I hope to share many more birthdays with all of you."

Satisfied, the children began begging her to cut the cake.

Colette helped Pierre down from his chair, and he ran to Charmaine with a small package in his hand. "Happy Birfday!" he said, giving her a kiss.

"What is this?"

"A birfday pwesent."

Charmaine lifted the lid to find a lovely, and certainly expensive, set of ivory hair combs within. "Wherever did you get them?" she asked Colette.

"At Maddy's mercantile. I asked Paul to select them." Colette indicated her accomplice.

"And you had better wear them," he warned drolly. "It took me all morning to decide which ones would suit you."

"Thank you," she said, wondering how she could ever reciprocate their generosity. "Each of you must share your birth date with me. Colette?"

Yvette answered for her mother. "Mama and Pierre's birthdays are the same: March thirty-first."

"Truly?"

With Colette's nod of confirmation, Charmaine looked at Paul.

"Don't worry, Charmaine," he said, cognizant of her motives for asking, "Fatima remembers every birthday in this house."

Satisfied, Charmaine began cutting the cake.

Wednesday, December 21, 1836

Paul was leaving Charmantes. He was traveling on the *Black Star*, a ship that had berthed on the island yesterday and would set sail the day after Christmas. He was headed to several Southern ports: Newportes Newes, Richmond, and Baltimore, then up to New York and lastly, Britain. In his three months abroad, he would commission the construction of three ships, purchase a fourth, and hire a new crew of indentured servants to clear and cultivate his new island, "Sacré Espoir," pronounced "Sock-ray Es-pwahr," meaning "Sacred Hope." When finished, he'd travel home and begin developing it. He was very happy.

Charmaine was melancholy. Though Paul promised to be back before Easter, the coming weeks would be long and empty. She was falling in love with him, a disturbing condition exacerbated by the fact that he'd kept her at arm's length for nearly three months now. Still, she would miss him, miss his presence in the house each night, miss his easy banter, miss the times when he'd pull out her chair or hold the door open for her, miss his handsome smile that set her heart racing. If only he had kissed her, just once.

Tonight Stephen Westphal was to visit again. He, Paul, and Frederic would make final arrangements. Frederic would sign vouchers, and Paul would be set for the voyage ahead of him. Mr. Westphal would stay for dinner.

Agatha Ward seemed pleased and traipsed happily about the house the entire day, leaving Colette and Charmaine to wonder over her uncommon behavior.

In the late afternoon, just after the banker had arrived, Colette and Charmaine shared a glass of chilled tea on the front portico. The weather was pleasant, and the children were playing on the lawn, running here and there. Jeannette took charge of Pierre, mindful of his well-being. They chuckled over their antics.

When the moment seemed right, Charmaine withdrew two envelopes from her apron pocket. Both Jeannette and Yvette had written to their brother this time, and she looked to Colette for advice. "Do you think Paul would mind if I asked him to deliver these letters to John? He mentioned stopping in Richmond."

"He will not mind," she answered firmly, aware of Charmaine's misgivings. "For all their rivalry, they're still brothers and very close."

"That is not the way it appears."

"They're brothers," Colette reiterated, "and brothers often quarrel. I know I used to with Pierre."

"Pierre?"

Colette laughed now. "My brother, Pierre. He and my mother died shortly after the twins were born."

"I'm sorry," Charmaine whispered.

Colette suppressed the painful memory. "He was born a cripple and unable to walk. Now he is at peace . . . in heaven."

"What of your father?" Charmaine asked cautiously.

"He died when I was very young," she answered, her voice no longer sorrowful. "I hardly remember him. My mother had a difficult time raising us. We were gentry, so my father lost a great deal of his fortune in the years following the French Revolution. By the time I attended a lady's school in Paris, my mother's funds were nearly depleted."

"Why Paris, then?"

Colette grew distant. "It was near the university and offered an opportunity to meet a rich gentleman . . . or at least the son of a rich gentleman. You see, my brother was constantly ill, the physicians' fees mounting. A wealthy husband could resolve my mother's financial difficulties, perhaps foster Pierre's cure. Or so I was told."

"Is that why you married Mr. Duvoisin?"

Colette knew the question was coming, had encouraged it. "That was one of the reasons, but there were others. The situation became complicated."

"He must have been very handsome," Charmaine encouraged.

"He still is," Colette averred, smiling now. "And I was attracted to him from the moment we met. But I was intimidated by him as well."

The minutes gathered. "Frederic is a good man, Charmaine. He's instilled in his sons values they don't even credit to him. And he's been a good husband to me. I know at times he appears gruff, but his stroke has left deep scars."

"I realize that," Charmaine said.

"When we were first married, Frederic restored my mother to a comfortable life. In addition, he took care of my brother and all his medical expenses. Pierre wanted for nothing that last year, receiving the best treatment the Duvoisin money could buy. And of course, he gave me two beautiful daughters . . . and a handsome son."

Charmaine breathed deeply. "Did you ever love him?" she probed, sad that this woman had sacrificed herself for the welfare of her family.

"I love him still," she said, her voice cracking. "But it wasn't easy for Frederic after the girls were born. I was forbidden to have any more children."

"It had to be just as difficult for you," Charmaine reasoned.

"Yes and no," she replied, turning away. "As I said, it became very complicated." The subject was closed, and they fell silent.

Colette considered Charmaine and wondered when the younger woman would speak about her own past. She instinctively knew Charmaine's recollections contained elements of pain as well. *If not today, soon.* Her musings were interrupted by a most unexpected question.

"What is John like?"

Colette weighed her answer, determined to give an unbiased opinion. "He's an enigma—a one of a kind."

"The good kind or the bad kind?"

Colette smiled. "That depends on who's describing him. There are those who despise him to the core, and there are those who love him until it hurts. With John there is no middle ground. You either hate him or love him, and it's usually in that order."

"The men of this family certainly don't love him."

Colette hesitated again, as if she were looking for the right words to explain a paradoxical dilemma. "Due to my husband's stroke, Paul and Frederic *think* they hate John, and he, in turn *thinks* he hates them. I'm certain you've heard all the rumors, Charmaine. Most of them are true. John and Frederic had a terrible altercation and when it was over, Frederic was left as he is today—crippled, in mind as well as body. Paul was there, and he blames John for what happened. Unfortunately, the wound has yet to heal."

"Why don't you blame John?"

Colette sighed forlornly. "He isn't to blame and was hurt as well. Everyone sided with Frederic, including me. I'm afraid John hates me for it. He harbors the same asperity that eats away at his father. They are alike in so many ways. Yet, each of them would vehemently deny any similarity."

"Alike?" Charmaine pursued. "How so?"

"Their charisma, their self-assuredness, the manner in which they assess a person. Once John passes judgment, he rarely changes it, and more often than not, his assessment is correct. Heaven forbid if his judgment is damning. There is all hell to pay, and hell is a sight more lenient than John's sharp tongue. Frederic is the same way—uncompromising to a fault."

"Do *you* like him?"

"Who? John?" Colette laughed. "Look at my daughters, Charmaine. They'd have my head if they heard me say otherwise. But when I first met John, I despised him." She grew thoughtful, her eyes cast beyond her surroundings as if she could see across time. "Someday," she said softly, "you will meet him and understand what I mean . . . Just remember, Charmaine, you hate him first."

The front doors clapped open, and Paul and Stephen strode onto the portico with Agatha tucked comfortably between them. Colette frowned at the trio, but her attention was diverted as the children came bounding across the lawn. Yvette was shouting enthusiastically, reaching the colonnade first. "Mama!" she heaved, completely out of breath. "Chastity is going to have a foal!"

Jeannette and Pierre drew up alongside her. All three had wandered over to the paddock when Gerald, the head groom, had led the chestnut mare into the yard. "That's right, Mama," Jeannette added, "Gerald says she'll have her baby sometime in August. Isn't that wonderful?"

"That is wonderful," Colette answered with a smile. "And I can just imagine what's going to happen when that filly or colt is born. Mademoiselle Charmaine and I won't be able to get the three of you out of the barn."

Yvette agreed with a happy nod. "Do you think Martin will have to come when it's time for her to foal?"

"Perhaps . . . but only if there is some difficulty," Colette replied. "Why?"

"He was teaching me how to spit the last time he was here," Yvette answered proudly. "But I don't have it down just right."

"Yvette!" her mother chastised, mumbling something about Martin being a vile man.

Dinner was served at seven. Charmaine brushed out her hair and decided to wear it down. Using the combs she'd received for her birthday, she swept it back from her face and placed a comb high above each ear. The entire mane cascaded down her back. She was a fetching sight when she entered the dining room, and Paul drew a ragged breath, glad to know her birthday gift would encourage her to wear the lovely locks in such a fashion.

Stephen Westphal was astonished when Paul beckoned the governess to sit in the chair Agatha had occupied the last time he had dined at the Duvoisin manor. *So the pretty governess has caught Paul's fancy,* he thought. *Agatha's concerns are warranted.*

A five-course meal was served, beginning with a delicious pea soup. Fatima Henderson, her wide hips swinging, bustled in and out of the kitchen with more ease than Felicia and Anna, who often dawdled. Since Colette's reprimand, Felicia found the evening meal less interesting—she was no longer allowed to flirt with Paul—and she dillydallied over her serving chores. Why the maid was kept on at the manor, Charmaine could only wonder.

George appeared minutes later. He'd obviously been apprised of the banker's visit this time, for he greeted the man cordially and elected to sit near Charmaine. With Jeannette between them, he leaned in and struck up a conversation. Before long, Charmaine and Jeannette were giggling.

Paul preferred having George sit opposite the governess, where he was able to control their repartees, but now their heads were bent overtop his sister, and he experienced an unusually sharp stab of jealousy. *It's time George and I had a little talk,* he decided.

Thus resolved, he turned back to Stephen. "I'll be contacting Thomas and James Harrison when I arrive in Liverpool. Father dealt with their shipping line when he had the *Vagabond* manufactured. Though I'll be commissioning the vessels in the States, they've become renowned, so I'll take under advisement any recommendation they can make concerning steam propulsion."

"Right," the banker agreed, and so it went for the better part of the dinner.

Agatha chafed at the seating arrangement that placed her far from the financier. She had hoped to participate in Paul's business discussion. She couldn't do so from where she sat; there was too much chatter between them.

As dessert was served, the conversation turned to personal matters. "I'll need an endorsed note for the Bank of Virginia," Paul said. "I'll deposit funds there, liquidate half, and then draw from one resource." He paused for a moment. When he spoke again, his words were hard. "John is not to be involved, Stephen, so I'd prefer you not share this with your daughter."

"Anne?" he asked in surprise.

"You mentioned some months ago that John was courting her."

"Yes," Stephen confirmed. "In fact, I just received a letter from her. She hints an engagement is imminent. A marvelous match, wouldn't you say?"

"Marvelous," Paul muttered, thinking of all the money his brother would come into. But John had never cared about such things. How then, had the widow London caught his fancy? She was attractive, most likely in her late twenties, but Paul didn't think she was John's type.

As if reading his thoughts, Yvette added her own two cents. "I don't think Johnny will marry her."

George chuckled. "Why not, Yvette?" he asked.

"He told me the woman he loved was already married and he'd never marry anyone else."

"There you have it!" the banker piped up. "All these years he's harbored the hope that one day Anne would be free to wed. I knew he was enamored of her when I visited Richmond some years ago."

Paul snorted.

"You don't believe me?" the man queried, clearly insulted. "Well, then, time will tell the tale."

Paul's stormy gaze shifted to Colette, but the woman was whispering to Pierre. "You are right, Stephen," he said. "But in either case, Anne is in contact with my brother, and I do not want him informed of this undertaking."

Westphal grunted derisively. "And how do you expect to keep this from him once you've initiated transactions with the Virginia bank?"

"I don't," Paul answered smugly, savoring the thought of John in the dark for a change. "But by the time he figures it all out, contracts will be signed, monies will be withdrawn, and any unpleasantness will have been avoided."

"Unpleasantness?"

"Come, Stephen, you know my brother. Is an explanation necessary?"

"What of the legal issues? Richecourt or Larabee is sure to contact him."

"Visiting their firm is foremost on my agenda once I reach Richmond. John has made an enemy of Edward Richecourt. That being said, Mr. Richecourt will be more than happy to deal with this matter in an expeditious and confidential manner. He is well aware that my father's business dealings keep his practice solvent. Therefore, he can be trusted to keep quiet about Espoir."

Colette cringed over Paul's surreptitious plans. Not that she blamed him. John's needling was relentless. It was that very type of unpleasantness Paul was trying to avoid. However, this scheme was certain to backfire on him. John always found out, simply because he was far more unscrupulous than Paul. John was the inventor of breaking all the rules.

"That being understood," Paul continued, "can I count on you to keep this to yourself, Stephen?"

"If that is what you want, Anne won't be told."

Satisfied, Paul leaned back in his chair. "So, what else does Anne write? Any Richmond events I need to know about before traveling there?"

"Actually . . ." the banker said, clearing his throat, his eyes darting down the table, catching Agatha's raised brow. "She writes about your new governess."

Intensely interested with this unexpected topic, Paul leaned forward and gave Westphal his complete attention. "Really? What does she write?"

"Well," he said, clearing his throat again and shifting uneasily in his chair, aware that every eye was on him. "I don't think I should say—not in front of the children, anyway."

Charmaine's heart accelerated. Disaster was about to strike, and she had no way of stopping it.

Paul scratched his head. The man had obviously uncovered something scandalous if he felt it was only fit for adult ears. "How would your daughter know about our governess?" he mused. "Are you saying some sordid information accidentally fell into her lap and she just happened to write to you about it?"

"Actually, Mrs. Ward expressed her concerns a few months ago," he replied. "She was anxious about Miss Ryan's background. She came into the bank and asked if Anne might make some inquiries."

"Agatha?" Paul queried, bemused yet annoyed. He peered down the table and questioned her directly. "On whose request?"

"My own," she replied haughtily. "I took it upon myself to petition Stephen. I had legitimate misgivings about Miss Ryan, and when no one else seemed concerned, when no references were required other than those Loretta Harrington provided, I was compelled—for the sake of the children—to investigate." She breathed deeply. "Thank goodness Stephen's daughter agreed to assist. I fear the children are at grave risk. Not even I was prepared for what she uncovered. It is far worse than any of us could have imagined."

Colette checked her anger. "I think Mr. Westphal's allegations, whatever they may be, had best be left for another day. My children have no place in this conversation."

"Colette is right," Paul concurred. "Rose, would you take the children to the nursery?"

Charmaine's reprieve lasted but a moment; Rose quickly jumped to do his bidding, ushering the children from the room, unmindful of Yvette's protests.

Colette cast turbulent eyes down the table at Paul, her stormy countenance rivaled only by George's. Paul remained unperturbed. "All right, Stephen," he breathed. "You now have leave to speak. Tell us, what have you found out?"

Mortified, Charmaine pushed from the table. But Paul foiled her escape, grasping her arm and holding her to the spot. She would be forced to listen to the macabre story, relive it, while those she had come to love sat in judgment over the terrible secrets she had kept. Tonight, they would brand her the offspring of a maniac, a murderer, and she had no defense against the horrific truth. Great shame washed over her, and she bowed her head.

Paul's grip tightened, the pain igniting her wrath, and she glared at him furiously. But he seemed oblivious, his eyes fixed on the banker. "Out with it man!" he snarled, aggravated by Westphal's hesitation.

"If I had known sooner," the man wavered, uncertain if Paul really wanted the truth, "I would have come to you with the information immediately. But as you know, the ships were delayed. Anne's letter is weeks old."

"Yes, yes, get on with it."

"Actually," he faltered again, beads of perspiration dotting his upper lip. "I regret it has fallen to me to reveal the deplorable facts." He glanced down the table. Colette appeared as irate as Paul. Only Agatha remained smug.

"Tell him, Stephen," the dowager prompted, her satisfied eyes leveled on Charmaine. "It is best he and Colette know the type of person they have hired and are harboring in their home."

"Yes, Stephen," Paul agreed. "You've primed us for this terrible tale. Let's have it out! What has Miss Ryan done that we must know about, lest the children come to harm?"

"It is not what *she's* done. It's her father."

"And?"

"He is—a murderer."

The room fell deadly silent, all of Charmaine's deepest fears realized. Even the sounds from the kitchen ceased, as if ears were pressed against the swinging door. The truth was out, and now Paul, who had allied himself with Agatha during her interview, could gloat. He'd been right about her all along.

Charmaine refused to look his way again. With her disgrace mounting, she renewed her efforts to escape, twisting against his unyielding fist. "Please," she whimpered, to no avail.

"What exactly are you saying, Stephen?"

"Miss Ryan's father is a murderer," he reiterated, "did in fact murder her mother."

"Have you proof?"

"Most assuredly," the financier stated, taking courage from Paul's sudden interest in the facts. "According to Anne, who spoke to one of the Harringtons' housemaids, John Ryan barged into the Harrington house late one night. When Joshua Harrington sent him on his way, he went home and attacked his own wife. Of course, Anne wanted to make certain the story wasn't fabricated, so she contacted the sheriff and was shocked to find that not only had John Ryan committed murder, but is still at large, a fugitive. Apparently, the sheriff was relieved to let the case drop once the hullabaloo calmed down, because the Ryans were nothing more than white trash, living in a shanty in the slums of the city."

"How did Mr. Ryan kill his wife?"

"He beat her to death. According to the sheriff, those beatings were a common occurrence. This time it just got out of hand. Miss Ryan"—and the banker nodded across the table toward

Charmaine—"came home to find the body near death and cried on the Harringtons' shoulders once it had grown cold in order to get the sheriff involved. Sheriff Briggs conveyed to Anne his disdain for being pulled into the nasty affair."

Charmaine had had enough. She had allowed the man to humiliate her, to expose her deception and label her as riffraff, no better than her father. But she refused to allow him to degrade her mother. With eyes flashing, she shot to her feet. "That 'body' as you call it, was *my mother*, a good and kind woman, whom I loved and lost because of my wretched father!" In spite of her anger, her eyes were flooding with unwanted tears, her anguish painfully apparent in the words she could barely force out. "And yes," she hissed, "he beat her, beat her often, and there was no one to turn to, no one to stop him! Not even when she lay dying. If it wasn't for Joshua and Loretta Harrington, no one would have even cared. Mr. Harrington petitioned the sheriff, but little good that did! It's over a year since my mother's death, and still, my father walks free. I know he will never pay for his heinous crime. So cringe if you will. I tell you, there is no one who despises John Ryan more than I—no one who seeks justice more than I. But that will never happen, will it?" The rhetorical question echoed about the room.

Paul sympathized with the young woman who had yet to look his way. *This is why she is wary of me.* Her father had never given her a reason to love any man, had in fact terrified her. Paul was filled with the desire to comfort her, to hold her in his arms and shield her from all she had suffered.

"No, I thought not," she said in answer to her own question. "There is only one reason my father remains at large, and that is owing to people like you, Mr. Westphal, who are more interested in blaming the innocent rather than looking for the guilty." She turned on Paul. "Punish an easy victim. I'm right here. Now," she snarled, twisting against his hand, "if you'd release my arm, I'd like to retire. I refuse to be further humiliated!"

George stood, enraged. The inquisition had gone on too long. "You are too polite, Charmaine," he growled, his eyes riveted on her manacled wrist. "This room reeks of a different kind of trash, and I, for one, have lost my appetite." He pushed the chair aside and placed a comforting arm around her shoulder, challenging Paul to hold her one moment longer.

The threat was acknowledged, and Paul's hand relaxed. Charmaine pulled free and turned in George's embrace. When they reached the foyer, she broke down and cried. "You had best go back," she heaved, "or they'll be angry with you as well."

George snorted. "I don't care how angry they get."

"I was so happy here. I don't know where I will go now."

"What do you mean?" he asked. "You can't believe Colette would dismiss you on account of a bit of scandalmongery? If you do, you're not giving her credit for the good and kind woman she is."

Charmaine considered him, her tears subsiding.

"Colette loves you, Charmaine. The children love you. Even Paul . . . I'll warrant he is telling them where they can go, if you get my meaning."

"Then why did he treat me like that? Holding me like a trapped animal?"

"He wanted you to face them, with your head held high. Paul has endured years of ridicule because of his illegitimacy and has learned never to allow the accuser the upper hand. Kowtowing, running away—it gives credence to every insinuation, fact or not. I'm just annoyed he allowed them to badger you for as long as they did."

Charmaine comprehended his wisdom and prayed he was right. If so, she had sorely misjudged Paul.

"We all have secrets we'd prefer to keep, Charmaine, something we're not proud of. My mother ran off with a sailor when I was only a year old, leaving my father a broken man. I was fortunate to have my grandmother here."

Charmaine looked tenderly at the man who had just revealed an aspect of his own life that had to be painful. "Thank you, George," she whispered.

"Don't mention it," he smiled, thinking how lovely she looked tonight. If Paul weren't so damned possessive, he'd court Charmaine Ryan himself.

She sighed raggedly. "I think I'll check on the children."

With George's nod, she turned and climbed the stairs to the nursery.

The aspersions continued to mount. The contention: John Ryan's blood ran through his daughter's veins and would someday manifest itself with mortal consequences.

"I've heard enough!" Paul sneered.

"As have I," Colette agreed, throwing down her napkin and standing, her poise long gone. "I've neglected my children and would like to give them a kiss before they go to sleep." She stepped from the table, but abruptly stopped. "I also need to speak with Miss Ryan. Despite your mean-spirited warnings, she will retain her position here."

Stephen had risen with Colette and attempted to apologize. "Madame, I only had the children's best interest—"

"Mr. Westphal," she accused, disgusted by his pretentious contrition, "if you had *anyone's* best interest at heart, you would have brought this matter to me privately and not to my dinner table. What you forced Miss Ryan to endure tonight was revolting." Without a backward glance, she left the room.

Stephen sent imploring eyes to Paul, who only shrugged. "I'm afraid I have to agree with her, Stephen. Charmaine Ryan is an asset to this family and will remain in my father's employ as long as Colette sees fit. I've never held to the belief that the sins of the father are visited upon his children. If that were the case, most men would be damned. Your sentiments smack of European aristocracy." He paused a moment, allowing his statements to sink in, deploring the classes and labels established by bluebloods and their countless imitators. "I have much to do in the morning," he concluded. "I don't want to appear a poor host, Stephen, but I think it is time to call for your carriage." Not waiting for a reply, he walked to the foyer, pleased when the banker scurried after him.

Charmaine patted her face dry and opened the nursery door.

"Mademoiselle!" Jeannette called, running to her. "Are you all right?"

Yvette did the same, and together, they pulled her into the chamber. "You were crying," she said, her voice quivering.

"I'm fine now," Charmaine answered, sitting on the girl's bed. She glanced at Rose, who also wore a worried expression.

"You're still our governess, aren't you?" Jeannette pleaded.

Charmaine's eyes welled again. "I don't know," she whispered.

"We won't let anyone send you away!" Yvette expostulated, arms wrapped around her. "We love you!"

Charmaine returned the embrace, profoundly touched.

Jeannette noticed her mother standing in the doorway first. "Mama!" she cried, "you're not going to send Mademoiselle Charmaine away, are you?"

"Absolutely not," she replied, her serious face giving way to a smile, then a giggle, and soon they were all laughing.

Later, Charmaine and Colette strolled along the balcony, their soft whispers melding with the evening breezes. They wound up in

Colette's boudoir, where Charmaine disclosed the details of her home life. Colette was a compassionate confidante. By the time Charmaine returned to her own room, a heavy yoke had been lifted from her shoulders.

Paul had wanted to speak to Charmaine, but she was not in the nursery, nor in her room. Tomorrow . . . he would talk with her tomorrow.

Saturday, December 24, 1836

Fatima bustled around the kitchen, humming carols as she put the finishing touches on the dozen food baskets she had prepared at Colette's request. She'd cooked nonstop for two days. Now, she stood back and smiled at the delicious Yuletide delights that would be delivered to the bondsmen's keep that afternoon, an annual tradition, which had commenced nine years ago. Fatima very much approved of Colette's charity, but her exuberance turned to worry when the mistress of the manor entered the kitchen well before noon.

"Miss Colette, what are you planning on doing dressed like that?"

"You know very well what I'm planning," she answered.

"But Master Paul told me he was taking care of the victuals this year."

"His idea, not mine," Colette replied, arranging the loaves of crusty bread into one basket. "I'm quite capable of riding out to the fields in a carriage."

Fatima sucked in her cheeks. "That ain't a good idea."

"Why not? Why should this Christmas be any different?"

" 'Cause you been feeling poorly, that's why," the stern cook replied. When it appeared as if Colette wasn't listening, Fatima pressed on. "Master Frederic ain't gonna like it!"

Colette only laughed. "He didn't like it the first time, either."

"No, he didn't. That's why—"

"And he adjusted his way of thinking, did he not?" Colette interrupted.

"That was then and this is now. He's a mite more concerned 'bout your health than the men-folk gnawing on this here food."

"He won't even know I am gone. Unless, of course, you tell him."

Fatima shook her head, realizing the folly of further argument. When Colette got her dander up, there was no stopping her. A slow smile broke across Fatima's face. It had been a long time since she'd seen even a fleck of that dander, a hint of the Colette of old. A spark had flared the night of the banker's visit, and Fatima was of a mind to see it burn brightly again. Therefore, she set aside her perturbation with one final injunction. "No lifting them baskets. Joseph can go with you to do the carrying."

"That is fine, but I am also taking the girls along to help distribute the food."

Fatima stopped dead in her tracks. "Why are you gonna do that?"

"It is time they learn that a life of privilege comes with certain responsibilities. I don't want them growing up pampered beauties with warm smiles and cold hearts."

Even after nine years, Colette's wisdom and concern, the depth of her heart, amazed Fatima. Nodding her approval, she turned back to her work.

The preparations were completed and the carriage readied. When the baskets were secured in the landau's boot, the girls, Colette, and Joseph Thornfield departed the grounds, leaving Charmaine and Pierre to wave their good-byes from the top step of the portico. No one noticed Frederic standing on the second-story veranda, a scowl marking his brow.

Later that evening, when Colette had retired and Charmaine

coaxed the girls into bed, the twins were still whispering about the huge building they had visited and the strange men they had met. Jeannette had thoroughly enjoyed herself, but Yvette wrinkled her nose in disgust. "I don't understand why we had to go out there," she complained. "It was horrible: smelly and filthy!"

"Mama says we wouldn't be half so rich if those men didn't work for Papa," Jeannette offered affably. "She says we should be thankful, and bringing a Christmas feast is just a small way to show our gratitude."

"I know what she said," Yvette replied peevishly.

Jeannette shrugged and snuggled deep into her covers.

Charmaine gave them a kiss, pulled a blanket over an already slumbering Pierre, and tiptoed from the room. She knew what Colette had hoped to teach her daughters today, but evidently, only Jeannette embraced the charitable lesson.

Colette was brushing out her hair when Frederic stepped into her boudoir. Though he had knocked, he hadn't waited for an answer. She studied him through the looking glass, unnerved as he moved toward her, self-conscious of her state of undress.

"You went out to the keep today," he commented.

"It is Christmas Eve," she answered.

"With the twins."

"Yes." She pushed out of her chair and faced him, struggling to maintain her composure. "Should I not teach them to care for those less fortunate than they? Isn't that what tomorrow is all about—the Christ child born in a lowly manger?"

His eyes swept her from head to toe, an assessing perusal that took her breath away. "They are criminals, Colette," he rasped. "I'm concerned for the girls' safety—your safety. Beyond that, you are not well. I don't want you leaving the grounds without telling me."

Colette stiffened. "Am I a prisoner in my own home? You attempted to make it so once before. I tell you now, it will not happen. I will come and go as I please!"

Frederic clenched his teeth. "And I told you, I don't care if you leave. My daughters, on the other hand, *are* my concern."

Colette felt a surge of tears rush to her eyes. She would not allow him to see her anguish, the pain he could so easily inflict. Belting her robe, she pushed past him and marched into her bedroom, slamming the door behind her.

Frederic stared long and hard at it. Coming to an abrupt decision, he rushed forward. But his lame foot caught the edge of the carpet, and he stumbled. His right hand flew out, grabbing hold of a chair. As his cane clattered to the floor, he swore under his breath. His heart was racing and his limbs shook fiercely. Only when his breathing grew regular did he let go. Beads of perspiration dotted his brow, and he wiped them away with his forearm. Bending over, he retrieved the cane, realizing it marked what he had become. Appalled, he slowly returned to his own quarters.

Sunday, December 25, 1836

Christmas morning was greeted with Mass at dawn and a bountiful breakfast, after which Colette gathered her children and took them to their father's apartments, a rare occurrence, as Frederic generally visited them once a week in the nursery. Charmaine was grateful these encounters occurred in that safer territory, a neutral arena of civility—painful civility.

Awaiting their return, Charmaine walked into the drawing room and found Paul there. They had not spoken since the night of Stephen Westphal's visit. He'd been preoccupied with his upcoming trip, poring over documents in preparation of his imminent business negotiations. Tomorrow, he'd be leaving. As she stepped into the room, he stood.

"I'm sorry," she apologized. "I didn't mean to disturb you."

"You didn't. I wanted to speak with you, anyway. Where are the children?"

"With your father."

"Come and join me then," he invited, indicating the chair opposite him.

When she had complied, he tossed his papers aside, sat, and studied her at length. "I want to apologize," he began.

"For what?"

"For allowing you to think I wasn't on your side the other night. When I realized you were going to flee, I was compelled to stop you. I've learned it is best never to turn one's back on the enemy. I feared you were going to do just that."

She was astonished. George had been right.

"If you had looked my way," he was saying, "I would have conveyed that advice to you, but you were far too determined to lambaste Mr. Westphal. I'm sorry if I bruised your wrist."

She had been absentmindedly massaging her arm. "It's fine," she whispered self-consciously. "Thank you for defending me—even in light of the truth. I know you did not approve of me at first."

"I was wrong," he replied. "The children are fortunate to have you here."

"Still, you could have judged me by the deeds of my father."

His eyes were warm on her, and he shifted forward in his chair. "No," he breathed, "I could never have done that."

She was so lovely, and he was going to miss her during his months away. He realized she'd be missing him, too, perhaps more so. He'd been the perfect gentleman over the past few months, true to his word and true to his agreement. It had worked in his favor. He knew she was attracted to him. Right now, she longed to be kissed. Unlike two months ago, she felt at ease in his presence.

Nevertheless, she was distraught that he had made no further advances. Poor Charmaine Ryan; she was positively confused! The woman in her demanded passion, the little girl, safety, and then there was the female her father had wrought, the one who screamed, *Every man must be avoided at all costs.* How he longed to wash away her fears and show her the way to womanhood.

Absence . . . His three-month absence would make her heart grow fonder, and when he returned, he'd read hunger in her eyes. Let her dream of him while he was away. It would make his homecoming that much sweeter. He just needed to give her something to remember him by.

"Come dawn, I'll be sailing with the tide," he murmured. "I shall miss you."

Charmaine was reeling. He was going to kiss her; his hands had gripped the arms of her chair, and she was trapped between them. She closed her eyes, but did not lean away. His cheek brushed against hers as he nuzzled her ear. Her heart was pounding so loudly she couldn't understand what he whispered. To steady her soaring senses, she grabbed hold of his arms.

"There you are!"

The moment was shattered as Agatha entered the room. Paul broke away and immediately stood. Charmaine averted her crimson face. Once composed, she retreated to the foyer without a glance in Paul's direction.

Chapter 7

"QUICKLY, Robert!" Agatha urged. "She's having trouble breathing!"

Charmaine huddled in the archway of the drawing room, the twins drawn tight against her and Pierre clasped to her breast. As the doctor rushed up the stairs, Jeannette began to cry. "Is Mama going to be all right, Mademoiselle?"

"Of course she is," Charmaine breathed, attempting to disguise her own anxiety. "Now that Dr. Blackford is here, she'll be fine." She carried Pierre back into the room and sat him on the piano bench. "Let us sing together. A few songs might help us feel better."

The children brightened, but Charmaine remained worried. *Why did I encourage Colette to accompany us on our Sunday outing?* Of course, no one could have predicted the storm that had blown in, not from the beautiful skies that morning. By the time they reached the house, they were drenched to the skin and chilled to the bone. Colette fell prey to a fever almost immediately. Pneumonia—that's what Dr. Blackford called it, explaining she suffered from mucus in the lungs, which made breathing difficult. Agatha's alarmed mien added to Charmaine's perturbation; this had to be serious.

The day drew on. Robert departed Colette's chambers. He reached the open doorway of the nursery and cleared his throat, startling them.

"How is my mother?" Yvette demanded.

"There has been a minor improvement," he stated sourly.

Robert Blackford could have been a handsome man—tall and lean, with dark, aristocratic features. But he never smiled, his brow permanently severe, his jaw perpetually clenched.

"If you want her well again," he continued, "you are not to disturb her until I give permission. She has pneumonia thanks to your little outing on Sunday."

Charmaine had a great deal of trouble getting the girls to sleep that night. She thought Pierre would present the bigger problem, for he had cried nearly an hour the evening before. Without Nana Rose's able hands—the old woman had been abed for the better part of a week with rheumatism—Charmaine feared she was in for another bout of torrential tears. Not so; he fell asleep quickly. The girls, on the other hand, were guilt-ridden and anguished over their mother. Charmaine encouraged them to pray, but it was only as she read to them that their eyes grew heavy, and they succumbed to exhaustion.

Now she was free to fret on her own. Colette had not been well for the better part of two months, her health deteriorating rapidly since Christmas. Charmaine had thought the fresh air and sunshine of Sunday would do her some good. But Agatha was right. She wasn't a physician and should have left well enough alone; thanks to her, Colette was worse than ever. Robert Blackford's every-other-day visits would certainly turn into daily visits now.

She went down to the kitchen and chatted with Fatima Henderson. "This house is just too empty," the cook complained. It was true. Because Paul was away, George was overburdened. During the past weeks, they'd seen very little of him. Charmaine despaired anew. While Paul resided in the house, she felt protected. In his absence, havoc had reigned, the days longer, the nights wretched. Once the children were abed, there was little to do to while away the hours.

She needed a distraction and meandered into the drawing room, walking over to the piano. Maybe if she played something elaborate it would serve such a purpose and cheer her. She rummaged through the side table drawer until she found the dog-eared pages of a complicated piece. She propped them up, rearranged her skirts, and set her fingers on the keys.

She played the first sixteen measures, the last four a sequence that introduced the secondary theme. She sighed. The arrangement was difficult, lovely, yet sad. She played it again and again, reveling in the resonance of the finely crafted piano. This composition would never have sounded so beautiful on Loretta Harrington's upright. It was a masterpiece intended for a master instrument, its haunting strains echoing off the drawing room walls.

One more time over the ivory keys and Charmaine smiled. The notes were becoming familiar. She had faltered only once that last time, and now the rapturous rhapsody blossomed in all its glory, like an anxious flower bud bursting open to the beckoning sun.

Though the dissonant secondary theme defiled the perfect harmonies of the first, they were suitably entwined: lovers racing to the climax, expectancy building with each successive, addictive chord, exploding into a furious arpeggio that thundered up the keyboard, then tumbled back down. After three full measures of silence, a solitary, naked chord answered the fury, bringing the piece to a close: desolate, lost, hopeless . . .

The evening was too warm, the quiescent air too stifling in the confining chamber, and Colette knew the panic of suffocation. She left the bed and pattered barefoot across the soft carpet to the French doors, pulling them open. There she stood, welcoming the brisk March wind that buffeted her face and carried her golden hair off her shoulders, praying it would clear her senses.

This is only a minor setback, she reasoned. Yes, her head throbbed, her throat was constricted with needling pain, and her chest was congested. *But a severe infirmity of the lungs?* No, she silently denied, she wasn't that ill, though Agatha and Robert would like everyone to believe she was. And yet, after two days of coughing and fever, this afternoon she had lost the will to oppose their ministrations. She succumbed to Robert's wicked serum and Agatha's demanded round-the-clock bed rest.

That had been hours ago. Tonight, with the mansion so quiet and her contaminated room so oppressive, she escaped to the veranda. Breathing deeply, she welcomed the rejuvenating night air, until a hearty gale hit her full force. Shivering, she quickly latched the glass panels and wrapped herself in a plush velvet robe. Just as quickly, the sweats returned.

She should lie down. *No!* She'd not return to the rumpled bed where she had passed the better part of three days. Instead, she slipped her numb feet into soft slippers. She'd check on the children.

She was abreast of the staircase when she first heard it—a torpid melody long abandoned yet well remembered . . . Then, it was gone, indifferent of the emotion it had evoked. She hadn't heard it. It was all in her clouded mind. She shouldn't have stood in the night air. The exertion was taking its toll. Perhaps she should return to her apartments. No, that was foolish. She'd come this far, and she needed to see her children. If she just steadied herself for a moment, she'd be fine. There, she felt better already.

The children slept soundly. Thanks to Charmaine, they'd been tenderly mothered in her absence. She kissed each child's forehead, tucked in a cover here, moved a head back on the pillow there. Content, she tiptoed from the room.

Everything was shrouded in silence, and yet, as Colette crossed the hallway, the familiar strain was there again, meeting her at the top of the staircase. It was beckoning her, tugging at her very soul. Yes, it was stronger now and not a bitter disappointment of the imagination. It was real! All she had to do was reach the drawing room. Already her heart beat wildly with incautious desire, the rhapsody embracing her, mocking her turmoil and demanding but one thing: she come!

Charmaine played on, the power of the piece quintessential. No poet could pen words more plaintive than the haunting sorrow dwelling in this composer's masterpiece. She was merely the medium called upon to give it life, its spellbound prisoner, just now realizing there was more here than just the music, much more. Her hands floated flawlessly across the keyboard, her fingers exalting untamed territory. The composition consumed her in its desire to proclaim its plight: charades that hide the truth, injustices that persecute the living, and choices far from resolved . . . Charmaine had lived them all and wanted to weep.

The door slapped open, and she jumped, her hands crucifying the keys.

Relief flooded over her as she faced the startling wraith. "*Colette?*"

The mistress of the manor appeared dazed, her liquid eyes distant and her pupils dilated. Her face was flushed, and her breathing erratic. When she didn't respond, Charmaine crossed the room and placed an arm around her frail shoulders. Colette swayed and began coughing fitfully. When the spasm passed, Charmaine coaxed her into the nearest chair. "Are you all right? Can I get you something? Perhaps a drink? Or should I have Travis send for the doctor?"

The last query snared Colette's attention, and her detachment receded. "No," she whispered. "I'll be fine . . . in a minute. Just give me a minute." Her eyes darted about the room as if she were looking for someone. Eventually, they came to rest on Charmaine. "You . . . you were playing the piano just now?"

"Yes."

Colette frowned. "I didn't know you could play so—well." Her words trailed off, and again she scanned the darkened room. *Is he standing in the shadows?*

"I didn't think I could play like that, either. It was as if the composition possessed me."

Colette's regard sharpened.

Unnerved by that gaze, Charmaine said, "You should be in bed."

"No, I'm fine. I was just checking on the children when I heard the music. You played it so beautifully, almost as if . . . as if you'd composed it . . ."

Charmaine laughed softly, incredulously. "I could never have done that."

". . . as if you were a part of it," Colette continued, ignoring Charmaine's denial. "As if you belonged to it."

Charmaine could not disagree. "It's exquisite. I just wish I were able to play it properly."

"You will," Colette encouraged, "with time and patience, you will."

"Perhaps, but it will take a great deal of practice." Charmaine lifted the sheets of music from the piano and studied them in the lamplight. "There are a few chords here that flow in the most unusual direction. I need to better understand their placement before I do it justice. Right now, my fingers are inclined to change the dissonant measures; they're too unhappy."

Colette's eyes sparkled with tears. "An astute observation. The piece needs your touch to see it resolved."

"Resolved?" Charmaine declared, upset she'd suggested interfering with the imperfectly perfect score. "I wouldn't dream of tampering with it."

"Not tamper," Colette corrected, "enhance. The music as it stands cries out to be understood. The manner in which it is played—a gentle hand, a commitment to each measure—will enrich it. A few notes sent in a new direction will replace the sadness and sorrow with happiness and joy. You have the strength of character to do that, Charmaine, to bend the masterpiece, but not break it, to possess it, as it has possessed you. And when your love *is* the music, the harmony will be perfect."

Peculiar sentiments, Charmaine thought. "Who composed it?" she asked.

"Obviously someone who has borne a great deal of pain."

"Yes," Charmaine agreed, "and that pain must have become his inspiration."

Colette nodded, content for a second time that night. "Would you play it again? It has been so long. I'd like to hear it one last time."

Charmaine placed her fingers on the keys and resurrected the rhapsody.

Wednesday, March 8, 1837

Colette sat at her desk, breathing as deeply as her constricted lungs would allow. Agatha and Robert had finally left her, and she had a moment's peace. She refused to stay abed, certain she had exerted more energy arguing with the doctor and his sister than walking the short distance from bedchamber to sitting room. Still, she admitted the physician's remedies had had some positive effect. Though her cough persisted, his mustard plaster had eased the piercing pain she'd experienced yesterday when her hacking had been uncontrollable. His constant care had also cured her of a two-day fever and chills.

She had slept very little last night, and yet, this morning she felt strangely untroubled and refreshed. Charmaine Ryan had pointed the way; she knew what she must do.

Picking up her quill, she began to write, allowing her heart to determine the words. More than once, tears splattered the stationery, but she chased them away with the back of her hand. Tears were for the past, smiles were for tomorrow. She would think only of smiles.

So deep were her thoughts, she did not hear her chamber door open.

"Colette, why are you out of bed?"

She jumped, nearly upsetting the inkwell, a hand flying to her mouth. "Frederic," she gasped, "what are you doing here?" *Was he reading over my shoulder?* No, his eyes betrayed only concern.

"I've come to see how you are," he answered gently.

She sighed in relief, but the expulsion of air ended in another coughing fit. When she looked up at him, he was scowling.

"Robert told me you've refused his advice. Must I set Gladys up as guard to make certain you stay in bed?"

"Do what you like, Frederic," she retaliated, "but I won't be bullied!"

She remembered a time when such a retort would have incensed him further, but today his countenance softened dolefully. "I am not trying to bully you, Colette. I only wish to see you well again."

"Why?" she asked, suddenly on the verge of tears. "What does it matter?"

"The children need you."

"The children . . . *Just* the children?" She bit her bottom lip and, for one breathless moment, thought he was going to speak the words she longed to hear.

Instead he asked, "Where were you last night?"

Confused, a multitude of thoughts raced through her mind: the suffocating room, the need to see the children, the music . . . and then, this peculiar question. "You were here?" she asked, noting the accusatory gleam that flickered in his eyes. *Dear God, he still mistrusts me!*

"Robert has painted a grim picture. I was worried and couldn't sleep."

"Neither could I. I went to check on the children."

"Strange," he snorted, "I did the same thing, and you weren't there."

"I *did* look in on the children," she said. "Afterward, I went downstairs. But if you want to believe the worst about me, if that eases your pain—"

She was coughing again, so fiercely she doubled over, unaware of his despair. "Colette," he urged, his hale arm pulling her to her feet, "you must get back into bed. I won't disturb you if you remain in bed."

Friday, March 31, 1837

Colette's health continued to deteriorate after her bout with pneumonia, and her absences from the nursery became commonplace. Not so today. If Colette couldn't come to the children, the children would go to her. It was her birthday. Charmaine made all the preparations: a day's excursion with the girls and Pierre, and a visit to their mother's chambers after dinner, where they would give her the locket they had picked out at the mercantile earlier that week.

Charmaine had just finished tying Pierre's laces, when Frederic appeared in the nursery doorway. "Are you going somewhere?" he asked.

"Yes, sir," she answered, quickly straightening up.

She remained ill at ease with the man, their first encounter forever etched in her mind. It was a condition she'd been forced to confront on a daily basis now. Over the past month, he'd come to visit nearly every morning, as if he were attempting to make up to his children the time they'd normally have spent with their mother, that precious time that had been stolen from them.

"Mademoiselle Charmaine is taking us on a picnic," Jeannette offered. "Would you like to come, Papa?"

"I think not. But I do have a present for Pierre. I believe he is three today."

The little boy beamed in delight. "I am! Where's my pwesent?"

Frederic produced a package from behind his back, and the boy quickly dove into the wrapping. He lifted from the paper a wooden ship, a replica of the Duvoisin vessels that sailed the Atlantic. Laughing, he gave his father a fierce hug. "Tank you, Papa!"

Charmaine smiled down at him, satisfied with his manners and delighted with his joy. Already he was on hands and knees pretending to sail the toy.

Yvette frowned in disappointment. "Pierre got a present on our birthday," she remarked sullenly. "Why don't we get one on his?"

"Would a visit to see your mother suffice?" her father asked. "I know she would love a visit from you. She's feeling a bit better today."

The invitation had a magical effect, Charmaine's planned outing quickly forgotten. As they raced out of the room, Frederic called after them. "One thing," he lightly warned. "No jumping on her bed, and don't forget to say 'Happy Birthday.'"

"Of course we wouldn't forget that!" Yvette exclaimed.

In an instant they were gone, and Charmaine was left alone with the taciturn man. He stepped slightly aside and, with the wave of his hand, encouraged her to precede him down the hallway. She did so, wondering if she had become accustomed to his labored steps, or if those steps had improved in the months she had come to know him; he did not seem to struggle as fiercely as he had before.

They found the children in Colette's bedroom. Though the French doors were thrown open and sunlight spilled into the chamber, the room was dismal. Colette, propped among many pillows, did not look well. Large, dark circles lay claim to sunken eyes, and the smile that reached them was more sad than happy.

The children seemed unaware of the severity of her illness. Pierre was nestled beside her, Jeannette sat next to him, and Yvette stood opposite them, near her mother's pillow, grasping one of her hands. They were innocently happy just to be in her presence.

"We are going on a picnic today," Yvette was saying. "We can't wait until you are well enough to come with us again!"

"That's a lovely way to spend Pierre's birthday," Colette answered. "Next year, when I'm better, we'll plan something special to do together."

"I'm fwee!" Pierre announced proudly.

"Yes, I know, *mon caillou*," she replied. "You are growing so handsome. Soon you will look just like your father." She brushed back the soft brown hair that fell on his brow and drew him close for a tender kiss. "I missed you."

"When are you gonna be better, Mama?"

"Soon, I hope . . . very soon."

Frederic cleared his throat. "I didn't hear anyone say 'Happy Birthday.'"

"Oh yes, Mama," they all chimed in, "Happy Birthday!"

"I'm so glad we're visiting now," Jeannette said. "Mademoiselle didn't think we'd be allowed until later, but Papa knew we wanted to see you this morning."

Colette's eyes filled with tears as she looked from one child to the next. Then she met her husband's gaze across the room. "Thank you," she whispered, her gratitude rivaled only by her astonishment.

Earlier that morning, she had had a dispute with Robert Blackford, gaining nothing save a warning she not leave her bed lest he summon her husband. When Agatha had hurried off to do just that, Colette had been certain she'd be denied yet another visit with her children. But Frederic had defied them.

The children spent only a short time with her, presenting the wrapped gift Charmaine remembered to bring. She kissed each of them, savoring those they offered in return. Her eyes remained wistful after they'd left.

Frederic stepped closer and, sitting on the edge of the bed, took her hand in his. In spite of her illness, her pulse quickened and her fingers tingled. *Is he aware of the emotion he evokes?* His eyes told her, *No.*

"Thank you," she whispered again. "They will cure me faster than any of Robert's tonics."

Frederic didn't respond, the weight of his regard unsettling. "If you promise to heed Robert's advice," he said, "I will bring the children in to see you whenever you wish. How would that be?"

She weakly squeezed his hand. "That would be wonderful."

He patted her hand before tucking it beneath the coverlet. With some effort, he pushed off the bed and turned to leave. "I need you, too," he murmured.

She watched him limp from the room, blinking back tears. Though her strength was waning, his vigor was waxing. It was too late for them, she realized. In resignation, she accepted that as best for everyone concerned.

Sunday, April 2, 1837

Wade Remmen climbed the front steps and stood before the large oak doors of the Duvoisin mansion. He knocked on the door and waited, turning to survey the beautiful lawns from the height of the portico. A mere two years ago, his life had been wretched. He'd certainly come up in the world. But he wanted more. Someday, he'd acquire his own fortune and build a palatial estate such as this; then his future could mock his past. *My sister would love to be here right now. Someday* . . . The front door opened, and the butler invited him in.

George was eating heartily. He motioned for Wade to take the seat across from him and asked Fatima to dish up the same fare.

After a good portion of the meal was consumed, Wade was still pondering the reason for his second invitation to the manor. The first had come months ago—a luncheon offered in gratitude for his intervention at the mill the day before.

In all his nineteen years, Wade had never panicked in an emergency. Likewise, he never feared standing up for himself. These attributes, along with his determination to work hard, had earned him Paul Duvoisin's respect. When the sawmill's foreman sliced open his arm in early November, exposing the bone and nearly bleeding to death on the spot, Wade had swiftly wrapped a tourniquet on the upper limb and ordered a man to run for the doctor. After he'd sent another man in search of Paul or George, he returned to the labor at hand. The crew began to grumble, but he insisted a bit of blood wasn't going to shut down production. When their objections grew vehement, he threw himself into the job, ignoring them. In less than five minutes, everyone was back to work. In the end, a life had been saved, and just as much lumber milled. Paul had been pleased.

Today, Wade wondered what feat awaited him, for he knew Paul was away and George had been carrying the workload of two. His intrigue was piqued when Harold Browning entered the room and the same meal was set before him.

"I have a problem," George finally said. "I must leave Charmantes for a couple of weeks, and I need the two of you to take over while I'm away, or until Paul returns, which I expect will be any day now."

Harold was befuddled. "May I ask where you are traveling?"

"Virginia," he replied tersely, closing the topic to further probes. "Now, can I count on you at the mill, Wade? You've handled it before. This time you'll be in complete control for a fortnight, perhaps more."

"As long as the men know I'm boss, there shouldn't be a problem."

"I'll speak to them first thing in the morning," George answered, shifting his consideration to Harold. "You'll have the greater challenge, managing both the sugarcane and tobacco crews. Jake and Buck can take care of the harbor: warehousing the harvests, coordinating the unloading and loading of any ships that make port. With any luck, Paul will be on the first one from Europe. Once he's home, he can take over."

"Does Frederic know you are leaving?" Harold asked.

George leaned back in his chair. "He will soon enough," he replied vaguely, pleased when Charmaine and the children entered the room.

"George," she greeted with a buoyant smile. She could count on her fingers the number of times she had seen him since Paul's departure three months ago, and she was truly happy to find him at the table now. "What brings you home?"

Before he could answer, her attention was drawn to the other two men, who'd come to their feet as she stepped closer. She nodded to Harold Browning and then the younger man beside him. She couldn't remember his name, though he'd dined with them once before in the fall. The hint of a grin tweaked the corners of his mouth, and she was instantly struck by his good looks, recalling Colette's admiration when he'd departed the house last time. Tall and lanky, he was clean-shaven with a broad nose and full lips. His lazy smile reached his dark eyes. They matched the color of his hair, which was cropped short. Muscular arms and swarthy skin attested to the many hours he'd toiled under the blazing tropical sun. He was young, perhaps her age, yet sure of himself as if he were much older.

"I remember Miss Ryan," he said as George introduced them.

George didn't dally. "I've a great deal to do today."

Charmaine watched all three men depart. She would have liked to socialize with George, but instead was left to the company of the children. Jeannette's crestfallen expression mirrored Charmaine's mood.

"Is something troubling you, sweetheart?" she asked.

"I wish Mr. Remmen could have stayed awhile longer, that's all."

Mr. Remmen and Mr. Richards, Charmaine thought.

Thursday, April 6, 1837

Dark clouds gathered swiftly, blotting out the sun and rumbling with thunder, but the growling masses did not match the lamentations that shook Charmantes' mansion from within. The entire household was aware of the plight of their frail mistress, who lay near death. The pneumonia had taken a greater hold; any imagined improvement was just that, a delusion, and now Colette was fighting for her life.

Frederic was consumed with despair. He paced his chambers in broken misery, as impotent to fight his wife's infirmity as he was powerless to heal himself. The heavy thump of one boot, the crisp click of the cane, and the sad scrape of his lame leg, could be heard without, again and again and again . . . He had left Colette's bedside only a short while ago, but Robert's hushed words continued to haunt him: "I fear she is dying, Frederic. All we can do now is pray."

Dear God, it couldn't be so! She was too young, too beautiful, so full of life. *No,* he admitted to himself in sour self-contempt, *the last hadn't been true for a long time,* not since the day he had shackled her to him with manacles of guilt. The vivacious wench grew into a reserved lady. Sorrow and defeat had snuffed out laughter and fire, her once brilliantly blue eyes now smoky-gray. He was about to lose her more surely than he had all those years ago, and it was his own fault. She didn't want to live, for he'd seen to it her life was not worth living. Sadly, there was nothing he could do at this late hour but pace and pray.

The house shook beneath the violent storm. The door banged open and was swiftly slammed shut, a mock echo of the tempest. Drenched, Paul mopped the hair from his eyes, doffed his saturated cape, and handed it to Travis.

"How was your trip, sir?" the manservant asked.

"Fine—fine!" Paul snapped. "What the hell has happened here? I return after three and a half months abroad to find the island in chaos. George is nowhere to be found. Jake Watson and Harold Browning are tight-lipped as to his whereabouts, and only Wade Remmen is man enough to suggest he's left Charmantes altogether. But that's insane! To make matters worse, we're in the middle of a raging thunderstorm with little of the island secured."

"Certainly it is nothing to fret over, sir," Travis placated, "after all, it's not yet hurricane season."

Paul snorted. "Why did I expect things to run smoothly in my absence?"

"The house has been in turmoil over the past two days," Travis attempted to explain, his voice taut. "Miss Colette is dreadfully ill. Dr. Blackford has been in constant attendance and allows no one to enter her chambers without his authorization. Even Mrs. Ward is beside herself with worry."

Paul's irritability vanished. The butler's manner left little doubt to the gravity of the situation. "My father"—he demanded urgently—"does he know?"

"Everyone knows, sir, and everyone is praying, most especially the children."

The children, Paul thought. *They will be devastated if anything happens to their mother.* Unbidden came visions of Charmaine, but he shook off the profane musings. The dampness was seeping in. "I'm in need of a bath and a change of clothing. After I've eaten, I'd like to see my father."

"Yes, sir," Travis nodded eagerly, glad to be put to work. "I'll have Joseph draw the water, and I'll tell Fatima to prepare you a tray of food. Then I'll let your father know you are home."

Paul was halfway up the stairs before he remembered the first news that had accosted him when he'd set foot on Charmantes. "Travis, where *is* George?"

"He left three days ago on the *Rogue,* sir."

"*What?* Why?"

Travis recalled George's instructions: *Tell Paul or Frederic only if they ask,* and quickly relayed the message, "Miss Colette asked him to deliver a letter to Virginia—"

"Jesus Christ Almighty! Has he gone mad? Does my father know?"

"No sir, he never asked me."

"God Almighty," Paul cursed again as the impending scenario played out before him. George's absence would create many managerial problems over the course of the next few weeks, especially progress on Espoir; however, thoughts of George's desertion were far from pertinent in light of the greater disaster awaiting them all. Paul rubbed his throbbing forehead, but the pain only intensified.

He considered Colette. She must be contemplating death if she sent George on such a mission. But why? What would it gain her, save pain and havoc for everyone concerned? Ultimately, it threatened the collapse of this faltering fortress—on their heads. Paul shuddered.

Charmaine attempted to amuse the children, but their minds were far from the game of hide-and-seek she had suggested they play. "Come away from the door, Jeannette," she pleaded. "Your father will call us when your mother awakens."

"He said that yesterday, but still we weren't allowed to see her."

"And the day before, we saw her for only ten minutes!" Yvette chimed in.

Charmaine sighed, at a loss for encouraging words. "Yes, I know, but still, we must wait. If your mother needs rest, it's best we don't disturb her. You want to see her completely well again, don't you?"

Jeannette nodded in resignation, but Yvette was not so inclined. "We've been told that over and over and over again! I'll wager Father never comes today. He's so worried, he's forgotten about us."

Jeannette's eyes filled with tears. "Do you think that's true, Mademoiselle Charmaine? Papa promised we would see Mama today."

"I wanna see her, too!" Pierre began to cry, crawling from beneath the bed, where he'd been hiding. "I miss Mama. When are we gowin' to her room?"

Charmaine picked him up and sat on his bed. "Now listen to me," she said. "I know Dr. Blackford and your father are doing all they can to make your mother better; therefore, we must heed their advice. But, if your mother asks to see you—which I'm certain she will—you'll not be forgotten, will you?" When they shook their heads "no" and Pierre's tears subsided, she continued. "We must be patient. All right?" They nodded.

Colette's chest pulsated with pain, her breathing shallow as if the weight of the world pressed down on it. Hot one moment and cold the next, she quaked beneath dampened bed clothing, changed not an hour ago, yet already saturated with perspiration. Still, she fought valiantly, her eyes snapping open when a cool cloth was placed to her burning brow.

"Ssh . . ." Rose Richards whispered, "lie still . . . don't try to talk."

Colette sighed. The old woman had been so good to her, more of a mother than her own mother had ever been, and she felt comforted. Time wore on, and Rose continued to apply the compresses.

"Try to sleep, Colette," Rose encouraged, "a nice, deep sleep."

The words had the opposite effect; Colette's eyes opened again. "Nan—"

"Ssh . . ." she admonished. "Save your strength. There's no need to talk."

Colette licked her cracked lips. "Nan," she pressed weakly. "I need to know . . . did George . . ."

"Yes, child," Rose soothed. "He left Charmantes days ago. He will deliver your letter. Now, lie back and rest. You must close your eyes and rest."

"It's important . . . so important . . ."

"Yes, yes, I know."

"No!" she argued, alarmed by the thread of pacification she heard in the old woman's voice, struggling now to sit up. "I'm not trying to make more trouble."

"Colette, you've never made trouble, and the letter *is* in George's hands. It *will* be delivered. Lie back and sleep."

Drained, yet satisfied, Colette relaxed into the pillows and closed her eyes.

"What the deuce . . . ?"

Robert Blackford was livid as he took in the French doors thrown wide to the raging storm and the cold compress Rose Richards was applying to the brow of his flushed patient. "I thought I told you the woman is in my care!"

Rose met fire with fire. "My remedies may seem old-fashioned to you, Robert, but they will do Colette more good than this contaminated room."

"Woman, you are mad! I tell you now, I've tried everything, even cupping."

Rose's mind raced. "Surely you haven't bled her!"

"Of course not! She's too weak to withstand that absurd treatment. But your concoctions are not helping her, either. You'd best take out your rosary beads and visit the chapel. That will be the best home remedy you can practice today."

Rose paled with the baleful declaration, and Robert's anger ebbed. "I'm sorry," he muttered bleakly. "I'm at a loss as to what to do for her."

Rose had only seen him like this once before—the night his sister had died—and the memory filled her with dread. "Surely she'll recover."

"The congestion in her lungs is not the only complication

threatening her life. But that is a matter between Colette, Frederic, and the priest."

"Father Benito?" Rose asked, her alarm multiplying twofold.

Robert nodded solemnly. "She asked for him this morning. He's come and gone only an hour ago. Perhaps he has left her with some measure of peace."

Peace? There was no peace in Colette's contorted face. Her serene smile had been stolen away, her beauty supplanted by hollow eyes and protruding cheekbones that cut harshly into her once angelic visage.

"Come, Rose," the physician cajoled. "She's sleeping now. At present, there is nothing you can do for her. Go, say your prayers. This family needs them."

Rose left the room, a morose nod given to Agatha as they passed on the chamber's threshold.

"Papa, can we see Mama now?" Jeannette implored.

Frederic limped into the nursery. "She is sleeping, princess, but I will take you to her room once she awakens. I told Dr. Blackford I would be here," he continued, reading Yvette's stormy countenance. "When he calls for me, you may come, too, if that pleases you."

They nodded optimistically.

"What have you been studying today?" he asked, quickly changing the subject. "Perhaps I can help Miss Ryan with your lessons."

For the first time, Charmaine was pleased Frederic had come to visit.

He must be with Colette, Paul thought when he found his father's chambers empty. He knocked on the adjoining door. Agatha opened it.

"Paul," she exclaimed, stepping forward to hug him, "you're home!"

He suffered the unexpected greeting as she drew him into the room. "Where is my father?"

"I don't know. I thought he was in his apartments."

"How is Colette?"

Her manner turned lugubrious. "Not well, I'm afraid. Not well at all."

"May I see her?"

"I don't think that is wise. Robert is with her now—"

"I'd like to see her," Paul stated.

He crossed the room and opened the bedroom door, ignoring her objections, and reached the foot of the bed just as Robert glanced around. "I must ask you to leave," the man ordered sharply, "she is not well enough to receive visitors."

Paul was not listening, his face a mask of horror as he looked down at Colette. Her eyes were closed, and he was grateful for that, fearing what they might tell him if they opened. Then they were open, and he nearly cried as she attempted to smile. "Good God, Colette," he muttered impulsively.

"Do I look that wretched?" Her lame laugh erupted into a racking cough.

"Out!" Robert commanded. "I want you out of here! You're upsetting her!"

"No!" she begged. "Please—" Before she could finish, she was coughing again.

"I said, you're upsetting her!"

Paul was hearing none of Robert's fulminating nonsense. He rounded the far side of the bed and attempted to help Colette sit up to catch her breath. She burned beneath his touch.

"I'm all right now," she whispered. "I'd just like a drink."

"Paul, you must leave!"

"Get her a goddamn drink!" Paul barked.

Agatha scurried to the pitcher and poured a glass of water, bringing it to him. Colette swallowed only a sip before collapsing back into the pillows. Beads of perspiration dotted her brow, and Paul wiped them away.

"Thank you," she breathed, clearing her throat.

"Can I get you anything else?"

"The children . . . Robert refuses . . . but I want to see my children . . ."

Paul nodded. "Then you shall."

As he returned to the sitting room, Robert was right on his heels, closing the door between the two chambers. "You cannot mean to bring them here. She doesn't have the strength—"

"What kind of physician are you, anyway?" Paul growled, facing him. "She's been under your care for nearly a year now and look at her!" Receiving no answer, he snorted in disgust. "Stay out of my way!"

"This is not my fault!" Blackford rallied, calling to his back. "She has pneumonia. Your little governess took her on a picnic in the pouring rain. She caught a chill, and her lungs have filled with mucus. She's been fighting this newest malady for a full month now."

Paul rounded on him, but his ire flagged as swiftly as it had spiked. He shook his head and left the room.

"One moment, Yvette!" Charmaine reproved as she opened the door.

"Miss Ryan," Paul greeted, her lovely face erasing the memory of Colette's ghastly visage.

"Paul!" she exclaimed, glad beyond words.

At the mention of his name, everyone in the room perked up, and even Frederic brightened, releasing Pierre who had been sitting in his lap. "Come in, please come in," she invited. "When did you arrive?"

"An hour ago," he answered, ruffling Pierre's hair and hugging Jeannette who had scampered over to greet him.

Yvette remained next to her father, who sat at her desk. "Mama is very ill," she informed him, as if that were the only thing that mattered now.

"Yes, I know. She's been asking for you. Would you like to see her?"

"Oh yes!" they answered in unison.

"But"—he admonished—"she has a high fever. You mustn't force her to talk, and you may stay only a short time. Do you understand?"

They nodded.

He had just lifted Pierre into his arms when Agatha appeared in the doorway, her face ashen. "It is time. Robert fears it is time."

Death . . . it hung in the room with a life of its own. The gathered assembly could feel it—smell it—taste it. There was no escaping the sound of it: Colette's labored wheezing, the dogged coughing, and now the whimpers of her loved ones. Charmaine closed her eyes to the telltale finale. *Why in heaven's name did we bring the children here?*

In the throes of her extremity, Colette's unique beauty was only a memory, scarred by the unholy battle she had fought: hooded eyes sunken, lips chafed raw, sallow complexion drawn over skeletal cheeks, lovely hair matted and coarse.

Yvette faced the truth first, bravely inching closer, silent tears trickling down her cheeks. "Mama, I'm here," she said, taking her hand.

Colette attempted to smile up at her.

Jeannette followed, falling to her knees beside the bed. When

Colette closed her eyes, she buried her face in the bed linen and wept.

"Don't cry," Colette beseeched, mustering the strength to stroke her daughter's hair. "I'm happy—" The remark hung unfinished as she suffered through another fitful cough.

Blackford sidestepped Paul, who stood sentry against interference. "The children have had their time," he directed, reaching the bed. "This visit is upsetting everyone, specifically Colette. No good will come of it."

It was true, but Paul couldn't ignore Colette's tormented entreaty of: "No! Please! A moment longer . . ." He passed Pierre to Charmaine, then pulled Robert aside. "I want you to stay," Colette was saying, her voice low and raspy.

"We will, Mama," Yvette whispered, fighting the fire in her throat. "We'll stay as long as you like."

Colette considered Jeannette again, the child's sobs increasing. "Sweetheart, you mustn't cry . . ."

"I—I can't help it!" Jeannette gasped. "You can't die! I—I—won't let you die! I love you too much!" She rose from her knees, leaned across the bed, and wrapped her arms around her mother, as if she could squeeze the demon of death from her.

Charmaine's embrace quickened around Pierre. His whimpers had intensified, yet, she took succor from him, grateful to have someone to hold. She pressed his head to her bosom and shielded him from the avalanche of grief.

Rose stepped out of the shadows and bent over Jeannette. "Come, darling," she comforted, separating the girl from Colette, "say goodbye to your mother."

"No!" Jeannette cried, struggling to be free. "I won't leave her!"

Colette broke into another rattling cough, unable to catch her breath this time, the convulsion worse than the others.

Robert rushed forward again, pulling her upright and striking her back until the spasm subsided. "She cannot withstand this strain!" he remonstrated sharply, his accusatory gaze leveled on Jeannette, who'd retreated, terror-stricken, to the edge of the bed.

"I'm all right," Colette panted, sucking in shallow pockets of air.

"Come, Jeannette," Rose cajoled, gathering her in tender arms, "your mother must rest. Give her a kiss."

Jeannette obeyed, her lips lingering on her mother's cheek. "Mama? I love you Mama."

Colette's hand found hers. "And I love you," she murmured, her grip tightening momentarily.

Jeannette abruptly stood and tore from the room.

Paul followed.

Yvette stood fast, her eyes fixed on her mother, aware that Rose had come round to her side of the bed. "Mama? You'll be all right without me?"

Colette shook her head slightly. "I won't be without you. I'll always be here . . . in this house . . . with you, Yvette." She cleared her throat. "Yvette . . . you'll take care of your brother and sister for me? You're very strong. Promise me . . . promise me you'll always stay together."

"I promise, Mama. Don't worry about them."

Satisfied, Colette beckoned for a final embrace, her arms like deadweights as they closed over Yvette's shoulders.

"Good-bye, Mama," Yvette choked out. "I love you!" With a swift kiss, she broke free and fled.

Colette turned her head aside and, unmindful of the doctor's reprimands, wept. Her anguish spiraled when she realized Rose and Charmaine were leaving as well. "Please!" she gasped, her voice barely audible. "Please . . . my son . . . I want to hold my son."

No one seemed to hear. Robert was wiping her brow, and Agatha was whispering in his ear. The governess was leaving, and she had not kissed her son goodbye. "Please!" she called out desperately.

As Charmaine reached the doorway, Frederic detained her, allowing only Rose to pass. "My wife wants to see Pierre," he said, nodding toward the bed.

Slowly, Charmaine turned back into the room.

"Pierre," Colette sighed, reaching out feebly. "Pierre," she called again, smiling weakly when Charmaine sat him on the bed.

Her joy was swiftly snuffed out. The three-year-old was terrified and wanted nothing to do with her, moaning loudly as she caressed his head. He clambered to the edge of the mattress, reaching for Charmaine.

The woman in this bed was not his mother. His mama was gentle and beautiful, not ravaged and worn. He pulled himself to his knees and buried his face in Charmaine's skirts.

Colette closed her eyes to sorrow. When she opened them again, they held the light of resignation. "Charmaine," she breathed, hand extended.

Charmaine grabbed hold quickly and squeezed Colette's fingers.

"You'll . . . you'll take care of him?"

"You needn't worry. Colette. I'll take good care of Pierre and the girls."

"And . . . you'll give him . . . all the love he needs."

"Yes, Colette. I shall love him as if he were my own. Now, please, don't try to speak anymore. Please rest."

"But him!" Colette struggled anew, as if Charmaine hadn't understood. Frantically, she grasped at Pierre in an attempt to reach his governess. "He needs you the most . . . because he's the most vulnerable . . . and I wasn't able to give him . . . what he—"

"Pierre will be fine," Charmaine promised, lifting him clear off the bed, chasing away her tears with the back of one hand.

Colette nodded and, drained, closed her eyes again.

"Goodbye, Colette," she forced out, returning Pierre's tenacious hug. "Thank you for all you've given me, my dear, *dear* friend."

Colette heard the earnest declaration, took it to her heart. *Love him*, she prayed again.

The door closed softly behind Charmaine, leaving only three to their grim vigil. Frederic's deep voice shattered the solemnity. "Leave us."

Robert faced him. "Frederic, there is little time for that now."

"Leave us, man, and leave us now. I will give my wife everything she needs. Now clear out!"

The physician's mouth clamped shut. In less than a minute, he and his sister were gone, the bedroom suddenly empty. Empty—so cruel in its irony. Would his heart always brim with grief when he felt most empty? He had made it so.

It was a long time before Colette's children slipped into the oblivion of sleep. Paul and Rose attempted to console them, and Rose finally succeeded in getting Pierre to close his eyes. But in the end, Charmaine's gentleness dried the girls' tears. When Paul and Rose departed, they spoke for a long time. Charmaine had, after all, lost her own mother. But she refused to listen to talk of death. "Your mother is sleeping just down the hallway," she insisted. "We're not giving up hope. Let us say our prayers. Let us pray to St. Jude. Miracles can happen."

When they were asleep, Charmaine went down to the drawing room, something she hadn't done for a long time. She was happy to find Paul there, even though he was discussing Colette's condition with Agatha, Robert, and Rose. As she entered the parlor, Agatha threw her a nasty look, but Paul welcomed her into their company.

"As I was saying," the doctor continued, "any strength Colette possessed deteriorated long before the pneumonia set in. She was, and still is, ill equipped to fight such a malady. The next twenty-four hours should tell the tale."

"Meaning?" Paul bit out.

"If she can hold on until the fever breaks, she may have a chance."

"Is there nothing you can give her in the interim?"

"Unfortunately, she has eaten little and has vomited the rest, including my strongest compounds." Blackford shook his head. "No, she must fight this on her own. Now, if you'll excuse me, I must see—"

Paul grabbed hold of his arm. "Robert, my father is with her. Give them some time alone."

The doctor looked down at the hand that waylaid him and abruptly pulled away. "An hour—I'll give him one hour." With that, he was gone.

"Paul," Agatha began, "Robert has tried, really, he has. I can attest to the hours he's passed over Colette's bedside. He's forfeited his other patients just to be here, round the clock."

"I'm sure," Paul grumbled, rubbing the back of his neck.

"Agatha is right," Rose interjected. "Robert has done everything in his power to combat this illness."

"It's my fault," Charmaine added, guilt-ridden over the part she had played. "Colette was feeling better a month ago, and I suggested a picnic. If we had arrived home before the rainstorm, she would never have caught a chill."

"Exactly!" Agatha piped in disdainfully. "It is beyond my comprehension that an *educated* person would coerce a frail woman into traipsing far from her home in the first place."

"Coerce?" Paul replied. "Come, Agatha, if Colette didn't feel well enough to go on this picnic, she would have had the good

sense to stay home. As for Charmaine, how could she have predicted inclement weather? No one is to blame here. I'm just trying
to determine if something else can be done. Colette is a young
woman with three children who will be devastated if she—" He
feared finishing the thought.

Insulted, Agatha left the room.

Paul turned to Rose. "I've more faith in your remedies than all
of Robert's prescriptions combined. If you will consider passing
the night at Colette's bedside, I will tell him not to step foot in that
room unless he is summoned."

"I'm at a loss," she confided woefully, "but I would be pleased
to sit beside Colette for as long as I am permitted."

Paul nodded, then watched her leave.

Charmaine regarded him. She'd so looked forward to his return, felt terrible he'd come home to heartache. "It has been miserable here without you."

In spite of himself, he smiled. "I suppose that means you
missed me."

"I *did* miss you. It was as if disaster befell Colette the moment
you left."

"She hasn't been ill all that time, has she?"

"She's never been truly well," Charmaine said. "After Christmas her health continued to decline. Dr. Blackford's biweekly visits became every-other-day visits. Some days, she'd seem improved,
but when we grew hopeful, she'd have another relapse. Then she
contracted this 'pneumonia.' After that, Dr. Blackford was here
nearly every day. It has been a terrible ordeal, as much for the children as for Colette."

"At least they have you, Charmaine. Colette is a wise woman.
She was right about you."

Embarrassed, Charmaine lowered her eyes, but Paul pressed

on. "I don't want you blaming yourself. Colette has been weak for quite some time. She should never have had Pierre . . ."

His words trailed off and he stared far into the distance—across time.

"I must check on the children," she said. "They've not been sleeping well."

Her voice drew him away from a multitude of disturbing thoughts. "Yes, and I had better find Robert. Tonight he will not disturb Colette with *his* educated ministrations."

Frederic mopped Colette's brow with the cool cloth.

Her eyes fluttered open. "You don't have to stay—"

"Yes, I do," he interrupted, his voice stern, but not harsh. "Close your eyes and rest, Colette."

But her gaze remained fixed on him as he turned back to the basin of water, her parched lips trembling when she spoke. "Promise—promise me you'll not send Charmaine away if I—"

Frederic's head jerked round, his severe regard stifling the ominous words.

"Please, Frederic . . . promise me," she finished instead.

"If you will close your eyes, I will promise you anything, Colette. Charmaine will always be welcome in this house, you needn't fear otherwise."

Allayed, Colette closed her eyes.

With difficulty, Frederic dragged the heavy armchair close to the head of the bed. There he remained, continually changing the compresses as soon as they became warm, thankful when no one returned to steal away this private time.

After a while, the heat gave way to severe chills, and though Frederic thought she slept, Colette's eyes flew open, and she began to shiver uncontrollably. At a loss for what to do, he stood and walked round the bed, settling on the mattress. He drew her into his embrace and tucked the coverlet around her. Soon the warm cocoon relieved the violent shudders. Her cheek rested upon his chest, and slowly he felt her arm encircle his waist. He shifted, pulling her more tightly against him. As he stroked her hair, her rapid breathing grew easy and regular. He knew exactly when she had fallen asleep.

The minutes ticked by, and Frederic thought back on all they'd been through together, everything that had propelled them to this moment. He savored the scorching heat that radiated from her cheek, breasts, belly, and legs, branding him through the clothing and healing his body with an infusion of pleasure.

The door creaked open, and Rose softly entered. Her eyes immediately fell on the couple. Frederic's finger came to his lips, warning her to remain silent. She nodded and withdrew to the sitting room, where she reclined on the settee. A great calm swept over her, and she wondered if God had sent this egregious tribulation to rectify the pain the family had suffered these past few years. For the first time in years, Rose entertained the possibility of hope.

Frederic, too, experienced an enormous surge of contentment. Kissing his wife's head, he pressed his own back into the pillows, closed his eyes, and slept.

Friday, April 7, 1837

Morning dawned glorious. The storm had washed Charmantes clean, and the mistress's suite reveled in the same redolent splendor. Colette was improved.

She woke to find her cheek pressed to her husband's chest and his arms encircling her. He was snoring, and she cherished the sound of it. Her nightgown clung to her, but she luxuriated in the warmth of his body and, with a soft cough, cuddled closer. The movement awoke him. Before he could speak, she hugged him. His embrace quickened in response. Then, he stroked her brow and caressed her cheek.

Cool to the touch. Frederic closed his eyes in silent prayer, thanking God for answering his supplication.. He'd never waste another moment with this woman.

Someone knocked, and he attempted to move, but Colette held him fast. He smiled down at her, pleased when she shifted to look up at him.

"Tell whomever it is to go away," she whispered.

His fingers spanned her jaw, his thumb resting under her chin, nudging her head farther back into his shoulder. Leaning forward, he tenderly kissed her parched lips. She was unhappy when he drew away.

"I'll not leave you again, *ma fuyarde précieuse*," he vowed, "not ever again."

She choked back tears, devouring the words "my precious runaway," that special endearment she had not heard for so many years.

Rose and Paul were at the door. "How is she?" they asked.

"Better," Frederic answered, "the fever broke during the night."

"Thank God."

Frederic nodded. "Rose, could you have Fatima prepare broth, something light? She hasn't eaten for days. And Paul, would you tell the children they might visit later in the morning? They went through a terrible ordeal last night."

"What about you?" Paul asked. "Don't you want to eat? Get some rest?"

Frederic shook his head. "I'm fine. I'm going to stay right here."

Paul's brow tipped upward, befuddled. His father should be

tired, instead he was cheerful, energized, the aura emanating from him more than relief. Rose must have felt it, too, for as they left the mistress's quarters, she was humming.

Paul's thoughts rapidly turned to the other island. He'd be able to transport the bondsmen there today and get them settled, something he thought would have to wait.

Charmaine and the children were breakfasting when he delivered the miraculous news. The twins became animated and bubbly, already planning for the wondrous future. Charmaine's exuberance ebbed, however, when Paul mentioned spending the day and upcoming night on Espoir, insisting he must take advantage of Colette's recovery and at least establish the new crew on the island. In his three-month absence, doom had reigned supreme. His return had chased it away. But now he was leaving again, and Charmaine feared the consequences of his desertion.

The arrival of Agatha and Robert in the dining room heightened her anxiety, their somber faces overshadowing the children's ebullience.

Paul leaned back in his chair and regarded them. "The fever broke," he informed them.

Blackford's brow rose in surprise. "And shall I commend Rose Richards for her nursing prowess?" he queried sarcastically.

"Actually, my father cared for Colette throughout the night," Paul replied. "Apparently, he was all she needed."

"I would warn against an early celebration," Robert rejoined. "We've seen her improve before, just to have our hopes dashed."

Paul's face hardened, aware of the children's interest in the matter. "She will recover completely this time, Robert," he threatened.

The doctor snorted. "What is being done for her this morning?"

"When I left, Gladys and Millie were drawing her a bath, and Fatima is preparing her something to eat."

"*A bath?* They are preparing her a bath? Have they gone mad? Even if the fever has abated, she could easily catch another chill and fall more gravely ill than before."

Paul shrugged. "It is what she requested."

Robert rubbed his brow before throwing his sister a beseeching look, as if no one in the house, save her, would support him. "The food," he continued, "I hope it is something light, like soup or broth?"

"I believe so. But you can check with Fatima."

Fatima scurried around the kitchen, preparing not one, but two trays. If the mistress was up to eating, so was the master, she told Rose.

Rose agreed and helped lay serviettes and utensils on the trays. "She's better, Robert," the elderly woman blithely announced as the physician and his sister entered the kitchen, "and ready to eat something."

"So I've heard."

He watched as the broth was ladled out, the toast buttered, and the coffee poured. "I'll take this one," he offered as he picked up Colette's tray of food. Fatima nodded and turned to ring for Anna or Felicia. "That won't be necessary," he said. "Agatha is coming with me. She can carry Frederic's tray."

Fatima held open the swinging door as sister and brother headed for the mistress's chambers.

Frederic ate most of the food laid before him. But Colette's tray would have to wait. His wife was in the middle of her bath, he informed Robert and Agatha, and when she was finished, *he* would make sure she consumed something. Colette wanted to rest, undisturbed.

Again, Agatha bristled at the intended slight and sauntered toward the door. Robert, on the other hand, warned Frederic of the danger he was courting. "Her condition is fragile, Frederic.

You and I both know she has had relapses before. As for this bath, it is sheer folly. Mark my words: her fever will return before day's end. If you are wise, you will insist she eat and rest, nothing more."

Frederic nodded, but refused to speak.

"I will remain at the house," Blackford continued, "in case I am needed."

Supported on either side by Gladys and Millie, Colette stepped from the tepid tub water and walked the short distance to the arm-chair, where they helped her dress. Though she shivered, she was glad to be clean.

Millie began brushing out her hair, clicking her tongue in dismay as many golden strands were pulled free. "I fear this illness has damaged your hair, Miss Colette," she lamented, gaining her mother's immediate frown and swift shake of the head. The last thing Gladys needed was her mistress asking for a mirror and fretting over her cadaverous appearance. Colette needed happy words right now.

They had just finished changing the bed linens when Frederic rejoined his wife. Millie cast nervous eyes to the floor and curtseyed, but Gladys smiled. "I'll send Joseph in for the tub, sir," she said as she ushered her daughter from the room. "Will there be anything else, sir?"

"Would you bring the food tray in?"

She complied, then quickly departed.

Frederic turned loving eyes on Colette. "Fatima prepared something for you to eat. Do you think you could manage some broth?"

She nodded with smiling eyes. Her face was so very drawn, and yet today, it possessed a radiance he'd not seen for years. To Frederic, she was beautiful.

She took a small bite of toast and found even chewing an effort. When she reached for the spoon, her fingers refused to work. "My hands are numb," she complained.

Frederic drew a chair closer and took the utensil from her. "I never thought I'd live to see this day, Colette," he quipped, "or perhaps you'd have me believe I am the stronger one."

"We do make a pair," she jested with a chuckle. It only served to trigger another convulsive cough, which she struggled to subdue, exhausted by the time it had subsided. "I'm afraid it will be some time before I'm improved."

"You've improved already," he countered lightly. "No more talk of illness. We are going to nurse one another back to health."

He extended the first spoonful of broth to her lips, but the liquid had grown cold. The tray was sent back to the kitchen with Joseph, who had come in for the tub, with orders the coffee and broth be reheated.

In the interim, Frederic encouraged Colette to enjoy the fresh air out on the veranda, and a chair was moved into the morning sun. It was there the children found her.

"Mademoiselle Charmaine was right," Jeannette laughed, "miracles can happen! I'm going to say extra prayers to thank Jesus and Mary *and* St. Jude."

Frederic smiled at his daughters, happy for their happiness. He regarded Pierre, who sat on a bench next to his mother, content to let her stroke his hair. Today, he did not cry or pull away; today, he recognized the woman who leaned forward and kissed his head. Frederic would also thank God.

When Colette's tray of food arrived, Charmaine nudged her charges. "Come children, we have lessons, and it is important your mother eat and rest so she recovers completely."

Their father concurred. "You may see your mother again tomorrow."

Pacified, they gave Colette one last kiss and scampered happily across the balcony and back to the nursery. Once again, Frederic proceeded to feed his wife. This time, the broth was hot and the coffee, heavenly.

"Now," he breathed as she finished the last few drops, surprised by how much she had actually eaten, "it is time you were back in bed, napping. I'll send Rose in to sit with you while I see to myself." When her eyes grew alarmed, he added, "I won't be gone for more than a half hour, and I promise, no pestering from Agatha or Robert today. I told them to stay far away earlier this morning."

"Thank you, Frederic."

He gently drew her out of the wing chair and into his arms. Her frail body was soft and feminine against him, evoking exquisite, scintillating sensations where the two met. For the first time in years, he kissed her as a man kisses a woman, the tender embrace blossoming into passion as his mouth opened hers.

She grabbed hold of him to steady her reeling senses, intoxicated by the power, the smell, the feel, the very essence of him. Slowly, his lips traveled on, across her cheek and to her neck, where he buried his head in her hair and whispered endearments near her ear.

"I love you, Colette. I've always loved you."

Recalling the last time she had heard those words, she turned her face into his shirtfront and whimpered joyfully.

When she was back in bed, she remembered the letter she had written and wondered if she had done the right thing. A voice from within whispered she had. She closed her eyes and fell into a peaceful sleep.

Frederic had barely finished dressing when there came a fervid knocking on his dressing room door. Travis opened it, muttering something about patience. His wife stood there, ashen-faced. "It's Miss Colette—she's ill again!"

Robert Blackford was quickly summoned. Frederic was thankful the man had remained in the house, but he cursed himself for ignoring the physician's advice. Her fever raged anew, and now, she was vomiting with acute stomach cramps. What had happened? He knew: the bath, the food on an empty stomach, and her excursion from the bed.

Blackford attempted to give her a draught of elixir, but she expelled that right away, doubling over in agony. He stood, shook his head in trepidation, and glared contemptuously at Frederic.

Frederic was grateful he didn't say, "I warned you."

Rose took up her post at Colette's bed, mopping her fiery brow with a cool cloth. Agatha demanded Gladys wash the chamber pot, bring fresh linens, and draw cool water.

Frederic threw himself into the nearest armchair and buried his head in his hands. A relapse . . . how many times had she had them over the past year? Many, though none this severe. Still, she had had them. *Why then, did I tempt fate?*

The day drew on, and Colette remained violently ill, coughing and laboring to breathe. She didn't have the strength to sit up and needed help to lean forward when overcome with a wave of nausea. She became delirious, soiled the bed, and slipped in and out of a fitful slumber in which she uttered strange words and names.

Frederic forbade anyone to tell the children, and so, their afternoon passed by happily. But Charmaine began to worry when they took supper alone. No Rose, no Agatha, and no Robert Blackford, though she knew they were all in the house. If only Paul were home . . .

As twilight fell, a calm pervaded the infirm room. Colette's vomiting had subsided. Only the fever remained. Still, the two men and two women kept up their bedside vigil. When the clock tolled nine, Frederic broke the solemnity. "Robert, Agatha, Rose, why don't you three have supper and retire? Colette has been resting for some time now. If I need you, I will send Travis."

They nodded, knowing there was little more anyone could do, except wait and pray. Perhaps this night would be as kind as the last.

"If there is any change whatsoever—if she deteriorates or improves," Robert admonished, "I want to be called immediately. I will not abide any more of these old-fashioned remedies. She is my patient. I'm the one who will see her well again, God willing."

His heart heavy with guilt, Frederic nodded. "As you say, Robert."

When they were alone, he limped to the bed. This morning he'd felt whole; tonight, he was weary, crippled again. "Colette?" he queried softly, the mattress sagging under his weight. "Colette?" he called again, grasping her fiery hand.

She was awake, the glassy gaze now regarding him, revealing she had heard every word. He was shaken by her scrutiny. It was as if she were trying to see into his heart, to know whether the last hours they had spent together had been real. Suddenly, he wanted her to see every fiber of his agony, and his eyes welled.

"I love you, too," she whispered.

He was astounded, and the ache in his breast ruptured. "Oh God, Colette, for so many years I've waited to hear those words. Why now?"

"I thought I hated you," she choked out. "Because of my injured pride, I wanted to hate you . . . I was a fool, Frederic. Later, when I knew, when I longed to tell you, I thought it was too late . . . I thought you despised me." She was crying, too, her eyes swimming with tears. "Frederic, I'm sorry. Can you forgive me?"

She struggled to reach his arm, the fist pressed against mouth, but her hand dropped away. He grabbed hold of it and drew her fingers to his lips. "Only if you can forgive me," he pleaded hoarsely.

"I did that a long time ago."

She yearned for him to hold her again, yet she knew she must broach the subject that could send him away forever. "John," she breathed, bravely forging forward, "he needs your love, even more than I do . . . I'm worried for you both, Frederic. I'm not going to get better. Please promise me—"

"Ssh," he said, placing a finger to her lips. "I love him as much as I love you, Colette. The past is over. Let us look to the future—together."

The hatred of yesterday was gone. Today, love prevailed, and for the first time in her life, she didn't fear tomorrow. Closing her eyes, a great calm washed over her. "Hold me tightly like you did last night," she entreated. "I want your arms around me again."

Frederic doffed his clothing and climbed into the bed. Like the night before, she was burning up with fever and shivered as a wave of cool air wafted beneath the blanket. Quickly, she nestled against him, caressing his chest, savoring the warmth of his body stretched full length next to hers, the strong arms that encircled her. He stroked her hair, her shoulders, her back as he kissed the top of her head again and again. She closed her eyes in unsurpassed happiness. *Is there any better way to leave this world?* she wondered with a prayer of thanksgiving. They fell into a peaceful slumber, one from which Colette never awoke.

Chapter 8

I N a shower of spring brilliance and crystal-blue skies, Colette Duvoisin was laid to rest. As the sun climbed to its zenith, a throng of mourners left the manor's chapel and headed north to the estate's private cemetery, a gnarled, ill-kept plot of land populated with brambles, wild flowers, and stark, jutting headstones that reached heavenward. Here the morbid procession stopped, allowing the pallbearers room to lay down their feather-light burden on the cushioning briars. Then the circle closed around the pine coffin, the mourners drawing solace from one another as they awaited the closing eulogy.

Finality greater than death gripped them, an overwhelming loss that continued to intensify. Yesterday, they had walked in a daze. But today, the firmament illuminated the unfathomable truth, the mortal truth: Colette Duvoisin was dead, and no one—no private prayers, nor dreams of the past—would bring her back. She was gone from them forever, and many weeks would pass before the pain subsided.

The twins were unusually silent, their blue eyes spent of tears, their stoic stance belying the torture Charmaine knew ravaged their hearts. Yesterday, those eyes had not been dry for more than a moment at a time, and poor little Pierre, too young to truly comprehend the finite event, was caught up in their acute remorse, sobbing over their distress. Today, Rose had remained behind with him, maintaining the cemetery was no place for a three-year-old and she would visit it soon enough. But Colette's daughters were determined to join the procession, sitting ramrod straight throughout the entire funeral Mass, standing and following the pallbearers from the chapel without so much as a glance in anyone's direction, their eyes trained on the coffin that held their beloved mother. Charmaine's breast ached for their terrible loss, all the more excruciating in her inability to comfort them.

She remembered Jeannette's innocent query when they received the devastating news. "What happened to our miracle, Mademoiselle Charmaine?"

"I know what happened!" Yvette burst out. "God was only pretending to hear our prayers! I'm never going to pray to Him *or* St. Jude ever again!"

"You don't mean that," Charmaine consoled. "It's your pain talking."

"I do mean it!" she shouted, erupting into tears. "I do!"

Charmaine had searched for words of solace, but they eluded her. She attempted to recall Father Michael Andrews's eulogy at her own mother's funeral, to no avail. Either her grief had been too profound to hear the priest's kind words or his remorse too great to impart them. She embraced Yvette instead and allowed her to cry into her skirts, stroking her hair until she was worn out and heaving. Jeannette wept next, and it was thus they passed that first awful day.

Today, as Charmaine stood on the knoll, memories of her own mother's death besieged her. She relived the suffering of those first few days, her feelings of abject hopelessness. She had been older than the girls, an adult really. Yvette and Jeannette, on the other hand, were so young. How would they endure? Suddenly, Charmaine's prayers changed. She no longer offered them for Colette. The fair woman rested in heaven. Instead, Charmaine prayed for the twin sisters, that the weeks ahead would heal their hearts. Last night, they had cried out in their sleep for her, and that was a good sign. Charmaine would always be there for them, just as she had promised Colette.

As Father Benito St. Giovanni stepped forward, Charmaine surveyed the assembly that numbered nearly a hundred strong. It seemed the entire town, or at least its workers, had traveled the nine-mile distance to pay their final respects. As for those who lived and worked on the Duvoisin estate, only George and his grandmother were absent.

Again she puzzled over the man's whereabouts this past week and remembered Rose's words. "He's attending to an errand for Colette." *What did that mean?* Charmaine thought it wise not to ask. But just yesterday, she'd been privy to the whispered gossip coming from Felicia and Anna. "He's traveled to Virginia." *But why?* The answers would have to await his return.

Charmaine's gaze continued to travel from face to foreign face, alighting on two she recognized: Harold Browning and Wade Remmen. Slowly, warily, her eyes left the arc and settled for one uncomfortable moment upon the two men standing apart from the crowd.

Frederic shunned the large circle of mourners, leaning heavily on his black cane, dismissing the stalwart son who flanked his left side. Like his daughters, his heart was locked away. He had not emerged from his chambers since leaving his wife's deathbed, and Charmaine surmised those quarters would once again become his prison. She was mistaken in believing he'd come to console the children yesterday or this morning, for he refused to even look their way, his eyes trained on his wife's coffin. Charmaine sadly realized his easy dismissal of the girls and Pierre was as much a punishment for himself as it would become for them. Their mutual sorrow and the comfort they could have drawn from one another might have been the start of healing, but such was not to be the case. Why, then, had he labored from chapel to graveyard, this man who wanted to brood alone, who wanted no one to console him, who rarely left his rooms, this effete man whose love of wife Charmaine had often doubted? Why had he taken up his place beside Colette's casket this morning? *Because he loved her . . . just as Colette had loved him.*

As the crowd pressed forward to better hear Father Benito's final benediction, Frederic held his ground, his eyes barren, the polar opposite of Friday, when they had visited Colette on the balcony. Instantly, Charmaine's heart was rent by another devastating thought: Colette's dreadful illness had drawn them together, ending their estrangement. How terribly tragic that love had come too late—that their eleventh hour affection had been laid to waste at the toll of twelve. No wonder Frederic wanted to mourn alone. He was damning the world, damning himself. Charmaine shuddered, though the April sun was quite warm. With growing alarm, she wondered where the mortal event would lead this already embittered man. Instinctively, she knew the days and weeks ahead would be bleak, more so than she had feared at the start of this dreadful day.

Late the next evening, Paul knocked on the nursery door. Charmaine, happy to have a moment alone with him, stepped out into the hallway.

"How are they?" he whispered.

"They're sleeping now, but I don't know for how long."

He studied her face compassionately. "How are you?"

"Better than the girls," she murmured.

"But you've been crying."

"For them. They're devastated, Paul. I don't know who's more upset, the girls or Pierre." Her voice grew raspier. "He doesn't understand why he can't go to see his mother and—"

Paul was not immune to her tears, and his eyes welled in response, but he hid the unmanly display behind the hand he brought to his brow.

"They refuse to eat," she finally continued. "I'm at a loss as to what to do."

"There is nothing you can do, Charmaine. Give them time. They need to be sad for a while."

"Do you think your father would let them visit his chambers?" she asked hopefully. "I think he would be a comfort to them, and they to him."

"No," Paul replied, unsettled by the suggestion. "His grief is too great."

Though dissatisfied with his answer, she didn't press him. She needed to draw strength from someone. "At least you're here for them," she said instead.

He inhaled. "Actually—I have to leave for Espoir at dawn. I spent today getting the business on Charmantes in order, but I'm needed there. Until George returns, I'm extremely pressed. You do understand, don't you?"

"Yes, you're abandoning us again," she blurted out.

"That's a harsh statement," he objected, grimacing inwardly. "The lumber has been delivered, the foundation for the new house laid, and, now, before the rains are upon us, I need to enclose the building. I've hired carpenters and contracted an architect, who can only remain in the Caribbean for a month. Aside from that, the men are awaiting work. I have to be there."

"You're right," she tried to agree. "It will be better for you to keep busy."

Her conciliatory sentiment cut more deeply than her accusatory one, and he found himself torn. "I promise to return by week's end. We can take the children on an outing together, lift their spirits."

"They should like that," she replied, forcing a smile.

"Good. Then it's a date."

The weekend came, but Paul never returned. Word was sent that a "catastrophe" prevented him from leaving Espoir. He'd see them sometime during the following week. It was just as well. The girls were still grieving; they'd never have agreed to go anywhere.

Sunday, April 30, 1837

Colette had been dead for three weeks, and conditions in the manor had not improved, leastwise not where the children were concerned. The "date" Paul had planned weeks ago had finally arrived, but the girls refused to participate, their remarks disdainful.

"If they do not want to go, don't force them," he rejoined curtly, annoyed he'd suspended his grueling schedule specifically to be with them. A confrontation with his father earlier in the morning had set the mood for an aggravating day, and now he wished he hadn't returned at all.

Exasperated, Charmaine decided to leave them to lament. She and Pierre would accompany Paul into town, and as they departed the grounds, the girls might possibly change their minds. They didn't, and only Rose waved goodbye when the landau pulled away, promising to look in on the twins throughout the afternoon.

Unlike his sisters, Pierre was happy, recovered. Innocent of the grave event that had shaken the rest of the house, he showered Charmaine with the love he had once bestowed upon his mother and blew kisses to Nana Rose as he tried to lean farther out the window of the conveyance and shout "bye-bye."

The closed carriage bobbed down the quiet road, but the silence within was not peaceful. Paul stared pensively out the window, his countenance dour.

Charmaine spoke first. "How is your father?"

He snorted, then rubbed the back of his neck. "Not well, I'm afraid. More despondent than my sisters, in fact. I think I made matters worse this morning."

"I don't see how," she commented derisively. "The children haven't seen him since the funeral. They've not only lost their mother, but their father as well."

"I'm afraid you're wrong, Charmaine. Matters *can* grow worse, much worse. My father has vowed to follow Colette to the grave," he whispered, fearful Pierre might understand, "and I'm beside myself as to what to do."

Charmaine shuddered at the thought. "Perhaps he *should* see the children, see what he'd be leaving behind."

"Do you really want to subject them to that, Charmaine?"

Again she shuddered, and the remainder of the ride passed in silence.

Charmaine was uncertain if it was Pierre's exuberance or the bustling town that lightened their moods, but the afternoon turned somewhat pleasant as they strolled along the boardwalks, greeting people they met, mostly Paul's acquaintances. They arrived at the mercantile where Madeline Thompson welcomed them. "My goodness, Pierre, how you've grown in just a month!"

The boy giggled, happily accepting the peppermint stick she offered.

"Where are the girls?"

"I'm afraid they're still in mourning, Maddy," Paul explained.

The woman's eyes filled with tears. "Why don't you take them two sweets as well?" she said, allowing Pierre to choose.

They browsed a bit. Charmaine kept returning to a bolt of yard goods and finally decided to purchase a length of the pretty fabric. "Jeannette has taken quite an interest in sewing, and Yvette may perk up if I suggest she design a frock."

Paul smiled down at her, glad his sisters had Charmaine to fret over them. He refused to allow her to pay, telling Maddy to add the cost of the material to his monthly bill. He insisted she select something for herself, but she dismissed the idea, telling Pierre to choose a toy instead.

Shortly afterward, they left the store. They'd been away from the house for little more than two hours, but when Paul asked, "Where to next?" he knew Charmaine had had enough of the town.

"I really should be getting back to check on the girls."

"You are a wonder, Miss Ryan," he said, white teeth flashing for the first time that day. She looked innocently up at him, and he had the impulse to kiss her right there in the middle of the public thoroughfare. But that would surely inhibit the friendship growing between them, a friendship similar to the one he had shared with Colette. His passionate bend was swept away. He scooped up Pierre instead, and together, they crossed the street.

They had just arrived at the livery when Buck Mathers hailed them down, out of breath. "They need you at the dock, Mr. Paul. There's a big problem."

Paul shook his head in vexation, but Charmaine soothed the situation. "You go ahead. We have a carriage and a driver. We can find our way home."

"I'll be there for dinner," he promised, setting Pierre to the ground.

Charmaine nodded, encouraging the three-year-old to wave as the two men rushed off.

Thursday, May 11, 1837

Charmaine massaged her throbbing temples and collapsed into the armchair. The evening air was silent, but not peacefully so. Not one sniffle wafted on the breeze, though the French doors were open in the adjoining room. The unknowing ear would assume the children slept, but she knew better, certain that two sets of eyes stared dismally into space.

She hadn't meant to speak harshly to them, upsetting little Pierre in the process, but Yvette and Jeannette's depression—their drawn faces—could no longer be borne. They consumed very little food, and the effect was haunting. They'd become miniature replicas of their mother in the days before her death and, from what Charmaine had heard whispered, imitators of their father. Time would heal them, everyone kept insisting, time and limitless love, yet these had yielded little. Even Rose seemed incapable of mitigating their grief.

The blessing of sisterhood was now a liability, and the desolation they read in each other's faces was beginning to affect Pierre, who already cherished memories of his mother. Just tonight, they cruelly chastised him when he innocently called Charmaine "Mama" instead of "Mainie." With bottom lip quivering, he ran to her, crying hysterically as he buried his face in her skirts.

It was the last straw. "This sniveling has gone on long enough!" she struck out, furious. "Look what you've done, making Pierre feel guilty just because he's happy again. *Why?* Do you want to add to your mother's suffering?"

Yvette retaliated with: "Mama isn't suffering anymore—only we are!"

"You think not?" Charmaine countered. "You think she's found peace knowing her children can't be happy without her? How can she even think about heaven when the two of you hold her bound to earth, imprisoned in this very room with your self-pity?"

The plausible words sent Jeannette into tears. "You—you make it sound as if we shouldn't miss her—as if—as if we shouldn't cry for her!"

Charmaine's face softened, yet her voice remained hard. If a dose of severity were efficacious in getting them to talk to her, she'd lace her words with it. "You're not crying for your mother. You're crying for yourselves."

"What's wrong with that?" Yvette demanded.

"Not a thing, had it been a month ago or a few times each day. But you have been crying every hour of every day for too many days now. You're not even trying to accept the Good Lord's decision to take your Mama to paradise with Him. She should be at peace now, not worrying over you. But you've not thought of anyone but yourselves—not your brother, not your father, nor anyone else in this house who grieves as you do. Poor Mrs. Henderson, she's so upset you won't touch the special treats she's prepared just for you, that you're withering away. And Nana Rose, she's known your mama longer than the two of you have, and have you hugged her even once? Or your brother Paul, who took time out of his busy schedule to spend the day with you? You cast aside his attempt to console you and hurt him. I'm ashamed of you! And what of me? Do you realize how difficult it's been for me to watch you like this?"

Charmaine sighed deeply, her voice growing irenic. "I understand your tears, and I know there will be many more over the months to come, *but not like this.* Right now, they've become a terrible burden to all of us. If you really miss your mother, if you truly want to make her happy, you'd best dry those eyes and start living. I'm certain wherever you run, wherever you play, your mother will be watching from heaven. I'm equally certain she'd enjoy seeing you smile a great deal more than she would seeing you cry."

The room fell silent. Surprisingly, neither offered a rebuttal.

Charmaine walked over to Pierre, pleased to find her lecture had lulled him to sleep. She crossed to the doorway and stopped. "You can't bring your mother back with tears," she concluded. "I wish you could, but you can't. She's been dead for over a month now, and during that month, you've ravaged her soul in much the same way her illness ravaged her body. It is time to show her how much you really love her."

Now, minutes later, sitting alone in her bedroom, Charmaine wondered if they had listened or shut her out. Had she been too hard on them? Hurt them? Suddenly, she was angry with herself. Returning to the nursery, she was astonished to find them asleep. Maybe they had heard. Maybe God would answer her prayers this night.

Wednesday, May 17, 1837

Disgusted, Agatha Ward lifted the untouched tray of food and left the master's quarters. Frederic refused to eat, deciding two weeks ago this was the easiest way to follow his wife to the grave. He had not wavered from his insane plan. Nor had he budged from the chair that faced Colette's bedchamber, as if she still lay on the other side of the connecting portal.

Starvation was an ugly thing, but Agatha would not allow him that final triumph. She'd arrest the situation before it was too late. To that end, she swiftly stepped in for Travis Thornfield, horrified to learn ten days had lapsed. The manservant, beside himself with worry, was only too happy to allow her to take charge.

That had been three days ago, three days of ineffectual empathizing, coaxing, reasoning, entreating, and finally, ranting. Agatha's thoughts raced to Paul, wishing him home. But even if the younger man were here, what could he do that she hadn't already tried? Nothing.

Frederic, refusing everything but water, was a wretched sight to behold, with a full fortnight's beard, disheveled hair, gaunt cheeks, and crazed eyes. His tailored clothing hung limp from his emaciated body. But his weakness was deceptive: cross the line, challenge his suicidal crusade, and his despondency evaporated like a drop of water in a scorching desert, replaced by a rabid fury that shook even his stalwart sister-in-law.

Tonight, Agatha would not be shaken or deterred. Tonight she would win this unholy war. She looked down at the tray once more, then back at the closed door. If Frederic wanted to dwell on his dead wife, she would make him think again. The time had come to remind him exactly what type of woman Colette had been—to make him reconsider his misplaced affections. A drastic measure, perhaps, but dire circumstances called for merciless intervention.

Robert Blackford hastened to the Duvoisin estate and waited patiently in the drawing room as Travis went in search of his sister. He didn't need to be told why he'd been urgently summoned at so late an hour, though Agatha's swiftly penned note painted a gruesome picture. He'd heard of Frederic's "grief" from any number of patients throughout the week; the entire island loved gossip, especially Duvoisin gossip. Apparently, Frederic was not adjusting to his wife's demise.

If the rumors were as bad as they sounded, present conditions threatened to eclipse those of the distant past. He chuckled with the irony of it. Even the players were the same, save the wives. A score and eight years ago, that role had been played by his younger sister, Elizabeth. Her death had shaken the great Frederic

Duvoisin's sanity as surely as Colette's death shook it now. There
had also been a child involved, an infant—John. Robert shuddered with the memory, and even today, wondered how Frederic
had survived intact. He remembered fearing for his own life;
Frederic had held him responsible for Elizabeth's death. But then,
Robert blamed himself as well. True, the baby had been breech, a
dangerous delivery at best, but he had needed her to live, his own
happiness contingent upon her recovery. Yet, she slipped into unconsciousness and never awoke, and Frederic had never forgiven
him.

But Elizabeth was not the problem this night, Colette was: A
new time, a new event, and for all the mirrored circumstances, a
new pain. There was Frederic's age to consider, as well. He was no
longer a man of thirty-three, in the prime of life. He was over sixty
and badly beaten by a harsh world. He was also intent upon giving
up, bolstering the probability of success. Though the outcome
should have pleased Robert, bringing the long and winding road to
an end, he feared Frederic's death would destroy Agatha. This
compelled him to intercede. For his twin sister, he would put a
stop to the man's self-destruction.

At the sound of the drawing room door opening, he pivoted
around, placing under lock and key the painful decision he had
just made. "Miss Ryan," he acknowledged in surprise, having expected a servant or his sister.

"Dr. Blackford," she nodded, equally surprised. She had not
seen the man since Colette's death and wondered why he was here
now.

"I suppose the children are abed?" he asked.

"Well over an hour ago," Charmaine answered. "It's quite
late."

"So it is," he said, checking his pocket watch. He snapped it
shut, replaced it, then considered her speculatively. Agatha held

the girl both inadequate and insubordinate. Still, Robert wondered what information he might garner if he drew her out. "How *are* the children?"

Stunned, Charmaine canted her head. The man had never conversed with her before. "Better," she replied cautiously. "They've accepted their mother's passing, but as for their grief, it remains. They have not forgotten her."

"Nor should they. Nevertheless, you are to be congratulated on seeing them through this terrible time," he praised. "Agatha tells me you have worked wonders. If only I could be that effective when meeting with their father tonight."

Charmaine didn't require an explanation. Frederic had not emerged from his impenetrable quarters since Colette's death, and the rumor he was starving himself had taken root. Thankfully, Jeannette had stopped asking to visit him. Charmaine didn't want the children exposed to that horror.

Agatha arrived and whisked Robert away. Feeling lonely, Charmaine rummaged through the music drawer and found the piece she was seeking. It was perfect for this night: why not a haunting melody to release the ghosts that trampled her soul? She propped the pages on the piano stand, arranged her skirts, and let her fingers sing.

Frederic remained slumped in the high-backed armchair, contemplating death and the ease with which it evaded him. A knock at the door, and his listlessness gave way to ire. Damn them! When would they accept his decision to die? Was he not master of this house? Why, then, was everyone hell-bent on stopping him? He *would* follow Colette into the next world, and those of this world be damned if they didn't like it!

He ignored the second rap, the third, and the fourth. But the persistent intruders would not retreat. After the fifth knock, they entered without permission. Now, sister and brother hovered nearby, assessing him as if he were not present. Robert stepped closer still, abruptly gripping the arms of his chair. He leaned over and looked him square in the face, willing his hooded eyes to lift in acknowledgment. "Frederic?" he demanded.

Frederic remained impassive, affording not the slightest indication he'd heard or was aware of the "visitors" who had come to converse with him.

Blackford straightened up and faced his sister, hands on hips.

"Didn't I tell you?" Agatha whispered as if she knew he was listening, yet not hushed enough to be inaudible. "He has been like this for the better part of two weeks—since Paul left for Espoir."

"And this will come to an end," Blackford snarled. "Frederic—look at me!"

Frederic tilted his head back and shot him a piercing glare.

The raw condemnation shook Robert. "That's better," he muttered, nervously adjusting his waistcoat. He dragged a chair even with Frederic, sat, and forced himself to meet the enraged gaze levelly. With Agatha standing behind him, he could do this. "It is time we talked," he began. "Colette is dead, and nothing can change that. You, on the other hand, are very much alive. This lunacy stops tonight."

The declaration elicited no reply, and though the eyes remained stormy, Robert began doubting the man's coherency. "Frederic—are you listening to me?" he pressed. "Do you understand what I'm telling you? You cannot go on like this! Surely you don't intend to meet such an end?" Still no response, just the branding eyes. "I tell you, I won't permit it," he threatened. "Even if I have to order you held down and force fed! *Do you hear me?*"

"The good doctor, come to save my life," Frederic remarked, his deep voice raspy, as if he worked hard at speaking. But for all his difficulty, the chilling statement was not lost on brother and sister, who were taken aback.

"Yes," Blackford reaffirmed as he squirmed in his chair, "if need be."

Frederic grunted. "I desire death, and you, *dear friend*, come to interfere?"

The query was a slap in the face. "You don't know what you are about!" Robert railed, reflecting on the countless services he had performed for this man for the better part of thirty years. "You are mad if you think the afterlife is going to reward you with what you desire!"

"*What I desire?*" Frederic thundered. "*What I desire?* I'll tell you what I desire. I desire what you've taken from me! Not once, but twice!"

Blackford bristled. The man *did* blame him! "I've taken nothing from you," he answered softly.

"Haven't you?" Frederic sneered through parched lips. "Elizabeth wasn't enough—"

"There was nothing I could do!" Blackford expostulated, losing his composure. "John's was a breech birth and he—he alone stole Elizabeth's life. I thought you comprehended the severity of that delivery!"

Frederic's eyes grew baleful. "Leave me alone. I don't want to hear your excuses. I accepted them once, but never again." He bowed his throbbing head and grumbled, "You cannot explain away Colette's death so easily."

"I will not be blamed again for a situation beyond my control!"

Frederic's head snapped up. "*Beyond your control, man?* She was under your constant care for nearly a year! How, in God's name, did the situation get beyond your control? And don't talk to me about this fancy condition you call 'pneumonia'! If it was as deadly as you knew it to be, it should have been arrested in its infancy. You were by her bedside for weeks! So tell me, *Doctor*—how can you stand there and maintain the situation was 'beyond your control'?"

"Because it was," Robert bit out malignantly. "Colette did not die of pneumonia, though it contributed to her weakness. I told you years ago: No more children. Delivering twins was too much for her. But did you listen? No, you pressed yourself upon her, and she found herself carrying Pierre."

Frederic's jaw grew rigid, but Robert callously continued. "Again, another strain, yet you were lucky, and she survived. But she did not recover unscathed. Last spring, you almost lost her; the most minor illness can easily take hold. And that is exactly what happened with the pneumonia. But there's more, Frederic. Not one week after she contracted that infirmity, she suffered a miscarriage."

Frederic inhaled sharply, and Robert fed on the man's horrified expression, his courage suddenly limitless. "That's right—a miscarriage. Her weakened constitution made it impossible to carry the baby to term, and for days, I was unable to stem the bleeding. That bath was the worst thing for her. I warned her. She knew the risks."

Then the shock was gone, supplanted by a demonic rage that brought Frederic up and out of his chair like a man possessed.

Robert did not cower or gloat, his gaunt visage merely compassionate now.

Frederic halted in his tracks, revolted by the man's show of pity. "You realize what you are insinuating?"

"I realize what I have withheld from you," Blackford answered flatly.

"By God, why?" he exploded, swiping a nearby table clean with his cane. The childish tantrum only incensed him further. "Why was this information withheld? *Why?*"

Robert came to his own feet, feeling at a disadvantage while the fulminating man towered above him. "I knew the child could not be yours," he admitted freely, "and in Colette's best interest, I did as she requested. I held silent."

Frederic felt a wave of nausea rising in the back of his throat. He swallowed it, focusing instead on the questions he must ask. "And after her death? Why didn't you tell me then?"

"I feared for *your* well-being. What good would it do, except to put you through the turmoil you now suffer? I had hoped to spare you that."

"When—when did she conceive?"

"Before Christmastide—perhaps November," Blackford answered coolly, "judging by the baby's size."

Frederic glared at him—Agatha next—but found nothing in their faces to refute the brand of infidelity. "Get out," he snarled.

Robert faltered, his sorrowful eyes questioning the edict.

"You heard me, man! The two of you—out! I won't be deterred by a lie!"

Agatha stepped forward beseechingly. "Frederic, you are torturing yourself, but this will never do. You have three children to consider. They need you. Colette . . ." she paused, carefully choosing her words ". . . was not Elizabeth. Yes, I know what you saw in her, the many similarities. I saw them, too!" She breathed deeply, reading Frederic's surprise, pleased to know she was getting somewhere. "Naturally you were attracted to her. You thought of Colette as your second chance. But she was not Elizabeth! Elizabeth was a good and decent wife, a faithful wife. *Elizabeth* loved you. But Colette, she never loved you as—"

"I've heard enough! I've made my decision—will see it to its end."

Robert shook his head. "Very well, Frederic. Think what you will. Believe we are mendacious villains. But while you sit in your chair and contemplate what I've told you, remember that in discrediting me, you've danced to the tune Colette has piped. Not many a man would mourn a woman who has cuckolded him in his own home, under his very nose."

"Get out!" Frederic hissed, spitting venom at the man who had completely overstepped his bounds. "Get out, or I'll have you thrown out!"

Robert relented and, with his sister close behind, left the tortured man. Frederic would have to make up his own mind.

Frederic had been alone for all of five minutes, yet that short space of time was an eternity, an eternity to ponder one word: betrayal. He'd been betrayed, not once, but again and again! This last time, the worst of all! How had she lain in his arms those last two nights of her life, pretending at love, uttering precious words that were nothing more than another lie? How he would love to hold her again, for he'd take great pleasure in squeezing that life from her with his bare hands! Yes, he wanted to murder, longed for its satisfying, bittersweet taste.

He had mourned her for weeks, cursed himself for the hell he had created for the two of them. Now he laughed with the ironic insanity of it! He was the only one who had suffered, while she surreptitiously crept from her rooms in the middle of the night and into the arms of another. He'd been a fool—even in that last month, when he had been beside himself with worry. He remembered the night he'd gone to check on her. She wasn't resting as Blackford had ordered, and she wasn't with the children! Again the cane slammed down on the table. *Who was her lover?*

How she must be laughing! She had slyly made him feel guilty. Well, no more! She had been the root of his misery for nearly ten long years—a whore today, a whore since the day they'd met, and all those days in between! Agatha was right: he'd hoped to replace

Elizabeth with a snip of a girl who stirred sweet memories. But she was not Elizabeth! She was a conniving, highborn slut, who had nearly destroyed his family.

Bile rose in his throat again, and as he spewed the caustic acid into the chamber pot, he hated more fiercely than ever before.

No one answered the bellpull. With clenched jaw, he forfeited a third yank and savagely pulled open the hallway door. He limped from his prison, surprised when the foyer clock tolled ten. But the late hour did not deter him, and he nearly toppled Millie Thornfield as he reached the staircase.

The maid stifled a shriek, a hand flying to her mouth. "May I help you, sir?"

"Where is your father?" he demanded, leaning heavily on his cane, bone weary and irked by the girl's gawking.

Millie hesitated, shaken by the master's maniacal eyes. She didn't know her father's whereabouts, but didn't dare say so. "I'll— I'll find him, sir."

"When you do, have him summon Benito Giovanni to the house. Immediately!"

"Father Benito?"

"You heard me, girl! Now be about it! You are dallying!"

She bobbed before him, then raced down the stairs. But just when she thought she was safe, his voice halted her. Looking up, she awaited a possible countermand. But he stood deathly still, head cocked to one side, eyes staring into space as he registered the strains of the melody that carried from the drawing room. "Sir?" she incautiously interrupted. "Was there something else?"

"Where is that music coming from?"

"From the front parlor, sir. Miss Ryan has been practicing that piece all evening, sir."

"Well, tell her to stop practicing it! Tell her to destroy it!"

"Sir?" Millie queried in renewed consternation.

"Tell her I forbid her to play it. Tell her, if I hear so much as one note of that particular piece again, she will be dismissed. Go! Tell her!"

He is mad! Millie chanced one last look at the man. In a flurry of skirts, she scrambled down the remaining stairs and fled the foyer. Moments later, the haunting melody ceased and silence blanketed the great house.

Father Benito St. Giovanni was rudely awoken at the ungodly hour of eleven. The pummeling of a fist on his cabin door brought him up and out of bed. In less than an hour, the priest, who owed his life to both John and Paul Duvoisin, stood before their notorious father. Aware of Frederic's suicidal fast, he had expected to find the man near death. Not so. Why, then, had he been summoned? Frederic's stormy eyes cued him the reason was not pleasant. Thus, he bowed his head slightly and waited.

"Now, Father," the patriarch of Charmantes began, taking a long draw off a tall glass of brandy, relishing the fiery path it blazed down his throat. It hadn't dulled his senses or eased his anguish. So much the better; it fueled his wrath and kept him focused. "I want a name, and I want it now."

Benito frowned slightly, but wisely held his tongue, forcing the tormented man to expound.

Frederic leaned back in his chair, bemused by the padre's charade of ignorance. The initial query had been spoken levelly. Obviously, Giovanni thought he had nothing to fear. Well, he'd soon find out how mistaken he was. If this man of the cloth needed further explanation, Frederic would oblige him. "Come, Father, there's no need to pretend you don't know why you're here. Surely you knew I'd find out?" Frederic chuckled wryly.

The priest's gaze remained fixed on the floor, and Frederic began to enjoy his discomfiture. "Now," and he paused for effect, taking another swig. "I know my wife received the Last Rites at your hands. Therefore, I'm certain you hold the information I seek." His voice turned sharp and deadly. "I want the name of the man who fathered the bastard child she was carrying!"

Benito closed his eyes and digested the unexpected, searing revelation. *Where did Frederic obtain this information? What am I to say to him?* He held silent, fighting his pounding heart and channeling his racing thoughts.

"*Well?*" Frederic demanded, his patience spent. The game was up. Time to have it out! "Don't deny having the name. I knew my wife too well. For all her adultery, I'm certain she'd confess every mortal sin if she knew she was dying. And she knew. Now, I was here when you were called to her bedside. I know you absolved her of her sins—all of them. Again, I want the name of my wife's lover, and if you know what is good for you, you will tell me quickly. I promise he will wish he had never been born, and not you, nor anyone else on this goddamned island, will deny me the satisfaction of confronting him!"

The priest paled, certain no matter how he answered, his position on Charmantes was in jeopardy. Somehow, he must appease the man. He raised his head and responded with compassion. "Sadly, you believe the worst about your deceased wife. However, what she did or did not reveal to me under the Sacrament of Extreme Unction will never leave my lips. You know I am sworn to silence. You cannot ask me to break my sacred vow."

"Damn it, man! I will have his name, and he will pay!"

"No, Frederic," the priest countered placidly. "Even if she confessed this sin, she needn't have spoken a name to receive absolution."

Frederic sat stunned. Either Giovanni was smarter than he thought, or he spoke the truth. "You lie. She named her lover. I can see it in your eyes."

"Whoever he is, God forgive him," Benito rejoined, noting the man's waning vehemence. "Forget this libertine and bury the past, Frederic. Murder is a far greater offense than adultery. Your wife is dead and her sins forgiven. Why contaminate your own soul with thoughts of retribution?"

"Get out, old man!" Frederic ordered. "You are no better than Robert and Agatha—laying all blame on Colette. Yes, I would love to confront her face-to-face and reward her for her unfaithfulness, but she is gone. However, there is another here on Charmantes, alive and well. I tell you now: he will suffer for his venery. Before I leave this world—he *will* suffer!"

Sunday, May 21, 1837

Frederic sat on Pierre's bed awaiting the return of his children and their governess from Mass. He was more presentable than last week this time. Even so, he was extremely thin, not having regained his appetite.

Charmaine was humming as she swept into the room behind Pierre. She hoped to see Paul today, but her eyes widened when Pierre shouted, "Papa!" and Jeannette rushed past her. "Papa, you're here!" She hugged him fiercely. "I'm so glad you've come to visit us! We missed you!"

"Me, too!" Pierre giggled. "Where were you?"

The man swallowed hard, suddenly realizing how foolish he had been. How could he have thought to abandon this world—that his son was better equipped to take his place? He regarded Yvette, who stood ramrod straight, so much like Colette. "I've been mourning the death of your mother," he said softly, "but that is over now. It is time to move on."

"That's what Mademoiselle Charmaine told us," Yvette said, pleased with his explanation. She embraced him, too. "You loved Mama, didn't you?"

"Yes," he whispered.

Charmaine was not so forgiving. No matter how great his suffering, Frederic had selfishly added to his children's terrible ordeal. Unable to set aside her condemnation, she started toward her bedchamber. "I shall leave you alone."

He must have read her thoughts. "Miss Ryan, stay," he petitioned. "I want to apologize to you, as well as to my children. I'm sorry I wasn't here for them over the past few weeks. I'm also sorry it fell to you to comfort them."

What could she say? It served no purpose to remain angry. "I am glad you've recovered, sir," she offered. "The children were worried about you. Even I was worried about you."

"Worried?"

Agatha stood at the nursery door, her haughty inquiry hanging in the air.

Charmaine grimaced. The dowager had taken great pleasure in berating her over the past six weeks. With Colette gone and Paul away most of the time, no one was there to curb her.

"I was merely commenting on the children's happiness to see their father again," Charmaine attempted to explain.

"Really? It sounded to me as if you were speaking of your own happiness."

"Agatha," Frederic interceded, "I am spending some time with my children. You wouldn't infringe on that, would you?"

"Certainly not, Frederic," she replied with a striking smile, departing as quietly as she had come.

Later that evening, she visited Frederic in his apartments. It was time to make her ardent dream a reality—now—before another young woman, and the governess no less, stepped in. He desperately needed comforting, was famished for a woman's love. Tonight, he'd forget those other two who pretended at love just to enjoy his fortune.

Wednesday, June 14, 1837

"Are you mad?" Paul expostulated in disbelief. "You *are* mad, that is the only explanation for this lunacy!"

The day had been all but pleasant. First, he'd been forced to return to the main island midweek due to a shipping mix-up that threatened to delay the next stage of development on Espoir. No sooner had he set foot on Charmantes than a score of other crises erupted, each one more pressing than the one before. Without George there, his troubles continued to multiply. He snorted when he numbered the weeks his *friend* had been gone—over ten to date—and it greatly irritated him. How long did it take to travel to Richmond and back again? Was George on holiday now? Unfortunately, there was nothing he could do about it. However, the last thing he needed, the last thing he expected to be embroiled in at the end of this deplorable day was this absurd conversation with his father, whose sudden silence could have been mistaken for deep reflection had his visage been pensive. But the man's eyes were stormy, his jaw set behind grinding teeth. Frustrated, Paul took to pacing, no closer to understanding the workings of his parent's mind, his polar loyalty.

In the months before Christmas, Paul would have sworn that only mistrust and anger existed between Colette and his sire. Then, after his return from Europe, he'd witnessed a myriad of astonishing emotions: ostensible despair when Colette had hovered near death, relief and happiness when it seemed she'd overcome her malady, and, finally, incomprehensible grief when her shaky recovery had ended tragically. After the third week of mourning, Colette's words, spoken in the gardens, haunted him: "He loved me once . . . did you know that? He loved me once." Had that love never died? Possibly. Nevertheless, Paul could not dismiss the distant past, and remained uncertain. Yet today, as he walked the streets of Charmantes, he heard the gossip: *Yes, he's on the mend . . . He's given up the fast . . . of course he still loves her, but he's thinking of the children now . . .*

Paul recalled the suicidal scheme his father had initiated in early May. When he arrived home, Rose confirmed the aborted effort. Though relieved to hear it was over, he was ashamed he'd been absent for it all, annoyed no one had sent word to Espoir. Today he was convinced his sire had loved Colette, even into the grave, and for the first time, Paul comprehended why the man had been so embittered for all those years. It wasn't just hate, it was heartbreak. He had it all figured out.

But no, just moments ago, his father had changed course again, annihilating those logical deductions. Now Colette was to be "forgotten." That was the word he'd used. Aside from the children, no one nearest him was to even speak of her: no reminders of her in his room, no artifact that would spoil the pristine world from which she had been purged.

Fine! He could tolerate that, humor his parent, pretend Colette no longer existed. But this other thing? Never! He would never condone this day's nonsense! And he'd be damned if he'd allow the revolting idea to be kindled. He would snuff it out before it flared out of control.

"I tell you again, you are mad! And I won't allow it!"

"Allow it?" Frederic returned. "I'm the father, or have you forgotten?"

Paul flung himself into a chair. "No, I haven't forgotten," he mumbled.

"Good. Then I can count on you to make all the arrangements?"

"No," Paul answered tightly, his eyes every bit as turbulent as his father's. "I'll play no part in it."

Frederic cocked his head to one side, attempting to read his son's mind, unprepared for *this* reaction, erupting before he had a chance to explain. "Why are you so opposed to this?" he asked. "What does it matter to you?"

"It matters because it is a grave mistake you will live to regret. Have you no regard for Colette? Yes"—he bit out—"I dare to speak her name! She has been dead for two months. Two months! Not even the lowest wife would be set aside so quickly. But Colette was not lowly. She was good and kind, fair inside and out. And no, don't you dare argue that point!" He held up a hand. "For all your condemnation, for all your accusations, you know my words are true."

"I know no such thing!"

"The hell you don't!" Paul exploded. "She made a mistake, one terrible mistake you crucify her for over and over again! Can't you see the forest for the trees? How can you judge Colette so severely and not see Agatha for what *she* is! To mention them in the same breath is abhorrent!"

"Do not speak of her so. She is to become my wife."

"Haven't you heard a single word I've said?" Paul shouted. "You cannot wed this woman! You cannot!"

"She will make me forget," Frederic answered tightly, straying far from the issue now. "I need to forget."

"She'll make you *wish* to forget! Nothing more. If you think you knew what hell was married to Colette—if you think you know what it is now—just wait!"

"That's enough!" Frederic snarled, further perplexed by his son's outburst; yet Paul's fierce opposition cemented his resolve to make Agatha Blackford Ward his third wife. "I do not expect you to see it my way. Not now, anyway. But all of this is done for a good reason, a reason I ask you to respect."

"Reason?" Paul choked out, far from appeased. "I see no reason. You haven't spoken of anything remotely linked to reason."

"Isn't it enough that I say it exists? Would you strip me of all pride by suggesting I'm incapable of making my own decisions?"

Paul faltered; he'd overstepped his bounds. "As you say, it is your decision to make," he capitulated. "But, be warned, Father, my sentiments will not change. And I will never, *never* acknowledge Agatha as my stepmother."

"I don't expect you to," Frederic grumbled, suddenly ambivalent in his noble intentions.

Saturday, July 1, 1837

Not three months after Colette's death, Frederic took Agatha Blackford Ward for his third wife. The couple ventured to the mansion's stone chapel early one Saturday morning for the private ceremony. Without the knowledge of family and friends, Benito St. Giovanni blessed the peculiar marriage in the presence of only two witnesses: Paul and the island's doctor. Robert Blackford became Frederic's brother-in-law for a second time.

If Frederic had hoped to receive a more favorable response from his younger children, he was disappointed. As he left Agatha and entered the nursery to tell them of his marriage, he was greeted by Yvette's stormy face. "Is it true?" she demanded, pushing past Charmaine. "Tell me it's not true?"

"Is what true?" Frederic asked in surprise.

"Joseph's father told him you were marrying Mrs. Ward today. It's not true, is it? He was lying. Please tell me he was lying, Father!"

Frederic experienced an overwhelming pang of regret. "It *is* true," he answered curtly. "Agatha and I were married a short while ago."

Charmaine's stomach plummeted. In a panic, she grabbed hold of a bedpost, distantly aware of Pierre hugging her legs.

Yvette's belligerent cry, "See, Mademoiselle Charmaine!" ricocheted off the walls. "I told you it was true! Joseph never lies to me."

Jeannette burst into tears. "But, Father, why? Why would you marry *her*?"

When he did not explain, Yvette berated him fiercely. "If you had to remarry, why didn't you pick Mademoiselle Charmaine?"

Charmaine was aghast, and she found Frederic assessing her as if he were weighing his daughter's words. *Where did Yvette come up with her ideas?*

The man took the comment in stride, a lopsided smile tugging at the corner of his mouth. "Is that why you are upset? You'd rather Mademoiselle Charmaine replace your mother?"

"I didn't say that!" Yvette scolded, annoyed her father had misunderstood. "No one can replace Mama. You should know that! You told me you loved her. Were you lying? Mama was good and kind and beautiful. How could you marry someone who is bad and mean and ugly? Now we have a stepmother worse than any we've ever read about in fairytale books!"

Frederic's eyes narrowed. "Enough, young lady! Agatha *is* your stepmother now, and as such, you will respect her." He indicated Charmaine menacingly. "And your governess will see to it that you do."

Charmaine's moment of sympathy vanished, but she bit her tongue, willing herself not to side with the twin. "Sir," she said instead, "Yvette is only speaking from her grief. She misses her mother. Surely you can understand that."

"It does not give her the right to grow ill mannered," he returned stiffly. "I'll not abide insults directed at my new wife. Is that understood?"

"Yes, sir," Charmaine answered meekly, her position precarious.

Perhaps the children sensed her dilemma, for they, too, fell mute.

Yvette's eyes welled with tears, and she blinked them away.

The unusual sight shook Frederic more than her ire had, but there was no turning back. Certain it was best to guard a harsh resolve, he bade them good day.

"You must not anger your father," Charmaine cautioned once they were alone. "There is nothing you can do to change the situation, and insulting your new stepmother will make matters worse."

Thankfully, the girl and her sister nodded.

"Remember," she continued, forcing a smile, "I'll always love you." She hugged them, determined to overcome this newest impediment to their recovery.

Later, Charmaine wondered over Frederic's decision to remarry so soon after his second wife's demise. How could he dismiss Colette so quickly, set her from his heart with so little respect? Why had he attempted to end his own life, if his love had not been intense and consuming? What did it all mean? Perhaps Agatha charmed him in his grief. If nothing else, she *had* helped save his life. Charmaine concluded that Frederic had never seen Agatha's cruel side, and had not the slightest idea of the repulsive conditions to which his children would be subjected.

Agatha inhaled deeply, enjoying the salty scent of the ocean air, sighing as she retreated to her sitting room. "That will be all, Gladys. I shall ring for you in the morning."

Gladys, who had just finished removing Colette's clothing, bobbed and left.

Agatha moved to the jewelry chest atop the dressing table. She lifted the lid and smiled down at the many gems sparkling within the velvet-lined box. She had stopped Gladys before they, too, were taken away, stored until the day the twins were old enough to wear them. She smiled when she found Elizabeth's valuables amongst Colette's. If the second wife could enjoy the first wife's jewels, then so would the third. Of course, she knew why Frederic had allowed Colette to touch his *precious* Elizabeth's possessions. He thought of the two women as one and the same. Agatha dismissed the disturbing thought. Today was too wonderful to dwell on the past. The painful journey was over, and finally, the future belonged to her. She closed the chest and moved about the chamber, arranging things more to her liking.

When Frederic entered, she gave him a dazzling smile. He limped over to her, as handsome as he'd been this morning, as handsome as ever.

He caressed her cheek. "Happy?" he queried softly.

Her eyes filled with tears. "Very happy," she whispered. "I've loved you Frederic . . . for so very long."

He nodded soberly. "I know. Perhaps we *are* destined to be together."

"Perhaps? No, Frederic," she insisted, "there is no 'perhaps' on this glorious day. I *shall* make you happy, and the sadness of the past will remain there."

"For my children's sake, I hope you are right. It seems I'm regarded as the sinister patriarch, and I am weary of it."

Agatha laughed. "Sinister, Frederic? Never! But then, no one understands you the way I do." She stroked his chest, her eyes clouded with passion. "Come," she whispered, pulling him into his chambers and the bed that awaited them.

Sunday, July 2, 1837

On Sunday, Paul joined Charmaine and the children for Mass. As she smiled up at him, she was rewarded with a wink that set her heart to racing. She wondered how long he'd remain on Charmantes, but didn't ask, deciding to enjoy the splendid moment while it lasted.

It didn't. At the close of the service, Agatha intercepted the house staff at the chapel door, and Paul rushed off. She instructed them to reconvene in the great hall in one hour's time.

"I will be assigning additional duties to each of you," she stated obtrusively. The underlying message was inauspicious, and Charmaine fretted over the lecture that awaited them. "That will be all," she concluded, turning her attention to Father Benito, who had requested a minute of her time.

Charmaine gathered the children together, stifling a smile when it became apparent Agatha was annoyed at the priest.

"I don't see why I should have to donate anything," she hissed.

"Mrs. Duvoisin," Benito replied pointedly, "you agreed to abandon your heretical ties to the Church of England on the day of your marriage—agreed to convert to Catholicism. Presently your duties as mistress extend far beyond this grand manor. Charmantes awaits you. As the wife of its benefactor, altruistic obligations fall to you. Surely you were aware of that." Agatha glowered at him, but the priest smiled benevolently. "Miss Colette was extremely charitable, until she fell so violently ill."

Charmaine followed the children through the ballroom, Agatha's voice receding behind her. *So, the new Mrs. Duvoisin is about to find a life of luxury comes with a price.* Hopefully, the priest's philanthropic work proved long and arduous.

An hour later, she returned to the banquet hall and withstood Agatha Duvoisin's dictatorial oration. In less than five minutes, the new mistress revoked any shred of freedom the staff had previously enjoyed. Charmaine watched as Mrs. Faraday left in a huff, followed by a fiery Fatima Henderson and a downtrodden Gladys Thornfield. Felicia and Anna skulked away, permitting Charmaine a moment of vicarious pleasure as she imagined them working for their wages. With that happy thought, she headed for the foyer, certain Rose would be glad when she returned.

"Miss Ryan, you seem amused."

Charmaine abandoned her reverie. "Pardon me?"

"I was wondering if you found my instructions amusing?" Agatha inquired stiffly. "You seem quite pleased with yourself."

"No, ma'am," Charmaine replied, her smile wiped clean.

"Good. I would like to speak with you privately in the study. The comfortable position you've held in this house is in need of a review."

"Review?" Charmaine asked with growing dread.

"We shall discuss it later, at four o'clock. And Miss Ryan—do be prompt."

Charmaine was left quaking; this private meeting portended trouble, and even Rose could not convince her otherwise. She remembered Frederic's threatening words of just the morning before. If she didn't tread carefully, she would be sent packing. Sadly, she realized she would sustain as great a heartache as the children if she were dismissed; she loved them so.

At three-thirty, Charmaine once again left them with Rose. She'd be more than punctual, limiting the ammunition Agatha might use against her.

Of late, nothing was going Paul's way. He crossed the emerald lawn with an agitated gait, took the stone steps of the portico in two strides, and stormed the manor's double doors. He slapped a brown folder against his left thigh, the rhythm working his revolving thoughts into a frothing frenzy, until he found himself contemplating the circle's inception once again: his father's mismatched marriage, his ponderous schedule between Charmantes and Espoir, George's prolonged absence, the new manor's halted construction, and lastly, the circle's end—the sorest point of all—his brother, John, and the missing shipping invoices that were not with the other, unimportant, papers he held in his hand.

"Why does he do this to me?" he seethed aloud, the habit of talking to himself most prevalent when John provoked him. "I know why," he ground out, barging into the study and slamming the door shut with such force the glass rattled in the French doors across the room. "He knows it will foster havoc on Charmantes and I will have to deal with it! I bet he's been snickering for months just thinking about it."

He reached the desk in another five strides, flinging the folder atop the other papers lying there, its contents spilling out. The childish act yielded momentary gratification; he swung around to find Charmaine staring at him wide-eyed from the high-backed chair. "How long have you been sitting there?" he demanded, his temper spiking as he realized what she had witnessed. "Well? Answer me!"

"A long time, sir," she replied docilely, fueling his feeling of foolishness.

Instantly, his anger was gone, and he closed his eyes and rubbed his brow. *Sir . . . she's calling me sir again.* "I'm sorry, Charmaine. I didn't mean to snap at you like that. I've been plagued with countless worries, and I'm at my wit's end."

"I guess we're in the same predicament," she replied.

He heard the apprehension in her voice. "Is something amiss?"

Is something amiss? she thought. *Surely he jests!* But how would he know of the troubles facing the entire Duvoisin staff, and her in particular? "There will be many changes in the house within the next few days," she said, dropping her eyes to the hands in her lap. "Some of them frighten me."

"What changes could possibly frighten you?"

"I'm to have a private meeting with Mrs. Duvoisin in a few minutes."

Agatha . . . his stepmother . . . the new Mrs. Duvoisin . . . Suddenly, he was rankled by more than the title she bore. He didn't need an explanation to deduce the woman's motives, nor the distasteful outcome she would attempt to script.

He immediately summoned Travis Thornfield and dispatched a message. The manservant was to inform the new mistress her meeting with the governess had been canceled. "If she complains," Paul concluded, "refer her to me. Miss Ryan is firmly established in this house. There is no pertinent reason to interrupt her strict schedule. That will be all, Travis."

The butler departed, wearing an uncommon smile.

Charmaine was astonished. Once again, Paul stood beside her. When was she going to realize she had nothing to fear from him? *Perhaps today,* her heart whispered, the thought leaving her giddy. *Is it possible he's grown more handsome in the past moments?* She had her answer as he casually walked across the room and towered over her, her heart beating wildly in her chest.

"There," he said with a wicked smile, teeth flashing below his moustache. "She'll not be pleased, but she'll think twice before threatening your position again."

Charmaine was not so certain, though she was grateful for his efforts. "I don't know . . ."

"Charmaine," he chided lightly, sitting in the chair adjacent to hers. He leaned forward and cradled her hand. "You needn't fear Agatha. Though she's determined to prove herself mistress of the manor, I have my father's support in this matter. He'll not dismiss you, no matter her vehemence."

"Thank you, Paul," she said in a small voice. His warm hand made breathing difficult, and she found it equally difficult to concentrate. "You have lifted a heavy burden. I don't know what I'd tell the children if I were forced to leave. I've become quite attached to them."

His smile turned warm. "I know you have, Charmaine, and they feel the same way about you. My father knows that."

"I hope he does. After yesterday, I'm not so certain."

Paul frowned. "What happened?"

She told him about the girls' reaction to Frederic's unexpected marriage, and his smile returned. "Yvette has gained my respect," he said. "I told my father much the same thing. I'm glad he's heard it from someone other than me. I can imagine how upset he was."

"Yes, but it doesn't make any difference, does it? What's done is done."

"Unfortunately, you are right, Charmaine. It is just one of many things that has added to a deplorable week."

"I'm sure. I wish I could resolve your dilemmas as swiftly as you have mine. Unfortunately, all I can offer is sympathy."

Paul's demeanor abruptly changed. His eyes sparkled beneath raised brows, and a roguish smile spread across his face. "Don't depreciate that offer. I'd love to indulge in a bit of sympathy and forget my troubles for a time."

She knew where his words were leading, where the invitation would take her if she allowed it. That was the key, allowed it. She'd enjoyed his company for almost a year now. Once his flirtatious advances had frightened her; today she found them exciting. Suddenly, she wanted more, wanted to know he wasn't just toying with her, that he was truly attracted to her, wanted to know what it felt like to have his mouth upon hers. Intuitively, she knew the lust that had sparked his first proposition in the gardens those many months ago had blossomed into something more. And yet, he had never kissed her. Why? On Christmas Day, he had almost done so, but they had been interrupted. And once he'd returned home, they'd been thrown into the turmoil of Colette's death. Beyond that, there was Espoir and his merciless work schedule, his treks home few and far between. Today was the first time they'd been alone in ages. She returned his dazzling smile. Let him think what he would. She wanted him to kiss her right here and now. As if reading her thoughts, his gaze traveled to her lips.

Paul had watched numerous emotions play across her comely face, yet was no closer to figuring her out. The risqué invitation didn't seem to upset her, yet she didn't speak. She was so lovely, and he longed to make love to her, slowly and sweetly. He had no use for this little cat-and-mouse game and was annoyed with himself. "Charmaine? Did you hear what I said?"

Her coyness vanished. "I heard," she replied, more evenly than she thought possible.

"And?"

He released her hand to cradle her cheek and chin, his thumb brushing across her lips. She closed her eyes to the sensual caress. She couldn't breathe and broke away, standing and turning her back to him.

"And?" he pressed again, moving behind her.

"And"—she faltered—"I don't see how I could possibly help you."

So, he thought, *she's playing to a new set of rules: Don't act offended, but don't give in.* He had dallied too long, and the dreamy moment was dissolving. He felt cheated and chuckled ruefully, his breath catching in her hair.

Embarrassed now, she stepped farther away and composed herself. Finally, she faced him. "Perhaps if you explained some of your problems . . ."

"Some?" he derided suavely. "Where would you like me to begin? Agatha? George? Or perhaps John, the biggest problem of all. There's nothing you can do to rectify that headache."

"Let me be the judge of that," she said.

He laughed outright. But when her stance remained set, arms folded one over the other, her eyes serious, he strode to the desk and lifted the sheaf of papers he'd thrown there earlier. "Very well. These are invoices. They—"

"I know what invoices are," she cut in.

He nodded, then explained why those he held were so perplexing.

Apparently, a ship had docked on Charmantes midweek and had sat in the harbor for five days, her cargo untouched. The captain and Jake Watson had disputed over which goods were intended for Charmantes and which were to be shipped on to Virginia.

"The captain maintained the supplies packed for Charmantes were at the rear of the hold," Paul was saying. "Jake was confused and demanded to see both the European and Virginia invoices. He didn't believe even a new captain could be so dimwitted as to bury our goods behind those that would be discharged at a later time. The captain bristled, probably because Jake's estimation of him was accurate. Again, Jake insisted on seeing John's invoices, informing the captain not one cask would be hoisted without proof of merchandise. The captain hemmed and hawed, eventually admitting that—although he *thought* John had given him the proper paperwork—the invoices he carried were, in fact, invalid. When Jake saw these, he had had enough."

"Enough of what?" Charmaine asked.

"Enough of John's antics! I didn't rant and rave when he changed the shipping routes last year, so he has come up with another scheme to impede the work on Charmantes. Once our staples were loaded in Richmond, John removed the legitimate paperwork and gave the captain these instead."

Paul waved a pile of papers under her nose. When they stopped flapping, Charmaine caught sight of several crude drawings with accompanying notes, which he abruptly withdrew and shoved back into the folder.

"He used invoice sheets for his artwork just to make certain I knew the entire mix-up was intentional." Paul slapped the folder against his thigh again, his agitation escalating. "When Jake saw the sketches, he was furious. Apparently, he called the captain a few choice names and informed the man that if his crew unladed the packet, he was storing every last cask, including the merchandise for Virginia, in our warehouses until I returned from Espoir and decided otherwise. The captain lost his temper and stood sentry against Jake's threat. And so, the ship has sat in our harbor for five days! *Five days!*" he bellowed in exasperation. "Her European cargo losing hundreds of dollars in market value."

"Why didn't Mr. Watson talk to you when you returned on Friday?"

"Friday *night,* Charmaine," he corrected. "*Late* Friday night. Everyone was at Dulcie's, and I just assumed the ship had been unloaded, reloaded with sugar, and was ready to depart for Richmond. I should have known better! We spent the better part of two hours climbing over barrels to find out whether those in the stern contained island supplies. Without the invoices, I couldn't be certain, and John would love to learn I had spent the entire day shifting hogsheads just to find nothing at the back was ours!"

Charmaine knew he was chasing circles and felt sorry for him. "Why would your brother create such confusion? He has just as much to lose as your father and you do, doesn't he? That's what Colette used to say."

"He will pay any price, Charmaine, *any price,* if he knows he's upset me or, better yet, made my hard day's work harder."

She was appalled. "If that's true, you have to turn the tables on him."

"How could I possibly do that?"

"Send the ship back to him, just the way it is. Or better still, keep all the merchandise."

Paul disagreed. "Sending it back will deprive us of valuable supplies, especially grain. Keeping it would cost my father a fortune. His buyers in Virginia would be none too pleased, either. John knows all this."

Charmaine nodded to his final declaration, but turned back to her original suggestion. "Are you certain Charmantes couldn't survive without the grain?"

"Of course we could survive, but it accomplishes nothing."

"Nothing, except sending the problem back to your brother. Maybe you should include your own set of drawings, telling him a thing or two!"

Paul chuckled. He certainly would love to see John's face when he began unloading the vessel and found his mean-spirited tomfoolery had backfired—that *he* was the one facing a laborious day on the docks. Let the captain talk his way out of that one, and let John deal with the buffoon he had hired. Yes, it was a most pleasing fantasy . . . Then Paul was struck by a new thought. Perhaps John knew about Espoir and had hoped to sabotage his efforts by creating more work on Charmantes. But no, Stephen Westphal and Edward Richecourt were sworn to secrecy, so John couldn't know—unless George had spilled the beans. But that was impossible. The *Heir* would have left Richmond before George got there.

"Paul?"

He came around when Charmaine called his name a second time. "I'm sorry, Charmaine. Not to worry. I'll sort it out."

"Very well, but I wouldn't stand for such nonsense!"

Her eyes flashed with fervor, and thoughts of his brother vanished. Damn, she was desirable, and he ached to hold her, to release the dark locks pinned at her nape and stroke the abundant mane as it cascaded down her back, to possess her petulant mouth. He stepped closer, but her eyes remained hard, oblivious to the fire she had stoked. He stopped. *Now is not the time,* he thought, steeling himself against his carnal appetite. *We'll only be interrupted again. But soon, very soon, another opportunity will present itself. Perhaps late one night when everyone else is abed* . . . Yes, he fancied that idea. Then he would conquer her.

"Excuse me, sir."

Paul chuckled with the anticipated interruption. "Yes, Travis?"

"I'm afraid Mrs. Duvoisin wants to speak to you now, sir. I tried to tell her you were preoccupied—"

Before he could finish, Agatha pushed her way into the room. "So," she accused, "the governess is overburdened with her duties and cannot make time for an interview with me. And here I thought those duties involved the children."

"At present, Miss Ryan happens to be helping me," Paul replied stiffly.

Agatha's eyes raced up and down Charmaine's slender form, eagerly searching for some incriminating evidence to feed her evil assumptions. "Helping you? I can just imagine how."

"Charmaine *is* helping me, Agatha," Paul bit out, his jaw twitching with contained anger. "If you'd care to notice, we are sorting through a stack of invoices that accompanied the *Heir.*" He produced the folder to support his statement. "John has created another headache by misplacing the most important papers. Charmaine was merely—"

Agatha's face turned livid. "John—always John! How do you withstand it? Why does your father *force* you to withstand it?"

"I don't know," Paul answered, baffled by her reaction. "I believe you wanted to speak to me about Miss Ryan?"

"Yes," she agreed reluctantly, scrutinizing Charmaine again. "I think I have the right, as the children's stepmother, to determine who cares for and educates them."

"No, Agatha, you don't have that right," Paul countered. "Your marriage to my father changes nothing. However, since we disagree, I suggest we take the matter to him immediately, and have *him* settle it."

"Very well," she hesitated.

"Good. Let's have done with it."

Charmaine was trembling as she preceded Paul out of the study, bewildered when he led her to the nursery. "There's no need to accompany us, Charmaine. I'll let you know how everything turns out." With that, he nudged a miffed Agatha toward his father's quarters.

Charmaine entered the nursery. Rose, who had been reading to the children, lifted her brow in silent inquiry, but Charmaine only shrugged, aware Yvette was all ears. "Well?" the precocious twin asked. "Don't you think we should know what happened?"

"Yes, Mademoiselle," Jeannette agreed. "We're worried. We don't ever want to lose you."

"I don't think you will," Charmaine offered gently. "Paul is determined to override any harsh decision your stepmother attempts to make."

"What does that mean?" Jeannette asked.

"It means he is doing what Johnny would do if he were here," Yvette explained, "and I'm proud of him."

Charmaine chuckled, remembering Paul's earlier words about Yvette. "Paul is speaking with your father right now. He wasn't in the mood to hear Agatha's complaints."

"Why not?" Yvette asked.

Charmaine eyed her for a moment, uncertain if she should tell the eight-year-old what she had learned from Paul. "He was upset with your brother over some missing invoices."

"Johnny? Do you think Paul is talking to Father about him, too?"

"I don't know . . . Maybe . . . Why?"

"No reason," Yvette answered nonchalantly. "I don't want Johnny to get into any more trouble, that's all."

Not long after, she left the nursery saying she needed to use the water closet.

Agatha cast a series of aspersions against the governess, saving the worst for last: Charmaine Ryan's background.

Renitent, Frederic sat back in his chair, folded his arms across his chest, and looked her straight in the eye. Thanks to Paul, he'd heard it all many months ago. "Charmaine Ryan was chosen by Colette to care for the children," he said. "They remain her children, not yours, Agatha. If for no other reason than to respect her wishes, Miss Ryan will retain her position in this house."

"But Frederic—" she demurred.

"No buts, no more discussion. I am pleased with Miss Ryan. Regardless of her past, she's demonstrated great love and affection while mothering my children. That is what they need right now, Agatha, a mother. I do not see you lending a hand with them."

Chastised, Agatha turned aside, saying, "I shan't bring the matter up again."

"Good."

She recovered quickly, spurred on by a new thought. "I fear the entire incident has been blown out of proportion. I had only intended to speak with Miss Ryan today. I would never have dismissed her as Paul has led you to believe. He was upset over other matters and misunderstood."

"What other matters?" Frederic asked, his regard diverted to his son.

Paul still clutched the folder from the *Heir*. "John, just John," he answered, tossing the invoices into his father's lap.

"What has he done this time?"

His ire rekindled, Paul delved into the aggravating story, forgetting Agatha was there. His father listened patiently, shaking his head on occasion. His eyes hardened as he viewed the salacious sketches, complete with obscene remarks. "He's up to no good again," Frederic snarled, "as if he has nothing better to do with his time."

"May I see those?" Agatha asked, arm outstretched.

"No." Frederic shoved the papers back into the folder and threw them into the dustbin.

Agatha bristled. "Why do you allow Paul to suffer such non-sense?"

"Yes, Father," Paul interjected, capitalizing on Agatha's propitious allegiance. "Why must I abide his malicious antics? We're no longer children. John refuses to behave like an adult, and yet, he's in charge."

Frederic smiled sardonically. "You are in charge here, and John is in charge in Virginia."

"That's not how I see it. John is in charge above and beyond the Virginia operations. John changed the shipping routes, which led to this fiasco. We never had this problem before. Direct packets carry island supplies, nothing else."

Frederic nodded, but remained silent.

Paul pressed on, venting his anger. "Beyond that, you and I both know John controls the purse strings that affect the growth of your entire estate."

"That is owing to the fact he lives on the mainland," Frederic said, bringing folded hands to his lips. "What would you have me do?"

"Take him off the will!" Agatha cut in. "Then he shall see where his vicious games have gotten him."

"Really? You think we have problems now?" Frederic paused for a moment, allowing the question to sink in. "We need John in Virginia. For all his faults, Paul knows no one else could command

John's end of the family business as well as John does. As for re-moving him from the will—if John enjoys a prank when he holds a vested interest in Duvoisin enterprises, what games do you think he'll play if he knows his actions hurt or benefit only Paul? You can't begin to guess. He'd have a heyday."

Paul had not considered this; his father was a wise man. He glanced at Agatha, who seemed to be searching for a rational re-buttal. There was no love lost between aunt and nephew. John was downright cruel to her, and she preferred he remain abroad. With her marriage to Frederic, Paul surmised she worried over her future should his father die and John inherit. He snickered to think of his brother ousting Agatha from the house, if not the island. Clearly, she needed an ally, and he had been chosen. But the Duvoisin em-pire needed John. As long as John resided in Virginia, he would remain the heir apparent.

Yvette had been gone a long time. Suspicious, Charmaine left the nursery. "Yvette?" she called, knocking on the privy door. "Are you all right?"

"I had a stomachache. But I'm feeling better now. I'll be out in a minute."

She returned, followed by Paul. He had wonderful news: Charmaine had his father's approval. Agatha would not question her position again.

"Mademoiselle said a ship docked from Virginia," Yvette inter-jected when the adult discourse ebbed. "Were there any letters from Johnny?"

"No, there weren't any *letters* from Johnny," he answered curtly. "But there was a letter for Miss Ryan, which completely slipped my mind."

Paul pulled an envelope from his shirt pocket, addressed in Loretta Harrington's hand. Charmaine eagerly accepted it. It had been months since she'd heard from the woman, and her eyes flew over the contents.

"What does it say, Mademoiselle Charmaine?" Jeannette asked.

"Mrs. Harrington writes of the new railway into Richmond."

"Railway?"

"Last year there was much ado about it, but I left Richmond before I had the chance to see the station. She, Gwendolyn, and Mr. Harrington booked passage to Fredericksburg, where two of her sons live, and rode directly behind the huge steam engine."

Charmaine looked from eager face to eager face. Even Pierre showed interest. The children had been reading about the locomotives in a periodical Paul had brought back from Europe.

"In just over an hour they traveled fifty miles and arrived in Fredericksburg without delay!"

"Was that city named after Papa?" Jeannette asked innocently.

"No, sweetheart," Charmaine replied as Pierre climbed into her lap.

"That is why I want to visit Johnny in Virginia," Yvette announced. "I want to have a ride on that great big steam engine."

"Me, too!" Pierre piped in.

Charmaine hugged him. "Maybe someday we will visit there," she said, befuddled to find Paul frowning when she smiled up at him.

Saturday, July 16, 1837

Agatha sorted through the papers strewn atop her husband's desk. He was visiting with the children, which afforded her an hour to tidy up. She was astonished when she came across his will. Had he removed it from the safe because he intended to change something? Had he given some thought to her comments concerning John?

She had just finished reading it when Frederic entered the room. He instantly realized what she held and turned livid. "How dare you rummage through my personal things?"

Agatha replaced the document with a great show of dignity. "I wasn't rummaging, Frederic. I was merely straightening out this mess. Your will was amid the papers." She crossed the room, then stopped. "I am your wife now. I didn't think it was a secret. Obviously, I was wrong, and now I know why."

Frederic's rage diminished. "If there is something you want to know, ask."

"Paul is going to be devastated," she choked out, tears glistening in her eyes. "You realize that, don't you? If he finds out, he's going to be devastated."

"Finds out what?"

Frederic grimaced. Paul stood in the doorway. "Agatha has read my will," he replied hesitantly. "It names Pierre as second in line to inherit—after John."

The room plummeted into a paralyzing silence. Only a sense of betrayal hung in the air. Paul forced himself to speak, to break free of his father's perfidy. "I see . . . I mean, it makes sense . . . After all . . . he is legitimate."

"Paul," his father beseeched, his sorrowful eyes growing steely when it looked as if Agatha would interrupt. "You know this has nothing to do with legitimacy. I have tried to provide for all three of you. That is why I've given you Espoir. My will is merely a formality. In fact, I was preparing a new docu—"

"Father, you don't have to explain," Paul cut in, his throat constricted with emotion. He was angry with himself, revolted by the wave of jealousy that engulfed him, the harsh judgment he'd been ready to pass. "As you say, you've given me Espoir. You've financed the entire operation, including the shipping. I've no right to ask for more, to be envious of Pierre or John."

"But I should have told you about Pierre," Frederic murmured. "I'm sorry you found out this way."

"No, Father," Paul countered. "There's no need to apologize, not when you've given me so much."

Sunday, July 30, 1837

Frederic pored over the documents he held, studying each element and computing each figure with swift precision. When the papers offered no further information, he placed them aside and turned a satisfied smile on his son, who waited patiently for his opinion. "They appear to be in order."

Paul concurred. "I'm very pleased. In fact, I'm surprised we've not confronted any delays since taking over the defaulted contracts in January. The shipbuilders have been prompt in meeting our schedule. They were relieved to have someone step in and purchase the titles. The financial panic made it difficult for them to come up with the capital to finish the vessels. We enabled them to put their men back to work and remain solvent at the same time."

Paul gestured toward the papers on his father's desk. "Once you've signed the remaining documents, I'll see them transported to Mr. Larabee when the next ship sets sail. On his end, he'll liquidate the securities and instruct Edward Richecourt to proceed with the final installment of funds. It was wise to go with the New York firm, and a stroke of luck to boot. Newportes Newes and Baltimore held promise, but I'm glad I continued north. Because the vessels were well under construction, they'll be ready in a third of the time, and we've obtained three ships for one hundred and fifty thousand dollars when we expected to pay one-eighty."

"You are not disappointed with fully rigged merchantmen?"

"From what Thomas Harrison indicated, it will be years before the merits of steam outweigh wind propulsion. Paddlewheels may be faster, but fueling their engines becomes a concern. No, we're better off waiting until they are perfected. I'm quite pleased with the three-masted clippers. Their hulls sit high out of the water, a brilliant bit of engineering that will greatly reduce the time at sea."

Frederic nodded. "And on this end?" he queried. "Will Espoir be ready?"

"We've expanded the dock. Two ships can berth simultaneously. The house is nearly completed and beautiful. The architect proved reputable. He returned to Europe two months ago with a list of furnishings, which he will purchase on my behalf and transport to Espoir when the vessels make their maiden runs. As for island operations, the men have cleared half the land, and three fields have been sown. By next year, they will be on a one-tract-per-month rotation."

"We may need to increase the size of the fleet," Frederic said with a smile.

"Let's see how the routes work out first," Paul advised.

Frederic's smile broadened. His son had a good head on his shoulders. "I'm proud of you, Paul, very proud. You've met your own grueling schedule despite the chaos and tragedy of the past four months. I realize the burden hasn't been light, and yet, you've continued to manage operations on Charmantes amid the press of Espoir's development. You haven't shirked your responsibilities, even though you've lost George's able hands."

Paul frowned. He hadn't mentioned George and wondered how his father knew of his prolonged absence. He doubted Travis had shared the information.

"I know about George," Frederic said. "When do you expect him back?"

"I have no idea," Paul grunted. "You realize he went to Virginia?"

"So I've heard."

"What do you think is going to happen?"

"I don't know, Paul," his father replied, rubbing his chin, "I don't know."

"If it hasn't happened by now, George will probably come home alone."

Frederic remained silent, deep in thought as he stared into the distance. When he did speak, he was directing his attention back to the documents, lifting them from his desk and rereading them.

"I know you were upset about Pierre and my will," he commented, to Paul's discomfort. "But I want you to know I realize which son has remained beside me, who deserves the credit for nurturing enormous profits here on Charmantes, even in the face of our depleted cane fields. It was for this reason I placed Espoir in your hands and invested in its future. I would like to know that when I die, you will own a share of what you've helped to build."

"Yes, sir," Paul said, embarrassed by his father's praise. "Thank you, sir."

They were interrupted by a knock on the door. "Agatha, come in," Frederic invited. "I would like to place you in charge of something."

Though he knew she was pleased with his enthusiastic welcome, she eyed him suspiciously. He chuckled. "I've been thinking about this for some time now, but I shall need help with the details. I'm certain it will meet with your approval." He breathed deeply, then shifted in his chair. "Paul predicts the ships will make their maiden crossing before Christmastide. Correct?"

"Yes," Paul confirmed, though he, too, appeared apprehensive.

"This is what I propose: we plan a grand celebration on Charmantes over the Christmas holiday."

"Celebration?" The word dropped in unison from Paul and Agatha's lips.

"Yes." Frederic regarded his son. "According to you, it will take a year before Espoir is in full production. In that time, it would be foolish to forge the Atlantic with half-empty ships. I say we bring Paul Duvoisin to the public eye, set him before the world market-place. Why not advertise to farmers—both in Virginia and the Caribbean—the availability of your new fleet, and allow these to-bacco, cane, and cocoa farmers, as well as their brokers, to bid on your transport services?"

He paused, enjoying their reactions. His wife's eyes twinkled in burgeoning excitement, while his son appeared thunderstruck.

He pressed on. "Why place all your coins on one bet? Yes, I'm certain Espoir will produce profitable harvests for years to come, but the ships may prove more lucrative in the long run. Additional vessels can always be commissioned if need be, and so much the better if that becomes necessary."

Agatha was elated. "This is marvelous, Frederic, just marvel-ous! If Paul is jumping into the shipping world, men of influence must be told. And what better way than to invite them here to Charmantes for an unforgettable event?"

"Exactly," Frederic agreed. "We shall plan a week of activities, which will include the unveiling of Espoir, the christening of Paul's fleet, and the signing of contracts. We'll extend invitations to well-known businessmen, brokers, and prosperous farmers both in Virginia and the West Indies. Let these landowners see what we Duvoisins have built; witness our undisputed success. Let them bid on cargo space or better still, invest in additional ships."

"Let them long for a piece of it!" Agatha interjected dramati-cally.

Frederic nodded. "And then, after all the proper connections have been made, we will culminate the festivities with a grand din-ner and ball."

"Father," Paul breathed, "what can I say?"

"I gather you approve?" Frederic asked.

"I do, but . . ." His words dropped off as concern for his father's health came to the fore.

"Yes?" Frederic queried.

"Are you fit for this?"

"I'll be fit," he vowed. "For you, Paul, I'll make every effort to be fit. I shall write to Larabee and Richecourt in Virginia. They can supply the names of the men we should contact in the States. After the invitations go out and the positive responses begin to reach us, I'll rely on you, Agatha, to coordinate the other arrangements. You can do that, can't you?"

"Absolutely!" she purred.

"Then it's settled. My only reservation is burdening you with additional work, Paul."

"On the contrary," his son responded. "Espoir has fallen into its own routine, the overseers conscientious. By the end of next month, I should be able to manage its production from Charmantes, traveling there every week or so. As for this venture"—and he shook his head, still in awe of what his father had planned—"it sounds as if you and Agatha will be taking on far more than I. I'm dumbfounded, actually. This is wonderful!"

When Frederic was alone, he sighed, happy for the first time in months.

Charmaine entered the drawing room. Pierre was sound asleep, and now she turned her attention on the girls. They begged to stay up a bit longer, playing a duet on the piano. When Paul smiled her way, Charmaine capitulated. He'd dined with them for the first time in two weeks and hadn't rushed off as he normally did directly after dinner. He'd been exceptionally charming throughout the meal, his countenance every bit as amiable now. If she insisted the twins retire, she'd no longer have a reason to return to the drawing room once they were in bed. She'd be wise to make the most of the next few minutes.

Unfortunately, they were not alone. Agatha sat with her needlepoint, Rose with her knitting. Bravely, Charmaine crossed the room and settled next to Paul on the settee, gaining a lazy smile that widened into an intense perusal.

He relaxed into the cushions, his arm outstretched across the back of the sofa. "Now, isn't this nice?" he whispered.

She blushed.

"I wish I were home more often," he continued softly.

"You're returning to Espoir in the morning?" she asked.

"Unfortunately, yes. However, the work is progressing nicely there, the house nearly finished. It won't be long before I can rely on my overseers full-time. Then, you'll be seeing a great deal more of me." He shifted a discernible degree closer. "Would you like that?"

Her blush deepened. It was answer enough. Her innocence and visible discomfiture fed a quickening in his loins. It was what he loved most about her.

Shortly afterward, Rose stood to say good night, and Charmaine and the girls did the same. Paul watched them go, then flipped open a periodical.

Agatha looked up. They were alone, an unprecedented occasion. She set her needlepoint aside and studied him. He was so very handsome, so much like his father. "Paul," she began cautiously, waiting for him to give her his full attention, accepting the frown of annoyance he shot her way as he dragged his eyes from the newspaper. "I know you don't like me."

He began to object, but she waved him off. "Please, allow me to say what I have to say, and then you can respond."

He leaned forward.

"I realize you were unhappy when your father and I wed, but I intend to make him happy, truly happy. I've loved him for a very long time."

"Since I was a boy," he supplied.

"Yes," she agreed. "But I wasn't at liberty to marry him then." She bit her bottom lip, distraught. "Don't judge me harshly, Paul. Thomas, God rest his soul, was a good man, and I loved him as well, but never as I have loved your father."

"And?"

"And I thought perhaps we could come to an understanding."

"What type of understanding?"

"I like you, Paul. When you were young and I would come to visit, you were always polite, always respectful—unlike your brother." She grimaced in repugnance, pausing for emphasis. "This afternoon, I was proud to be included in these plans your father is making. I would like this enterprise to succeed beyond your wildest expectations. But mostly, I'd like your approval as I lend a hand in the coming months."

"Agatha, any effort that contributes to the success of this event will gain my approbation. I am glad my father is getting involved again, and if this new venture gives him purpose, so much the better. Likewise, if you lend a hand in raising him out of his misery, I commend you on that as well."

"Thank you, Paul." Her smile was genuine—beautiful. "I've no doubt you will do well for yourself. You are more than just a handsome young man . . ." She let her words fall where they would, then stood and bade him good night.

For the second time that day, he was astonished.

Chapter 9

Friday, August 18, 1837

By nine o'clock the children were sound asleep, and Charmaine had time to herself. She dismissed the idea of spending the remainder of the evening in the drawing room. Only Agatha and Rose would be there, and although Agatha no longer harassed her, Charmaine still avoided her. She did not need companionship that badly, so she rang for Millie, deciding to take a bath instead.

An hour later, she was finished and sat at her dressing table, working out the tangles in her damp hair. "It's too darn curly!" she grumbled. Like so many other nights, she tossed the comb aside and grabbed her wooden hairbrush, but it failed just as miserably. She was not in the mood and abruptly sent the brush sailing, where it hit the door and dropped to the floor. Dissatisfied still, she fingered the sewing shears on the table. In the building humidity, it would take hours for the thick mane to dry. How easy it would be to clip it short. But she couldn't bring herself to do it. Pushing back from the dressing table, she moved to the French doors. There she stood, allowing the evening breeze to lift the heavy locks off her neck, her fingers absentmindedly raking through the snarls.

Footsteps resounded on the portico below. Paul was on his way to the stable. Charmaine hadn't realized he was home and frowned at her decision to remain in her chambers. Nothing was going right. If she had known he was in the house, she'd have gladly withstood Agatha's disapproving airs to be in his presence.

She shook her head free of the thought. He'd confounded her over the past two months: setting her heart to racing, yet remaining aloof, always flirting, suggesting he found her attractive, yet never whispering words of endearment. He had turned her world upside down, and she didn't like it. She had always been sure of herself, not flustered and confused.

A sound from across the lawns drew her away from her musings. She looked toward the paddock. Paul emerged from the stables and walked back to the house. Evidently, he wasn't leaving, just checking on Chastity, the mare due to foal.

She hung her head, knowing it was best to stop thinking about him. She'd come to the conclusion she was merely a distraction—someone to toy with when she was present, but easily forgotten when she wasn't. Hadn't he dismissed her from his thoughts each time he left for Espoir? Certainly, she didn't plague his waking hours as he did hers. After all, she was only the governess. He had made it quite clear she would please him in bed. As for a decent proposal, it would never happen. Thus, she'd be wise to avoid him. What had Colette said? *He's a ladies' man . . . I'd hate to see you give your heart to someone who has no intention of returning your love.* If she didn't heed Colette's warning, she'd be nursing a broken heart. *Put him from your mind,* she reasoned, *forget what his kiss would have been like. Be happy you were in your room tonight. The less you see of Paul, the better.*

A knock resounded on her door, and she invited Millie and

Joseph Thornfield into the chamber. They'd come to empty the tub and take it away. Charmaine waited until the boy had waddled off with two brimming buckets, then spoke nonchalantly to his sister. "I noticed Master Paul going into the stables, but he didn't leave. It's awfully late. Is something amiss?"

"He is worried about the mare," Millie replied as she straightened from the tub, a third bucket in hand. "She's been whinnying all evening, but it's too early for her to foal. He's sent for Martin."

"Martin?"

"The town farrier," Millie explained, then shuddered in exaggerated revulsion. "A disgusting man, who's full of himself, if you know what I mean. Once he's been asked to help with the horses, he makes himself right at home. I just hope he doesn't barge in here like he did the last time—midnight it was—rousing the entire house so someone would make him something to eat."

Charmaine had never met this Martin, but she seemed to remember Yvette mentioning him once. "I don't think you need worry," she said. "Surely he won't behave badly with Master Paul at home."

"You think not?" Millie countered. "He's downright rude to Master Paul, and Master Paul indulges him—all because Dr. Blackford refuses to minister to horses anymore."

Joseph returned and refilled his buckets. This time, Millie left with him. One more trip, and the tub was removed, and Charmaine was once again alone.

Thunder rumbled far off, and the drapes flapped in a hearty breeze. She closed the French doors and tiptoed into the children's room. Yvette was sleeping ramrod straight, her thin blanket tucked under each arm. Jeannette's linens had been kicked aside, and Charmaine drew them over her again. Pierre was nearly snoring, one fat thumb stuck in his pudgy mouth, the other hand clutching his stuffed lamb. Stroking back his hair, she kissed him on the forehead, her love abounding as she considered him a moment longer. Then, hearing the first droplets of rain, she latched the glass doors and returned to her room.

The storm was rapidly approaching, the thunder growing louder, bringing with it a sense of dread. She turned down the oil lamp on the night table, knelt to say her prayers, and climbed into bed. Already the night resurrected memories of Colette, simulating that terrible day before her demise. Charmaine hugged her pillow and squeezed her eyes shut, awaiting the worst . . .

But the worst did not come. The foyer clock tolled eleven, and the storm continued to toy with them. Though it rumbled, it did not roar, as if it were purposefully holding back, circling them, waiting for the kill.

Footsteps on the staircase eased the tension. Paul was retiring. Perhaps now she'd be able to sleep, knowing he was close by and would protect her.

That comforting thought soon took wing. The heavens ripped apart, and the tempest unleashed its full fury on the house. Violent, sporadic wind drove sheets of rain into the French doors. They rattled loudly in objection. Blinding lightning lit up the room, and earsplitting thunder replied, the former rivaling the latter in its power, as if the two were fighting for the upper hand. Then, they were lashing out simultaneously, and Charmaine shrunk under the blanket, curled up and trembling, bracing herself for each explosion, frightened of the interim silence as well, a void that amplified other eerie sounds . . .

She attempted to ignore the rustling of clothing near her bed, but the cold, clammy hand that touched her arm was real, and she screamed, throwing back the linens to escape. Thankfully, the sound was swallowed by another roar of thunder, for there, standing next to her bed, was a quaking Jeannette and in the doorway to the children's room, Yvette, patting back a wide yawn.

"Sweet Jesus!" Charmaine cried, clamping a hand over her bosom. "I'm sorry, Jeannette, but you frightened me." She laughed in gargantuan relief, holding out her arms to the petrified girl, who eagerly fell into them.

Yvette moved to the foot of the bed. "You're afraid of this storm?" she queried in disgust.

Charmaine nodded, feeling quite foolish now. "Even more than Jeannette."

"She isn't frightened of thunderstorms," Yvette countered.

"No? Then why are you here?" Charmaine asked, looking down at the twin who had yet to speak.

"Someone was standing over my bed," Jeannette whimpered, trembling.

"That's what woke her," Yvette added. "She didn't believe me when I said it was you, coming to check on us."

Charmaine smoothed back Jeannette's hair. "Yvette is right. I did look in on you, sweetheart. I even covered you up. I'm sorry if I disturbed you."

But the girl shook her head adamantly, fear sparkling in her wide eyes. "It wasn't you. It was a ghost that ran away when I turned over!"

Charmaine gave her another hug. "You must have been dreaming, a nightmare brought on by the storm, no doubt. Come," she encouraged, taking the lamp from her night table, "back to bed with you."

"I wasn't dreaming!" Jeannette cried. "I wasn't! I saw it, and it wasn't you. It ran out the French doors. It's on the veranda right now, waiting for me!"

"I wouldn't let anything harm you, Jeannette," Charmaine averred, "but I can't be brave alone. Won't you help me? We'll go back into your room together, and with the light of the lamp, you will see there is nothing there to frighten you. All right?"

Jeannette nodded tremulously, taking Charmaine's hand. As they entered the nursery, they were buffeted by a chilling draft. The French doors were swinging on their hinges, the room at the mercy of the storm.

"Why didn't you close them?" Charmaine demanded, placing the lamp on the dresser. But as she rushed over to the wind-beaten panels, face turned away from the pelting rain, a spine-tingling aura took hold, and she came up short. Petrified, she slammed the doors shut, slipped the latch into place, and jumped back, grateful no ghost had appeared from beyond.

Expelling a shuddering breath, she surveyed the damage. The drapes and rug were drenched. Laundering them would have to wait until morning, but she pulled a towel from the bureau and mopped up the floor.

Next she checked on Pierre. He hadn't budged, which seemed almost unnatural. The storm hadn't subsided. In fact, with the French doors open, it had been magnified, yet he'd slept through it all.

"As you can see, there was no one on the balcony," she said. "I think your ghost was nothing more than those billowing drapes, Jeannette. After all, your bed is the closest to the veranda."

The girl remained unconvinced, complaining that without a lock, the doors could open again.

"I know what will help you go back to sleep," Charmaine announced, hoping to defuse Jeannette's fears, "warm milk and cookies. Now, climb into bed, and I'll go get them. How would that be?"

Jeannette nodded, but jumped into bed with Yvette. "I'll wait here," she whispered. In the next moment, they were snuggling under the covers together, giggling softly.

Charmaine donned her robe, then lifted the lamp. But Jeannette immediately objected, begging her to leave it, so Charmaine lit a small candle instead. "I'll be back in a short while," she said.

As she walked down the hallway, the flickering flame cast grotesque shadows on the far walls, feeding her apprehension. Though she was getting good at timing the lightning and thunder, she was unprepared for the first toll of midnight and nearly jumped out of her skin when the foyer clock struck the hour. "Goodness," she scolded herself, grabbing hold of the stairway balustrade, "what's the matter with me? I'm acting like a frightened rabbit. There is no such thing as ghosts!" Then she began her descent.

With his dressing room door slightly ajar, Paul heard the sound of footfalls beyond, a shaky voice accompanying them. He opened the door and leaned casually against the frame, admiring the lovely vision before him. Charmaine Ryan was indeed a fetching sight, even more so in her state of dishabille: hair unbound and thin robe drawn taut, accentuating her slender waist and shapely hips. She had turned into a temptress, and his mind wandered back to the night in the drawing room, some two weeks ago, when she had brazenly chosen to sit next to him. She was ready for the plucking, of that he was certain, but it was exceedingly difficult to corner her alone . . . until tonight. He smiled wickedly. Hadn't he hoped for an occasion such as this? What better time than when everyone else was in bed? Yes, what better time indeed!

Although the storm had lulled, Charmaine was by no means relieved. The house was shrouded in darkness, her passage illuminated only by the candle and the erratic flashes of lightning. Beyond that, she could not shake the feeling she was being watched, though it appeared as if everyone had retired. Fear tied a knot in the pit of her belly, and she hastened past the study, through the dining room, and into the kitchen. "I was a fool to suggest coming down here."

She began humming to blot out the creaks and ticks emanating from the dark recesses of the kitchen. The haunting melody she had been forbidden to play on the piano spontaneously came to her lips, and oddly, she felt at ease, secure. Haunting, indeed! She warmed the milk without spilling it and found the cookies Mrs. Henderson had baked that morning, placing everything, including her nearly extinguished candle, on a serving tray. Then she retraced her steps.

As she emerged from the dining room, a burst of lightning silhouetted the figure of a man standing near the study doorway. Darkness instantly enveloped the corridor, and he was gone. Charmaine gasped, but the ensuing roar of thunder muffled the sound.

"*Who's there?*" she called, praying her eyes had deceived her.

The apparition was real. Paul stepped into the circle of candlelight, bringing with him a draining relief that left her weak in the knees. "I didn't mean to startle you," he said, moving closer, his hair mussed, his robe askew.

"I didn't know anyone was awake," she sputtered, slowly recovering.

"I heard you on the stairs and thought perhaps you were in need of company. But I can see I was mistaken." He indicated the tray she balanced in her arms. "It was hunger, and not loneliness, that has you roaming the house at this late hour."

Charmaine glanced down and laughed self-consciously. "This isn't for me. It's for the twins. They were awakened by the storm, and I thought a snack might help them fall back to sleep."

"I suppose I shouldn't detain you," he said with a dynamic smile, "but I shall. Come . . ." He walked into the dark study.

Though his manner seemed benign, an inner voice counseled her not to follow. She went no farther than the door. "I really must see to the children. They were frightened," she added lamely, "and if I don't return shortly, they'll begin to worry."

"I'm certain they'll survive a few moments longer," he replied. "In fact, when you do return, you are likely to find them asleep." He hoped his words proved true; the hour would be late when she left him. "Besides, Charmaine, aren't you the least interested as to why I really followed you down here?"

She was intrigued, but before she could reply, he turned his back on her again and felt his way to the table with the tinderbox. There he struck the flint and lit the lamp, adjusting the wick. Its flame flared high, chasing the darkness to the far reaches of the library.

The rumbling storm lost its ferocity, and Charmaine relished a sense of security that made it easy to ignore her rational mind and enter the room. She obeyed him when he spoke over his shoulder and casually told her to set the tray of food down. But her momentary calm was shattered when he faced her and she read the raw passion in his eyes. Cauterized, a sudden spasm shook her.

"Are you cold?" he inquired softly.

"No," she whispered, his magnetism pulling at the core of her being.

"Are you afraid of me?" he queried.

Yes, her mind screamed, *and of myself! Dear Lord, we're alone, and I am bewitched.* But she said none of this. Heaven forbid! "Should I be afraid of you?" she asked instead, cleverly setting aside his question.

"That depends on what you're afraid of," he answered just as cleverly, cocking his head to one side.

Dear Lord, he's handsome, Charmaine thought, one stray lock of hair curling on his brow, bidding her to stroke it back into place. She dismissed the temptation, certain that such familiarity would send her straight into his arms.

Lightning flashed again, and the thunder answered. A fierce draft skirted across the floor, grabbing at her robe and wrapping it around her legs; then it was gone. In that eternity of passionate thoughts, neither of them spoke.

Paul's eyes blazed brighter as he admired her lithe form, her innocent beauty highlighted by the copious tresses that fell over her shoulders to her waist. His smoldering gaze returned to her lovely face and the dark eyes that lacked the carefree abandon the moment demanded. There, he noted the last shred of wariness. He moved toward her, much like a panther stalking its prey.

Though unknowingly she flinched, Charmaine did not flee. Rather, she stood her ground until they were but a breath apart. She tilted her head back to look up into his face, her heart leaping when his callused hand caressed her cheek.

"You are most desirable, my sweet," he murmured huskily, confident of the romantic web he was spinning, savoring the spell she had cast on him as well, his own pulse thundering in his ears. "That is why I sought you out, and now, I would ask for a kiss."

His eyes lingered on her lips, and her eyelids fluttered closed. There was no turning back—she didn't want to turn back—and she leaned forward, relishing the quintessential moment. He grasped her shoulders and slowly drew her into his embrace. His head descended, and he delivered a tender kiss meant to put her at ease. Then his mouth turned persuasive, testing and tasting, his moustache coarse and prickly, masculine. Abruptly, he pulled her hard against him, his mouth cutting across her lips and devouring them. One hand traveled to her nape, the other caressed her back.

Charmaine's head was spinning with the onslaught, and she kissed him in return, rising on the tips of her toes, her hands creeping up his sinewy arms and grasping his shoulders, molding her body to his. Her brazen response belied her innocence, and her unleashed ardor sent his desires soaring.

Sharp laughter rang from the doorway.

Paul quickly disengaged himself, an oath dying on his lips.

"That's the ticket, Paul. Bring her home, put a roof over her head, strip the bit of clothing off her back, bed her, and then, when you've tired of her, out she goes on her fondled ass with little money spent!"

Mortified, Charmaine turned toward the doorway and the resonant voice that dared utter such vulgarity. A bedraggled stranger stood there, badly beaten by the storm, drenched from face to foot, with the stubble of a beard on his cheeks, and a leather cap cocked to the back of his head. With the slightest movement, she espied Paul out of the corner of her eye. He was straightening his robe, a mock display at dignity, yet he held silent, making not the slightest inquiry as to why the man was in the house.

The intruder strode unceremoniously into the room, and though his wet attire should have placed him at a disadvantage, he did not seem ill at ease. He proceeded to audaciously circle them, and Charmaine was unable to move out of sheer embarrassment, appalled when his assessing regard raked her from head to toe, measuring her worth as if she were on display at an auction. His eyes met hers, and she dropped her gaze to his boots. He'd tracked a considerable amount of mud on the carpet, as if he had come from the stables. And then she knew: He was the livery hand who'd been called to help with the foal. Still, she couldn't understand why Paul would suffer such insolence.

But there was no time to think, for the derelict held them captive. His wandering gaze fell on the tray of cookies and milk, and a smile broke across his face, revealing gleaming white teeth that were not perfectly straight, but perfectly aligned with his sardonic demeanor.

"How cozy," he mused wickedly, "a passionate kiss followed by refreshments." He settled into one of the chairs, crossed his arms over his chest, and said, "Do carry on! I was *moved* by this romantic performance. Your lines were fabulous! Could you repeat that one again, Paul, about wanting a kiss? I never thought to ask before." He chuckled deeply.

Charmaine's ire boiled over. "You rude, despicable cur!" she spat out, emboldened by her temper. "From which filthy hole have you crawled? No!" she quickly added, holding up a hand and wrinkling her nose in overemphasized revulsion. "I don't want to know!"

His smile broadened, the whole of his face one enormous jeer now. It could not be borne, and she lashed out again. "Thank God I live here and need never place name to your arrogant face!"

The grin ruptured into rich laughter, trampling her bravado. She lifted her chin and grabbed hold of the snack tray. But as she marched from the room, his voice followed her. "Give us a kiss, you saucy, brazen wench!"

Once outside the study, Charmaine gave in to her trembling, unable to steady her frayed nerves, let alone soothe her wounded pride. *A wench. A brazen wench. A saucy, brazen wench!* She had never been called a wench in her life! She looked down at the tray and saw the candle was snuffed out. If she didn't know better, she'd place the blame on the reprobate who was still closeted in the study with Paul. At least he lived in town, and she wouldn't have to see him again. Pacified, she pushed the debasing episode out of her mind and groped her way up the stairs, no longer afraid of the dark.

"What are you doing here, John?" Paul asked pointedly, moving to the brandy decanter and pouring himself a stiff drink.

"It was high time I checked on business."

"Really?" Paul snorted.

"Really. Lucky for me the ship was delayed by the storm—" With Paul's raised brow, he added "—or I would have missed you pressing the house help into working the night watch with you.

You horny bastard!" He smiled. "She really *loves* her job, doesn't she?"

"Drop it, John."

The room fell silent as Paul took a draught of brandy.

"She cares not who I am," John mused. "Perhaps she'll change her mind in the morning."

"I doubt it," Paul answered listlessly, his plans for the evening neatly laid to waste. Leave it to John to screw things up for him. "She's different."

"Really? Not from what I just saw."

"Just leave her be!" Paul growled, unable to check his anger any longer.

"Leave her for you, you mean. Isn't that right, Paulie? So . . . you haven't had your way with her yet."

"I'm not going to discuss this with you."

"No?" John clicked his tongue and canted his head, giving the matter some thought. "My assumption must be correct. Tonight was your first tryst with the vixen."

"It wasn't a tryst!" Paul sneered.

"Then you're in love with her?" John pressed, receiving only a scowl. "I didn't think so. In that case, she is fair game. We shall see who is the better player." Chuckling again, he stood and strode from the room, leaving a puddle of murky water at the foot of the chair he had vacated.

When she needed the lightning to illuminate the way, it refused to burst forth, and Charmaine realized the storm was over. The staircase was dark, and she clutched the balustrade tightly. When she reached the top, she fumbled down the wide hallway, straining to see. Her hand found the doorknob to the children's room. She was never more relieved as when she pushed the door inward and was bathed in lamplight.

The girls were asleep as Paul had predicted. What a fool to have wandered the house at midnight! Not even the memory of Paul's kiss annulled the humiliation she had suffered. *No! I won't think about that!*

She turned her mind to the twins, coaxing a sleep-drugged Jeannette back into her own bed, frowning when she glanced at the French doors and found them slightly ajar. A shiver chased up her spine, and she walked cautiously toward the glass panels, securing them again. She could not shake the uneasiness that engulfed her, for it was ludicrous to think either the girls or Pierre had opened them. It must be a faulty latch. Yes, that seemed plausible. She would mention it to Travis Thornfield in the morning.

She lit another candle and turned the lamp down low. Taking the tray of treats, lest the children eat them before breakfast, she stepped into her own bedchamber and closed the door, safe at last.

In his aggravation over the unpleasant turn the evening had taken, Paul hadn't considered John's destination after leaving the study. Even now, he did not remember that the governess occupied his brother's former bedchamber, for his mind was still relishing the taste of her sweet lips, the feel of her soft body in his arms, her impassioned response to his advance. Had he set aside his glass of brandy and allowed his mind to clear, the implications of the bedroom arrangements would have been manifest, and he'd have been none too pleased.

John fumbled in the darkness as he entered his dressing room. "Blast it all!" he snarled. "Where's the confounded tinderbox?" Despite his rummaging, his efforts came up futile. Frustrated, he groped his way to the bedroom door, hoping to have more success there. He was wet and miserable, and in desperate need of a hot bath. He knew the bath would have to wait until morning, but a good night's sleep in a dry bed after a week aboard the *Destiny,* which had traveled from New York, would be a pleasant accommodation.

He was stunned when he flung the door open and found his brother's concubine climbing into his bed. In fact, he was so surprised, he gave no thought to her reaction: the speed with which she jumped up. He drew a deep breath and released it slowly, his shock giving way to a crooked grin. She was bewitching. Perhaps he didn't need that full night's sleep after all.

"Well, well, well, and well again. Aren't you the little minx?" he chuckled significantly. "Do you always entertain total strangers?"

Charmaine was too petrified to speak. She only knew she had been set upon by a beast, one that was tracking her now, and in her mounting fear, all she could do was plaster herself against the wall.

"Now how did you know where I'd be bedding down for the night?" he pondered amusedly, closing the distance between them.

Charmaine realized she must act, or all would be lost. Pushing off from the wall, she flew like a wild thing, reaching the children's door in a heartbeat. But in the instant it took to grab the doorknob, her arm was caught from behind, and she was pulled back with one forceful tug. Her scream was stifled as the man's other hand clamped down on her mouth and she was propelled around, coming face to face with the tormenting demon. Her eyes grew wide at his leering grin, her face turning crimson as she fought to hold her breath against the foul odor she was sure he radiated.

Reading the repugnance and terror in her eyes, John relaxed his grip. She didn't seem to know who he was, but that didn't coincide with the fact she knew where his chambers were located.

Perceiving his moment of weakness, she began to struggle again. Given an inch, she had taken a yard, and John released her mouth to subdue her thrashing feet that were doing little in the way of assaulting his shins, but much in the way of inflaming his ardor.

"Calm yourself, Madame," he hissed, pinning her against the door when she didn't comply. "I just want some answers to my questions. However, if you'd like me to continue where Paul left off, I'd be more than happy to oblige."

She submitted, quaking now. His words buffeted her cheek, and she cringed, anticipating acrid, whisky breath. She smelled wet clothing, little more.

"Why are you in here?" he demanded.

"This is my bedroom!" she pleaded. "I work here! This is where I sleep!"

The conviction in her voice held the ring of truth. "So you *don't* know who I am?"

She grew courageous when his hands dropped away. "You're probably a convict escaped from some filthy prison!" she rallied, bent upon insulting him as he had her. "You should have rotted there!" But even as she blurted out the retort, the light began to dawn: *He isn't Martin, the livery hand.*

She gasped when he pulled her to his chest and buried his face in her hair, his lips close to her ear. "Ah, a prison indeed," he whispered passionately, "but can you guess what I was convicted of?"

"I'll scream if you don't release me!" she cried, the tremor in her voice nullifying her threat. In truth, she was far too frightened to scream, certain that any outburst would prompt him to ravish her.

His head lifted from the sweet fragrance of her wild hair. When he chuckled softly, Charmaine knew he was only toying with her. Then his laughing eyes became serious, and quite abruptly, he released her, stepping back apace.

She was an all-too-feminine distraction, and he was finding it exceedingly difficult to leave her company. But, he would not cajole her to his bed like his brother, and he certainly wouldn't force her.

She'd come of her own accord, or not at all, and he knew she wasn't going to do that. He backed away, grateful he was as tired as he was.

Still, he was having fun with this little encounter, so he wasn't of a mind to leave just yet. *She must be the governess,* he surmised. *Colette must have given her this room to be close to the children.*

He moved around the chamber, noticing the feminine changes she had made. Her possessions were meager, but they warmed the room in a way his belongings never had. He exhaled, causing her to jump. She hadn't moved from the doorway, and he realized something besides the change of inhabitant was different, but he couldn't pinpoint what it was.

"Are you going to leave?" she inquired, hugging herself rigidly against his penetrating gaze.

"Patience, patience," he chided, eyeing the tray of cookies. He took one and popped it into his mouth, chasing it down with a glass of milk. "Wouldn't you like to join me? It would be a shame to waste these, and since Paul won't be *coming,* not here, anyway, we might as well—"

"Won't you *please* leave?" she cut in, ignoring his chuckle. "It is very late, and I have a great deal to do in the morning!"

"Oh, don't worry about that," he reassured with the wave of his hand, "I'll see to it you're allowed to sleep in the morning, especially since you've entertained not one, but two gentlemen this evening. A hard night's work!"

When her mouth flew open to protest, he only winked at her, popped another cookie into his mouth and turned to leave. As he strode to the hallway door, something splintered underfoot. He picked up the hairbrush she had thrown across the room earlier that evening. It was broken in two. He studied the pieces for a moment, then tossed them onto the bed. With that, he tipped his cap, opened the door, and left the room.

Charmaine flew to the door and locked it. She ran to the

dressing room door to do the same, only to find it did not have a lock. She fretted for a time, but when the adjoining room remained mercifully silent, she began to relax. She got into bed and picked up the remnants of her hairbrush, letting out a sigh of relief.

Paul sat heavily on his bed, realizing just how desolate his bed-chamber was . . . "Shit!" he swore, shooting to his feet. "Shit!"

He sped to the door, but thinking better of it, exited through the French doors. In seconds, he was around the corner of the south wing balcony, past the children's rooms, and standing at the glass doors of John's old bedroom. They were closed, but he peered in. Mercifully, Charmaine was sitting in the middle of her bed, alone. He pushed into the room, his eyes raking the chamber, making certain his brother wasn't lurking in the shadows.

Startled, she gasped, but when she realized it was Paul, her hand dropped from her breast.

"Are you all right?" he queried with genuine concern.

"I am now!" she bit out.

"Was he here?"

"Of course he was here! This is his room!"

"Did he—"

"No!"

Paul's apparent relief fueled her ire. "Why didn't you tell me who he was downstairs? I made a complete fool of myself, ranting and raving the way I did! And if that wasn't bad enough, you let me come up here and . . ."

Her words dropped off as he rounded the foot of the bed. Again, she jumped off the mattress. *You've entertained not one, but two gentlemen this evening* . . . Already John Duvoisin's words were haunting her, and she was furious with Paul for placing her in such a humiliating situation. "You told me he'd never return! You promised me that when you suggested I move into this room!"

"He shouldn't have come back," Paul admitted softly, "and I was just as surprised as you. That's why I was at a loss for words."

Charmaine read the displeasure in his eyes, and her anger waned.

"I wanted to save you the embarrassment of an introduction, which John would have exploited. And I *completely* forgot about the sleeping arrangements until I returned to my room. I'm sorry, Charmaine."

He continued to advance, so close now her heart thudded in her ears, the beat no longer heated but heady.

"Forgive me?" he petitioned.

With her slight nod and timid smile, he leaned forward.

The moment was at hand. But above the sound of her racing pulse came a resonant, mocking voice: *Well, well, well, and well again . . . Aren't you the little minx? You saucy, brazen wench!*

Charmaine stepped back; she'd play no part in those vulgar declarations. "You had better go."

Paul accepted her refusal with a soft snort of disappointment. His gaze swept the length of her, then he departed the room the way he had come, leaving her confused and shaken. She had been vulnerable, and again he had acted the gentleman.

She climbed into bed, sitting on the broken brush. She pulled the two pieces from beneath her and thought of John and Paul. *Two gentlemen tonight* . . . She'd hardly call John Duvoisin a gentleman. She set the hairbrush aside. At least it was the only thing she had lost this night.

Saturday, August 19, 1837

Paul knocked on Frederic's chamber door at dawn. His father might still be sleeping. He knocked again, and the door opened to a quizzical Travis Thornfield. "Your father is in his bedroom having breakfast."

"I must speak with him immediately."

Travis stepped aside, and Paul crossed the antechamber for the inner room.

Frederic looked up in surprise and closed the journal next to his plate.

"John is home," Paul stated.

Frederic sat back in his chair and allowed the news to sink in, his heart besieged with elation, apprehension, and ultimately, despair.

Uncomfortable with his parent's pensiveness, Paul felt compelled to say more. "He arrived on the *Destiny*. She was delayed by the storm and didn't lay anchor until evening."

"Did you see him?"

"I was in the study when he arrived."

"Did you speak with him?"

"Briefly. It was late. I was tired. He was soaked." Paul tried hard to read his father's expression, one he'd never seen before. "He's here to check on business, or so he says."

Frederic stood, leaned heavily on his cane, and limped to the French doors. "Thank you for letting me know," he murmured.

When he realized his father would say no more, Paul left.

Frederic stared down into the courtyard. John was home. He'd been afraid to hope for this day. Now it had come, he wasn't truly prepared for it.

Charmaine hadn't fallen asleep until the first rays of dawn streaked the sky an inky orange, only succumbing to fatigue after reliving her ordeal at least a thousand times. Now, light poured into her room, and she awoke with a start. It had to be late morning. She rose and hurriedly crossed to the children's bedchamber. A sheet of paper had been slipped under the adjoining door.

Mlle. Chazmaine,

It is morning and you are still sleeping. We are with Nana Rose.

Jeannette, Yvette, and Pierre

Charmaine smiled in relief; Jeannette and Yvette must have told Rose they had been unable to sleep last night. Last night . . . the storm . . . the children . . . the specter . . . the midnight snack . . . Paul—John!

She sat down on her bed, rubbing her throbbing temple, and looked at the clock on her dresser: eight-thirty. She didn't want to face the day, inevitably confronting John Duvoisin along the way, but she knew she must. Otherwise, she could never save face.

John Duvoisin. She'd finally met the heir to the Duvoisin fortune, the man she'd heard so much about, mostly bad. Now she knew why. In their two brief encounters, hadn't he proven himself deserving of every epithet? She cringed, recalling the words she had spat in his face. *You rude, despicable cur . . . From which filthy hole have you crawled? . . . Thank God I live here and need never place name to your arrogant face . . . You're probably a convict escaped from some filthy prison . . .* She groaned and buried her face in her hands.

A convict indeed! How could she have been so verbal—dim-witted? Even if she hadn't figured out who he was in the study, his identity had been glaringly obvious once he'd invaded her bedchamber. He hadn't been stalking her, and he wasn't some stable-hand either! He'd merely been seeking his bed. Her cheeks flushed as she remembered the assumption he had made when he'd found her climbing into it. *Do you always entertain total strangers?* Dear God! It was too much to think about! Her head pounded, and her eyes stung from lack of sleep.

She had nothing to be embarrassed about, she resolved, then moaned. Who was she fooling? She *did* have something to be embarrassed about. He'd caught her in his brother's arms. She might not be guilty of "entertaining" a total stranger, but she was guilty of a late-night rendezvous with Paul. To make matters worse, he had found them in their nightclothes and had drawn all the worst conclusions. She couldn't even enjoy the memory of her first thrilling kiss, for the prurient man defiled it.

John Duvoisin. What would she say to him? If nothing else, she must face him with her head held high.

The nursery door burst open, and the children came bounding in, unmindful of the impropriety of storming her room. Fully dressed, they bounced on the bed in glee, their laughter ricocheting off the walls.

"Have you just awoken?" Yvette exclaimed incredulously. "It is so late! You must hurry and get dressed, Mademoiselle Charmaine."

"Why? What is the rush?"

"Nana Rose told us we are not to go downstairs for breakfast without you, and we are ready for breakfast now!"

There was a knock on the outer door, and Charmaine opened it to Mrs. Faraday, who bustled into the chamber with a stack of fresh linens.

"You must hurry, Mademoiselle Charmaine, or we'll be too late!" Jeannette piped in, taking up where her sister had left off.

"Huwwy, Mainie!" Pierre echoed.

Confused, Charmaine took in their effervescent faces. "Too late for what?"

Mrs. Faraday explained. "Master John returned late last night, and the children are anxious to see him. He is in the dining room, eating as we speak."

"Master John?" Charmaine queried in feigned ignorance.

"Their elder brother. The girls expect him to shower them with gifts as he did the last time he arrived unexpectedly from Virginia. Apparently, Master Paul was still awake when he came in and has just now told Rose."

Charmaine felt the blood rush to her cheeks. The telltale blush was not lost on the housekeeper, whose assessing eye rested momentarily on her face. Then she babbled on. "She is the only one in the house truly pleased to have him back, though I cannot, for the life of me, figure out why. She is as bad as the children, rushing off to her room to make herself presentable before seeing him."

"We're glad he's come home!" Yvette countered. "I'll wager he has a great stack of presents for us! Maybe something bigger than a piano this time!" She stood on her tiptoes and reached as high as she could in indication of the magnitude of wonders that awaited them with the return of her beloved brother.

"And Pierre wants to meet him!" Jeannette added. "Don't you, Pierre?"

"Uh-huh!" he agreed with an alacritous nod. "I never saw him before."

Tying back the drapes, Mrs. Faraday shook her head. "He can be a rascal," she proceeded, eager to impart what she knew of the man, "a bad influence on the children, teaching them disrespect the likes of which I've never seen." She leveled her gaze on Yvette as if to fortify her point, then motioned toward the tray of half-eaten cookies. "What would you have me do with this, miss?"

"I'm finished with it, thank you."

Yvette eyed the discarded snack. "You *did* bring them for us! We waited and waited for you, but you never came back last night."

Charmaine caught the housekeeper's raised brow. "It took a while to warm the milk. By the time I returned, the two of you were fast asleep."

"So you ate the cookies yourself?"

"No—I mean—I didn't eat them all."

Mrs. Faraday frowned in bewilderment, taking the tray with her as she left.

"Oh Mademoiselle Charmaine, please hurry and get dressed! We want to see Johnny before he's gone for the day!"

"Very well," she ceded. Best to get the introduction over with.

The children returned to the nursery, and she began washing up, splashing water in her face, brushing out her hair and securing it in a tight bun. As she pulled a dress from her armoire, she realized her heart was racing. She inhaled deeply. What would Mrs. Harrington do if she were in this predicament? Perhaps the situation wasn't so dire. If she presented herself with dignity and grace, a warm smile and friendly greeting, they could start afresh. She recalled Joshua Harrington's opinion of John Duvoisin and grimaced. Somehow, she knew this was wishful thinking. But see the man she must. *You owe him nothing,* she thought, and then groaned. *Nothing but respect.*

She was fastening the last button on her plain dress when a pummeling resounded on the door. "All right, all right!" she laughed artificially as she opened it. Three eager bodies spilled into the room, dashing to the hallway door.

"What are you waiting for?" Yvette cried over her shoulder, disappearing into the corridor. "Come quickly!"

Charmaine followed, but by the time she reached the crest of the staircase, the twins were far below, slowed only by Pierre, who was trying to keep pace. Even in her excitement, Jeannette lovingly took his hand and helped him along. Next, they were jumping off the landing and racing out of sight, the patter of feet marking their passage. Charmaine lifted her skirts and hurried her descent, knowing it would be better to enter the dining room with the children.

She was too late; their voices echoed in unison, attesting to their boundless joy.

"Johnny!"

The name shook her to the core. He was still present at the table, most probably alone. But even if he wasn't, she felt certain he'd take pleasure in taunting her. She passed the study and braced herself, sighing in relief when she reached the archway and found his back was turned to her. She could observe him first, inconspicuously.

He lounged in Paul's seat, his boots propped on George's chair. The children were clustered around him. Jeannette was sitting in his lap, Pierre leaned against his left leg, wearing the widest of grins he'd ever bestowed upon a stranger, and Yvette, his staunchest ally, stood to his right, fiercely hugging his arm. Charmaine was astounded by the raw emotion betrayed with this reunion. One look at the girls' adoring faces, and she knew she had seriously underestimated how much they loved him. Even more striking was her impression the man reciprocated the feelings, his attention fixed on the twins, a hand rubbing Pierre's back.

"Where are our presents?" Yvette asked presumptuously.

"Presents?" John queried. "What presents? I didn't bring any presents." His voice was deep and crisp, and quite pleasing to the ear.

"Oh really? Then why did you wink at Jeannette just now?"

"I wasn't winking," he insisted, "I had something in my eye."

Yvette wasn't fooled. "Well, then, what's in that large sack under the table?"

"My, haven't we sharp eyes," he laughed in that chuckle that was already disturbingly familiar to Charmaine. "See for yourself."

Yvette clambered under the table to fetch her loot. She was soon forgotten as Pierre tugged on John's leg. "We hab a gubberness," he said, smiling up at the man, who leaned forward to lend his full attention.

"Do you?" John asked, and Charmaine could tell he was smiling. "Is she old and ugly like Nana Rose?"

"Oh no," Pierre pronounced seriously, the cruel remark lost on the innocent child. "She's boo-tee-full and I love her!" He hugged John's leg all the harder to emphasize his point, exacting another chuckle from the man.

"There she is!" Yvette pointed as she crawled from beneath the table.

John turned, and Charmaine's breath caught in her throat. Lifting Jeannette off his lap and setting her on her feet, he stood, and their eyes met, his lazy gaze holding her prisoner as he assessed her in the light of this new day.

So this is John Duvoisin, Charmaine thought. He was tall, though perhaps not as tall as his brother, with broad shoulders and a slender waist. Unlike last night, he appeared distinguished, his attire that of a gentleman. The cut of his face possessed a rugged handsomeness she had missed yesterday. Now there was no mistaking his identity. The resemblance to Frederic was distinct: brown eyes, long curved nose, square jaw, and thin lips. Even had his visage been blank, she would have known he was a Duvoisin, such was his bearing and stance—one that radiated the power wielded by the men of this family.

As if reading her mind, his thick brow tipped upward, touching the light brown locks that covered the whole of his forehead. She wanted to look away, except he seemed to challenge her to do so, his scrutiny supercilious, mocking her fear. She shivered at the thought of her future resting in his hands: she'd never be free of the tormenting fires he had stoked just a few short hours ago when he had come barging into her sheltered life. An inkling of the pain he would bring her caused her to recoil.

"I believe we've already met," he said with a crooked smile, "though we don't know each other's name."

"I know who you are!" she responded heatedly, her anxiety gone.

His brow raised further. "Well, now, for someone who thanked God never to 'place name to my arrogant face,' it certainly didn't take you long to scrape up all the details."

She gaped at him, nettled by his precise recollection. His respectable appearance was not going to foster polite conversation.

He, in turn, was amused by her blatant outrage. She was playing the lady wronged, though he knew she was no lady. Her self-righteousness would prove interesting indeed. "Come, Mademoiselle—it is Mademoiselle, isn't it?" With her rigid nod, he continued, "You act as if I'm still the water rat come in from the rain. Or perhaps in dry attire, I'm just a rat?"

"I never called you a rat!" she replied defensively.

"No?" he queried snidely. "What else but a rat crawls from a filthy hole? But then, considering we've only just met, perhaps I'm wrong. Surely you couldn't have formed a fair opinion of me, unless someone has influenced you. My brother hasn't been filling your head with nasty stories about me, has he?"

Her silence was answer enough, and he chuckled softly.

His merriment pierced her deeply, yet she could only glare at him, realizing he had manipulated her into betraying Paul.

"Don't look so chagrined, Mademoiselle," he commented. "You haven't told me anything that I didn't already know."

"I haven't told you anything!"

"That's right, you haven't, Miss . . . ?" He didn't know her name, and suddenly feeling at a disadvantage—he never tolerated that; putting others at a disadvantage was *his* forte—he pressed on. "You do have a name, don't you?"

Charmaine was intimidated by his directness. She thought of Anne London and grew wary of his motives. According to Stephen

Westphal, John was engaged to the widow. He had to know her name—and more! She'd not open herself to further ridicule by answering. Instead, she spoke to the children, who were seated at the table, watching them avidly. "I'm going to ask Mrs. Henderson to prepare a breakfast tray. We can eat—"

"I asked for your name, Mademoiselle," John cut in curtly.

There was no avoiding it. "Charmaine Ryan," she threw over her shoulder, praying her assumption was wrong, yet hastening toward the kitchen in case it wasn't.

"Well, then, Charmaine Ryan," he replied slowly, testing the sound of it. "You and the children shall breakfast with me. Come now, no need to be afraid."

Though his gibe halted her step, curiosity turned her about face; his voice betrayed not the slightest indication he knew who she was.

He, in turn, canted his head to study her. Somehow, she seemed familiar, though he was certain he had never met her before. "Charmaine Ryan," he murmured again as he pulled out the chair he had propped his feet on earlier and gestured for her to sit. "Since you are guardian of the children, I would just like to talk—become better acquainted with you *and* your moral conduct in my home."

She stood stunned. How would she ever reclaim her dignity? She considered leaving the room, but that would lend credence to his lewd conclusions. More important, she couldn't abandon the children; he'd hold that against her as well.

"I'm sorry, John," Paul called as he entered the room, "but Miss Ryan and the children are breakfasting with me."

Charmaine sighed in relief.

"How charming!" John chortled, leaning back against the table and crossing his arms and legs. "If it isn't the knight in shining armor come to rescue the damsel in distress." The twins giggled. "And I'm not invited?"

"You can join us, Johnny!" Yvette interjected.

Paul grunted. "Come Charmaine," he said, taking her arm, "we can eat in the kitchen."

"Don't bother," John replied, pushing off from the table. "I know when I'm not wanted."

"Don't go, Johnny!" Jeannette implored. "We haven't visited with you yet."

"I will come to see you later," he promised. And then, on an afterthought, he asked, "Why hasn't your mother joined you this morning? Is she taking breakfast in her chambers?"

The girl froze, her astonishment mirrored by Yvette. He turned befuddled eyes upon Paul, who struggled with a response.

"John—I—"

Then Jeannette was crying, and John's mounting perturbation was diverted. "What is it? What is the matter, Jeannette?"

"Mama is dead, Johnny," Yvette whispered unsteadily. "She died in April."

A tumult ran rampant across John's face, and suddenly, Charmaine felt sorry for him. He obviously had no idea about Colette's death.

"When were you planning on telling me this, Paul?" he snarled.

"I didn't know you hadn't been told—"

"The hell you didn't!"

The moment held until John headed toward the foyer in large, angry strides. Paul rushed after him. "Where are you going?"

"To see Father and find out what other secrets he's been keeping!"

Paul grabbed his arm. "No, John! You hurt him enough last time."

John ripped free, his face contorted, a feral gleam in his eyes. "*I hurt him?*" he thundered. "*I* hurt him?" Then he fell on Paul in volcanic fury, grabbing great fistfuls of his shirtfront and slamming him into the wall.

Charmaine wasn't sure if the impact or her scream brought Fatima Henderson racing from the kitchen.

"What's going on in here?" the cook demanded, her voice bringing John to his senses. "Master John, what's gotten into you?"

John's grip relaxed, and Paul pushed him away. They glared at one another, refusing to meet the woman's reprimanding eyes, Paul adjusting his jacket as if he were the conqueror instead of the vanquished.

"Miss Charmaine," Fatima pressed when neither man would answer her, "what are these two up to, already at each other's throats and Master John not even home a day yet? Are they fighting over you?"

"No, Fatima," Paul refuted coldly, his eyes fixed on his brother. "We're not fighting over Charmaine. John just doesn't like hearing the truth."

Reality began to sink in, and John's wrath caved in to desolation. His face had gone white, and Charmaine read his anguish. He bowed his head and left.

She regarded Paul, silently beseeching an explanation.

"Fatima," he directed, "please see to the children while I speak with Charmaine."

Fatima took charge of Pierre's plate, giving Jeannette a comforting pat on the shoulder. The girl continued to sniffle, her cheeks wet.

Paul looked to Yvette. "When you're finished, you are to take your brother and sister back to the nursery. Mademoiselle Ryan will meet you there."

Yvette nodded. It was clear from his tone he'd brook no resistance.

John reached the landing, head down, when his eyes fell upon the bottom of her gown. His gaze lifted, taking in the folded hands, her bust, and finally, her breathtaking face, smiling down at him from the portrait, young and innocent, and suddenly dead. *Too late, I've arrived too late.*

His name echoed from above. He tore his eyes from Colette's lovely face and looked at his aunt.

"So it *is* true," Agatha said as she descended, "you've returned."

"So I have," John muttered, "and unfortunately, so have you."

Unperturbed, she smiled triumphantly, eyebrow arching. "Apparently, you haven't heard *all* the news. Unlike Colette's unfortunate passing, there has been a joyous wedding in the manor. I am pleased to tell you your father and I were married in July."

John thought he would vomit. His aunt's smug mien fired him anew, and he took a threatening step toward her.

Her smile broadened, unalarmed. "It was inevitable. Frederic and I have been in love for many years now. Had I been widowed sooner, I would have become the second Mrs. Duvoisin, rather than the third. Colette was much too young for your father, really. After all, she could have been his daughter. He needs a *woman* to love him, not a little girl."

John would have taken great pleasure in slapping her face if Rose had not called to him from the crest of the north wing staircase.

"John, you *are* home! I was just coming down to see you."

He spun around, masking his emotions. "I'm afraid I can't talk right now, Nan. My father is waiting to see me."

"John," Rose admonished gently, warily, "please . . . be kind."

"As you say, Nan," he bit out, before pushing past Agatha.

His mind was a maelstrom of words and images. What had George said? *Colette fears Agatha . . . fears the hold she may exert over Paul . . . fears for the children . . .* Clearly, his aunt had been after bigger game and had bagged it.

Agatha's twisted smile followed him. When he was gone, she threw a knowing look to Rose, then turned and climbed the stairs.

Rose offered a silent prayer. She had hoped to have a moment alone with John, but she was too late and headed to the dining room instead.

Paul closed the study door and leaned back against it.

"What happened out there?" Charmaine asked.

"You needn't be concerned about it," he replied with an exasperated sigh.

"Needn't be concerned? I was terrified! He attacked you!"

"My brother is easily incensed. He imagines slights against him when none exist, and then he carries on as he did just now."

"But not having been told about Colette *is* a slight. And although I'm not fond of your brother, surely he was justified in being angry about that!"

"He was informed about her failing health months ago," Paul stated flatly. "Her death shouldn't have come as a shock."

"Then why was he so angry?"

"As I said, he doesn't like to hear the truth. He's hurt members of this family with this sort of behavior. Even Colette, as good and kind as she tried to be to him, suffered at his hands."

Charmaine gaped at him in disbelief. She shuddered to think episodes similar to the one she'd just witnessed had taken place in the past. God forbid, had the man been violent to Colette? She didn't dare ask. "But why?"

"Ever since I can remember, John has been determined to do things his way, and his way invariably runs afoul of our father's wishes. My father has good reason to be angry with him on many accounts. Likewise, John hates the fact that our father is still in charge. It is the very thing that fuels his fury."

She could not speak. The picture Paul painted was all too reminiscent of her parents' home. Fear was nipping at her heels again, that same gnawing apprehension she had constantly lived with when her father was around.

"Charmaine, you've heard me speak of my brother before. You saw for yourself how he is, both last night and this morning. Even so, you needn't worry. You can trust me to watch out for you."

"I hope I can."

"You must. Rough times are ahead. John will see to it. He always does."

"Master John?"

Grave concern creased Travis Thornfield's brow, and he stood his ground, blocking John's entrance to his father's chambers.

"Let him in, Travis."

Travis stepped back, and John stalked into the bright dressing room.

Frederic was standing, and though he appeared at ease, his pulse was racing.

"Leave us alone, Travis," John growled, his anger fed by his father's calm demeanor and restored health.

"Sir?" the manservant questioned, his eyes traveling to Frederic.

Frederic only nodded, and Travis deserted the electrified room.

The day was still in its infancy when Charmaine carried her breakfast tray upstairs. Her steps were slow and burdened, lack of

answer, just the sound of scurrying footfalls. She called out again.
"Are you in there?" Still, no reply. She pondered momentarily what
to do. Perhaps it wasn't the children. Jeannette would not have
held silent. And yet, anyone else would have responded. Hence,
she opened the door.

A gust of wind rushed past her, swirling around her legs and
taking up her skirts, sweeping a ream of stationery off the nearby
desk and raining its many sheets on the immaculate floor. As she
stepped into the empty chamber, a second gale burst through the
French doors, taking more paper to wing. Now she had a mess to
clean up.

She closed the door to stem the stiff breeze and set to work.
There were scores of blank sheets. Slowly, she straightened and replaced them. She abruptly stopped. There was a letter here—a very
wrinkled and worn letter. Charmaine recognized the hand immediately, and her heartbeat quickened. It belonged to Colette. She

quickly placed the three pages in order and gasped when she found the first sheet.

My dearest John,

I cannot know your present state of mind. It is not my intention to cause you greater pain . . .

John stood before his father, seething.

"Why don't you sit down, John?" Frederic offered.

"I won't be staying long," came the rigid reply.

Frederic exhaled. "Welcome home."

John snorted, further revolted by the false greeting. "I see Colette's painting still hangs in the center hallway, Father. When will you be commissioning the artist to paint your third wife's portrait?"

Frederic received the heavy sarcasm evenly. "You've seen Agatha?"

"Right after I found out about Colette's death," John answered virulently. "Not one slap in the face, but two! Tell me, Father, couldn't you wait for Colette's body to turn cold before you took another wife?"

"My marriage to Agatha has nothing to do with Colette."

"You amaze me, Father. I think I've left a cripple behind, but look at you: you're up and about, a veritable newlywed! Poor Paul, he thinks you can't withstand another confrontation with me, but you *have* withstood two young wives, the last of which gave you a real run for your money. And here you are, only four months after Colette's death, working on wife number three!" He shook his head in theatrical astonishment. "You must be slipping, though. Agatha's rather old. I would have put money on the new governess catching your eye. She's more in line with your taste for virgin flesh, isn't she?"

If Frederic had hoped John's journey home was for any reason other than continuing where they had left off four years ago, he was mistaken. With his prayers for the morning swiftly desecrated, his heart took up a new beat, and his blood began to boil. And still John was talking, his words ruthless and baiting.

"Or could it be you're ready to admit you're too old for someone as young and fetching as Miss Ryan?" He paused for a moment, pretending at thought. "No, that can't be it. You still have all that money to spend! And any young, impressionable maiden would salivate at your feet if you wagged that fortune in front of her, wouldn't she?" He paused again, placing a fist under his chin as if the problem were too perplexing to figure out. Then, he lifted a finger in mock comprehension. "I know what it must be! Paul has laid claim to her and you wouldn't dream of interfering. After all, he's your shining star."

Frederic had heard his fill. "You've come home to insult me, is that it?"

"Not quite," John denied. "I came home because Colette wrote to me. You were aware of that, weren't you?"

He relished the fire in his father's eyes and eagerly pressed on. "She feared for the children. Now, let me see, what were her exact words? Ah yes: 'If your father cannot put his bitterness behind him, the only love the children will have when I am gone is that of their governess and Nana Rose.' But here's the problem: Rose is terribly old, their governess is a little trollop falling all over Paul, and then there's you, the father they never see—the bitter one. Such a happy family, isn't it? Oh, but I forgot, now they have a stepmother. Won't she make their lives just wonderful?"

"That's enough!" Frederic ground out, his jaw clenched and twitching.

John smiled wickedly; he'd gained the desired result. "How does it feel, Father, to know your wife wrote to her *stepson* to request his aid in supplying the children with the love and affection they'd never get from you?"

"I am not surprised she wrote such a letter, John," his father fired back. "She's played you for the fool more than she has me."

"And what is that supposed to mean?"

"Let us just say I was married to her for nine long years and came to know her in ways you can't hope to imagine."

John resisted the urge to deliver a hammering blow to his sire's face. Instead, he damned him silently, a hatred unmatched, then turned away and escaped the room, slamming the door behind him. Agatha stood in the hallway, a tight smile of victory on her lips. John contemplated striking her, but curbed that weakness as well. With blood pounding in his ears, he headed for his chambers.

"Some things never change," Frederic mumbled as he slouched into the armchair. "When will I accept that?" Burying his face in his hands, he massaged his brow. He had an excruciating headache.

Charmaine's hands were trembling as her eyes flew over the letter. *Why had Colette written to John, especially after the way he had treated her?*

She quickly folded the sheets and placed them back on the desk. But they unfolded slowly, inviting her to read on, and she glimpsed the date at the top of the first page: Wednesday, March 8, 1837—exactly one month before Colette's death!

The penned endearment shouted up at her—*My dearest John*—words reserved for a loved one. According to Paul, Colette had suffered at John's hands, and Colette had said John was angry with her. *Dear God*, Charmaine murmured, unable to attach reason to it. Then again, Colette would have put aside rancor to make peace, to convert the demon with temperance.

Charmaine picked up the letter again, her eyes falling to the first paragraph, drinking in phrases not intended for her eyes.

> *. . . I pray you receive this letter. I have every faith in George to deliver it into your hands.*

George? The gossip was true! He *had* traveled to Virginia! The letter must have been extremely important to warrant the abandoning of his duties these many months. Charmaine continued to read, this time in the middle.

> *. . . I do not want to die knowing he will shortly follow me in such a state of mind. The ferocity of his anger belies the depth of his love, but he needs somebody to show him the way. I was unable to do so, but I know you are. If you have ever truly . . .*

Suddenly, the hallway door banged open, and John stormed the chamber, grabbing hold of the rebounding door and slamming it shut with such force the walls vibrated. He was halfway into the room before he realized she was there, her loud gasp breaking through his violent thoughts.

What is she doing here?

And then he knew: clutched to her breast was a letter—his letter. This unsavory act was the last straw, and he exploded. "How dare you sneak into my room and rummage through my drawers for what you could find?"

Charmaine was too terrified to speak, her slackened jaw quivering. She was guilty of violating his privacy, and nothing could exonerate her.

"I'm waiting for an answer, demoiselle!"

"I—I'm sorry!" she sputtered, bursting into tears.

The letter slipped to the floor, and her legs propelled her forward. She didn't get far. He caught hold of her as she skirted past, jerking her around to face him.

"Not so fast!" he snarled. "Why are you in my room?" He gave her a hard shake, his hands like vises biting into her flesh.

"I'm sorry!" she sobbed, writhing against his brutal fingers. "I didn't know it was your room!"

Although her contrition was convincing, a torrid torment roiled in his heart, making it easy, satisfying in fact, to vent his wrath on this wench, who was digging herself into a deeper hole of dubious conduct every time he ran into her. Perhaps she wasn't the vicious, manipulative Agatha Blackford Ward, the new Mrs. Frederic Duvoisin, but she was a conniving Jezebel all the same.

"You expect me to believe that?" he chortled insanely.

"I was looking for the children!" she cried.

"In my desk drawer?"

She wrenched one arm free, but his fist yanked the other painfully higher. "You're hurting me!"

"Just as I suspected!" he sneered demonically. "You have no answer!"

He pushed her away, and she fell backward into the bed, sitting with a thump, massaging her throbbing arm. Although tears smudged her cheeks, her eyes were suddenly dry. They flashed with hatred, hatred for this man, another "John," who was so much like her father. He had just sealed his fate. From this moment forward, their discourse could never be civil. He was a dog and would forever remain so. No matter Colette had written kind words to him, trying to reach his blackest of souls. But Charmaine was not Colette, did not have the fortitude to selflessly forgive.

Experience had taught her such attempts at peacemaking were futile. With jaw set, she pushed off the bed.

John didn't falter under her display of courage. The moment she moved, so did he, checking her escape. "Now," he growled icily, "I want the truth from you, or you'll have more than a sore arm to rub when you leave this room!"

Charmaine shivered momentarily, but the embers of hatred had been stoked, and its fire eclipsed her fear. "I've told you the truth. I was searching for the children. I heard noises coming from inside this room, but when I called to them and they didn't answer, I assumed they were up to some mischief. That's when I opened the door. A draft blew the papers to the floor. I was merely picking—"

"Behind closed doors?" he demanded incredulously. "Do you take me for a fool, Mademoiselle? I placed that letter in the desk drawer. So tell me, Charmaine Ryan, how did the wind manage to blow it from *that* spot?"

Charmaine fleetingly puzzled over his declaration and dismissed it as swiftly as she thought: *The desk drawer? Colette's letter was not in a drawer. He's hell-bent upon venting his anger, and I've become an easy victim.*

John perceived her confusion, her partial innocence, and his temper cooled.

"I've told you the truth," she hissed, squaring her shoulders. "Let me pass."

"You've lied."

"I haven't lied, but I can see the truth makes little difference to the likes of you. Go ahead and strike me if you must. I'm sure it will be the victory you've been seeking all morning."

Stung by the accurate remark, John hesitated, then stepped aside.

Charmaine was shocked and could not move.

"Well, *my Charm . . .*" he drawled obsequiously, the mock endearment of her name a slap in the face. "What keeps you from departing? Perhaps you are awaiting my leave?"

She stiffened, then raised her chin and dashed around him. As she reached the door, she threw a defiant glare over her shoulder, but the gesture offered little satisfaction, for he responded by bowing low like a courtesan showing great respect for a noble lady.

Once free, she was overcome by blinding tears and collided with George just as she reached the nursery. "Charmaine?" he queried. "What is the matter?"

She struggled to pull away until she realized who he was. "George! You're home!" Then she sobbed harder, luxuriating in the safety of his arms.

"There, now," he soothed, taking courage to stroke her back. "It's all right." He had only seen her in this state once before, and he wondered what could have upset her so. Then, as if struck by lightning, he knew.

Charmaine shyly lifted her head, wiping dry her cheeks. "I'm sorry, George," she laughed self-consciously, "I didn't mean to cry on your shoulder."

"That's all right," he countered. "What are shoulders for, anyway?" Then the levity was gone. "Would you mind me asking why you were crying?"

"It was nothing," she lied, averting her gaze.

"Nothing but John," he mumbled.

Astonished, her eyes shot back to his face. "How did you know that?"

"I just know. What did he say to upset you?"

"I don't want to talk about it."

She seemed about to cry again, so he refrained from pressing her for details. "You would be wise to avoid John for a while. He's come home to sad news. I'm certain he's not taking it well."

"Why are you telling me this?" she asked charily. "Are you defending him?"

"John is like a brother to me. He's not a bad man, just a troubled one."

"I'm sorry, George, but I'm afraid I've seen the real John Duvoisin, a side he'd never show another man—that of the devil!"

George willed himself not to smile, having heard similar sentiments many times before. "Very well." He sighed. "Just stay away from him. *Far* away."

"Don't worry," Charmaine avowed. "I intend to."

"Good. Now, before I talk with the *devil*, I'm supposed to tell you the children are with my grandmother in her chambers."

"How did you know where they were?"

"After four months away, my first order of business was to visit my grandmother. The children were with her when I knocked on her door."

"I had better see to them," Charmaine replied.

George watched her go. Shaking his head, he strode to the guestroom John now occupied. According to his grandmother, the man had been apprised of all the events leading up to his return home, namely Colette's death and Agatha's reign. John had to be furious if he'd confronted Frederic already. George cringed with the thought of facing his friend just yet. Perhaps this was not a good time, he concluded, the fist he'd held suspended dropping to his side.

Monday, August 21, 1837

Sunday was mercifully uneventful, and when the day ended, Charmaine thanked the Lord she had been spared John Duvoisin on the Sabbath. She'd anxiously anticipated another rancorous altercation with him, but her worries had been needless. He hadn't attended Holy Mass and was absent for all three meals, locking himself away in his chambers, his presence signaled only by the footfalls of Anna or Felicia as they scurried to his door to deliver another bottle of spirits. Nevertheless, Charmaine had been afraid to venture from her own quarters. Their dispute over Colette's letter was too fresh in her mind, and she hoped to postpone their next confrontation for as long as possible.

For that reason, she rose early today and hastily ushered the children down to breakfast. With any luck, the detestable man would abstain from eating again, or would rise late, and she could successfully evade him for a second day.

As Fatima set four steaming bowls of porridge on the table, Charmaine reeled with the realization she loathed a man she had only known for forty-eight hours. Her conscience chastised her, but she reasoned others were suffering his return as well, the house teetering on an undercurrent of tension. Family and servants alike seemed to be awaiting his next move, the thundering crash, the ultimate explosion. Charmaine vowed to be absent for it.

To that end, she was determined to finish breakfast with the children as quickly as possible and retreat to the safety of their rooms. However, Yvette was just as determined to sabotage her plan. She dallied through the meal, distracting Jeannette and Pierre. Every time Charmaine pointed a finger at her cereal, the girl protested. "Too many lumps!" So, the oatmeal grew cold, and Charmaine had run out of threats.

"I'm going to get some milk!" Yvette announced. "I'm incredibly thirsty!"

"You stay right there," Charmaine enjoined. "I will get it for you."

Upon returning to the dining room, Yvette was nowhere in sight. "Where is your sister?" Charmaine demanded.

"Gone," Pierre replied, taking hold of his glass and sloshing milk down his shirt before greedily drinking it.

"Back to our room," Jeannette elaborated. "She changed her mind."

Charmaine did not believe it for a second, and wiped Pierre's dampened chest in rigid restraint. Sure enough, the nursery proved empty. Now she feared the worst: the eight-year-old had begged all weekend long to visit her older brother's apartments. *That* was her destination.

When Jeannette promised to read to Pierre, Charmaine took a deep breath and set out in pursuit of the errant twin. She walked quietly along the veranda, stopping just shy of John's quarters, head cocked, listening. No voices, though the French doors were open. Tiptoeing closer, she peered in at an angle, a small section of the chamber visible. Nothing—nobody. She leaned forward and spied the foot of the bed. A little farther, and boots came into view. She jumped back, stumbling over her own feet and nearly falling, plastering herself against the face of the manor. Someone was reclining there—John! When her heart stopped hammering, she chuckled softly, foolishly, and relaxed. He was alone; she'd been wrong.

Where to look now? She crossed through her room and began with the second floor of the north wing, next the servant's staircase to the kitchen, then the kitchen itself. No Yvette. She cracked the door that opened onto the dining room, relieved to find only Anna and Felicia moving around the table, setting down teacups and saucers. She walked casually across the room, ignoring their sidelong glances, and entered the study. It was empty as well. She was growing more frustrated by the minute and feared her original assumption was correct: Yvette had stealthily made her way up to John's chambers.

Gritting her teeth, she stepped into the drawing room and circled the piano, the two sofas, the high-back chairs, and the coffee table. She looked behind the curtains. Still, no Yvette. She moved to a table near the French doors. It was covered with a lace cloth that fell to the floor. She had just bent over to peer under it when a crisp, masculine voice resounded behind her.

"Searching for something, Mademoiselle?"

Charmaine's heart leapt into her throat, and she straightened so quickly she nearly toppled the table.

John leaned placidly against the hallway doorframe, arms and legs crossed, a bemused smile on his lips. The easy portrait ended there: his eyes were bloodshot, his complexion ruddy, and his cheeks covered in stubble. He seemed oblivious of his unsteady state as he persisted in demeaning her.

"You didn't have to straighten up so fast. Your derrière is the finest bit of fluff I've had the pleasure to see in quite some time, save for the other night."

Charmaine reddened, irate more than embarrassed.

His smile broadened. "What are you searching for so diligently? Perhaps I could help locate it? If not, I'd be happy to assist with anything else that comes to mind." His eyes, which had scanned the room, now raked her from head to toe, indifferent that she was deeply offended.

She steeled her emotions and walked briskly toward the archway where he stood. He did not step aside; rather he placed his palm flat against the doorjamb, blocking her path.

"Once again, Mademoiselle," he stated in irritation, "you haven't answered my question. Perhaps you thought the wind had blown a letter under the table, and you felt it your duty to pick it up and *read it.*"

He expected an angry response and was unprepared when she ducked under his extended arm and raced into the main foyer. She had reached the steps by the time he'd whirled around, but his chuckle followed her up the stairs.

Safe in her bedchamber, she cursed herself for running from him like some frightened child, or worse yet, a guilty one. She should have stood up to him, and she stamped her foot. "Oh, that miserable, despicable man!"

She entered the nursery, praying that by some miracle Yvette had returned.

"Did you find her?" Jeannette asked, looking up from the book.

"No," Charmaine replied in exasperation, only half-aware of Pierre, who had left his sister's lap to give her a big hug. "Jeannette, do you have any idea where she could be?"

Jeannette's negative response set her to pacing. Soon the household would be stirring, and she fretted over the mistress's severe reprimand should Yvette turn up in some forbidden area. Her heart missed a beat when there was an unexpected rap on the hallway door. *Agatha already?*

Charmaine reached it, cringing when Yvette bounded in, leaving her to face not Agatha, but John.

"I'm returning one missing twin to where she belongs at this hour in the morning," he said. "She was what you were looking for, yes?"

"Yes," Charmaine replied curtly. "Thank you."

She pushed the door closed, not caring it would shut in his face. But he braced his hand against it, stopping it midway. "Before you lock me out," he smirked, "I'd like to have a word with you."

"You've already had a word with me," she rejoined audaciously.

"I'll have another word with you, then," he countered sharply, gesturing for her to step into the hallway.

For all her bravado, his temper was unsettling, and so she complied, counseling herself calm as he closed the door, hands folded primly before her, eyes lowered.

"Aren't you the least bit interested in where I found her?"

"No," she replied stubbornly.

"I see," he mused. "Incompetent *and* stupid."

Charmaine's eyes widened, both hurt and angry, but she didn't have the opportunity to defend herself.

"You would be wise to remember the children are your responsibility, Mademoiselle, at least for now. Yvette has no business eavesdropping on adult conversations, which she undoubtedly will hear if she escapes your eye and takes cover in the drawing room. Yes, that is where I found her."

Charmaine burned, his supercilious stance and smug smile giving rise to the words, "May I ask you if you are annoyed with me—or yourself?"

His brow raised in surprise. "Mademoiselle, Yvette is your responsibility."

"And I fail to see how she would have come to harm in the drawing room, unless you are embarrassed by what she overheard: your adult conversation—derrière and all! Furthermore, if you hadn't interrupted my search, she wouldn't have remained hidden for long."

John found her outburst entertaining, her large eyes just as diverting. But it wouldn't lead to victory, not even a small one. He'd sparred with intimidating opponents in his day and always won. *What else can I say to fire her up and garner more ammunition to use against her?*

"I don't care what she heard, Miss Ryan, and even less by whom. But *I* am the exception in this household. I know Mrs. Duvoisin, or even my dear brother wouldn't take too kindly to Yvette eavesdropping on them. If *they* find her in some hidden niche, I guarantee there will be all hell to pay, and the bill that hell charges will come directly to you. That will be all, *my Charm*."

It was the last straw. As he walked away, Charmaine pursued

him. "No, that won't be all!" she spat at his back, drawing him round as he reached the crest of the staircase and took one step down. She stepped in front of him, closer to eye level now, her temper out of control. "There is one more thing, *Master* John. You needn't remind me of my duties, and I take offense you've judged me incompetent. Obviously, you are unaware that I have managed quite well with the children for close to a year now, and not once has their welfare been jeopardized. But you are right about Mrs. Duvoisin: her reaction would have been just like yours. As for Paul, he has always supported me."

For the first time, John appeared stymied. Charmaine smiled triumphantly. He didn't remain mute for long, however. "Miss Ryan, I know you've made it well worth my brother's while to 'support' you, but you underestimate me."

"*Really?*" she returned, astounded by the scope of his crude conclusions. "You should know your father has also commended me."

John's eyes hardened. "*Miss* Ryan, you have no idea how miserable I can make your life if it strikes my fancy. It hasn't come to that—yet. But, use my father to threaten me, and it will."

Charmaine felt the blood drain from her face.

Mercifully, Agatha emerged from the south wing hallway, an unlikely buffer for her sudden intimidation. "What goes on here?" she demanded.

"Miss Ryan was just comparing the two of us," her nephew replied.

"Comparing us?" she choked out. "Surely there is no comparison!"

"Indeed!" John agreed wryly, raising his hand in salute.

Then he was gone, leaving Charmaine to contend with the confused woman. With a mumbled "good morning," she quickly retreated to the nursery.

There she spent the next four hours lamenting her loose tongue. Why had she spoken so brashly, boastfully? *Pride goeth before a fall* ... She'd grown overconfident and *had* underestimated John's authority. Should she take the matter up with Paul and tell him about the incident with the letter? She instantly discounted that idea; it would lead to more trouble. Yes, Paul might support her, but he was second in line. And if he went to his father, Frederic would never condone her unscrupulous behavior, no matter how she pleaded her case. Somehow, her future had been placed in John's hands. He held all the cards, had held them since Saturday morning. And if that wasn't bad enough, she'd just added more fuel to the fire. He was right—she was stupid!

The morning wore on, and the children grew bored. Charmaine had repeatedly quelled their requests to leave their sanctuary, but as lunchtime neared, she couldn't quarantine them any longer. Panic seized hold as they approached the dining room. What if John were there? Thankfully, he wasn't. Even so, his wraith was present; every little noise made Charmaine jump.

"Where is Johnny?" Yvette asked.

"I don't know," she replied, then added under her breath, "As long as he's not here, he can be anywhere he likes."

"You don't like him, do you?" Yvette demanded, canting her head.

"I never said that!"

"It doesn't matter. You'll change your mind sooner or later."

Charmaine nearly choked on her food. The child had never been more wrong in her life. She'd sooner declare her father a "man of God."

Lunch was over, but the children refused to return to the playroom. "I'm tired of playing with those silly toys or reading those fairytale books," Yvette protested. "We haven't left the nursery for days!"

She was right. They couldn't spend the rest of their lives se-questered. "Then let us have our piano lesson," Charmaine of-fered.

Yvette objected again. "Johnny might hear us, and I want to surprise him."

Charmaine sighed, but Jeannette's suggestion met with every-one's approval. "We wouldn't be spoiling the surprise if you played for us, Mademoiselle."

Minutes later, they clustered around the piano, and Char-maine placed her hands to the keys, performing her usual reper-toire of children's tunes while they sang along. Even Pierre joined in, the serious tremor in his voice spawning contagious giggles. All their woes were forgotten, and gaiety ruled the afternoon.

John was contemplating the ceiling and the dust motes sus-pended above him when the strains of a childhood melody floated into his bedchamber. "Damn good whisky," he mumbled, swing-ing his legs over the side of the bed. Still, he wasn't as drunk as he wanted to be. Grabbing the bottle he'd retrieved from the dining room earlier that morning, he uncorked it and poured a brimming glass. As he took a swig, the sound caught his ear again. His eyes went to the French doors where the curtains billowed in the breeze. The tune wasn't in the bottle, and it wasn't his besotted imagina-tion, either. Finding the music a welcome reprieve from his dismal abyss, he rose and headed to the balcony.

He wasn't prepared for the piercing light and squinted sharply, reaching for the balustrade, holding fast until his world stopped spinning and the throbbing in his head ebbed. The strains were clearer now, and he pictured the twins as they sang along. A femi-nine soprano rose above their voices, embellishing the melody. *How sweet,* he mused acrimoniously, *the governess plays the piano, too.* He looked at the glass he held, then hurled it over the banister, relishing the sound of shattering glass when it struck the cobble-stone drive.

"My, aren't we happy today!"

John leaned farther over the railing. An impish George Richards smiled up at him, his smile broadening when they made eye contact.

"You almost got me in a place I shouldn't mention."

"It would have done you some good, Georgie," John chortled. "What have you been up to today?"

"A better question is: what haven't I been up to? Paul keeps me going."

"Poor George," John cut in with pretended sympathy, "paying the piper for an extended excursion to America. Did he save all the work for you?"

"Not quite, but we've spent the morning going from one operation to the next. He's made a few changes and wanted to acquaint me with them."

"Changes?"

"He's put Wade Remmen in charge of the sawmill," George offered.

"Wade Remmen?"

"You don't know him. He arrived on the island about two years ago: ambition, brawn, and a sharp mind for business. He'll keep the lumber supply stocked while Paul turns his attention to tobacco. I'm glad Espoir is nearly running itself now. Even with Paul here, it will be a chore preparing the tracts for a new crop."

John listened, then snorted. "If Paul is going to be around, I guess we'll have more time to antagonize one another."

"Only if you want to, John," George stated bluntly, hating his role as middleman and peacemaker.

"That's right, George," John agreed coldly, "and he must want it pretty badly if he's shelved the building of his royal palace to plant tobacco and duel with me. But I'm up to the challenge, don't you worry about that!"

"John," George chided, "remember when the three of us ran around Charmantes from dawn to dusk? He's your brother, for God's sake!"

Running a hand through his tangled hair, John shook his head, unable to explain his festering misery. "I'm in a foul mood," he mumbled, suddenly feeling childish. "It's that blasted piano and the off-key singing."

"It's the liquor," George corrected.

"Yes, I suppose it is."

"You ought to give it up, John. It isn't doing you any good. Besides, the twins have been asking for you. They're anxious to see you."

"Yes, yes," John replied dismissively.

"Why don't you join us for dinner tonight?" George suggested. "I'll be there. So will my grandmother. She wants to see you. She's worried, you know."

John considered the invitation, then nodded. "Perhaps I will."

"Good," George said. "I have to keep moving. There's plenty to finish between now and then."

"Don't let me stop you," John quipped. "I wouldn't want to be blamed if Paul docks your pay for slacking off."

George chuckled and climbed the steps to the portico. He'd just ridden back from the harbor with Paul. Best to warn him John might dine with them. Not that he regretted coaxing John out of his isolation. Still, the man was drunk and bitter, a dangerous combination that could add up to fireworks.

He found Paul in the kitchen wolfing down a chicken leg and a thick slice of bread. "I invited John to join us for supper tonight," he said, nodding a thank-you to Fatima as she set a glass of cold water in front of him.

Paul coughed, swallowed, and then glared at him.

"I thought you should know," George added.

"I assume then, he accepted your kind offer?" Paul queried caustically.

"I think he did."

"Thank you, George, for all of us. I'm sure the meal will be as enjoyable as this one." He waved the bread in George's face before turning to leave.

George delayed him. "Paul, have a care, will you? John's your brother. He's licking his wounds, and they're deep. He could do with a bit of compassion."

"Those wounds, as you call them, are of his making."

"Perhaps, but they are still there."

Paul's eyes traveled to Fatima, who was dabbing her eyes with her apron. Uncomfortable with the converging fronts, he brusquely strode from the room.

Deep were his thoughts when he heard the piano. His perturbation evaporated as he moved to the drawing room doorway. He had ignored the music only minutes earlier in his rush to eat and get back to work. Now he needed it.

Charmaine struck the last chord of the long sonata she'd been playing in the hope the children would grow bored and ask to return to the playroom.

"Well done, Mademoiselle."

She cringed for only a second, then regarded her admirer, who stood tall and handsome in the archway. Paul returned her smile, and her heart soared. She rose from the piano bench as he stepped into the room, his gaze unwavering.

"Children," he directed, "run along and play outside. I want to speak with Miss Ryan. She will join you in a moment."

"Why should we?" Yvette objected, rolling her eyes at her sister. "We aren't babies anymore!"

Charmaine was appalled, but Paul was angry. "Yvette, I have told you what to do. Now, you will respect my wishes."

One look at his hardened face and Yvette capitulated, marching from the room in a huff, Jeannette and Pierre right behind her.

"Just like John," Paul mumbled under his breath.

"What is it you wanted?" Charmaine asked.

He stepped closer. *Will the children, the servants, and now, John, forever interrupt us? When will I find release from this gnawing desire?*

"Paul?" she queried, summoning him away from his dilemma.

"I'd like to escort you to dinner tonight," he said, "if you would permit me. I have reason to believe that, unlike last night or the night before, my brother will be present at the table this evening. He's been drinking and will do his level best to ruin an excellent meal. If I am at your side, he will think twice before he taunts you, as I suspect he might."

"Oh thank you, Paul! I do appreciate your concern."

He smiled down at her, impassioned by her ebullient gratitude. "Do you think I'd ever allow you to come to harm?" he murmured huskily.

Suddenly, she was discomposed. It was as if this were the first time she'd faced him after his fiery kiss on Friday night. She stepped back and dropped her gaze to the floor. "What time will you come for me?"

"I will be at your door just before seven o'clock."

"I'll be ready," she replied. Then, uncomfortable with the blood thundering in her ears, she quickly skirted past him and rushed outdoors.

Paul watched her go and smiled in satisfaction. "Here's to you,

John!" he toasted, raising an imaginary glass to his brother. *You make it so easy to play the chivalrous hero. And doesn't every impressionable young maiden love the hero?*

Rose took charge of the children while Charmaine dressed for dinner. Washing away the perspiration of the hot day, she donned her best dress, then stood before the full-length mirror, pirouetting to check herself at every angle. Though modest, it hugged her trim figure and shapely curves. Satisfied, she began brushing her hair. After a good hundred strokes, she wound it into a loose bun. The combs she'd received for her birthday were the finishing touch.

Before the clock tolled seven, she left her chamber and, with a tremulous smile on her ruby lips, made her way through the children's bedroom and into the playroom. To her surprise, only Paul was there, turning around at the sound of the door opening behind him.

"Good evening," she greeted shyly.

"Good evening," he returned suavely, an appreciative gleam lighting his eyes.

She looked away as he stepped forward. Her heart was already pounding, and she attempted to break the spell. "Where are the children?"

"I sent them downstairs with Rose. They were anxious for dinner, and I was anxious to see you again." He stepped closer. "Lovely," he murmured huskily, his hand caressing her cheek, "you are so lovely. I fear I haven't been of much use to anyone these past few days, for you have haunted my every waking hour."

The declaration was intoxicating, opening a floodgate of possibilities and leaving Charmaine vulnerable to the hand that traveled to her hair. Before she could protest, he released the thick tresses, catching hold of the locks as they tumbled down her back. Gently, persuasively, he pulled her head back. His mouth loomed above hers, his lips barely touching as he whispered an endearment. "You are the wraith that invades my dreams . . . the vision that follows me when I awake . . . my beautiful Charmaine . . ." He claimed his prize, his lips moving over hers with a ferocity that forced them apart, his probing tongue tasting its fill.

She fell into him, thunderstruck, eagerly returning kiss for flaming kiss, arms wrapped around his broad shoulders, pulling him closer as she reveled in the strong, sturdy body that held her. This time, no one interrupted, no one desecrated the rapturous embrace.

Abruptly, he pulled away, held her at arm's length, then turned his back on her, leaving her shaky and confused. She suffered the first pangs of lust, a foreign sensation of yearning and disappointment.

"I'm sorry, Charmaine," he murmured over his shoulder. *What is wrong with me? I would have taken her here, in the nursery, without a care of who might walk in on us. Damn! She is too damn tempting!*

"Is something wrong?" she queried, her voice small and laced with shame.

He inhaled before facing her again, commanding control of his raging desires. "Nothing," he reassured, a neat smile painted on his lips, "nothing at all."

"Then why did you apologize?"

"Because now is neither the time nor the place to kiss you like that. But you make me do wild things, Charmaine."

"Wild things?"

"Yes, like dreaming of you every night."

She delighted in his poetry, the musical sound of his voice, and her heart was fluttering again. "I'm sorry I plague you so," she whispered coyly.

"You may plague me, Charmaine, but it would be far worse if you fled me."

"Would it?" she asked seriously.

"It would," he answered earnestly. "Now, come, we've a dinner to attend."

Dinner . . . Amazingly, her earlier dread was no longer there. Paul's growing love eclipsed his brother's vicious hatred. With this man at her side, she could combat anything John hurled her way. Tonight, she would reign victorious.

Paul noted her poise. "You don't seem upset about the impending ordeal."

"With you there, how could I think of it as an ordeal?"

"You're a funny one, Charmaine Ryan," he laughed, recalling how she used to avoid him. "But you are correct. I will be at your side, and John will regret his efforts to come between us. Remember, I won't allow him to hurt you."

"I'll remember," she murmured, her throat tightening against her burgeoning emotions. Once, not so long ago, she had dreamed of laying all her burdens upon Paul's shoulders. Now, under his gentle insistence, she was finally moving in that direction. Could her dreams be coming true? It was best to remain anchored in reality, so she pushed the thrilling thoughts to the back of her mind.

He took her hand and began to lead her to the door, but she stopped. "Can you wait just a moment? I have to fix my hair."

"No," he objected, catching her arm before she dashed away. "No," he said again more gently. "Please leave it this way. It looks lovely."

She accepted his compliment and complied. The combs were still in place, holding the riotous curls away from her face. Unfortunately, she would be very warm with her hair down, but for Paul, she could endure the discomfort. With a final, wistful glance, they left the room.

For all her intrepid words, her hands turned clammy as they stepped into the dining room. The power of Paul's presence fortified her, but Charmaine prayed it would vanquish any defamatory information his brother might divulge concerning her actions of Saturday morning.

They were the last to arrive. Rose was seated between one of the twins and Pierre, helping them with their napkins. Although she had sworn not to, Charmaine's eyes went involuntarily to the end of the table, where John had lounged last Saturday morning—Paul's usual spot. She knew he was there; why did she bother to look? She was relieved to find her entrance was not having the same momentous effect upon him; he was engrossed in conversation with George.

George noticed her first, and his face lit up. "Good evening, Charmaine."

Grimacing, her eyes returned to John. She'd gained his attention. Though his face was clean-shaven and his apparel neat, alcohol had left its mark, his demeanor unsteady, his eyes bleary.

Paul stepped to the table and pulled out a chair for her. She would be seated close to John, but not directly to his left. She took her place with as much grace as she could muster.

When Paul turned to the chair she usually occupied, John appeared amused his brother intended to sit between them. But Paul did not take his seat. The chair seemed glued to the floor and would not budge.

"Are you going to sit down, Paul?" he queried merrily as he straightened up. "Or must we start without you? I daresay, we've been waiting for you and *Miss* Ryan for quite some time now. Whatever could have detained you?"

Irked, Paul yanked the stubborn chair, but instead of holding stiffly to the floor, it came up easily, and he stumbled backward, regaining his balance just short of a fall. The twins laughed, but he ignored them as he took his seat.

Charmaine cast cold eyes across the table, stifling the girls' mirth to an occasional snicker. She wondered what trick had caused the misfortune, her suspicions lying with the newcomer, whose eyes sparkled deviously.

The table fell quiet as the meal was laid before them—though not for long.

"I heard someone playing the piano today," John mused aloud.

Everyone looked up, save Charmaine, who fixed her gaze on her plate.

"The music was quite good . . . whoever was playing it."

Mutinously, her eyes connected with his. "Yes, quite good," he reiterated casually, his regard steadfast and challenging. "An assortment of lullabies and even an attempted sonata . . . Very—how shall I say—? *Sweet.*"

Silverware clanked on china and Charmaine cursed the blood that rushed to her cheeks, advertising her disquiet. His jeering gaze refused to release her, and so, she broke away first.

Thus dismissed, John turned his attention to his brother, who seemed oblivious to his calculated comments. Evidently, Paul had not yet recovered from his skirmish with the chair. Well, Paul's fatal flaw was his temper. John's was never leaving well enough alone. Even now, he was wondering: *How far need I push the governess before she lashes out and Paul rushes to the rescue?*

"Might I ask who was playing that beautiful piece this afternoon?" he continued most politely, a masterful performance of cordiality.

Charmaine knew he was goading her and refused to answer, picking up her fork instead.

"Nobody knows?" he pressed, eyeing Yvette. "Perhaps it was a ghost."

"I know who it was!" the girl offered eagerly.

Charmaine groaned inwardly. *Why didn't I just answer the ridiculous question, instead of allowing him to intimidate me?*

"Well?" John probed.

"Information costs money," Yvette informed him curtly. "How much are you willing to pay?"

Charmaine was revolted, but George chortled softly.

"Don't laugh, George," John quipped. "I fear your avaricious streak is rubbing off on my sister."

George's face dropped, and John turned back to Yvette, who was waiting for a monetary bid. "Now, Yvette, you wouldn't be expecting a bribe, would you? For if you are, Auntie over there might be interested in that little matter we discussed in the drawing room this morning."

Agatha leaned forward, suddenly interested in the story that was emerging from the opposite end of the table.

Yvette answered quickly. "Mademoiselle Charmaine was playing."

Charmaine was livid. Now that the answer was out, she simmered over the methods used to extract it. To think the man would actually coerce an eight-year-old child for his own gain! Unfortunately, his tactics had worked, and his laughing eyes were upon her again. Charmaine gulped back the bile rising in her throat, surprised when a reprieve came from the foot of the table.

"What is this matter concerning Yvette?" Agatha demanded of John.

He raised a hand to wave her off. "You can live without it, Auntie."

Sputtering momentarily, she quickly regained her aplomb. "You may call me Madame Duvoisin if you wish to address me!"

"Address you?" John shot back. "Rest assured I will never wish to address you anything—*Auntie*—and certainly not with *my* name. No, you will always be 'Auntie Hagatha' to me."

"Well, I never! Your father will hear of this!"

"Fine," John responded wryly, "why don't you rush up there

right now and tell him? Then perhaps the rest of us can eat in peace."

Seething, Agatha glared at him, but dismissed his suggestion. Then, unable to sling an equally debasive remark, she made a great show of ripping her gaze from him and turning her unspent fury upon her plate, forcefully plying her knife and fork into a slice of meat.

"Now," John sighed, turning back to Charmaine. "Is it true you play the piano, Mademoiselle Ryan?" His eyes rested momentarily on Paul, who shifted irately in his chair. "*Do* you play the piano?" he asked again.

"Yes," Charmaine answered flatly, looking directly at her tormentor now.

"You play quite well. Few are acquainted with the modern pianoforte and pound on it as if it were a harpsichord. Did you receive lessons from a maestro?"

His belittling sarcasm stymied her.

Rose sensed Charmaine's distress, aware John was no more interested in finding out where she had learned to play the piano than he was in giving up the alcohol he'd been nursing. It was time to intervene. "John," she scolded, "eat your dinner before it grows cold."

To Charmaine's stunned relief, John leaned back in his chair, glanced at Yvette, who found the reprimand quite delightful, then lifted a fork to eat. Charmaine turned back to her own plate, grateful for Rose's deliverance.

George studied John, his intimidation of Charmaine unfathomable. He remembered her tears on Saturday and sympathized with her plight. Over the years, he had seen many an unfortunate soul go down in defeat once they were in John's crosshairs, but those victims had always deserved it. He couldn't imagine what Charmaine, as sweet as she was, could have done to provoke John's wrath. "I saw Gummy Hoffstreicher in town yesterday, John," he began with a crooked smile and a dose of levity. "He actually asked me how you were doing!"

"And did you tell him I've been rather miserable lately?" John replied gruffly. "He should be pleased to hear that."

"After what you did to him," George chuckled, "I'd say he would!"

"What did Johnny do?" Yvette asked.

George's chuckle deepened. "When we were boys," he reminisced, "perhaps a bit older than you, John, Paul, and I used to go fishing off the main wharf in town. Fatima always packed a large lunch, and we'd be off for the day. Anyway, that's where Gummy always used to be."

"Gummy?" Jeannette queried. "Why was he called that?"

"John gave him that name. His real name is Gunther, but we called him Gummy because he was missing a good many of his front teeth."

The twins lit up, giggling at what Charmaine thought to be cruel. Looking askance at John, she noticed he was listening, but eating as well, his mind far from her. The conversation turned spontaneous, and she relaxed.

"He was always lurking about the harbor," George was explaining, "scavenging for food and hooks. He wasn't poor, mind you, just too lazy to bring his own lunch. So, if we didn't give him something to eat, he would steal the sandwiches out of our lunch sack when we weren't looking, and then we'd catch him 'gumming' down. Every day, we were one sandwich short, until John got angry enough to do something about it."

Felicia entered the room with a pitcher of water. Charmaine watched from the corner of her eye as the maid arrived at the head of the table. She leaned over to refill John's glass, her ample bosom straining against the tight uniform, top buttons undone, her obtrusive pose affording him a generous view. *What a lovely couple they make*, Charmaine mused. *They deserve each other!*

"The next day," George snickered, reliving the delicious revenge, "John cut open some fish and scraped out the guts. Then he poked out their eyes. Finally, he took the sandwiches and spread some eyes and guts on each one."

Charmaine's stomach heaved. George, however, was not so squeamish, guffawing with glee, tears brimming in his eyes and running down his gaunt cheeks. "I'll never forget Gummy's face when he bit into that sandwich. He spit it out so fast, well, I thought he was going to lose his breakfast, too!" His merriment washed over the table as Paul and John, then the children and Rose, began to laugh.

"And what about the eyes staring up at us from the dock?" Paul added, drawing an even louder howl from George.

"That was the last thing Gummy ever stole, at least from John, anyway!"

Charmaine found the entire tale distasteful, and she turned disbelieving eyes upon Paul, who was chortling even harder than George. Everyone found the tale hilarious, save Agatha and herself.

"I can find no humor in such barbarism!" the mistress declared.

Without thinking, Charmaine looked to John, certain his retort would be swift and sure. However, he caught her eyes upon him and said instead, "You see, Miss Ryan, my aunt and I are really not alike at all."

"That is precisely what I indicated this morning!" Agatha added.

In response, John raised his glass of brandy. "Here's to you, Auntie, I believe that is the first and only time we will ever agree!" He took a long draw.

Charmaine gasped when Yvette imitated him. Rose quickly confiscated her glass of water and reprimanded her softly. "That is not befitting a young lady." But Yvette's eyes remained fixed on John, wide and wistful with her brother's wink of approval.

Everyone went back to eating, and the table began to hum with clustered conversations. Paul and George exchanged ideas, but John remained reticent. With him unoccupied, Charmaine's nerves grew taut. Why had she surrendered Pierre to Rose's capable hands? Though the child ate his meal passively, seeing to his dish was the type of distraction she needed. Nevertheless, when she smiled at the boy who smiled back at her, she found John's gaze rested on him as well, and she thought better of having the child sitting next to her.

Thus, she concentrated on eating, forever mindful of her antagonist. *Surely he isn't constantly watching me!* She looked his way and cursed her stupidity. He instantly sensed her regard. The brow arched, and the amber-brown eyes mocked her. She rose to the challenge. She would not allow him the satisfaction of relentless intimidation. She would not!

As if comprehending her resolution, he addressed her directly. "Miss Ryan, I don't recall seeing you on Charmantes before I left a few years ago. I realize you would have been younger; however, you don't speak like an islander. In fact, I detect a Southern accent. I'd like to know how you obtained your position here."

To Charmaine's relief, Paul intervened, sparing the details. "Miss Ryan sailed from the States specifically to apply for the position of governess. She possessed all the necessary qualifications and was offered the job."

John propped his elbows on the table and tapped laced fingers against his lips. "Who decided Miss Ryan 'possessed all the necessary qualifications?' You? If so, perhaps those qualifications are not in the *children's* best interest."

His meaning was not lost on Charmaine nor Paul. The latter's jaw twitched menacingly, but his reply was temperate. "Colette conducted the interview. Miss Ryan was her choice."

Their eyes held in a silent, meaningful exchange.

"A most foolish choice if you ask me," Agatha interjected, drawing John's regard. "Miss Ryan has a most questionable past. She is nothing more than a sly opportunist who managed to slither her way into this household by clever pretense, preying on certain members of this family."

Paul's mouth flew open to protest, but John beat him to the punch. "Are you describing Miss Ryan or yourself, Auntie?"

Agatha gasped loudly, and he savored her outrage before continuing. "I don't think Miss Ryan is the consummate schemer you say she is. The refined conniver is never caught."

Fuming, Agatha fell into a stony silence.

Charmaine, on the other hand, shuddered at the man's tacit reference to Colette's letter, amazed at how effortlessly he discredited two people at the same time. Had she not been included in his double-edged remark, she would have appreciated the fact the mistress of the manor had met her match.

"Now, Miss Ryan," he proceeded, "what prompted you to leave your home and family, even your friends, to apply for a position so far away?"

For a second time, Paul attempted to answer, but John held up a hand. "Miss Ryan has a tongue, has she not? Allow *her* to answer the question, Paul. I fear that when you tell a story, I have to keep digging and digging until I get down to the truth of the matter."

The ensuing silence sent Charmaine's mind into a spiraling frenzy. Spontaneously, Paul winked at her, a gesture that drew a callous grunt from John. But it imbued her with valor; she could answer as concisely as he had. "My home was in Richmond," she said. "When my mother died, I needed to make a new life for myself. Friends in Richmond—the people I worked for—informed me of the opening for a governess here. They have family on the island."

"Really?"

"Yes, really! When I heard of the position and showed an interest in seeking an interview, they accompanied me."

The inevitable question followed. "And what of your father?"

Here it comes, Charmaine thought, *Anne London's nasty allegations.* She'd been right: John knew all about her past and had bided his time, carefully choosing the moment to defame her, and in front of the children, no less! She thought to flee. *I've learned never to turn my back on the enemy.*

"My father disappeared one day," she replied boldly, catching sight of Agatha's smug smile, "never to return."

"He just disappeared?" John scoffed. "Never to return? People don't just disappear, Miss Ryan. There must have been a reason why he deserted you. What type of man does such a thing?"

Rose's sympathetic eyes rested on the dedicated governess. Charmaine was undeserving of this insensitive inquisition. "John," she chided, "will you please stop talking and start eating? Your potatoes are getting cold."

"They're already cold," he stated flatly, not backing down as he had before, his eyes unwavering, "and my question has yet to be answered. I find your story hard to believe, Miss Ryan. Did your father really do that?"

"Yes," she whispered.

"Why?"

Charmaine clenched her jaw. Anger and humiliation collided, their union tantamount only to her loathing of this man. He played the game so well, pretending not to know the answers he probably had memorized, while insinuating she was the liar. "My father was responsible for my mother's death," she hissed. "He disappeared in order to escape punishment for his crime."

John regarded her skeptically. Her acting was superb—a hint of tears welling in her doe-like eyes—and for that she deserved credit. *But murder? Was she suggesting her father was guilty of murder?* One look at Paul's stark face and the macabre revelation was verified. "A great man," he commented mordantly.

"Are you satisfied?" she demanded. "Do you derive pleasure by demeaning me in front of the children, or are you out to prove me unfit to care for them?"

"I don't hold you responsible for your father's actions, if that is what you're implying, Miss Ryan, only your own. The man should have been horsewhipped and then hung at dawn for his evil deed. In future, when I ask a question, you should speak the truth, immediately. I'm an honest man, and I respect those who are honest with me. Perhaps we will get along if you heed my words."

Charmaine was both stunned and revolted by his condescending tirade. *An honest man? Bah!* "I fear you contradict yourself, sir, for when I dared to speak the truth to you on Saturday morning, you refused to believe a word I said!"

She immediately regretted bringing up the topic; Paul's puzzled regard was upon her. Even so, she could sense his applause.

John was not so easily captivated and laughed outright. He stood and walked over to the liquor cabinet, where he selected a bottle of wine. He uncorked it and poured himself another glass. "Don't play me for the fool, Miss Ryan," he sneered, turning back to her. "Poor innocent Charmaine Ryan just happened to venture into my chambers in search of her charges, when a gale force wind came along, opening a drawer and scattering papers on the floor. And just as she was doing her first good deed of the day by picking them up and *reading them,* that nasty ogre of a man, John Duvoisin, came storming into the room to persecute and defile her wholesome kindness with his blackhearted evilness—"

Paul shot to his feet, slamming his fists down on either side of his plate and sending the china clattering across the table. "You insist on making everyone here miserable, don't you?" he exploded. "*Don't you?*"

George jumped to his feet as well, shaking his head at a seething Paul before moving to John, whose eyes were dark with hatred. "John, just sit down and eat," he ordered, prodding him back to the table.

Surprisingly, John did not resist, and Paul, who awaited his brother's retreat, slowly sat as well. An implacable silence enveloped the room, leaving Charmaine to ponder this latest outburst. Surreptitiously, she glanced from Paul to John. The former blindly contemplated some object on the table, while the latter studied the crystal wineglass he rotated in his hand.

Minutes lapsed and the main course was eventually finished. Only dessert remained. Felicia returned with a generous tray of assorted cakes and turnovers. Charmaine declined, having lost her appetite long ago. Paul did the same, contenting himself with a cup of black coffee. John chose to nurse the wine in front of him. George, however, took three.

"You glutton," John commented, eyeing the stack.

Charmaine's anger flared. There wasn't a civil bone in the man's body.

"Why waste?" George shrugged, taking a large bite of the tart on top. "Besides," he continued with his mouth full, "tomorrow, they'll be stale."

"Yuk!"

All eyes turned to Jeannette, who had pushed her pastry away. "I hate nuts!"

Standing, she reached across the table for another, but Agatha swiftly confiscated the tray, slapping her hand away. "You've already chosen your dessert, young lady. You must be satisfied with it."

"But—"

"No buts!" Agatha reprimanded. "Nuts or no, you must eat the one you selected. A girl of your age and class should know it is uncultured to call attention to your plate and then attempt to snatch a second helping." The woman turned her accusatory eyes upon Charmaine, and the remonstration took on a twofold purpose. "It seems the children haven't received any lessons in table manners. First you"—and she flicked her hand at Yvette—"raising your glass like a common seaman at a tavern, and you"—she wrinkled her nose at Jeannette—"grabbing at the desserts like a starving beast. A proper young lady would be appalled!"

Charmaine bowed her head and silently sympathized with Jeannette.

"Furthermore, it is sinful to waste food," Agatha concluded.

John rose and walked to the foot of the table. His aunt cringed as he lifted the pastry tray. "Jeannette, if Auntie here is a paragon of propriety, then God help us. Personally, I think you are a fine young lady."

Enraged, Agatha's mouth flew open. "I will not tolerate your insolence!"

"Nor I yours. You've made it abundantly clear you fancy yourself 'Duchess-Countess-Empress-Your Royal Majesty, the Queen,' and I, for one, care not to have it shoved down my throat for dinner!"

"I am mistress of this house and demand your respect!"

"Ah, but one day I will be in charge here," John countered. "Take heed, Auntie. It is wise to stay in my good graces, for once my father passes from this world to the next, I won't hesitate to expel those who irritate me, relative or no."

Holding her breath, Charmaine glanced at Paul, surprised to see him smiling. One sweep around the room told her he was not the only one enjoying the duel. Anna and Felicia had stepped out of the kitchen, and Charmaine could vividly imagine Fatima Henderson from within, an ear pressed to the door.

"Your father will hear of this insult!" Agatha screeched, her face ruby red. "He shall hold you directly responsible for what you have said. Your drunken daze will not excuse you come the morrow!"

"I need no excuse," he replied, menacingly, "for drunk or no, I mean what I say. So take your little complaint to Papa as fast as your spindly legs will carry you. However, you will *never* receive an ounce of respect from me."

Though Agatha trembled with rage, John appeared insouciant, dismissing her as quickly as he presented the tray of pastries to Jeannette. "Which one would you like, Jeannie?"

"I wanted crème," she said softly, "but stepmother took the last one."

"Crème it shall be," John agreed before turning toward the kitchen and calling an unfamiliar name. "Cookie!"

Fatima hobbled into the room. "You want something, Master John?"

How clever, Charmaine thought wryly, *he nicknamed the cook "Cookie."*

He requested a crème pastry for Jeannette, and Yvette immediately jumped in, asking for another one, too. "And what about you, Pierre?" he inquired, looking to the boy who immediately turned around, a good portion of his half-eaten dessert smeared across his face. "I suppose not. Make that two crème pastries, Cookie, and next time, leave out the nuts. Jeannette doesn't like them."

"I like them!" George protested, plate miraculously clean, eyeing the one Jeannette had rejected.

"George, you would eat anything," John commented dryly. "If you were Gummy, we wouldn't have had a story to laugh over tonight."

He picked up the discarded tart, but instead of giving it to George, he placed it in front of Agatha. "Here you go, Auntie, you finish it. It's sinful to waste."

George laughed loudly, gladly forfeiting the pastry for Agatha's dressing down. Everyone else gaped. John's impudence was boundless, leaving Charmaine to wonder if he ever left well enough alone. Agatha continued to seethe, but said not a word as John returned to his seat.

Charmaine stole sidelong glances at the head of the table, studying him curiously. He had certainly fallen into his role of master of the house. How much power would Agatha wield with him countering her every move? A storm was brewing to be sure, and most exciting would be the final showdown, when the battle, as Agatha threatened, would be brought before Frederic. Who would the man stand by: his prodigal son or his witch of a wife?

Dessert was finished, and Paul stood. "Ladies, George," he suggested invidiously, "why don't we retire to the drawing room for the remainder of the evening?" He motioned toward the hall, then assisted Charmaine with her chair.

"I quite agree," Agatha added as if nothing untoward had happened, standing regally and running a hand over her costly gown. "Perhaps we could enjoy a glass of port. Yes, port would do me a world of good."

"I doubt anything would do her a world of good," John mumbled to George, rising as well, "excluding, of course, a stampede of wild boars."

George chortled again. "Why don't you join us?" he invited, leaving the table and patting John jovially across the back. "I need your advice on a land deal I've heard about near Richmond."

When John agreed, Charmaine's plans for the evening immediately changed. She moved around the foot of the table and lifted Pierre into her arms, placing a tender kiss on his chubby cheek.

"Mainie," he said, laying his head on her shoulder.

John's attention was drawn to the spectacle, and he frowned.

"This little one is ready for a bath and bedtime story," Rose commented as she stood and squeezed Pierre's pudgy leg. "Let me settle him in for the night."

"You've minded him for the entire dinner," Charmaine said, anxious to return to the nursery. "I'll take him."

Yvette stomped her foot. "I don't want to go to bed! It's too early. I want to go to the drawing room with everybody else."

"I didn't say you had to—"

"She is right, my Charm," John interrupted pleasantly. "It is much too early for the girls to retire."

Charmaine tensed; Paul was rankled by John's endearment of her name. "If you would have allowed me to finish," she replied stiffly, "I was about to say Yvette and Jeannette may stay."

"How noble of you," John taunted. "You relieve Nana Rose of caring for a small three-year-old, then ask her to mind two eight-year-olds."

"John," Rose admonished gently, "I love the children."

His face softened, and he considered Pierre, who snuggled contentedly in Charmaine's embrace. "I never doubted that. I know he's safe in *your* hands."

Insulted, Charmaine's arms quickened around the boy, but Rose was already coaxing him away.

"Allow Rose to see to Pierre tonight," Paul interjected. "We rarely have the pleasure of your company."

Defeated, she smiled across the table at him. Then her eyes traveled to John who was moving toward her, his raised brow and crooked grin unsettling.

"Let me," he said, reaching for Pierre. "I'll carry him upstairs for Rose."

The boy buried his head deeper into Charmaine's shoulder and refused to be cajoled into his brother's outstretched arms.

"I'll take him," Paul said, coming around the table.

This time Pierre lifted his head and smiled. Charmaine passed him over to Paul perturbed by the anger that smoldered in John's eyes.

"He knows me, John," Paul placated before leaving the room with Rose.

"Shall we?" George interrupted, defusing the vexing moment.

When they reached the front parlor, Jeannette crossed to John and clutched his hand. "Johnny? Is it true what Auntie Agatha said?"

"About what?" he asked.

"Are you really drunk?"

John seemed taken aback by her frank question. "Not quite yet," he said, bowing his head. "But a glass or two should see me to that end."

"Why haven't you visited us?" Yvette demanded, drawing up alongside her sister. "We waited in that boring playroom all weekend!"

"I was preoccupied with other matters, Yvette. I'm afraid I would not have been entertaining company."

He settled into a sofa, and the twins situated themselves on either side of him, a safe distance from Agatha, who took up the needlepoint she never seemed to finish. Paul returned, and he and George started discussing work priorities for the next day. As Charmaine suspected, the next unpleasant episode began.

"Wielding the whip again, Paul?" John observed dryly, joining them.

"That's right. After all, that is how we keep the business running, is it not?"

"Or how you keep George running," John retaliated, straddling the chair he'd pulled out and placed directly across from his brother. He folded his arms over the back and leaned forward. "You don't waste much of his time, do you?"

"No," Paul replied, "unlike you, I don't waste much of George's time."

"I thought you could run Charmantes with your hands tied behind your back."

"Once again, you are mistaken," Paul replied, his patience wearing thin. "I'm the first to admit my limitations, which happen to be far greater when George is not around to pull his weight."

George's chest inflated.

"But you did manage without him," John countered.

"Yes, I did. I'm not completely without resources."

George's chest deflated.

Pretending great interest, John continued his assiduous pestering. "You never cease to amaze me, Paulie, turning to virgin resources so the construction of your palace would not be delayed."

Paul was dumbfounded. "How did you know—?" He threw George a scowl and shook his head. "Never mind. It's a house, John, not a mausoleum."

"Well, then"—John proceeded with a chuckle—"if it's only a house, no wonder you were able to manage without George. And no, George didn't tell me. I already knew. So, how *did* you manage without him?"

"By relying on more dependable help," Paul answered, casting another emphasized glare at George. "In fact, the only real complication I had to confront and then rectify was of your making, dear brother."

Charmaine shuddered with the appellation, knowing it portended trouble. She watched John's lips curl amusedly, the devil dancing in his eyes.

"Complication?" he inquired innocently. "What complication?"

Paul resisted the urge to launch into the subject of missing invoices.

"Is there something wrong?" John asked, his tone all courtesy and concern. "No? Then may I ask a question?"

"Ask away," Paul ceded impatiently.

"You mentioned resources. Would it be too impertinent to ask who managed my inheritance when you went gallivanting across the seas to New York and Europe or your soon not-to-be-deserted island?"

"Father—he handled everything."

"Then he's only an invalid when he wants to be? I can't imagine him mounting his mighty steed and riding out to the fields each day. So, who *was* in charge while you were away? Or is that why the sugar crop has been so bad?"

Paul's temper flared. "You cannot be serious! I work my hands raw for the likes of you, while you sit back and wait for Father's fortune to fall squarely into your lap. Don't talk to me about gallivanting when it's you who've gallivanted on the mainland for these past ten years, choosing to do as little as possible!" When he received nothing more than John's crooked smile, he was needled into reproving his brother further. "In the words of Socrates: 'Let him that would move the world, first move himself.'"

"Really?" John yawned. "Well, Paulie, I'm more inclined to believe it is: 'better to do a little well, than a great deal badly.'"

Paul dropped the asinine volley.

John sighed loudly. "Now that we've gotten all that figured out, may we get back to the subject at hand?"

"And what would that be?" Paul ground out.

"The men you've put in charge—here on Charmantes." When Paul began to object again, John cut him off. "Just the names, please. That's all I want."

"Damn it, John, you know them all!"

"George mentioned a Wade Remmen. Who in hell is he?"

"Wade Remmen?" Jeannette inquired.

John nodded, looking to his sister. "Do you know him, Jeannie?"

"Oh yes! He's a handsome man!"

Charmaine smiled, aware of Jeannette's infatuation.

"He's quite handsome, is he?" John asked, his mien merry.

"Oh yes," Jeannette nodded eagerly.

"And who told you that?" he probed. "Miss Ryan perhaps? Tell me, does Mr. Remmen have a moustache?"

"No, Johnny," she denied, "Mama said he was handsome. Then I noticed."

Paul's furrowed brow gave way to a gratified grin.

John matched smile for smile. "Did you hear that, Paul? You have nothing to fear: Miss Ryan has eyes only for you."

"I know that!" Paul bit out, belatedly realizing how ridiculous he sounded.

Charmaine groaned inwardly, displeased her private affections were being broadcast to the entire room, breathing easier when Paul revisited the topic of Wade Remmen.

"When George disappeared four months ago, I asked Wade to run the lumber operation. He's managed it very well, his decisions sound. For that reason, I've placed him in charge permanently. George will now be free to oversee other important matters."

"Free to be at your beck and call, you mean," John rejoined. "Tell me, George, how do you like having your strings constantly pulled like a marionette?"

"I don't mind at all—so long as I'm well paid."

"I guess some things never change," John mused.

"That's an understatement," Paul mumbled.

Clapping his hands together, John pressed on. "This Mr. Remmen sounds quite industrious. How long has it taken him to reach such an elevated stature?"

Paul knew John couldn't care less about Wade Remmen or any other island employee, for that matter. The sole purpose of this inquisition was to perpetuate the game John enjoyed playing—that of heir to the family fortune—a game John knew chafed him greatly. So Paul steeled himself and put on a face of disinterest, determined not to allow his brother to succeed.

"Wade is from Virginia. When his parents died, he and a younger sister were left destitute. Unable to find work, they stowed away on one of our ships, hoping to build a better life here. The captain found them aboard the packet two days out of port and turned them over to me when the vessel docked. That was two years ago. Wade was seventeen, well built, and used to hard labor. He pleaded his case and promised to pay for the ship's passage if I gave him the chance. I had nothing to lose and haven't been disappointed. So it was only natural I relied on him when George deserted us."

"What a story!" John exclaimed with a dramatic shake of his head.

"Anything else you'd like to know?" Paul asked, ignoring the theatrics.

"Did Mr. Remmen ever pay for his passage?"

Charmaine was astounded at the man's stinginess, but Paul seemed accustomed to the financial interrogation and laughed spuriously. "Tell me, John, must I account for every penny that might slip past your wallet?"

"If you don't, our resident moneymonger George will. Right, George?"

"Right, John. And, no, I don't believe Wade paid for either fare."

"And why not?" John asked, his eyes leveled on Paul again.

"Because he has needed his wages to get settled," Paul replied, ripping his furious regard from George. "His salary has gone into purchasing the rundown Fields's cottage. He's done a fine job fixing it up."

"I should think so, having had two passages waived. A bit unfair, I'd say."

"I didn't waive them—"

"Miss Ryan wasn't given a grace period, was she? Two years can earn a fortune in interest."

"Impossible," Paul snorted, "it's impossible to speak intelligently with you."

"Since you are meting out charity from my pocket, shouldn't everyone get a share of the bounty?"

"Miss Ryan was not indigent," Paul responded snidely, certain John was pressing the issue simply to pit Charmaine against him. It wasn't working: not a hint of anger flashed in her lovely eyes. "Nor was she penniless. She held a comfortable position in Virginia, and could afford the crossing costs."

"Then why did she leave?" John demanded.

"We have been over this, John. She wanted to make a new life for herself."

"And that she has," John smiled wickedly, entertained by his brother's deepening scowl. "I'd like to meet this Wade Remmen. Indeed, I would."

"He's at the mill," Paul stated. "Whenever you come out of your inebriated daze you can look for him there."

He stepped over to the serving tray and poured three glasses of port, passing one to Agatha and another to Charmaine.

Charmaine accepted the libation grudgingly, taking a sip before setting it on the table. This evening had served as a vivid reminder of the detrimental effects of alcohol. It made angry men angrier. She'd be happy to never see a bottle of spirits again.

Yvette took advantage of the lull in the conversation and scurried over to the grand piano. "Johnny," she said in great excitement, "I have a surprise for you!"

Charmaine cringed. *Here it comes,* she thought. John had implied her abilities at the instrument were sadly lacking. Now he was about to discover she had taken it upon herself to teach his sisters the little she knew.

"What's that, Yvette?" he queried, the timbre of his voice unusually gentle.

"Just listen!" she exclaimed, commencing to play her favorite tune.

Charmaine resolved not to look John's way, yet her eyes mutinied. He did not seem to notice; he remained transfixed upon the simple recital.

"What do you think?" Yvette asked, swiveling around when she'd finished.

"I'm impressed. That was beautiful."

The girl was beaming, and Jeannette quickly joined her. "May I play now?"

With John's assent, she began. This time, his eyes traveled to Charmaine and remained there. She was uncertain what she read in his expression, but it was more than astonishment. Triumphant for the first time that night, she smiled defiantly at him.

"That was lovely, too, Jeannie," he said, turning his regard on both sisters. "I suppose Miss Ryan has been teaching you to play?"

Jeannette nodded. "But we swore her to secrecy so we could surprise you."

"Now I understand," he said, his half-smile sardonic. "Your governess wasn't at the keyboard after all this afternoon. You were just pretending it was she."

"Oh no, Johnny," his sister refuted earnestly. "It *was* Mademoiselle Charmaine. We don't play that well!"

"Do you think we play that well?" Yvette piped in.

"Nearly," he replied, satisfied he'd quashed Charmaine's gloating.

Jeannette moved from the piano to the chessboard across the room. "Will you teach me how to play chess, Mademoiselle? You promised you would."

"It's been so long since I've played. I wouldn't be a good teacher."

Paul capitalized on the request and left John and George, pulling a chair up to the table. "I challenge you to a game, Miss Ryan. Jeannette, I will instruct you as we play."

Charmaine stammered with an excuse. "I'm afraid I won't be much of an opponent. Perhaps George would like to play in my stead."

Her objection had fallen on deaf ears, for Paul was rotating the board so the white pieces were on her side. "Come, Charmaine," he coaxed debonairly, "I haven't played in a long time, either. We shall be equally matched."

She gave in reluctantly. Joshua Harrington had taught her the game's basic strategies, but she had never committed them to memory. Paul would handily gain control of the board, and although she didn't care in the least if she lost, she preferred her inadequacy not be exposed to his brother. And yet, John was conversing with George; perhaps he wouldn't notice.

". . . but George, if you purchase land that is nothing more than a swamp, you'll soon find yourself sinking into a quagmire of debt with that little devil of a lawyer Edward 'P.' Richecourt knocking on your cabin door. Now, I know you fantasize about accumulating unlimited wealth overnight," he continued facetiously, as Rose stepped into the room and moved closer to them, "but it won't happen if you go looking for bargains. Part with the money you've been hoarding, however, and I've a few prospects that might interest you—sound investments that could prove a real windfall over time."

Paul's eyes left the chessboard and shifted to John, but Rose interrupted. "How many times must I tell you not to sit in a chair that way, John Duvoisin? You are going to topple over."

John, who'd been balancing the chair on its back legs, stood and rearranged it. "I've been sitting that way for as long as I can remember," he complained good-naturedly, "and I have yet to fall."

"Don't argue with me," his one-time nanny warned, shaking a crooked finger at him. "I'm older than you, and if need be, I can still take a switch to you!"

The statement elicited giggles from the twins, who had lost interest in the chess game. "Did you really take a switch to his backside?" Yvette asked, her laughter renewed as John feigned a grimace of fear.

"On more than one occasion," he interjected, placing an affectionate arm around the older woman's bent shoulders and walking her nearer his sisters. Noticing he had everyone's attention where he liked it, he said, "In fact, I remember one occasion in particular when I was nine—not always a lucky number—"

"Do you mind?" Paul cut in. "I'm trying to concentrate."

Amazingly, John forfeited his story and gave Rose another squeeze before releasing her. "Is Pierre settled for the evening?"

"Sleeping like a newborn," she whispered, taking a seat near Charmaine.

"He's quite a boy," John commented, talking across the chessboard now. "I'm impressed by how well he speaks for a boy of—"

"John," Paul bit out, and then, "Please—take your conversation elsewhere."

"Am I not allowed to speak in my own parlor?" John asked innocently.

Turning slowly in his chair, Paul regarded his brother. "You may speak wherever you wish. I just ask that you spare me your domestic whims until I've finished playing this game with Miss Ryan."

"Now, Paul, I'd hardly be a gentleman if I allowed you to *play games* with Miss Ryan. Therefore, I will act as a chaperone and watch—quietly."

Vexed, Paul turned back to the chessboard, conscious of John surveying the game from behind him. Sliding his bishop five squares diagonally, he proclaimed Charmaine's king in check.

She was in a fine mess, and everyone was watching. Distracted, she pretended intense deliberation before edging her king one square forward. Belatedly, she realized she had laid her valuable queen open to attack.

Paul closed his eyes to the critical blunder, for capturing her queen would place her king in checkmate. Ignoring the decisive move, he took hold of his bishop. But John swiftly brushed his hand aside. "What sort of game is this, Paulie?" he needled, grabbing his brother's black queen and sweeping the white queen off the board. "That's checkmate."

Charmaine's eyes flew from John's taunting visage back to the chessboard. She was indeed in checkmate.

"You couldn't have missed that move!" John remarked with relish. "You were always better at this game than I. Or were you just allowing Miss Ryan a small victory before closing in for the kill?"

"That's it!" Paul snarled, his ire doubly stoked by the twins' chorus of laughter. "You've been at me all night, pressing my patience!"

"Have I now?"

"You know damn well you have!" Paul barked, coming out of his chair and standing toe to toe with his brother.

"Watch your language!" John admonished jovially, unperturbed. "There are ladies present, and we must at least act decently."

"What would you know about decency?"

"I don't know, Paul, why don't you—Mr. Epitome of Decency—tell me? Why don't you begin with an accounting of the money you've spent on Espoir and an explanation as to why you've concealed its development from me? Or could it be you don't want me to know how much of Charmantes' profits are financing your building project there?"

"So—the real issue comes to light! Why don't you take the matter up with Father?"

"I have all the figures," John smiled crookedly. When Paul turned on George, he added, "No, I didn't get them from George."

"Then who?"

"Your lawyer and mine, the distinguished Edward Richecourt."

"The hell you did!" Paul roared. "He was given explicit instructions—" As if caught, his words died in midsentence.

John paid no mind to what he already knew. "Ah, but given a choice, Mr. Richecourt wisely spoke up. You see, even though he despises me, he knows better than to bite the hand that will one day feed him."

"Very good," Paul applauded ruefully. "But what are you going to do about it, John? Tell Father how to spend *his* money? It's not yours yet!"

"I couldn't care less how *Papa* manages his affairs, and even less about his great estate. I've done fine on my own and, unlike you, will continue to do so without taking a single penny from his pocket."

"How dare you suggest I've taken money from this estate?"

"I wasn't *suggesting* at all, Paulie. I was merely stating the facts."

"Well, let me state a few facts for you, dear brother!" Paul thundered. "Unlike you, I don't draw a salary every month—which I'm certain has secured you a great many investments, not to mention the purchase of that additional plantation of yours in Virginia. Yes, John! I, too, know what's going on! So, let's just say I'm cashing in on ten years of wages I've never laid claim to."

"Any salary I draw is coming out of *my* future inheritance," John retaliated. "I believe I'm still first on father's will, am I not? Amazing, loyal as you are to him, you are not even mentioned in that document." John shook his head once, and clicked his tongue for emphasis. "That being the case, your island operation is costing me dearly!"

Paul stepped in close, his red face only inches from John's, his fists balled white. "You've gone too far this time!"

Before he could act, George grabbed John's arm. "You've had too much to drink," he chided sternly. Next, he scolded Paul. "And you've taken the bait. Now, John and I are going to say 'goodnight.'" He gave a slight nod, then shoved John toward the door.

When they were gone, Paul slumped into his chair, and Charmaine heaved a shuddering sigh of relief.

"Are you out of your mind?" George asked, his voice rising as they reached John's suite. "Why in hell did you say that to him? Why do you perpetuate this rivalry? It isn't Paul's fault your father favors him, is it?"

"I can't stand how he exploits it—he's a real *daddy's* boy."

"He may be a daddy's boy, John, but Paul was the one who held this family together four years ago. He was the shoulder all the tears were cried upon. He was the one who calmed everybody down and got life back to normal here."

John grunted in renewed disgust, but George wasn't silenced. "You were dead wrong accusing him of embezzling money from this estate!"

"Out of my way, George," he growled, pushing into the room.

"No, I won't get out of your way!" George expostulated, deliberately stepping in front of him. "You were at it all evening long, and not just with Paul. Why in heaven's name were you picking on Charmaine Ryan?"

"She's a sneaky little actress," John sneered.

"Charmaine?" George exclaimed incredulously. "You can't be serious!"

"She has you fooled, too, George?"

George frowned. "What are you talking about?"

"I caught her in here the other day riffling through my papers."

"Charmaine? I find that hard to believe. Are you sure?"

"No," John fired back sarcastically, "she was a mirage!"

"This doesn't sound like Charmaine. Did she explain?"

"She gave a lame excuse."

"She's not a liar," George maintained. "She's a decent, honest young lady."

"And what's this business about her father?"

"He was a wife-beater. One day it went too far. It has nothing to do with who she is, but it does upset her to talk about it."

"Ah . . ." John muttered snidely, "that explains it."

"Leave her alone, John, or you'll have me to contend with."

John was perturbed by George's adamant defense of the governess. Fleetingly, he wondered how she'd managed to charm both his brother and his friend. "You know what, George? You talk too much."

"Aye, I talk too much," George agreed, grabbing John's arm as he attempted to brush past him, pulling him round and looking him square in the eye. "But somebody needs to tell you a thing or two!"

"You can't tell me what I want to hear," John replied bitterly, "so why don't you get out and leave me alone?"

He wrenched free, but George beat him to the brandy decanter on the other side of the room, confiscating it. "No, I can't tell you what you want to hear, but liquor isn't going to wash it away, and even if it could, I doubt the past was any better than the present. You've been unconscious for three days now. If you can't pull yourself out of this stupor, you should leave. Go back to Virginia, so Yvette and Jeannette will remember you as you were four years ago, and Pierre, well . . ."

"Finish it, George," John prodded, his eyes sparking back to life. "So Pierre won't remember me at all. Right?"

"Damn it, John! Do you want him to grow up thinking of you as a drunk—an obnoxious oaf who spreads misery to everyone around him? Is that what you want?"

There was no point in preparing for bed; she would never fall asleep. Instead, Charmaine reread the letter she'd recently received from Loretta Harrington. A response was in order, the diversion she needed. She sat at the desk and set quill to paper. But when she had finished, she was no closer to tranquility. Yes, she had written about a variety of things, but the dominant subject was John Duvoisin.

Charmaine stared down at the pages. Committing her turbulent thoughts to paper had not exorcised the demon. It had only succeeded in anchoring his face more firmly before her. Wide awake . . . she was still wide awake! How was she to enjoy the serenity of this lavish bedroom when her mind returned over and over again to the night he had invaded her privacy here? With everything that had occurred since then, why did she still picture it so vividly—feel his hands on her, his hard body drawn up against hers, his breath buffeting her cheek? *No! I won't think about him! I won't! I'll think about Paul, his kiss before dinner, or his passionate embrace that stormy night when—*It was useless! She needed to escape. Suddenly, the night air beckoned, and she thought of the courtyard gardens. Yes, the gardens, where the ocean breezes mingled with the sweet scent of exotic flowers, a haven that might vanquish the odious image of John Duvoisin.

Paul propped his elbows on his knees and rested his chin on laced fingers. The cool breeze that wafted off the ocean did not ease his turmoil, for phantom figures continued to spurn and mock him. George was right. He had played the buffoon, played it to the tune his brother piped, leaving Charmaine sorely abused, and his dignity battered. John would never allow him to forget his illegitimacy, would always ridicule his efforts to prove himself worthy of the Duvoisin name. Why did it matter? *Because, down deep, I still respect him,* Paul admitted. Bastard . . . the label had dogged him for as long as he could remember, but up until four years ago, it had never mattered to John. Now, John used it as a weapon, skewering him every chance he got. Paul exhaled and closed his eyes. Suddenly, his father stood before him, hard and condescending. For all of Frederic's praise of his adopted son and vocal disapproval of his legitimate son, John remained sole heir to the Duvoisin empire, with Pierre second in line. Perhaps Paul had no right to pretend to something he wasn't, to claim a rank among the Duvoisin men who had gone before him. The circumstances of his birth denied him that right. Hadn't his uncontrolled temper this evening proven his worth as a gentleman? A true gentleman would never have behaved so badly, justified or not.

"Good evening . . ." The soft greeting was angelic.

"Good evening," Paul returned, standing and stepping closer to the feminine vision before him. "I thought you had retired long ago."

"No," Charmaine said shyly. "And what of you? Couldn't you sleep?"

"I had the good sense not to try. Would you walk with me?"

Charmaine agreed without hesitation, though she was disappointed when he turned pensive, clasping his hands behind his back, rather than taking her elbow.

"I'd like to apologize for my brother's behavior tonight," he finally said. "Actually, I'd like to apologize for *my* behavior. I allowed John to test my patience and, in so doing, hurt you. I'm sorry I broke my promise."

Charmaine studied him in confusion.

"Am I forgiven?" he inquired in earnest.

"Forgiven? Whatever for? You said you would be at my side, and you were. How could I ask for more? As for your brother, you need not plead forgiveness for him. He will have to do that himself, though I'll not hold my breath waiting. I find it amazing such a man can be called a gentleman. Why, a gentleman sets aside arguments diplomatically, as you attempted to do a number of times this evening. But when one is not dealing with a gentleman, then—"

"Charmaine," Paul chuckled, suddenly grasping her hand and squeezing it jubilantly, "you must have been sent by the very gods this night—you with your determination and conviction."

"I'm sorry?"

Though befuddled, she was caught up in his surge of joy.

"You've just restored my self-confidence, and I'm grateful. You see, John can have a sobering effect on people—force them to look at themselves no matter how hard they resist. And this evening, I fell victim."

"Sobering? That's one word I would never use in describing your brother."

"So it would appear," he agreed. "But just wait until he *is* sober. His mordant wit was a bit dull tonight. As a rule, he's far worse."

The moment's gaiety vanished.

"*Worse?*" she declared apprehensively. "Then, how am I to avoid him?"

Paul's elation did not diminish. "Take the children outdoors. The weather is beautiful. I'm certain they would enjoy a day abroad. Plan a picnic or two."

"That is a fine idea for tomorrow," Charmaine replied dejectedly, "but what of the next day, and the day after that?"

"John will tire of his little games. He has no reason to remain here."

"Then why *is* he here?"

Noting her deep interest, Paul deliberated his reply. "He's curious about Espoir. Once he's looked everything over and is satisfied with his assessment, he'll return to Virginia."

"Do you really think so?"

"I know so. Future chess games will be far different from tonight's."

"And next time you'll allow me to win?" she asked coyly, bravely.

Paul chuckled softly. "Mademoiselle, surely you didn't take my brother's assertions to heart?"

"Did he speak true? *Were* you allowing me to win?"

"And if I answer honestly, will you offer a reward?"

"That depends on what you request," she answered tremulously.

His eyes settled on her lips. "A kiss," he murmured.

"Very well," she responded breathlessly, their playful banter taking her into uncharted territory.

"Charmaine, I would let you win any game if it would afford me a kiss."

His words were muted by the thud of her heart and the sweeping motion that pulled her into his arms. She tilted her head back and closed her eyes, allowing him full access to her lips, savoring the coarseness of his moustache on her soft skin. When it seemed he could hold her no tighter, his embrace quickened, his ravenous mouth bruising, cutting across her lips and forcing them apart, his tongue thrusting into her mouth. This time he did not withdraw, and the splendid moment lengthened. Charmaine clung to him for support, returning his searing kiss with an ardor of her own. When his mouth traveled to her throat, she sighed, his breath warm on her neck, sending a chill of sensate pleasure down her spine. She was keenly aware of the love words he whispered close to her ear: "Sweet Jesus, Charmaine, my need is great . . . I long for you . . . long to make love to you . . . Come with me to my room . . ."

Reality took hold, overpowering that odd blend of expectancy and yearning. "I can't!" she cried, bracing her palms against his chest. "I just can't."

Tormented, Paul's iron embrace fell open, and the woman whom he wanted more than any other disappeared beyond the hedge. Although he was left in agony, he reassured himself time was on his side. It wouldn't be long before she succumbed.

Safe in her room, Charmaine went through the motions of preparing for bed, tears of frustration giving way to the pleasing memory of Paul's embrace. Yes, he had propositioned her again, but she was warmed by the knowledge he wanted her as a man wants a woman, yet respected her enough to set aside his passion in deference to her wishes. Perhaps in time the two would become one.

A⁺
AUTHOR
INSIGHTS,
EXTRAS, &
MORE...

FROM
**DeVa
GANTT**
AND
AVON A

1. What is the significance of the title *A Silent Ocean Away*?

Ocean conveys the image of vast distance. An ocean separates the members of the Duvoisin family, both literally and figuratively. Chapter 1 opens with this imagery. The Duvoisins' secrets and troubles are further compounded by silence: their refusal and failure to speak to one another truthfully, to attempt to reconcile before it is too late. The reader should identify the oceans of silence shared between key figures in the story.

2. How has Charmaine created an ocean of silence between herself and her past? Can anyone truly escape one's past? How has Charmaine's past influenced her ability to love and trust in the present?

Clearly, Charmaine attempts to suppress her past, fearful of the impact it will have on her future. The simplest way to do this is to hold silent. Yet the suppression itself magnifies the blemish and gives credence to her unfounded guilt. Until Charmaine embraces her past and accepts it, it is destined to haunt her, and yes, influence her ability to love and trust in the present. Paul's very analysis: *The woman in her demanded passion, the little girl, safety, and then there was the female her father had fashioned, the one who screamed: Every man must be avoided at all costs.* But as George Richards says: *We all have secrets we'd prefer to keep.* No one is perfect. We all have a past and it does influence who we are. The question is: Do we use it to grow or regress?

3. How has Colette contributed to the legacy of silence in this family?

Colette is the focal point of the silence. In her memories, the reader glimpses her uncertain relationship with Frederic. She is a young wife and mother unable to speak of her physical and emotional needs. This leads to infidelity and more silence, which drives portions of the story not yet revealed.

4. *A Silent Ocean Away* is only the first of the *Colette Trilogy*. What should the readers be paying attention to or looking for in Book 2, *Decision and Destiny*?

Readers should be looking for the answers to such questions as: Why is John an outcast in his own family, yet the heir apparent? Why did Colette write to him? What are Agatha's motives? Why does Frederic look at John's return as a day for which he had been afraid to hope—a day for which he was unprepared? If Paul and John are bitter rivals, why does Paul admit to respecting John? To what extent is John responsible for his father's incapacitated condition? What role will Charmaine play in the turmoil? And, how do the children fit in?

Readers should also realize the *Colette Trilogy* is a trilogy on several levels, many symbolic. In Books 2 and 3 the reader should be looking for sets of three, whether companion scenes or items. For example: there are three important piano encounters, three significant letters, three plaintive departures, three joyous returns, and so forth. As the reader begins Book 3, he/she should be looking for those triads. The number three is symbolic in and of itself.

5. You mentioned symbolism. Have you employed any other literary devices such as foreshadow in your novels?

Absolutely. Some are obvious, others unapparent until the trilogy is read in its entirety and perhaps reread. For example, Charmaine's thoughts concerning John: *John! How I hate that name!* Or when first they meet and Yvette's assurance that her negative opinion will someday change: *The child had never been more wrong in her life. She'd sooner declare her father a man of God.* As for symbolism: take note of Frederic's cane, John's cap, Pierre's stuffed lamb, weather conditions, and John and Paul's horses: Phantom and Alabaster.

6. Colette's death is tragic for nearly every member of the Duvoisin family. Was this difficult to write? Might it have been averted?

Tears were shed during the writing of Colette's death. As a writer, you walk in your characters' shoes, so experiencing Colette's death as the children or Frederic did was emotional. However, Colette's death is a turning point in the story and essential to the plot. Life is not always happy; a plausible story mirrors life and transcends time. There is also a message to be found in Colette's words: *I won't be without you. I'll always be here . . . in this house . . . with you.* The reader should also ponder to what extent Colette yielded herself to death, and why she did this.

7. How did you choose the name Duvoisin? Is this significant?

The Duvoisin family is French, so naturally choosing a French name was critical. Duvoisin translates to: *Of the neighbor*—an important theme in the sequel we have planned. Other names were also selected for a reason. Colette means *Reigns Victorious*. Pierre, or *mon caillou* as his mother calls him, means *rock* or *pebble*, and this is symbolic. Charmaine's name has its own mysterious roots.

8. Is writing historical fiction difficult? How much time was dedicated to detail?

The fiction is easy, especially if you have a lively imagination and enjoy writing. Researching traditional history is also easy. Understanding the nuances of the day—what was and wasn't invented, what the people ate, their manner of speech, how they dressed—is more difficult, but imperative if a writer desires credibility. In addition, the growing of tobacco and sugarcane had to be researched, the ships and shipping industry of the time, the Caribbean, and so forth. Thus a great deal of time was dedicated to detail.

9. What was the inspiration for this novel? Are any of the characters based upon people you know?

The inspiration was multilayered, influenced by a love of historical fiction. Add to that a lively imagination, self-confidence in writing, and a desire to write as a hobby. That hobby took on a life of its own and eventually grew into a passionate obsession.

As for the characters, most writers draw upon personality traits they observe in people they know. Some of our characters, such as John Ryan, embody such traits. The characters themselves, however, are fictional, their story original.

10. *A Silent Ocean Away* is a coauthored work that reads seamlessly. How was this accomplished?

First-draft scenes and sections were composed individually, and our personal writing styles were clearly evident. The arduous editing that took place once we decided to self-publish had the greatest impact on "blending" our writing styles. With each reading of the work—possibly fifty in all—we imposed our own technique upon the other, until it was one work, not two.

Following is a preview of the next book in the saga of the
Duvoisin family . . . their friends, their lovers,
and their foes . . .

Decision and Destiny

COLETTE'S LEGACY

Available April 2009 only from Avon Books

Chapter 1

Tuesday, August 22, 1837

Peace of mind! Oh, the oblivion of peace of mind! They were Charmaine's last thoughts as she drifted off to sleep. Like a prayer answered, she succumbed to a deep and restful slumber, the first she'd had in three long nights.

Songbirds in the great oak just outside her window awoke her, and she lay abed enjoying nature's symphony, a harbinger of the brilliant day ahead, one that was perfect for a picnic. She rose and peeked into the children's room. They were fast asleep. She began to dress, determined to get an early start.

The letter she had written to Loretta Harrington sat propped on her chest of drawers. She scanned the pages, resurrecting the turmoil of the past three days.

> *I was pleased to receive your letter ... I am quite well ... The children are a constant comfort to me and I enjoy my position on the island ... I still do not understand Mr. Duvoisin's marriage to so cruel a woman as Agatha Ward ... I avoid her whenever possible ... Paul is the consummate gentleman, and*

aside from Rose and George Richards, I sometimes feel he is the only friend I have in the house . . . George returned this past week, but you should not harbor hope of him as a possible suitor . . . my thoughts have been far from such concerns . . . John Duvoisin has ventured home, even though it is whispered his father forbade him to do so. His presence has rekindled my former reservations concerning matrimony. I can understand Frederic Duvoisin's disdain for his own flesh and blood, for John is a rude, ill-bred, detestable cur who spends his days closeted in his apartments drinking from dawn to dusk. I've tried to avoid him at all costs, but he appears at the worst possible times, and I find myself poorly equipped to respond to his sarcasm. He has taken a dislike to me for a number of reasons. He's learned of my father, undoubtedly through his intended bride, the widow Anne Westphal London . . . Do you know her? But I am not the only person he ridicules. He wages war with practically everyone, including his aunt or stepmother, as the case may be . . . Tell Mr. Harrington he was never more correct in his opinion of a person than he was of this man. Please give everyone my love . . .

Sighing, she tucked the letter into its envelope. Then she sat at her dressing table and began brushing out her unruly hair.

The serenity of the morning was shattered by a series of vociferous oaths that brought her straight to her feet and into the corridor. Joseph Thornfield was racing down the stairs, a wooden bucket tumbling after him, ricocheting off the walls and splattering water everywhere.

"Damn it, boy! I love hot baths almost as much as I love music, but I refuse to be scalded into singing soprano in a boy's choir!"

Charmaine turned toward the bellowing voice, and her jaw dropped. There stood John Duvoisin, dripping wet from head to toe, leaning far over the banister, and shouting after the servant boy. He was naked save a bath towel clasped around his waist, unperturbed by his indecent state of undress. Charmaine compared him to Paul—the gold standard by which she assessed all men—annoyed to find his toned body rivaled his brother's: wide shoulders, corded arms, and taut stomach, which sported a reddish hue. Belatedly, she realized she was no longer staring at his back. She grimaced as she lifted her gaze and her eyes connected with his. A jeering smile broke across his face, his pain apparently forgotten now that he had the governess for an audience.

"You're as red as a ripe apple, my Charm. I thought my brother had shown you a man's body, or did I interrupt that lesson in anatomy the other night?"

Degraded, Charmaine marched back into her bedchamber and slammed the door as hard as she could. Her gratification was minimal; it was a full minute before his laughter receded from the hallway.

It was still early when she left her room again. Her plans for a quiet breakfast had been dashed. John had effectively roused the entire household, except for Agatha, who ate in her boudoir. Paul, George, and Rose converged on the staircase. Charmaine prayed John would be delayed, but lately, none of her prayers were being answered. He appeared just as they reached the dining room.

"Good morning, everyone!" he greeted brightly, winking at her.

She glowered in response, but he dismissed her, settling at the table with the children, who were thrilled to see him. She hesitated, debating where to sit. With Paul still talking to George in the archway, she remained indecisive.

John noticed at once. "Do you plan on eating, Mademoiselle, or will you just stand there and watch us? You paint the picture of a wounded dog awaiting table scraps."

The demeaning declaration stung like salt in an open wound, the promise of a brilliant day rapidly fading. Taking courage, she stepped closer.

"Ah yes," he mused, pretending ignorance of her quandary and coming to his feet, "the lady expects a gentleman to help her with her chair, but since Paul is preoccupied right now, I suppose a *convict* like me will just have to do!"

He rounded the table and pulled the chair out for her. With a great flourish, he whisked a napkin through the air and dusted off the seat cushion, finishing his theatrics with a servile bow and a gesture she be seated. She did so with as much aplomb as she could rally, but as she spread her serviette in her lap, her eyes went to Paul, whose jaw was clenched in monumental self-control.

John returned to his own chair, and chatted with George, Rose, and the children, the meal uneventful until Jeannette produced the letter Charmaine had written to Loretta Harrington.

"Shall I give this to Joseph to post, Mademoiselle?"

Charmaine cringed. "Yes, please," she hastily replied.

Too late! The man's interest was piqued, his brow raised. She knew that expression: it meant trouble. Sure enough, he stopped Jeannette as she passed behind him and removed the envelope from her hand. "What have we here?"

"A letter," Paul snapped.

"A letter?" John mimicked. "Thank you for explaining, Paul. I'd almost forgotten what a letter looked like. But Miss Ryan hasn't forgotten, has she?"

Charmaine paled, but John pressed on, tapping the envelope against his lips. "Mrs. Joshua Harrington of Richmond, Virginia. Harrington . . . where have I heard that name before? Ah yes, the merchants' convention last year. Joshua Harrington was leading the protest against import tariffs. I remember him quite well now. A short-tempered man, if my memory doesn't fail me, short and short-tempered."

"I found him quite the contrary," Paul argued.

"Now, Paul," John countered jovially, "he isn't a *tall* man by any measure."

George snickered, but Paul's brow knitted in vexation. "I was speaking of his temperament!"

"Well, I don't know which side of him you saw, but he quickly lost his temper when I spoke with him."

"Were you taunting him, John?"

"Why would I do that? He just doesn't have a sense of humor, that's all. I simply commented that, with a name like Joshua, he had to be a prophet and should consult with God before delivering his next ludicrous speech. After that, he wanted nothing to do with me, which suited me just fine."

Paul closed his eyes and shook his head in exasperation.

"But that is neither here nor there, is it, Mademoiselle?" John continued, serious again. "You have correspondence to post, and Joseph normally sees to such errands. However, he is busy cleaning up the mess in my room. Therefore, I volunteer to deliver it to the mercantile for you."

"That is very noble of you, John," Paul responded before Charmaine could object. "However, Miss Ryan would like to know it was, in fact, delivered."

"Now, Paulie, are you suggesting I would drop this by the wayside?"

"Let us just say I, too, am gallant, John. Since you have no reason to travel into town, while that is my very destination today, let me take it."

"No, I think not, Paul. You see, I do have a reason to ride into town. I have my own letters to post, and since Miss Ryan doesn't trust me, this is the perfect opportunity to prove to her I'm not the scoundrel she imagines me to be—that her letter will be delivered to the mercantile, intact."

"John—"

"Admit it, Paul. You have an ulterior motive for visiting the mercantile. A tête-à-tête with Maddy Thompson perhaps?"

"I'm finished playing games with you, John," Paul snarled. "If you insist on posting the letter, then by all means, go ahead."

"Oh goodie!" John exclaimed, inciting a chorus of giggles from the girls.

For Charmaine, however, the fate of her correspondence was far from settled. "Had I known my letter would cause such a quibble," she laughed artificially, "I would have left it in my room. Best I post it myself." She leaned forward to remove it from John's hand, but he held it out of reach and disagreed glibly.

"The children have lessons, do they not? Surely you won't allow a personal matter to interfere with that? No? I didn't think so. But fear not! I give you my solemn oath as a gentleman; your letter will remain safe in my hands. If there is something else that troubles you, George will vouch for me when I tell you that—unlike a certain individual who shall remain unnamed—I have never bent so low as to read someone else's private mail."

Charmaine reddened.

"Besides, I don't need to read your letter to know what you think of me. You've made that abundantly clear on a number of occasions."

Charmaine remained closeted in the playroom with the children, hoping upon hope John would leave for town and she'd be free to arrange a picnic lunch with Fatima. It was nearly eleven and, unlike Paul, who had spent the morning in the study with George, John had dawdled the last three hours away. Where was his ambition to carry out the task he had so eagerly begged for at breakfast?

Presently, she turned her mind to an arithmetic lesson, trying not to dwell on her two latest predicaments: the postponed picnic and John's delivery of her letter to the mercantile. Would he read it? He could, and she'd never know! Fool that she was, she had committed her hatred to paper, and now the devil himself possessed it!

John Duvoisin. Yes, she hated him! Hated how he scorned and mocked her. Hated how he singled her out and ridiculed her just for the fun of it. Hated how he presumed to know so much about her character. Hated how he loved to make everyone miserable. Hated him like she hated her father. Hated him, hated him, hated him! Colette's words of long ago haunted her: *Just remember . . . you hate him first.* Hate him first? What came after that? She seemed to remember something about loving him. Ridiculous! She'd hate him first, second, third, and forever. She prayed fervently for the day when he would pack his bags and return to Richmond. It couldn't come soon enough.

Beyond the confining room, doors banged shut and footfalls resounded in the corridor, setting her on edge. She left Jeannette and Yvette to their problems, and stepped onto the veranda. The breeze was invitingly cool for August, rustling the leaves of the tall oak overhead. Looking toward the paddock, she was rewarded with the fine sight of Paul, who stood with arms akimbo, conversing with George and two stable-hands. Charmaine admired the authority he projected, lingering on his broad shoulders and lean torso, slim waist and well-defined legs, the muscles in his thighs sculpted against the dark fabric of his trousers. Highly polished ebony riding boots finished the lusty figure he cut. She closed her eyes to the heart-thundering image and remembered that first day on the *Raven*, his shirt doffed, the play of muscle across his broad back and arms, deeply tanned from the island sun. He was the embodiment of the perfect man, like the great Roman statues in the museums of Europe.

She thought of their kiss in the gardens last night, and her heart raced. His embrace had been passionate and longing, and despite her inhibition, she relished the pleasurable memory. His racy invitation simmered in her ears, and she breathed deeply, counseling herself to tread cautiously. She was playing with fire. It would be best to avoid another such encounter. Even now, she realized how difficult that would be, for as he clasped an easy arm around the shoulders of a young stable lad, she fancied herself in those strong arms once again.

The main door banged shut, and the vision was lost. Charmaine gingerly stepped forward and peered down, jumping back when the devil incarnate descended the portico steps. He wore a brown leather cap, white shirt, light brown trousers, and matching boots. His gait was lazy, yet deliberate, a self-assuredness she would love to see crushed. In her brief three-day experience, she knew this would never happen. She had never met anyone who exuded such confidence, not even Paul. Colette's remarks once again echoed in her ears: *He's an enigma . . . a one of a kind.* Thank God, one was quite enough!

He was halfway to the stables when Paul stepped out of the circle of men. Charmaine held her breath when they reached one another and Paul initiated an exchange, a concise remark she couldn't hear. John waved a letter in his brother's face: *one single solitary letter.* He spoke next, another short phrase that drew Paul around and sent his eyes traveling up the face of the mansion. Within a moment, he found her, a smile breaking across his lips. Charmaine shook her head. John must have known she was standing there, watching them. How had he known? Or had he? He was probably playing Paul for the fool and got lucky.

John disappeared into the stable, emerging minutes later with a great black stallion in tow: Phantom, according to the twins. The proud beast fought the bridle, his sable coat shimmering in the late morning sun.

A groom led another horse out. When George took the reins, Paul threw his hands up. "I won't be long!" George called from the saddle.

Everyone seemed to be waiting for John to mount up as well. No one, not even Paul, rode the "demon of the stable," so dubbed because he was constantly breaking out of his stall, jumping the corral fencing, evading stable-hands or nipping the other horses. Great care was taken to segregate him. Clearly, John intended to do what his brother had the good sense to avoid, and Charmaine planned to laugh loudly when the stallion threw him onto his conceited rear end.

The steed was growing zealous for the freedom of the road, pulling fiercely at the bit, but John appeared oblivious as he conversed with George. He casually produced something from his shirt pocket and raised it to the animal's large muzzle. The horse gobbled it up. John stroked his satin flank and then, with one fluid motion, swung into the saddle. The horse bolted, but John reined him in, his momentum ending in a lunging halt. With a loud whinny and a violent shake of his huge head, the horse began to circle in place. Charmaine snickered; the man was no horseman. Finally, a weakness to exploit when the moment was ripe!

"He's rarin' to go!" George averred. "He hasn't been ridden in ages."

John concurred. "I see my brother wasn't brave enough to work him out!"

"No, John, I value my neck too much!" Paul called back. "If he throws you, it will be your own folly. You won't control him until he's had a good long run!"

"We'll see, Paulie," John countered. "It won't take him long to remember all the tricks."

As if to fortify his contention, he leaned forward and patted the animal's sleek neck. A nudge to the flank, and the beast trotted toward Paul. John reached out and ruffled his brother's hair, laughing heartily as the horse completed a wide sweep of the area, hooves tapping out a perfect rhythm on the cobblestone drive. John snapped the reins hard, and the steed shot forward, speeding past George and exiting the compound, his legs a blur, tail and mane sailing in the wind. George spurred his own mount into motion and followed in hot pursuit, disappearing in a cloud of dust kicked up by the vagabond stallion.

Charmaine stepped out of the house and felt liberated. The children were gay, chasing butterflies and picking exotic flowers that grew with abandon in the grassy fields. Though it was hot, the sky was a deep azure and the breeze carried the sweet scent of ocean spray. The tropical paradise was a balm for her turbulent mind, a welcome respite from days of sequestration in the nursery.

They traipsed northwest through three fields, their destination a special picnicking spot the twins had chosen. Ahead was a wooded area, breached only by a dark, narrow path of craggy rocks that appeared to lead nowhere. They entered the copse, trudging up an incline that wasn't quite as treacherous as Charmaine had at first imagined. Soon the path leveled off and quite unexpectedly, opened onto a lush, grassy bluff that was enclosed on three sides by thick foliage. The western edge offered a lofty view of the ocean, a breathtaking vista.

"Oh girls, this is just beautiful," Charmaine sighed, returning their ebullient smiles. "Look at the flowers! And the sea—look how it shimmers in the sun!"

They giggled in reply, setting down the picnic basket. With her help, they spread a blanket in the shade of a tall cotton tree and laid out the bounty Fatima had packed for them: fried chicken, crusty bread, fresh oranges and bananas, cookies, and lemonade. Charmaine remembered many an evening in her impoverished home where soup and bread were the main course, portioned over a few days to make it last. If she were lucky, a feast such as this would adorn their Christmas table. She silently thanked God for her good fortune and prosperity this day. If only her mother could know how happy her life had become.

They delved into lunch, famished after their long hike. Even Pierre ate heartily, and Charmaine chuckled as he stuffed a third cookie into his greasy mouth. She wiped his face and hands clean as he squirmed away. Then he settled on the other side of the blanket and fell asleep from sheer exhaustion, content to take his afternoon nap in the open air.

John meandered into the kitchen in an attempt to shrug off the boredom that pervaded the study. The afternoon was drawing on, and there was no sign that lunch would be served any time soon. He had declined George's invitation to eat at Dulcie's. He wasn't in the mood to mingle with the men who caroused there. So, he returned alone. He'd grown accustomed to being alone, and most of the time, he preferred it that way. But now he was hungry.

"'Afternoon, Master John," Fatima greeted as she bustled around the sweltering room, setting a tray of warm muffins on the kitchen table.

"Good day, Cookie," he returned as he sat down. "God, it's hot in here! I still say that stove should be out in the cookhouse where it belongs."

"Mind your mouth and don't be giving your pa any ideas," she warned. "I like it right here. Saves me a lot of running. And don't go touching those muffins!" she threatened, catching sight of his avid eyes on them. "They're for dinner."

"I'm not after your muffins, but it's nearly two. Where's lunch?"

His question drew a grumble from Fatima, who was now stoking the oven. As she bent over, John snatched a muffin and concealed it under the table.

"There ain't no table lunch today, Master John."

"And why is that? Are you holding out for a raise in wages?"

"You know me better than that," she chided, well aware he teased her. "I already sent a tray of food up to your pa and Missus Agatha. I didn't expect you back for lunch."

"What about the children and their governess?" John asked,

stealing a bite of his muffin when Fatima visited the pantry and dropped potatoes into her apron.

"Miss Charmaine took the children on a picnic," she explained, turning back to the table to dump them there. "I fixed them a basket of food before they left."

"A picnic?"

Fatima eyed him suspiciously. "I know what you're thinking, Master John."

"What am I thinking?"

"If you're hungry, I'll fix you something, just leave Miss Charmaine alone."

"Leave her alone?"

"I heard you picking on her last night. She's a nice girl, and she don't know you. So you leave her be, before you frighten her right out of this house."

Fatima fetched a loaf of bread to make him a sandwich.

"A nice girl, eh?" he asked skeptically, grabbing another muffin and raising it to his mouth. "I keep hearing that. George is sweet on her, and my brother—"

His words were cut short when Fatima caught him red-handed. "My muffins!" she bellowed. "Now you put that back before I take a stick to you!"

John scrambled from the chair and was out the back door before she could maneuver her wide girth around the table. He sidestepped several frantic chickens that squawked as they scattered out of his way, then he nearly got tangled in the laundry on the clothesline. But he laughed loudly, knowing he'd escaped her.

"Go on, now," she scolded from the doorway, shaking a knife at him, "and don't you come back here 'til dinner!"

He tipped his cap, bowed cordially, and walked down the back lawn, chewing on the warm muffin he'd nearly swallowed whole. It only whetted his appetite; now he was really hungry. He knew where he could eat—and a fine lunch at that! He laughed again, realizing the afternoon would not be boring after all. Poor Miss Ryan! She'd be alone with him; no Paul to come to her rescue. Well, at least the children would be pleased to see him. His destination was simple, since he knew exactly where they'd be enjoying their picnic.

Charmaine removed her bonnet, relaxed on the blanket, and took in her surroundings again. "How romantic," she murmured, imagining herself in this paradise with Paul. "How ever did you girls find this place?"

"We didn't," Yvette replied matter-of-factly, "Johnny did. A long time ago."

At the mention of the man's name, Charmaine's eyes darted around, searching the shaded areas. *He's not going to jump out at me,* she reasoned. *He rode off to town, and we were gone long before he returned. He has no idea where we are . . .*

"What's the matter, Mademoiselle Charmaine?" Jeannette asked.

"Nothing. Tell me more about this spot. When did John show it to you?"

"When Mama was well. When we were little."

"And if we close our eyes," Yvette said, "we can pretend she is with us . . ."

Jeannette did as her sister suggested, and Charmaine indulged their poignant fantasy. "You mentioned John," she finally said. "He discovered this place?"

Yvette nodded. "When he was a boy, he used to go on expeditions with George. That's when they found these cliffs. Johnny swore George to secrecy. He told us, from then on, whenever he got angry with Paul or Papa, he would come to this hideaway because it was the one place on the island Paul didn't know about, the one place where he could be alone. When he knew we could be trusted, he brought us here, too. But we had to promise *never* to tell Paul."

Charmaine gritted her teeth. The gall of the man—setting the children against Paul.

"I decided you could be trusted, too," Yvette added thoughtfully. "And if . . ."

"And if what?" Charmaine asked suspiciously.

"And if Johnny wants company today, he's sure to look for us here."

Wants company? First he has to return from town, then discover we've left the house. Certain both could not possibly happen, Charmaine dismissed the thought, pleased when Yvette suggested a game of hide-and-seek.

She and her sister scurried off, declaring their governess the seeker and the blanket, "home." Charmaine covered her eyes and counted to fifty. Then she scanned the far edges of the encroaching forest, searching for any movement that would betray the girls' hiding places.

The crunch of leaves caught her ear, and she headed down the path by which they'd arrived. A snapping twig pointed to the brambles straight ahead. Determined to surprise them, she broke into a run and rounded the brush at top speed, lunging to a sudden halt when she nearly landed in John's arms, her bun falling loose and spilling its bounty onto her shoulders.

"Well, now," he exclaimed, "I didn't expect you to be *that* happy to see me!"

Fuming, she snubbed him, making a great show of turning away.

"Aren't you going to tag me?" he pressed.

"No!" she threw over her shoulder as she stomped back to the clearing, pulling pins free of her hair. Unfortunately, the man fell in step alongside her.

"Johnny!" Yvette and Jeannette called in tandem, running from opposite sides of the bluff to greet him. "You did find us!"

"I was looking for lunch, and Cookie told me she packed a picnic for you."

"You can have some!" Jeannette offered, pointing to the left-over food.

John walked over to the blanket and stared down at the slumbering Pierre. After a moment, he lifted a discarded plate and piled it high with food. Then he settled against the trunk of a tree and delved into his meal. Yvette sat next to him, while Jeannette prepared him a plate of cookies.

They ignored Charmaine, who continued to simmer as she coifed her hair. He obviously intended to stay. After an interminable silence, she found the nerve to speak. "Do you always intrude upon people uninvited?"

"Only when it's worth it. And always when they're unsuspecting."

"And what exactly does that mean?"

"Let's take you for example: My, my, the secrets I've uncovered by intruding on you!" His eyes twinkled, but he waved away her displeasure with the chicken bone he held, tossing it over his shoulder. "Today I'm only intruding for lunch. This is delicious. The blisters I got on the journey here were a small price to pay."

Charmaine bit her tongue and focused on cleaning up, grateful when the twins engaged his attention, asking him for stories about America.

Their voices woke Pierre, who sat up, rubbed his sleepy eyes, and smiled when he recognized John. Yawning, he left the blanket and walked deliberately toward the man, made a fist, and plunged a targeted punch into his shoulder.

"Pierre!" Charmaine cried in disbelief. The boy had never raised a hand to anyone before. She feared John's reaction, certain he'd use the child's bad behavior to discredit her. Instead, he doubled over as if seriously injured and, with a loud groan, flopped to the grass, where he lay perfectly still.

With great trepidation, Pierre stepped closer, oblivious of his sisters, who were winking at one another. No sooner had he crouched down, and John's eyes popped open with the cry: "Boo!" Pierre jumped, then chortled in glee, not satisfied until he'd played "boo" three more times.

When John tired of the game, he drew the boy into his lap, pulled his cap from his back pocket, and placed it on Pierre's head. It was too large and slid over his eyes and nose. Only his grinning lips were visible.

Charmaine leaned back against the tree and watched them guardedly. Pierre was warming up to his elder brother. Just what she needed, a third child begging to see John all day long.

"How'd ya get here?" the boy asked, peering up at John from under the cap.

"On Fang, silly!" Yvette interjected, casting all-knowing eyes to John.

"Fang?" Charmaine asked.

"Johnny's horse," Yvette replied presumptuously.

"Horse?" Charmaine expostulated, turning accusatory eyes upon the man. "I'm sure you'll never recover from your large *blisters*."

"I said I had blisters," he rejoined, "I didn't say where."

The girls bubbled with laughter.

Charmaine was not amused. "Your horse's name is Fang? If it's the horse you were riding this morning, I thought his name was Phantom."

"The grooms call him that because of his bad manners. A phantom stallion. Surely you've heard that expression before, my Charm?"

"Of course I have!" she snapped, thinking: *like master, like horse.*

John's smile broadened. "Anyway, his real name is Fang."

"Fang," she repeated sarcastically, "why, that's a dog's name."

"Dog or horse, it's still an animal's name." John winked at Yvette when Charmaine turned away. "And he was given the name for a very good reason."

On cue, Yvette skipped to Charmaine and grabbed her hand, insisting she examine the horse so she would understand his bizarre name. "Come, Mademoiselle Charmaine, we'll show you."

Unwittingly, she was drawn into the girl's enthusiasm, and before she could object, was trekking the pathway with Yvette. She glanced over her shoulder to find John close behind, Jeannette at his side and Pierre on his shoulders.

The boy attempted to wave from his lofty perch, but quickly changed his mind, clasping both hands over John's eyes. John peeled them away with the complaint: "I can't see, Pierre! If I trip, we'll be like Humpty Dumpty and all fall down." Charmaine giggled when the three-year-old let go of John's face only to grab fistfuls of his hair.

"That's not Humpty Dumpty," he declared, "that's Ring a Ring a Rosy."

Moments later, they found "Fang" grazing in the middle of a wild field, his great head bent to the long grass, his tail swishing in the breeze.

"Come quickly!" Yvette urged, breaking into a run.

"Yvette!" John shouted. "Wait for me."

She stopped immediately, arms akimbo. "Then hurry up!"

When he reached her, he set Pierre down and squatted, looking her straight in the eye. "I've told you never to go near Fang without me. I thought you understood."

Yvette bowed her head. "But—"

"There *are* no buts, Yvette. The horse can be dangerous if he's startled. You are not to go near him unless you are with me. Agreed?"

"Agreed," she replied meekly.

John's genuine concern surprised Charmaine. After patting Yvette's back, he placed his cap on her head, a privilege that regained her friendship. Now she tugged at his hand and called for Charmaine to follow.

"So, this is Fang," Charmaine remarked apprehensively, jumping when the horse shook its head.

"Yes," John acknowledged, stroking the black mane, "this is my horse." He threw an arm over the animal's neck and proceeded to introduce them. "Fang, this is Miss Ryan, formerly of Richmond, Virginia. Miss Ryan, this is Fang, my loyal steed."

The twins were giggling, and Pierre joined in.

Suddenly, the horse stepped forward and, to John's delight, neighed a greeting that petrified Charmaine. "That means 'pleased to make your acquaintance' in horse talk," he explained, drawing more laughter from the children.

Charmaine smiled in spite of herself.

"Do you like him, Mademoiselle Charmaine?" Jeannette asked.

"He is quite remarkable," she replied nervously, "however, I have yet to see why he's named Fang. I still say that's a dog's name."

John stepped closer. "You use the perfect word to describe Fang, Miss Ryan," he replied, taking hold of her wrist to lead her nearer the steed. "You see, Fang has a *remarkable* characteristic that distinguishes him from other horses."

She cringed with the contact of his warm hand and pulled away quickly.

"He was born with one overly large, very sharp, front tooth. Right, girls?"

They nodded vigorously.

"One overly large front tooth?" she asked. "Surely you jest."

"No, I do not. Fang has a reputation for nipping fingers and other horses. That's why they all steer clear of Fang. He uses his tooth as a weapon."

The twins hadn't stopped laughing. How had she been drawn into this ridiculous conversation? If the children weren't enjoying themselves so immensely, she'd be walking back to the blanket.

"You don't believe Johnny, do you?" Yvette demanded. "It's really true!" She looked up at her brother. "You better show her."

John pulled the stallion's head up from the grass and grabbed his muzzle. When Fang whickered in objection, Charmaine stepped back.

"Why are you moving away?" he asked. "Don't you want to see the oddity of the century? You'd pay a fee to glimpse something like this at the circus."

"Actually," Charmaine faltered, "I'd hate to put you through all that trouble. I'm sure I can do without seeing the 'oddity of the century.'"

"Go ahead, Mademoiselle," Yvette implored. "He won't bite you."

Charmaine wondered whether the girl was referring to the horse or John. She decided to placate them and be done with it, or she'd never hear the end of it.

John produced a lump of sugar from his pocket. The stallion's lips curled back, and the treat was devoured, but Charmaine witnessed nothing unusual.

"Did you see it?"

"Well, actually, no."

"How could you miss it? It was right there, plain as the nose on your face!"

"Now, Yvette," John chided, "give Miss Ryan a chance. She doesn't know where to look like you do. Perhaps if she stepped a bit closer, she'd see better."

This time when John held out the sugar, he drew back the horse's lips and Yvette pointed to the area of interest. "Look! See it there? See that big fang?"

Charmaine didn't see a thing, but the girl's huff of frustration prompted her to scrutinize the animal's mouth further.

John let go of the huge head and pressed his brow into the steed's neck. Charmaine frowned. *Is he ill?* He looked heavenward, his entire face one tremendous smile. Tears were welling in his eyes, and in a flash, she realized he was laughing. The twins rivaled his mirth, doubling over in painful glee, unable to speak. Even Pierre was giggling.

"You are the first grown-up that prank has worked on!" Yvette gasped.

Charmaine's heart plummeted. They were enjoying themselves at her expense! Suddenly, insidiously, her throat constricted with tears. Why was this man so determined to make a fool of her? Now he had the children ridiculing her! In great despair, she grabbed Pierre's hand and set a brisk pace back to the bluff.

"Mademoiselle!" Jeannette called after her, running to catch up. "You're not angry, are you? We didn't mean to make you angry. It was only a prank, but we wouldn't have done it if we thought you wouldn't find it funny, too!"

Charmaine struggled not to cry and was comforted when she received an affectionate hug from the gentle twin. Yvette and John were fast approaching, and she quickly composed herself, not wanting the man to know he had once again reduced her to tears.

He saw her dab at her eyes. *Such a deft little actress. Now I'm supposed to feel guilty because I made the little lady cry.* He shook his head derisively and chuckled to himself. *She is quite fetching with her curvaceous figure and wild hair—her best assets by far. And she uses that sidelong glance to disarm a man. No wonder Paul and George have fallen for her. Well, George is Mr. Earnest, and Paul likes to be the hero so he can seduce her. And Johnny? Well, Johnny isn't taken in so easily. Still, if she wants to play, then why not? Johnny has nothing to lose. With Paul in her pocket, she thinks she can take on the best of them. But she hasn't played with the likes of Johnny. Well, Miss Ryan, you shall see what it's like to play with Johnny.*

"Race you back to the blanket!" Yvette challenged. "The last one there has to carry the picnic basket home!" The girl broke into a run and bounded into the path, Jeannette and Pierre in hot pursuit.

John drew alongside Charmaine. "Don't you have a sense of humor?"

She was determined to ignore him and stared off into the distance. But he wasn't about to be dismissed, so he stepped in front of her. When she turned her face aside, he grabbed her chin and forced her to look at him. She slapped his hand away. "Don't touch me!"

He only chuckled. When she sidestepped him, he hastened to catch up. "I'm sorry if my jest offended you," he apologized, garnering her utter astonishment. "It's a prank the twins enjoy playing. I thought you'd go along with it."

Doubting his sincerity, Charmaine withheld comment, relieved when they reached the bluff.

"You didn't even try to catch us!" Yvette complained.

John scooped up Pierre, who had run to greet them, then set him down again. "Now, Yvette, you would have been pouting all day if I had outraced you."

"You couldn't have done that if you tried!"

Pulling his cap off her head, she brandished it before him. "I still have this! Let's play 'keep away' from Johnny!"

When John lunged at her, she darted out of reach. As he closed in, she sent the cap sailing through the air to her sister.

He grinned. "All right, Jeannie, now give it back."

She hesitated, then squealed as he dove at her, scurrying away with his cap in hand. Then she, too, sent it flying.

John played along, indulging their tossing escapade. With hands on hips, he strategically placed himself between them. But Yvette recognized the ploy and threw the cap to Charmaine this time. She caught it and was drawn into the game as well. Now John was tracking her.

"Are you going to give me the cap, my Charm?" he asked, arm extended.

"Don't give it to him, Mademoiselle!" Yvette cried. "Throw it to me!"

Charmaine launched the cap in Yvette's direction, breathing

easier when John swung away. When it eventually came sailing back, it fell short of its mark, hitting the ground near Pierre. He picked it up, giggled, and clumsily shuttled it to her, enabling John to close in. Charmaine tucked it behind her back and blindly retreated. John steadily advanced, blocking her view altogether. Her foot struck the trunk of the tree. She was trapped!

He was only inches away, and as her eyes traveled up from the buttons on his shirt, past his neck to his clean-shaven face, memories of their first encounter rushed in. Somehow, he seemed taller than that night, even more imposing than the morning he'd barged into his room and found her reading Colette's letter. But he wasn't angry now. He leaned in close and, with a victorious grin, placed his hands flat against the tree trunk, imprisoning her there. His eyes were magnetic. At that moment, he struck her as being very handsome, his wavy hair falling low on his brow, his usually stern features turned boyish. He seemed to read her thoughts, and the rakish smile widened, boring deep dimples into his smooth cheeks. All at once, the blood was thundering in her ears, and she felt her face grow crimson.

"May I have my cap back, my Charm?" he asked huskily, "or must I remove it from your backside forcibly?"

Her limbs were quaking as she handed it over. He stood there a moment longer, restoring it to its original shape, complaining of the damage done. "I'm afraid it hasn't fared well in the battle. It will never be the same."

Yvette was outraged. "You're lucky you even got it back!" She turned on Charmaine. "You're no fun! You didn't even try to keep it away from him!"

"Well, Yvette," John said, "all good things must come to an end. *Even games*." Though he spoke to his sister, his eyes remained fixed on Charmaine, who was still leaning against the tree. He fixed the cap on his head and walked over to Pierre, affectionately ruffling his hair.

The twins sneaked up behind him, bent upon dislodging the cap and engaging him in the game again. But he stepped out of their reach. They danced around him still, trying to jump high enough to snatch it. Charmaine had never seen them so gay.

"Up to no good again, eh?" he accused mischievously.

"Just like you, Johnny!" Yvette rejoined.

"Just like me? When am I up to no good?"

"You're always up to no good," Yvette exclaimed, as if it were common knowledge. "That's what Father says."

A black scowl darkened John's face. Impulsively, Charmaine took a step closer to Yvette, fearful he might strike the girl. Instead, he demanded more information. "He told you that?"

"No, not me. Just Paul."

"But you were there."

"Not exactly. Paul had something important to discuss with Father, and I wanted to know what it was. So, I went to the kitchen and took a glass from the cupboard and listened through the wall of the water closet next to Papa's dressing chamber. It worked fine, because I could hear every word they said. Paul was angry about something you did, something about sending a ship here without papers. Anyway, that's when Papa said you were up to no good."

Suddenly, John was laughing heartily. "A glass against the wall," he murmured, shaking his head in amazement.

Yvette nodded, pleased with his reaction. "You remember when you showed me how to do that, don't you?"

"Ah, yes," he sighed. "You are an astute pupil, Yvette."

Charmaine was both astonished and irate. "So, her eavesdropping on Saturday was my fault, but this incident is just splendid because the instruction came from you, is that it?"

John laughed harder and spoke to Yvette. "My advice to you, my little spy, is: keep up the good work, but take care *not* to get caught. If Paul finds you with that glass, he'll lock you up in the meetinghouse cellar with all the drunkards."

"Where you belong, no doubt!" Charmaine snapped.

"What do you mean by that?" John asked.

"You had better think twice before you teach the children your antics. They may come back to haunt you."

"I'll make a note of that," John replied in overemphasized seriousness. With a theatrical flourish, he produced an imaginary paper and quill and pretended to write. "Miss Ryan, an authority on high morals and untainted virtue, warns me I had better watch my step, or else!"

"Or else what?" Yvette asked.

"Paulie will give me a sound thrashing. Isn't that right, Mademoiselle?"

Charmaine's eyes narrowed, but she refused to answer, as once again her caustic retort failed to meet its mark.

When John saw she had nothing more to say, he chuckled softly and bid the children a farewell. He turned back to her, pulled the cap off his head, and held it over his heart. "Thank you, Miss Ryan, for graciously allowing me to join your picnic luncheon. I'm sure you'll agree it was most enjoyable, but please don't beg me to stay any longer, since I really must be leaving now."

Enjoyable indeed! She almost laughed outright at the absurd statement. Still, she sighed with relief when she realized he meant to depart. Not even the children were able to change his mind, and he soon disappeared down the pathway. Not long afterward, they, too, headed for home.

The workday is over, the dishes put away, and the children are tucked into bed. That's when **DeVa Gantt** settles down for an evening with the family. The other family, that is: the Duvoisins.

DeVa Gantt is a pseudonym for Debra and Valerie Gantt: sisters, career women, mothers, homemakers, and now, authors. The Colette Trilogy, commencing with *A Silent Ocean Away*, is the product of years of unwavering dedication to a dream.

The women began writing nearly thirty years ago. Deb was in college, Val a new teacher. Avid readers of historical fiction, the idea of authoring their own story blossomed from a conversation driving home one night. "We could write our own book. I can envision the main character." Within a day, an early plot had been hatched and the first scenes committed to paper. Three years later, the would-be authors had half of an elaborate novel written, numerous hand-drafted scenes, five hundred typed pages, and no idea how to tie up the complicated story threads. The book languished, life intervened, and the work was put on the back burner for two decades.

Both women assert the rejuvenating spark was peculiarly coincidental. Though Val and Deb live thirty miles apart, on Thanksgiving weekend 2002, unbeknownst to each other, they spontaneously picked up the unfinished manuscript and began to read. The following week, Deb e-mailed Val to tell her she'd been reading "the book." It was a wonderful work begging to be finished, and Deb had some fresh ideas. By January, the women's creative energies were flowing again.

Unlike twenty years earlier, Deb and Val had computer technology on their side, but there were different challenges. Their literary pursuit had to be worked into real life responsibilities: children, marriages, households, and jobs. The women stole every spare moment, working late at night, in the wee hours of morning, and on weekends. The dictionary, thesaurus, and grammar books became their close companions. Snow days were a gift. No school, no work. Deb could pack up overnight bags, and head to Val's house with her two children. The cousins played while the writers collaborated.

Wherever the women went, they brought the Duvoisins along. From sports and dance practices to doctors' offices, from business trips to vacations, an opportunity to work on their "masterpiece" was rarely wasted. One Fourth of July, Val and Deb edited away on their laptops on blankets in the middle of a New Hampshire baseball field while their families waited for night to fall and the fireworks to begin.

Both women agree the experience has been rewarding and unexpectedly broad in scope. Writing a story was only the beginning of a long endeavor that included extensive research, arduous editing, and painstaking proofreading. Next came the query letters sent to agents and publishers, each meeting a dead end. Self-publishing was the only option—a stepping-stone that would enable them to compile a portfolio of reviews and positive feedback. Thus they became adept at marketing their work, all in the pursuit of reaching a traditional publisher. Within two years an agent had stepped in and HarperCollins agreed to publish the work as a trilogy.

Today, the women look back at their accomplishment. The benefits have been immeasurable. Perhaps the dearest is the bond of sisterhood that deepened: they have shared a unique journey unknown to most sisters. Their greatest satisfaction, however, has been seeing their unfinished work come to fruition: the Duvoisin story has finally been told.